M. G.

THE FAVOURITE CHILD

Also by Freda Lightfoot

LUCKPENNY LAND

WISHING WATER

LARKRIGG FELL

LAKELAND LILY

THE BOBBIN GIRLS

MANCHESTER PRIDE

POLLY'S WAR

KITTY LITTLE

THE FAVOURITE CHILD

FREDA LIGHTFOOT

Hodder & Stoughton

Copyright © 2001 Freda Lightfoot

First published in 2001 by Hodder & Stoughton
A division of Hodder Headline

The right of Freda Lightfoot to be identified as the Author of
the Work has been asserted by her in accordance with the
Copyright, Designs and Patents Act 1988.

10 9 8 7 6 5 4 3 2 1

A CIP catalogue record for this title is available from the British Library

ISBN 0 340 76900 9

Typeset by Palimpsest Book Production Limited,
Polmont, Stirlingshire

Printed and bound in Great Britain by
Clays Ltd, St Ives plc.

Hodder & Stoughton
A division of Hodder Headline
338 Euston Road
London NW1 3BH

ACKNOWLEDGEMENTS

This book is dedicated to the memory of all the women who were pioneers in the provision of birth control and women's health care. In particular to Charis Frankenburg who together with Mary Stocks opened the real Salford and District Mothers' Clinic for Birth Control in 1926. My sincere thanks go to Mrs Frankenburg's daughter, Mrs Ursula Kennedy, for inspiring me with the idea in the first place and for her help in providing information on the work of the clinic from family papers. For anyone interested in learning more I would highly recommend they read her mother's autobiography, *Not Old, Madam, Vintage*. It sheds as much light on a remarkable woman as on the noble and worthwhile enterprise she helped to found.

The clinic depicted in this story, though it may bear some similarities to the original, certainly in its work and aims, is entirely fictitious, as are the characters. Salford is as real as I can make it. I would also like to acknowledge the unstinting help of the Librarians at the Manchester Central Library who always seem to know what I am looking for and how to find it.

1927

Chapter One

Isabella Ashton alighted from the tram car at the corner of Cross Lane and strode out along Liverpool Street, her boots ringing on setts polished by generations of clog irons, thick woollen skirt swinging against her long legs. The slanting rays of a weak winter sun glinted momentarily upon wet slate roofs before being blotted out by a belch of smoke from a forest of broken chimney pots. Two children passed her, one a girl of about seven or eight pushing an old pram containing a pitiful quantity of coal. Seated in the midst of it sat a grey-faced toddler chewing on a piece, dribbles of black soot running down its chin. In front, pulling with all his puny strength, was a child of no more than four or five years, a boy judging by his ragged trousers. The pair had evidently been visiting the coal yard on the corner of Denbigh Street and were returning home with their meagre prize which would barely keep a family warm for more than a day. Isabella's heart went out to them. How was it that small children must bear such onerous responsibilities?

As she paused to watch them go by, she took off the hated cloche hat and shook out her bobbed red-gold hair. Wildly curling it seemed, like its owner, utterly beyond control, refusing to be either confined or tidy, despite all efforts.

She wished she could have bought these children a wagon full of coal, had done so for others on numerous occasions, not to mention giving those in need countless loaves of bread, pairs of boots and whatever else she could think to supply. But Isabella knew that even she, daughter of Simeon Ashton, the well-to-do manager of a thriving cotton mill, couldn't afford to provide the whole of Salford with heat for their hearths and food for their kitchens. Not that it was easy to get them to accept anything at all. She'd learned to tread carefully with her well-meant offers of help, for fear of causing offence.

Tucking the hat into her pocket, she picked her way around puddles, and children skipping or playing hopscotch. Women shrouded in thick woollen shawls hurried by, many with yet more children clinging to their skirts. The lamplighter was just completing his round, setting his long pole against each gas lamp and bringing a warming glow to the cold street.

A man stepped out from the lighted doorway of a tripe shop, a stone jar of hot soup cradled in his hand. ''Ow do, Miss Bella.' A friendly voice, cap neb touched in deference. 'Tha's a sight for sore eyes on a raw neet like this.'

'And yourself, Joe.' Bella returned the greeting, hazel eyes bright with good humour. All her friends in these parts called her by the shortened form of her name, and she rather liked it.

'Night's drawing in. I wouldn't linger. Tara, chuck.' His voice drifted back to her as he hurried on home to his supper through the gathering evening mist that clung wraith-like around the gas lamps.

'Tara, Joe.' She tugged the collar of her coat closer about her neck, feeling the bite of a cold November day that, as he said, was rapidly fading into a damp evening. But Bella didn't even slow her pace as she hurried on through the gathering gloom. Somewhere in the direction of the cattle market she heard a clock start to chime. She lifted her chin, which her brother Edward claimed jutted with a stubborn forcefulness like all Ashton chins, and tilted her head to one side to listen. Six o'clock. She was going to be dreadfully late. Mother was already annoyed, having been abandoned outside the Midland

Hotel following their afternoon tea party with Mrs Prudy and her whining daughter. If Bella were not back in time to bathe and change for her brother's birthday dinner which had taken weeks of careful planning, hours of preparation by Mrs Dyson their overworked cook, and a large slice of Pa's hard-won income, Mother would be utterly furious.

'Why do you always have to be so perverse?' she had raged earlier as, mumbling excuses, Bella had leapt on to a passing tram car. *'I will not have you visiting your dreadful friends today of all days!'* Emily Ashton had personally hand-picked several delightful young ladies, selected from the twin cities of Salford and Manchester and miles beyond, to present to her darling son. If a prospective wife were not secured for him this evening, it would be no fault of hers.

Bella felt deeply relieved that she had long since given up hope of finding a husband for a recalcitrant daughter who, at very nearly twenty-four and with a most radical outlook on life, was quite beyond the pale. Riddled with self-pity after trying to start a family for nearly twelve years before finally succeeding, her mother had become crippled by the bitterness of her many disappointments, made worse when all she'd achieved by her efforts was a tomboy of a daughter and a son with no more spunk than limp lettuce – Simeon Ashton's description, which Emily furiously refuted. Edward had been given every advantage, including an expensive education quite unsuited to his nature, because it had been considered the right and proper thing to do. Bella, as a mere girl, had been condemned to spend her formative years at Miss Springfield's Academy for Young Ladies where she learned to speak bad French and do dreadful embroidery. A complete waste of money on both counts.

In truth, Edward's one passion had been to learn carpentry but his mother threw three fits if she ever saw him with a tool of any kind in his hand; while Bella had been forced to devour whatever books she could find, in secret under the bedclothes, yearning for knowledge and information with an unquenchable thirst. All these frustrated educational ambitions, Bella thought with a wry smile, had caused her to direct her energies into radical issues considered quite inappropriate in a young lady of her standing.

'I'll be no more than half an hour,' she'd shouted back above the rattle of wheels on tramlines, grinning broadly before climbing the curving staircase to the top deck. But the image of her mother's ashen-faced fury had remained with her as she'd collapsed, gasping for breath, on the hard wooden slatted seat, a shaming guilt stifling her rebellious giggles as she remembered her mother's vehemence. The mere fact that Emily had forgotten herself so far as to raise her voice in public spoke volumes.

Now Bella bent her head into the wind and hurried on. No matter what the outcome of this particular show of rebellion, she intended to make sure that the Stobbs children were on the road to recovery. She could not begin to enjoy Edward's party until she was certain they were taken care of. Her fingers curled around the pot of calves' foot jelly in her pocket. Small but rich in nourishment, Mrs Dyson had assured her, and you couldn't take risks with influenza. What if it developed into pneumonia or worse? What if she'd misdiagnosed the sickness and it was really the start of TB or pleurisy, or one of the other dread diseases that stalked these mean streets?

Bella shivered. Beneath her fine tweed coat she wore a warm jumper and a bright green skirt, and on her feet smart Russian boots to keep out the wet. There would be salmon for supper, and a large rib of beef succulent with gravy, followed by Mrs Dyson's apple turnovers that melted in the mouth. The Stobbs family, like many another, were not so fortunate. Guilt ate into her soul as Isabella thought of this other existence she led, one which seemed far removed from the reality of life in these streets.

''Alfpenny for a shrive o' bread, missus.' The thin, childish voice penetrated her thoughts and Isabella paused to rummage through pockets and purse. There must surely be a halfpenny somewhere. She couldn't have used all her coins on the tram fare. It was at that moment she heard the screams.

Jinnie had never felt so bad in all her short life, and she was no stranger to pain. She knew what it was to be cold and have nowhere to sleep but the hard pavement, wrapped in a newspaper like a piece of haddock, and she was certainly on close speaking terms with hunger. Who wasn't in these streets? Jinnie knew what it felt like to be desperate for food and yet have her stomach heave and refuse to digest it. Once, she'd been told that milk was the thing for a stomach shrivelled by starvation and had set off to walk to the country, Brindleheath way, meaning to try and find some. As if she would have the first idea how to catch a cow, let alone milk one. She'd only got as far as the 'Rec' ground, and there were no cows there, before coming over all queer and passing out.

That was the day she'd met Billy Quinn. And hadn't she been glad? He'd seemed like her salvation at the time. She'd learned different since, of course. Lord, but she was feeling proper queer now. 'It must be working, Sadie. Is it working?'

'Hush up, luv. I'll fill t'kettle. Clean you up a bit afore his lordship gets in.'

Dear God, yes. She had to get up and off this bed before he got home. For all his nasty ways, Billy Quinn was a Catholic and he'd kill her for sure if he ever found out what she'd done.

He'd carried her back here that day she'd gone to look for the cows; brought her to his home, or hovel more like, being one room without benefit of running water save for what seeped through the walls. But at least he'd given her sips of warm milk. Jinnie had been no more than twelve at the time and had been with him ever since; nearly four long years and she really shouldn't complain. He'd fed her, hadn't he? Except when his Irish luck failed him. Helped her find employment of sorts, charring, doing washing, or running errands for him. He'd provided a bed for her to sleep in, even if it was his own. And if sometimes she wanted to object to the things he demanded of her in the dark hours of the night, at least he'd never required her to warm anyone else's bed, which was saying a good deal.

But then, so far as Billy Quinn was concerned, she was his own private property and he could do with her as he willed.

'Don't ye owe yer bleedin' life to me? Me being the one what saved ye,' he'd remind her in his soft Irish brogue whenever she showed signs of wanting to move on. 'You do what I sez and ye'll be right as ninepence. Isn't that the truth?'

'Whatever you say, Quinn.' It was always safer to agree, using the name he liked to be known by. She'd not go so far as to call Billy Quinn her friend. Few, if any, could lay claim to such a state of affairs. But it was no bad thing to have him on your side. She'd learned the art of acceptance quite early in their relationship. To keep her trap shut. Tell no tales or she'd be sorry. Jinnie certainly hadn't told him that she'd fallen.

Now, clutching her stomach, she watched Sadie move to the fire, lift the blackened kettle with her skinny arm and then drop it in shock as a scream ricocheted around the tiny room. From some far distant place Jinnie became aware it must have been she who'd screamed. And no wonder! It was as if a knife had sliced through her groin. The pain ground into her, seeming to go on forever, filling her with terror and panic. A warm wetness ran down the inside of her leg and she struggled to get up off the bed so she would avoid messing it up. Quinn hated mess of any sort.

'Stay still. Stay still, child.'

The pain came again, dragging her down. So did the scream. Hammering in her head. Beating her to a bloody pulp. This time when it finally subsided Jinnie lay exhausted, drenched in a cold sweat of fear. 'Dear God, what have we done!'

'Nowt you won't be glad of come t'morning,' Sadie remarked in her no-nonsense fashion and, snatching up the kettle once more, hooked it back over the fire. 'Just lie still and rest.'

Every month since her courses had started, Jinnie had taken a weekly dose of Beecham's Pills, a sure way of preventing any 'accidents'. Or so she'd been assured by her neighbour here. Sadie lived in the rooms below and though it had seemed a bit odd that the wonder pills hadn't stopped her from having eight childer with another on the way, Jinnie had obediently swallowed them, regular as clockwork. When her monthlies had stopped, it hadn't taken long for her to realise what the matter was. Her small breasts had gone all sore and swollen, and she'd been sick every morning the minute she put her feet to the floor. A sure sign, Sadie had told her.

So the Beecham's Pills hadn't worked for her either. Nor had the Penny Royal, the turpentine balls, hot mustard baths or the jumping off the eighth step. But since Jinnie was only just turned sixteen and could barely manage to feed herself let alone a child, never mind endure the shame of bearing a bastard, she'd determined to get rid of it. Besides, who would want Billy Quinn's child, or to feel tied to him forever? Not she. It had needed Sadie's skills with a crochet hook to put her right. Now Jinnie lay in a pool of her own blood, writhing with agony.

Through the grimy window she could see the comforting glow of lamplight in the street below, hear the long pole clinking against glass and metal. She glanced across at her friend whose putty-pale face swam towards her in the gloom, wet dishcloth in hand as if that could possibly staunch the flow of life from her.

'*We have to get out of here!*' Jinnie felt certain she had screamed these words out loud and wondered why Sadie didn't respond, why she just kept on dabbing at her with the now soaking dishcloth, making those worrying little sounds in her throat.

Jinnie doubled up on a fresh whimper of terror as yet another bolt of hot pain struck her. Dear God, would it never end? She struggled to sit up, thinking this might ease the pain, but fell back gasping on to the filthy sheets and, as she did so, spotted her friend hurrying out through the door.

'Don't leave me! *Sadie!*' When the scream came again, the sound of it seemed to echo through the waves of rosy fog that swam before her eyes.

She was dying, Jinnie was sure of it. Thanks to Billy Quinn.

Would her soul go to hell if she did die? Jinnie had little truck with religion, believing God had given up on her many years ago when he'd taken her mother and two younger brothers with TB, but she wondered if she should try and say a prayer now, just in case.

'Sweet Jesus! What's happening here?'

She thought for a moment that she had indeed uttered a prayer, but then a face swam before her eyes: bright hazel eyes, a halo of red-gold hair that must surely belong to an angel.

Then arms were lifting her, half carrying, half dragging her to the door, and the world shifted and moved beneath her. Jinnie wondered if she was on a merry-go-round, the sort she'd heard of at Belle Vue. Not that she'd ever seen one, she thought inconsequentially, but it must feel like this. Swirling, whirling, dizzying. She gave herself up to the giddiness of it, welcoming the sensation as almost pleasurable.

All that long night as Jinnie hovered on the brink between life and death, Bella stayed by her bedside, waiting, watching and praying that this lovely young girl, who was barely old enough to have experienced anything of life's joys, would recover. As the hours of darkness dragged by, she watched anxiously as nurses came and went, silently lifting the frail wrist, counting the thready pulse, sighing softly as they tucked the bone-thin arm back beneath the covers.

'Don't let her die,' Bella cried, seeing one nurse shake her head in despair.

'We're doing our best to see that she doesn't, Miss Ashton, but these young lasses do daft things.' The woman clicked her tongue with disapproval, tugged the sheet reprovingly into place as if the very fact of Jinnie lying there made the place look untidy. 'They should know better than to interfere with God's work, and let nature take its course.'

'Have a child they can't afford to keep, you mean?'

'No woman can have a child without God's help.'

'This isn't a woman. This girl is little more than a child herself. Where's the sense in bringing a baby into the world if you live in one stinking room and are near starving yourself?'

The nurse's shocked face clearly showed her disapproval. 'You're surely not condoning this dreadful act? Abortion is illegal.' Then she glanced quickly about her as if she might be overheard, cheeks pink with embarrassment. 'Pardon me for being so blunt but I assume you understand summat of what goes on, due to the time you waste on these feckless layabouts.'

Bella felt a nudge of anger, partly because of the insinuation that a girl of her upbringing shouldn't be aware of, let alone discuss, such matters as childbearing, and partly because of the woman's obvious prejudice against poverty. 'My time is my own to waste, if I choose to do so.'

'Of course, Miss Ashton. I never meant to suggest otherwise.' The nurse shook the thermometer with a vigour which indicated how she might like to have shaken her patient, given half a chance, and thrust it beneath the girl's armpit.

'Besides, how do you know she's feckless?' Isabella persisted. 'She might be unable to find employment as many are these days, hard-working but poor through no fault of her own.'

'You don't kill a child through no fault of your own,' the nurse retorted and Bella had to concede that this was generally the case. 'That isn't always so though, is it? What if she's been . . . taken against her will? Raped?'

The nurse's cheeks were now scarlet and puffed with outrage. 'I thought never to hear such a dreadful word from the lips of a well-brought-up young lady such as yourself. We all know for a fact that there are them as works hard and gets rich – or at least comfortably off, shall we say – and the rest who is poor and gets children. That's the way of the world.'

'Yes, but why? Is there no way to stop the children from coming?'

'I'm sure I'll not hang around to hear this sort of blasphemy!' Whereupon the flustered nurse snatched back her thermometer, thrust it into her pocket without even glancing at it and stamped out of the room, leaving Bella frowning with puzzlement.

It was past midnight before she thought to send a message home via a young boy she discovered sitting on the hospital steps who readily carried it for sixpence. Bella apologised to her mother for missing the birthday dinner, saying she would explain later. She knew that would not be easy.

Dawn brought no improvement to the patient but finally, in the late morning, when everyone had quite given up hope, the girl opened her eyes and asked for a drink of water.

'Good. She's coming round.' It was a different nurse this time. Equally as brisk as the other, she blithely continued, 'Now we can send her home. Get her off our hands at last.'

'Back to that hovel, in her condition?' Bella was appalled. 'Whoever did this to her could very well abuse her all over again.'

'I dare say.' The nurse issued a sniff of disdain but was already peeling back the sheets and roughly shaking the girl's arm. 'Come on, lass. No malingering in this bed as if you had a right to it when there's folk what deserves it more. You're lucky we don't call the constable and have you charged.'

With an effort that seemed to Bella nothing short of Herculean, the girl dragged herself up into a sitting position. 'Give me five minutes for me head to stop swimming and I'll be off home in two shakes of a lamb's tail.'

Bella, however, had other ideas.

Chapter Two

'I can't believe you're even considering letting her stay. Have you gone quite mad?'

Emily Ashton perched stiff-backed on the edge of her best leather sofa and glared accusingly at her daughter. One fist was clenched tightly in her lap, holding fast to a lace handkerchief in case smelling salts should be called for. The other rested along the arm of the sofa, fingers drumming with fury. The sound echoed through the room. Even the aspidistra quivered. Mrs Ashton wore a dark olive green dress buttoned up to her firm pointed chin, a declaration of half mourning for her lost hopes of the previous evening. Her slender, upright figure seemed to blend into the gloom of the shadowed parlour as if requiring, along with the highly polished, heavy mahogany furniture, to be sheltered by the green paper blind drawn against the afternoon sun.

Or to hide our shame from prying eyes, Bella thought. She attempted a joke to lighten the atmosphere. 'The hospital staff had the opportunity this morning to put me into Bedlam but they clearly considered my behaviour perfectly normal, if somewhat eccentric.'

'*Eccentric!*' Emily lifted her eyes heavenward, pointedly indicating that this was the last word she would choose to describe her ungrateful and rebellious child. 'You know nothing about this – this street urchin.'

'She's a young girl, Mother.'

'You don't even know her name.'

'It's Jane Cook, known as Jinnie. And it's only for a couple of nights, until she's properly recovered. She certainly isn't fit enough to take care of herself. She nearly died.'

'And how did she manage to do that, might I enquire?' As if it were by some act of pure carelessness.

Bella judiciously decided against enlightening her irate parent on the precise details. Instead she crossed her fingers against the lie and pressed on with her plea. 'An accident with a runaway horse. She won't be a nuisance, I promise. You won't even know she's here. I shall have a bed made up in the room next to mine so she'll be no trouble to anyone. I'll be the one to attend her should she need care during the night.'

'No *trouble*? She's brought nothing *but* trouble upon this house from the minute you decided to wander the streets instead of coming home to your brother's coming-of-age dinner, as you were directed. There was pandemonium here last night when you did not arrive. *Pandemonium!*'

'I don't see why there should have been. It was Edward's party after all, not mine.'

'Don't quibble. We were desperately worried, particularly as it grew late and still you didn't appear. Your father very nearly called out the constabulary to look for you, while I was beset by one of my fainting fits. What our guests thought I daren't imagine. It was all most distressing.' Emily's agitation increased with the telling of this tale which Bella had already heard several times in the hour since her return. For as long as she could remember if there was any way her mother could put the blame for life's misfortunes upon her daughter's shoulders, she would do so, largely because Bella coped with them so much better than she.

'I'm sorry, Mother. I never meant to stay out all night. Events just flew out of control.'

'Why does that not surprise me? When will you stop this racketing life you lead? It's not at all proper for a gel of your station to be going about unchaperoned.' Emily was attempting to soften her blunt Lancashire accent with the more refined tones she considered appropriate for a mill manager's wife.

Having married slightly above her station with high hopes of a bright future, Emily Ashton was now a disappointed woman. Her husband she considered far too soft for his own good, save when it came to commenting upon her adored son who, sadly, had been an academic disappointment. Her daughter was a lost cause. As for life in the higher echelons of middle-class society, however carefully she might arrange the flowers on her polished hall table, however expensive the gowns she wore or the fineness of the food which graced her beautiful mahogany-furnished dining room, she still had to climb into the loneliness of her marital bed each evening. Disappointing was the only word Emily could find to describe every facet of her life. Was it any wonder if she lacked the confidence even to give proper instructions to her own servants, or to express her opinion on any matter which may provoke dispute? Emily had long since given up hope that anybody would listen to her, so any opportunity she could find to express her bitterness, she did so with relish.

'You shame us all with your recklessness. What your father's views on the matter will be, I shudder to contemplate.'

As one, the eyes of the two women swivelled to where Simeon himself stood in his favourite spot before the blazing fire, hands clasped behind his back in his usual stance, rocking on his heels from time to time as he listened, without comment, to his wife's words. Yet he seemed encouragingly relaxed, Bella noticed. But then, Pa was rarely anything else.

It was one of the things she loved best about her father, that and his comfortable girth. Just to look at him made her want to put her arms about him and give him a cuddle. He was a dumpy little man with a round, smiling face topped by crinkly red-gold hair very like her own, save for being better controlled with a daily splash of Brylcreem. He was the dearest, sweetest man, with the patience of a saint, and, as both mother and daughter were only too aware, would make no detrimental remark upon anything Bella chose to do. This was partly because above all things Simeon detested a scene but mainly because his beloved daughter could do no wrong in his eyes. However dictatorial he may be with the operatives at the mill, and however thrifty with his hard-earned brass, in the hands of the women of his own family he was soft as putty. He believed it to be the man's task in life to protect and indulge his womenfolk, and not a soul in the entire household, from Tilly the housemaid through the redoubtable Mrs Dyson to his own dear wife, and more particularly his only son and heir, was in any doubt that Isabella was his favourite.

What he said to her now, in gently scolding tones, was that this was no laughing matter. 'I'll not have your dear mother's plans thrown into disarray because of your fads and fancies. I tolerate a good deal of your reckless, unladylike behaviour but ill manners distress me. You should know that by now.'

'Yes, Father.' Bella flew to his side to place a loving kiss on his whiskered chin.

'I live in hope that one day this overdeveloped social conscience of yours will ease and you will take your rightful place in up-and-coming Manchester society.'

'Yes, Father,' she said again, attempting to sound contrite. 'And in the meantime — about Jinnie? She can stay?'

'What does she think of this plan of yours?'

'I haven't discussed it with her yet but I'm sure she'll be grateful.'

'Is that why you're doing it, to earn her gratitude?'

A dull rose pink suffused Bella's cheeks. 'Of course not! As if I would be. You surely know me better than that.'

Simeon heaved a sigh of resignation. 'She may stay for two days. Not a second longer.'

'Dear, dear Pa! No wonder I adore you.' And flinging her arms about his neck, Bella rained yet more kisses upon his ruddy cheeks while he tut-tutted in pretend protest.

Emily put one hand to her throat and made a small choking sound. 'We're to give in to this daft folly of hers then, as always?'

'Her kindness may be inconvenient for us, Emily, but it is well meant. No worse surely than my funding the Christmas Breakfast at the chapel?'

'It's entirely different,' Emily stormed, screwing her handkerchief into a tight ball in her fist. 'You sponsor the Breakfast out of a right and proper sense of duty and at no risk to yourself, while Isabella takes her life in her hands every time she walks alone through those dreadful streets.'

Simeon turned his benevolent gaze upon his daughter, peering at her from over his wire-framed spectacles. 'Your mother makes a fair point. The streets of Salford are not entirely safe for a young girl, particularly as night falls. Perhaps you could confine your good works to daylight hours.'

'If you wish it, Pa.'

Emily was on her feet now, voice shaking with rage. 'No, no, no! Why will no one listen to me? She must be stopped completely. I will not have *my* daughter demeaning herself in such a way. Forbid her to leave the house at all, except with myself as chaperonne.'

'Nay, Emily lass, that'd be a bit much, eh?'

'Small wonder no decent man will touch her, gallivanting about with ne'er-do-wells, ruffians and misfits! She deserves to be left on the shelf to grow into a sour old maid. But I will *not* have her spoil Edward's chances too.'

'That is *enough*, Emily!'

Both women flinched. It was not often Father laid down the law, Bella thought, but when he chose to, there was no mistaking that benevolent and tolerant though he may be, he was nonetheless master in his own home.

'I will hear no more on the subject. Is that clear?'

Emily tore her handkerchief into shreds and stalked from the room. As the door slammed shut behind her, Simeon let out a deep sigh. 'Now see what you've done. I shall be driven to eat humble pie for days to bring your poor mother out of the glums, and you, young madam, shall cudgel your brains over how to make up for last night's débâcle.'

'I will. I'm so sorry, Father.'

'So you should be. For God's sake, try to use at least an atom of common sense with these philanthropic notions of yours. Personally I shall be glad when you give over with this particular fad and settle down. Your mother makes a valid point. It's time you shaped yourself and found a good chap to wed afore it's too late. Now I must go to her.' He planted a kiss on Bella's brow. 'And happen you'll consider finding a more fitting occupation soon, d'you reckon? To please me?'

Bella screwed up her nose as she pretended to consider the matter, hazel eyes alight with laughter. 'I'll do my best to be careful, Pa, will that do?'

'I dare say it'll have to. For now.' With one hand on the door knob, he paused. Returning to her side, he pressed a sovereign into her hand. 'No doubt you'll need a few items of apparel for this latest lame duck of yours. But don't tell your mother.' And with a sideways grin and a knowing wink, he was gone.

Bella wasted no time in putting her plans into effect. Clean sheets were brought from the linen cupboard and Tilly set about making up the bed in the guest bedroom next to Bella's own. Young Sam, aged seventeen and known as the handyman by Simeon and the chauffeur by Emily, was instructed to fetch flowers and then post himself at the front door in order to alert her the moment their patient arrived. She needed him to be on hand as the poor girl would require help climbing the stairs. Bella herself prepared a tea tray and, while she did so, sweet-talked Mrs Dyson into producing some of her delicious shortbread.

'And no doubt you'll be wanting yet more calves' foot jelly as well?'

'I thought perhaps a little oxtail soup for supper? Something warming that'll cling to her ribs, eh? Dear Mrs Dyson, what a treasure you are.' And Bella hurried away, allowing no opportunity for protest.

On the dot of three an ambulance drew up outside the Ashtons' end-terrace house in Seedley Park Road, as expected. Emily herself stood on the doorstep to direct operations, if only to show the neighbours that she was in charge. Double-fronted and built of the finest dark red Accrington brick, the house possessed bay windows on both ground and upper floors, as Emily would proudly and frequently remind her many friends and acquaintances. She herself did not view the house as an end terrace, choosing to ignore the row of smaller houses attached to its back, since from the front it appeared detached. In addition, unlike many another in less affluent streets, it also possessed a front garden, admittedly minuscule but nonetheless neatly contained by a small privet hedge and a front gate which Emily now opened to permit the brawny young Sam to carry their guest inside.

Jinnie seemed bemused by all the attention, and barely awake. 'Where am I? What's happening?' was all she managed as she was gently put to bed by Bella's own hands.

She didn't want the tea; showed not a scrap of interest in Mrs Dyson's freshly baked shortbread. Within seconds her eyelids had drooped closed and she was fast asleep.

'Best thing,' Mrs Dyson wisely remarked. 'Sleep'll put her on her feet in no time.'

Bella tucked the sheet in more firmly and, smoothing a curl from Jinnie's cheek, looked down upon her patient with a soft smile. 'You're right, Mrs D. Sleep is exactly what she needs. I should think this is the most rest she's ever had in her entire life. And first thing tomorrow, while she sleeps, I shall take the opportunity to slip out and see the Stobbs family. I missed them completely last night, due to events. At least here she's safe from whoever did this dreadful thing to her. What I wouldn't do to him if ever I got my hands on him! He comes right at the bottom in the pecking order of decent humanity so far as I'm concerned. Selfish brute!'

Billy Quinn knew all about the pecking order and, so far as he was concerned, his position in it was right at the top. He'd arrived in Salford via Liverpool and the Ship Canal less than a decade ago when he was no more than a lad of fifteen. Leaving his large family behind in County Mayo, he'd come to the mainland seeking his fortune with a bag of clothes slung over his broad shoulders, a bit of luck money in his pocket and the devil in his eyes. He'd slept in ditches and under haystacks as well as common lodging houses, or 'kip' houses as they were often called, where he'd fight anyone for a place to lay his head, and generally win.

He'd dragged himself out of those ditches, working on farms and in factories, and finally got himself a good job on a building site; was even happy to be termed a navvy since the effort he put into the job was minimal as it wasn't his main source of income at all. It was merely a front, meant to provide the veneer of respectability he needed for his real work.

Billy Quinn was a bookie. Small-time as yet, but with a formidable reputation. Woe betide any punter who thought he could put one over on him.

As a result of his success, these days he was proud to have his own place, albeit only one rented room in an old terraced house on Liverpool Street. It stated loud and clear that he was on the up-and-up. He'd even got himself a steady girl. Except that this morning, after a long night spent running a particularly lucrative dog fight, he'd returned tired and hungry to find the room empty. No girl in evidence. Not a sign remained that she'd ever been there. Even the bed had been stripped of every sheet and blanket.

Too stunned at first to take in the fact that Jinnie had

finally summoned the nerve to leave him, for all she'd frequently threatened to do so, he told himself that she was the loser. His next move would have been to a proper house all his own, a two up and two down, and he would've taken her with him — if she'd played her cards right. But he was peeved by this sudden display of independence. No one walked out on Billy Quinn, not without his say so.

'Would ye know where she is?' The question was asked on a low growl of anger.

Rarely ever more than a few feet from Quinn's side, save for when his boss had a woman in tow, Len Jackson was expected to supply the answers to all his questions, which wasn't easy seeing as they were often a mite awkward, demanding answers bound to annoy. Len would've liked notice of this one in particular.

'Nay, Quinn. I know nowt about it. Wimmin is a mystery to me. Allus have been.' Len sidled over to the window to look down into the back entry, keeping an eye out for likely trouble. He could see Harold Cunliffe leaning nonchalantly against the back yard wall. Harold suddenly bent down to tie his laces and Len turned quickly back to Quinn.

'Hey up! There's rozzers about. Harold has just signalled.'

But for once Billy Quinn's mind wasn't on business. He smashed his fist down on the rickety table so hard that it almost buckled beneath the pressure. 'Then bleedin' well find out where she is.'

It was rare for him to swear. Despite his reputation for meanness, outwardly at least Billy Quinn's manner was mild, his voice a soft Irish brogue. Quinn saw himself as a gentleman, with the kind of good looks that made women swoon or wish they were eighteen again, the sort they paid sixpence to drool over at the Cromwell Picture House. Thick brown hair was swept back from his high brow and, unusually, he never used Brylcreem but left it soft and loose so that he could flick it back with an arrogant toss of his head whenever it fell forward. His eyes were sleepy, heavy-lidded, often half closed against the curl of blue smoke drifting from the cigarette frequently seen dangling from his lips, and his seductively piercing blue gaze asked only one question of a woman: Was she willing or would he need to use persuasion? For all he liked to have Jinnie around as his regular girl, since she was an attractive little waif, Quinn never disguised the fact that he was fond of other women. He would say that, after gambling, they were his favourite pastime. But he was most particular which ones he slept with. Once having declared an interest, however, it was for him to decide when the relationship should come to an end.

Jinnie had made a big mistake by leaving. A fact he would make plain to her when he caught up with her again. He wondered if their neighbour Sadie knew anything, and vowed to find out.

Len could sense this was not the moment to suggest that perhaps Quinn hadn't treated Jinnie quite as he should, or that it was a wonder she'd hung around as long as she had. He was grateful to be saved from the need to answer his boss by the door bursting open and Harold Cunliffe charging in.

'Didn't you catch me signal? The rozzers is here. Get moving, it's the real McCoy this time.'

To run a successful bookmaking business, Quinn and his punters were required to defy the law which stated that street betting was illegal. He'd been doing so with ease for some considerable time. Conducting his business from the back entry, he depended on runners to collect bets, and lookouts, known locally as dogger-outs, to keep watch. It was vital that Quinn himself wasn't caught. His success depended upon it. No punter would place bets with him ever again if their hard-earned money was confiscated by the police. What he needed now, therefore, was for someone to act as mug. Like the joker in a pack he would be the throw-away card, and since Harold was the only one handy who they could afford to lose, he was the one selected.

'Get down the entry, Harold. I'll see you right.'

'Aw, Billy lad, I've seven childer to feed, and the missus is badly. How would they manage if I got nicked?'

Quinn rested one large hand on each of Harold's skinny shoulders. 'Trust me, Harold. Would I let them starve?'

'Nay, I'm not suggesting you would, only ...'

'And remember,' Billy's tone dropped to a menacing whisper, 'there's worse that could happen to you, Harold, m'boy, than spending a few days in clink. Is there not?'

Recognising his cause to be lost and believing that all fines would be paid for him by Billy Quinn, as was normally the case with a bookmaker, Harold hightailed it out of the door and stationed himself at the end of the entry, as instructed. In his pocket were a sheaf of betting slips, none of them genuine.

It was well known that many raids were 'staged' since the police were largely sympathetic to the plight of the working man, being put on the wrong side of the law just because he wanted to place a threepenny each-way bet. They'd also no real wish to be made unpopular by acting as 'spoilsports' and enforcing the letter of the law too harshly. Every now and then, however, the Superintendent would take it into his head to stage a surprise raid, a genuine one, usually to please a magistrate or make the arrest sheet look better. Today was one of those days.

Arriving in force, the police spotted Harold, who was duly arrested and carted off to their van. As on previous raids it proved impossible to catch Quinn, or any of his other runners, as doors mysteriously opened and were as quickly found locked shut, with no sign of the perpetrators of this 'crime' anywhere. Quickly losing interest in the chase, the policemen gave up the search and withdrew, content to have at least one victim to show to the Chief.

Len, back at his lookout post and watching events over a corner of the back yard wall, said, 'You realise this was Harold's third offence. It'll cost you fifty quid to get him out.'

'Fifty quid?' Quinn stubbed out his cigarette and lit another before continuing to check betting slips. 'Over my dead body. He can do three months instead.'

'But his wife and childer. You said . . .'

Quinn paused in his counting, glanced up at Len through half-closed eyes. 'Did ye have something to say on the subject?'

Len swallowed. 'Nay, not me. I know nowt about owt, me.'

'Then ye'd best keep it that way.' And Billy Quinn returned to conducting his business as usual.

Chapter Three

Mrs Stobbs had tried Gregory Powder, liquorice, Fenning's Little Healers and California Syrup of Figs on her eldest, yet still the child complained of stomach ache and pains in her head. She also had no appetite and was sufficiently flushed to indicate a temperature. Bella was fast coming to the conclusion that a doctor should be called, yet knew she'd have a hard job persuading the mother of this fact. Doctors cost money and with nine other children to care for, Mrs Stobbs had little enough to spare.

As if reading Bella's mind she said, 'My friend Gladys give me this tonic for her to try. That's all she needs. A pick-me-up.' Mrs Stobbs went on to explain how she'd already tried rubbing the child's chest with vinegar and goose fat, administered a purgative to clear the bowels and purify the blood as well as wrapping a stocking soaked in tea leaves about her sore throat. All to no avail.

Bella was privately of the opinion that the awfulness of their surroundings may have something to do with the persistent ill health of the children, that and the fact that they all lived in this one room — the whole family sleeping together in one, not over-large, bed. Bugs fell from the ceiling, damp soaked through the walls, a pitiful fire burned in the grate. Only the newspaper covering the shelves and small wooden table was put on clean every day, thanks to Mr Stobbs' fondness for the *Evening News*. This was Mrs Stobbs' idea of hygiene.

Bella examined the bottle which claimed to contain an 'elixir for good health and a strengthener of the blood'. Taking out the glass stopper, she sniffed. A noxious aroma assailed her and she screwed up her nose in disgust. 'You'll never get Lizzie to take this! It smells revolting.'

Mrs Stobbs almost snatched the bottle from her grasp and began searching the cluttered table for a spoon. 'She'll take it if she knows what's good fer her.'

Bella drew a spoon from her bag and rubbed it clean on her pocket handkerchief. There was no sink or water in the house and she quailed at the idea of using the contents of the jug set by the bed. 'I still think a doctor would be best, Mrs Stobbs. She's running a fever.'

Bottle poised over the spoon, the woman glanced across at the child huddled in the chair by a puny fire, her gaze haunted, filled with pain and fear. Lizzie was ten years old now and surely past the most dangerous stages of childhood. Besides, she was a grand help to her mother with the little ones. How would she manage without her? The hand that held the spoon began to tremble and Bella gently took it from her. 'Here, let me. I'll see if I can get her to take it. The label says it's made from seaweed so the iron in that might well be of benefit. But if her temperature hasn't come down by morning, I shall bring the doctor myself, Mrs Stobbs, and pay for him too if need be.'

Two fat tears rolled down the woman's cheeks but she made no move to wipe them away since this would expend energy she didn't possess.

Recognising her exhaustion, Bella said, 'Maybe you should try a spoon or two of this yourself. You could do with a tonic too. It's been one thing after another lately, what with all of them going down with sniffles and coughs.'

Mrs Stobbs shook her head. Precious medicine was not to be wasted on tired adults when there were sick children in the house.

'Thanks for your concern, Bella luv, but we can manage now.'

'I wish I could do more. I'm no doctor and my knowledge of medicine is so inadequate. But I'll be back tomorrow to see how Lizzie is.'

Once out on the pavement she couldn't help heaving a sigh, partly from relief at escaping the sweet-sour stink of poverty but also out of sad resignation, for Bella knew well enough what would happen next. No doctor would ever be permitted over the threshold. Some quack or other would be found and the child dosed till she either revived by sheer good luck or will power or, alternatively, succumbed to the inevitable.

Mrs Stobbs, hovering on her none-too-clean doorstep, half glanced back over her shoulder then drew the door almost closed behind her in a bid for further privacy before beckoning Bella to come closer. She could almost taste the woman's foul breath but didn't turn away as the whisper came in her ear. '*I reckon ah'm off again.*'

'Lord, no. The baby is only — what? Five months?'

'Six!' As if that made all the difference. 'He only has to drop his trousers and ah'm up the spout.'

'I thought the doctor said you were to have no more children?'

'Aye, he did. But he niver told me how to stop 'em coming, did he?' Now she glanced up and down the street and Bella, heart already sinking with despair at this dreadful piece of news, began to feel utterly inadequate to the task facing her. Besides four miscarriages (at least two of which may have been procured) and one stillbirth, caused through fright according to her husband and exhaustion in Bella's opinion, Mrs Stobbs had almost died following her last confinement. It had taken weeks of careful nursing after the birth to get her well again. Even so, she'd run out of milk to feed the latest addition and the baby had never thrived. Bella brought what beneficial food she could for the child, but it rarely showed interest and spent much of its day in a sort of half-starved stupor.

'That's what I wanted to ask. Ah don't like to put this on

you, Bella luv, a young lass like yerself, but 'oo else can I ask? Doctor won't talk about such matters to the likes o'me, so I thought happen thee could find out what's what for me.'

'What's what?' Bella frowned, feeling utterly bemused.

'You know. *How to stop 'em coming.*' These words were hissed in an undertone, partly because women's matters were never referred to directly, but also because abortion was not only illegal but hopelessly confused with contraception. To make matters worse, of course, the Catholic Church was utterly opposed to family limitation in any form, save for what was considered natural. So you couldn't be too careful. 'He's not a bad 'usband as 'usbands go but careless, if you tek me meaning? Particularly after he's been on the booze. Don't say owt n'more now. Walls 'as ears. Just find out for me what I can do to stop it happening again, then I can go and get mesel' sorted.' Whereupon the door slammed shut in Bella's astonished face.

'Anyone would think I was some sort of miracle worker, the things they expect of me,' she complained volubly to Mrs Dyson as she sat in that good woman's kitchen later in the afternoon, warming her hands around a mug of tea. 'Where am I, a single young woman, going to find out about birth control? I'm not even supposed to know about such matters. And I can hardly ask Mother, can I? Or Pa. Perhaps the vicar could tell me? He seems to have an opinion on most things.'

Mrs Dyson chortled softly as she munched on her best shortbread between scalding sips of strong tea. 'Eeh, lass, you have a wicked sense of humour. I'm sure you'll find a way, Miss Bella. You allus do.'

'How? What I know about sex, which is precious little, I've learned from you, my dearest friend. Mother has never uttered a word on the subject. I think she imagines I still believe in the existence of the stork. But I think this one has even me beat, for all I'd love to find some way to prevent women like poor Mrs Stobbs and young Jinnie upstairs from feeling driven to take such risks with their lives.'

'You could always read that book by that doctor woman . . . whatzername? Marie Stopes.'

'Marie Stopes?' Bella considered Mrs Dyson with surprised interest, brow creased in thought. The name had a familiar ring to it, but she couldn't place just how or where she'd heard of it. 'What book?'

'*Married Love*. It caused quite a stir when it come out a few years back. Letters in the paper, speeches in the House of Commons, various Archbishops, protesting the whole shebang accusing her of "pandering to depraved sexual instincts", just because she'd told in a book how a woman can plan when she has childer, instead of them coming of their own free will like. But don't ask me what she says the answer is. I've been a widow too long to care about such matters. She's written another since, I believe, and opened a clinic in London to help in a more practical way, teaching women what to do.'

'Clinic? Book? Mrs D, you are, as ever, a treasure store of fascinating information. What would I do without you?'

'Go hungry?' the cook said, passing her the shortbread.

But Bella refused a second piece. She found it hard to eat after one of her visiting afternoons. 'I must go and see our patient. How is she?'

'Aye, well, tha's got another miracle to perform upstairs. That young madam has slept the clock round but is asking for you good and loud now, and she's not prepared to hang around waiting much longer. She's been making her demands felt since dinnertime, itching to be off back to wherever she come from. And in my view, it'd happen be no bad thing to let her.'

'Oh, Mrs D, don't you join the opposition too. You're my best mate.' And Bella put her arms about the plump figure and gave the old cook an affectionate hug.

'G'am with you, smarmy miss.' Pink-cheeked, Mrs Dyson pushed her gently away and started to ladle broth into a warmed dish. 'She hasn't eaten a thing in the whole twenty-four hours she's been here, so happen you can persuade her to try a morsel of me best pea broth. It'll set her up grand.'

'Not eaten? But that's appalling. How will she ever get well if she doesn't eat?'

'Aye, well, you can explain all of that to her. A bath would do her no harm neither. I've tried to persuade her but given it up as a bad job. She'll happen listen to you.'

It was clear to Bella the moment she entered the room that Jinnie wasn't in the mood to listen to anyone. She was sitting on the edge of the bed, her stick-like limbs and lacklustre skin as white as the sheets, yet her determination to leave only too evident. 'Where are me clothes?' she demanded, her voice high-pitched, almost querulous with anxiety. 'I don't know wheer the 'ell I am, but tha's no right to kidnap me and fotch me here. 'Oo the bloody hell dusta think thou are?'

Her eyes, Bella noticed, were dark as chocolate with long curling lashes but there was still evidence of violet bruises beneath each. The soft, pale mouth trembled slightly, revealing that the girl wasn't very far from tears despite the tendency of her top lip to curl upwards in derision. Certainly there was not a sign of the anticipated gratitude.

Bella's reply was gentle, couched in soothing tones. 'I was only trying to help. You nearly died.'

The girl tossed back thick skeins of brown hair as if she were proud of its greasy lankness. 'Well, that would've been my choice, wouldn't it? Happen it would've been no great loss.'

'Oh, don't say that. No one should be left in the state you were in when I found you. I took you to the hospital in the first place, so when they almost turned you out on the street the minute you woke up, I felt responsible . . .'

'Well, you needn't. No bugger's responsible fer me. I can look after meself, ta very much.' As if to prove this, she got to her feet, wobbling slightly as she glanced frantically about her. 'Wheer's me bleedin' clothes?'

'I'm sorry, I've burnt them.'

The expression on Jinnie's face was terrible to behold. Outrage vibrated through every weakened muscle and Bella almost flinched, thinking the girl was about to fly at her with claws outstretched like a frightened cat. 'You've *burnt* them? How can you 'ave burnt them? 'Oo give you the *right*?'

'I'm sorry. I can find you some fresh. You're welcome to some of mine.'

'I don't need no charity.'

If the poor child hadn't looked so dreadfully woebegone and deadly serious, Bella would have laughed at the incongruity of such a brave statement. Instead she attempted to placate her, gently reminding her that the clothes had been covered in blood, whereupon Jinnie bit her lip, shocked into silence at last by the appalling truth of what she had done.

'Wait there.' And Bella disappeared next door to her own bedroom, rummaging through her capacious wardrobe to return moments later with a good tweed skirt, blouse and jumper, plus various pieces of underwear, including a pair of warm woollen stockings and stout shoes.

'I hope they fit you, but if not we can always make the odd adjustment here and there.'

She held the bundle out and Jinnie scowled, looking almost as if she might refuse this generosity. But then, seeing no alternative, she turned her back, stripped off the flannel nightgown and began to dress hurriedly. The result was not encouraging. The clothes hung on the girl's skeletal frame as if it were a coat hanger and not a living, breathing body at all.

'Well, that looks splendid,' Bella brightly remarked, hiding her concern.

'This don't mean I'm stopping 'ere. I'm off this very minute in fact.' Jinnie set off for the door, not quite knowing where she was going, or why, but somehow mad as blazes to find matters taken out of her control and determined to make the point.

Bella took a sideways step, blocking her way. 'Where to exactly? Back to that stinking room and whoever put you in that condition in the first place?'

'It's *my* choice, *my* 'ome, stinking or not. I can do as I please.'

'Of course you can. And it could equally be your choice not to return, to take this opportunity to escape.'

'Why would I do that?' A voice in the nether regions of Jinnie's brain reminded her that she'd been trying to do exactly that for as long as she could remember but her obstinacy wouldn't allow her to admit as much. 'Toffee-nosed folk like you find it easy to look down on scum like me but you know nowt about it. *Nowt!*'

'I'm sure you're right, but I would like to understand. Who was it who did this to you? A friend? Not what I'd call a sign of friendship.'

Jinnie saw red. 'Sadie only done what I asked her to.'

'Yes, but *why* did you ask her? You're far too young to take such risks.'

'*I'll do what I bleedin' want!*' Jinnie was shouting now, feeling desperation close in. Again she made a move to the door which Bella swiftly blocked.

'Tell me, Jinnie, who put you in this condition? Who was the father of your child?'

Jinnie wanted to shout that there hadn't been any child, not a proper one anyroad. Just a load of blood and gore. And there was certainly no father. But how could she deny it when this know-all of a woman had seen everything? Even so there were some matters best kept to herself. The fewer people who knew of Billy Quinn's role in this affair, the safer she would be. From Quinn himself for one. Failed Catholic or no, he wouldn't take kindly to what Sadie had done that day, either to Jinnie herself or the beginnings of what might've been, in the fullness of time, his son.

'Don't matter 'oo he is, it's none o' your business.'

'I think it is, since you nearly died and . . .'

Rage coursed through Jinnie's veins and she wanted to smack the self-satisfied, condescending smile right off that lovely face which looked down upon her so pityingly. 'If you say that one more time there'll be blue murder done, I swear it. How d'you know I would've died? I might not 'ave. Anyroad, I'll thank you to keep your interfering, do-gooding nose out of what's none o'your bleedin' business.' Jinnie pushed her small face close up to Bella's. 'Have you got that into yer thick, middle-class skull?'

Bella sighed. 'Yes, Jinnie. I'm sorry.'

'Good! Then I'm off, and don't try to stop me.'

'If that's what you want.'

'It is.'

Bella stepped back, indicating with a gesture that the way was clear for her to leave and, after the smallest hesitation, Jinnie stuck her nose in the air and did just that, slamming the bedroom door behind her as if to prove her contempt.

She stamped down the long, sweeping staircase, filled with a sudden terror that she might fall over, her pins were that wobbly. It took several attempts before she finally managed to pull open the heavy mahogany door and gain the safety of the pavement outside the double-fronted terraced house whereupon she fell to her knees, gasping for breath. Head bowed and stomach clenched in agony, Jinnie muttered furiously to herself between long, deep intakes of breath.

'Just shows how much *she* cares, uppity madam. Picks me up and drops me off at her posh house without so much as a by-your-leave. Then lets me walk out without even a goodbye or a nice-to-have-met you.'

'Hello! Were you speaking to me?'

Jinnie almost fell over in shock at the sound of the deep voice so close by. It came from a man bending down beside her and she found herself gazing up into a pair of grey eyes regarding her not with pity but with open admiration. It wasn't the handsomest face she'd ever seen, not by a long chalk, having pale freckled skin and a thin bony nose, but it must surely have been the kindest. The mouth was wide and curled up at the corners, the eyes bright with curiosity. To Jinnie it seemed quite perfect, like the face of an overgrown choir boy. And somewhere deep inside, her stomach gave an odd little lurch.

'You must be Jinnie, the one who clashed with a horse.'

'Horse?' she said, bemused.

'Your accident with the runaway cart horse. Must've been quite a shaker.' He straightened, held out one hand to assist her, smiling warmly. 'Edward Ashton's the name. I'm Isabella's little brother, though not so little these days, I suppose.'

Not daring to touch the hand, Jinnie scrabbled to her feet unaided and gazed up at him in wonder. 'No. You're not – not *little* at all.' Now that they were both standing she could see how tall he was. Tall and thin, like a long drink of water as her mother would've said. But as it wouldn't have been appropriate to make such a personal remark and as no other sensible words came into her head, Jinnie remained silent.

'I hope you aren't off home just yet. I was looking forward to meeting you, once you'd recovered a little.'

'Were you?'

'Absolutely.'

'Oh!'

'Why don't you join me for a spot of tea and some sticky buns? It must be nearly four.' He held open the door for her to precede him into the house, and if he guessed she'd been leaving in a huff when really she looked like death walking, he gave no sign of it. 'Do say you'll join me, Jinnie. Can't resist sticky buns, can you?' And he smiled at her in that little-boy way.

If he'd asked her to stand on her head and count to a hundred, she would have done so. Jinnie's heart was hammering so fast against her breast bone she was sure he must hear it. With a shy smile, she smoothed down the borrowed tweed skirt and walked sedately back inside.

✫   ✫   ✫

Despite the obvious antagonism from Emily, Jinnie and Edward quickly became firm friends. Each evening when he came home from the mill where he worked as a clerk in the office, he would tap on her door and ask how she was. Then he would sit by her bed and talk, about anything and everything under the sun. He told her how at some place called the New York Stock Exchange they were now trading in foreign shares, which must be good for Lancashire cotton; and how he'd seen a brilliant young actor called Laurence Olivier in a new play.

'Eeh, we come from different planets, you and me.' And he'd laugh and say he was glad that she'd landed on his.

Edward liked to discuss politics and world affairs about which Jinnie knew nothing, and she loved to sit and listen to his gentle voice. He explained how women would soon have the vote and that she'd then have a voice to which politicians would be forced to listen. And in the next breath how 200 Welsh miners who'd marched to London to protest about unemployment had failed to persuade the Prime Minister, Mr Stanley Baldwin, to meet them.

'Doesn't that just prove no one listens?' Jinnie exclaimed. 'None of them toffs wants to know about our problems.'

'Quite right, Jinnie,' Edward firmly agreed. 'Is it surprising the miners sang "The Red Flag"? It's a wonder Bella didn't march with them. She's far more knowledgeable than I am about politics and such but I do my best to take an interest, don't you know.'

It made her go all wobbly in her stomach just to have him sitting there, so fresh-faced and attentive, chatting to her as if she were his equal.

In her turn Jinnie was happy enough to answer his questions about life on the streets of Salford, or some of them anyway. She'd talk of the old women clattering about in their clogs and shawls, of the struggle to find a bit of coal or a shrive of bread to keep body and soul together, the difficulties of finding lasting employment and the shame of being on parish relief. She never mentioned Billy Quinn, nor gave any further details of her so-called accident with Bella's imaginary horse, nor commented on why she didn't go home, having now recovered from it. She rather thought Edward assumed that simply returning to live in squalor again would make her ill. Jinnie even confided something of how she'd been forced to fend for herself since she was twelve, when her mam died.

'Didn't you have a father to take care of you?' he asked, appalled, to which she admitted that she hadn't the first idea who he might be, or even if she and her brothers had shared the same one.

'Mam never said owt about him, and I never asked. I reckon he died long since.'

Fortunately Edward was more interested in the present than the past, and he would assure her that she was safe now, need never go back to that grinding poverty. 'I keep worrying you might dash off again and then I wouldn't know where to find you.'

'Why would I do that?' Jinnie had no intention of leaving, not now that she'd met Edward.

Two weeks had gone by, the two days she'd first been allowed now forgotten, and not once had Jinnie made another bolt for the door, not since she'd first clapped eyes on him. But for all she meant never to leave of her own accord, not for a minute did she believe herself to be safe. A part of her looked on this merely as an interlude, a well-earned rest in a bleak existence. Each morning she expected Billy Quinn to turn up on the doorstep and march her home to beat the living daylights out of her for thinking she could escape. And if that happened, or rather *when* it happened, she'd deal with it as she always did. With fortitude. What did it matter while she had Edward to smile at her and make her heart race?

Chapter Four

Jinnie sensed that Mrs Ashton was sorely tempted on a number of occasions to throw her out, and would have done so were it not for the attentive presence of her son. Emily soon began to insist that Jinnie was well enough to be up and about every day, and not waste her time malingering in bed. After that the pair of them would sit in the front parlour and play cards or backgammon in the evenings, though Jinnie was careful not to loiter on the stairs or in the hall from which it was but a short step to the other side of the polished front door. She was right to be cautious for a sharp warning was swiftly received when Emily caught her on her own one day.

'I'm not sure where you think all this fuss and attention will get you, but you should realise that I'm not so easily taken in as my children seem to be. I don't give a jot for your opinion, a mere street urchin, but that of my son I hold in high esteem. No one can accuse me of being unkind to the poor, but nevertheless I'll not have him taken advantage of by some little money grabber. Do I make myself clear? I shall rid my house of your presence eventually, Jinnie Cook, though it may take time and must, of necessity, be done with complete discretion. I'm sure we understand each other.'

Jinnie wisely made no response to this blunt statement. She confined herself to spending endless days amidst the shadows of the front parlour, waiting for Edward to return home from the mill each evening, hoping he would find time to talk to her.

'Why don't you come out with me one afternoon if you're

bored?' Bella suggested. 'I'm off to see one of my favourite people, Violet Howarth. Do you know her? She has a large and noisy, though surprisingly healthy, family. They live in one of the small courts off Liverpool Street. Why don't you come? Violet is a tonic for anyone.'

Jinnie shook her head. 'Happen not. Best if I keep me head down, eh?'

'Why? Who are you afraid of?' But Jinnie wasn't saying. Instead, since it was a Saturday, Edward offered to take her to a matinée and so Bella went out alone, as usual.

Edward took Jinnie to see Charlie Chaplin, and the following Wednesday they saw Douglas Fairbanks in a swashbuckling film called *The Thief of Baghdad*. Jinnie confessed that it was the first time she'd ever been to the pictures. After this, it became a favourite occupation. Once he took her to the Picture House on Oxford Street to see *The Jazz Singer*. Jinnie had never been so amazed in all her life as when she heard Al Jolson say, 'Wait a minute, wait a minute, you ain't heard nothin' yet.'

'And then he actually *sang*,' she told Bella excitedly the next morning. 'Clear as a bell it were. I would never 'ave believed it, if I hadn't heard it with me own ears.'

'You and Edward seem to be best chums,' Bella teased. 'I think he's rather sweet on you.' And she laughed out loud to see Jinnie blush.

'Don't talk soft! As if he'd look twice at a girl like me. He's just being kind, that's all, and I really should be off 'ome, not hanging about here all day wi' nowt to do.'

'You must get properly well first, then we'll find you somewhere decent to live. There's no hurry.' And Jinnie was happy to leave it that way for, much as she'd be sorry to lose this lovely posh life she was leading, she'd be sorrier still to lose Edward.

Despite the huge difference in their backgrounds Edward discovered, quite by chance, that he actually had a great deal in common with Jinnie. She might always come out of her corner with fists raised, ready for a fight, but underneath she was shy and vulnerable, afraid of making mistakes, just as he was himself. And they both felt the lack of a father's love in their lives, Jinnie because she'd no idea who hers was, Edward because no matter how hard he tried to please Simeon, he always failed.

He found it easy to talk to her because she was so warm and understanding, cheekily amusing and yet kind and sympathetic. Edward told her how school had bored him and she didn't think this in the least odd, rather a perfectly normal state of affairs, having been at odds with her own teacher because she took so many days off. 'They was allus sending the truant officer round. If he could find where we were living, that is. As if I cared about bloody school when I'd a sick mam to tek care of.'

She also seemed to find it perfectly reasonable for him to have a chip on his shoulder about being the son of a mill manager, looked down upon as working-class by those with parents who made their money from rents or land or some respectable profession like medicine or the church. 'The parents of my school chums rarely earned their comfortable incomes through trade, or from anything which could remotely make their hands mucky,' he explained. 'So I always felt the odd one out, picked upon as the one who didn't fit in. Added to which, I wasn't the brightest boy in the school. Bella should have been the boy and given the education. Certainly she thinks so.'

'Were you bullied?' Jinnie asked, dark brown eyes wide and sympathetic in her pale face. Edward strove to maintain the image he'd created of himself, one of coping, of being able to deal with whatever life threw at him, but as he looked into that melting gaze, what he read there caused his heart to judder with shock. This girl didn't think any the less of him for being bullied. She didn't give him pitying glances as Mrs Prudy's daughter did, nor blame him or think it was his own fault he got beaten, as his father had when one Christmas holiday the young Edward had tried to explain away a black eye and various bruises. Jinnie simply wrapped her loving arms about his neck and hugged him. In that moment he knew that he loved her, and would do so to the end of his days. She was the sweetest, kindest, most loving creature he'd ever met, beyond his lovely sister, and he thanked his lucky stars that she'd fallen across his path that day.

The first time he kissed her was at the Deansgate Picture House during a romantic interlude in a Mary Pickford film. Jinnie thought she might faint clean away, she went that weak inside. There'd been moments in her past when Billy Quinn's attentions had stirred some need in her but she'd never experienced anything like this. They'd sit holding hands in the dark, blissfully aware of each other's closeness; do a bit of canoodling when the gas lights were turned down, but although Jinnie gently encouraged him to be more adventurous, Edward was a real gentleman and never went beyond what was proper. To her complete astonishment, he actually appeared to respect her. She'd never experienced anything like that with Billy Quinn either.

'I'd never hurt you, Jinnie,' Edward whispered to her in the dark, his hand gently stroking her knee. 'I think I've fallen madly in love with you, do you mind?'

'I-I'm not sure.' Flushed with love herself, Jinnie longed for him to pull her into his arms and have his wicked way with her right there on the cigarette butt-strewn floor, but because he thought so well of her, she never let on how she felt. She behaved as he wanted her to behave, like a lady. Even so, Jinnie worried what he'd say if he knew the truth about her: how she'd had a backstreet abortion, slept with Billy Quinn since she was twelve, even acted as a bookie's runner for his illegal street betting ring. Oh, but she didn't want him to find out, not ever. He wouldn't respect her then, would he? Or love her even a little bit. He'd treat her as she deserved to be treated, like dirt.

*   *   *

'Get your coat on, madam,' Emily announced one morning. She was already togged up in her own ankle-length, fur-trimmed number with a velvet toque pulled well down over her frowning brow. 'We're off out.'

Jinnie had been sitting in the front parlour with no one to talk to but the aspidistra, so was more than ready for an outing, though why Emily should wish to take her anywhere, she couldn't imagine. As they hopped aboard a tramcar at the corner of Derby Road and settled into their seats, Emily asked why it was that she didn't have a job and Jinnie struggled to explain.

'There's not much work about for girls like me. Employers take one look and turn up their noses. Once yer on a downward slide, there's no way back. I tried one or two places but gave up in the end.'

'Nonsense!' Emily tutted, as if she could single-handedly cure any employer's prejudices. 'There's always work to be had, if you look hard enough. And where exactly do you live when you're not begging favours from your betters?'

Jinnie squirmed with discomfort. 'No place that I'd want to go back to, if I'm honest.'

'Then we must find you somewhere better, something more appropriate. Life isn't difficult unless you make it so,' Emily admonished her, unclipping her purse and taking out a florin to pay the twopence fare. 'As I said, I'm no fool, Jinnie Cook. In my view your layabout way of life simply encourages immorality and promiscuity, and it's time you received the right sort of supervision. Perhaps went down on your knees and expressed penitence for your wicked ways.'

'Nay, I niver did owt wicked in me life. Not knowingly anyroad,' Jinnie countered, and Emily cast her a sideways smile of satisfaction, pleased at having finally flustered her quarry.

'It all depends how you define wickedness.'

Jinnie simply looked perplexed by this, privately wondering

how Emily would have held off Billy Quinn if she'd been half starved and in his clutches.

Emily took her to the Ebenezer Mission Home for Orphans. It was a dark, forbidding building with rows of windows looking out on to the street like blank eyes. It seemed to Jinnie very like a reformatory or a workhouse. She felt her knees quake with fear as she stood in a tiny, brown-painted office and listened to Mrs Ashton discuss with the woman in charge what was to become of her.

She was to sleep in a dormitory with fifty other girls and would work in the laundry, bleaching and scrubbing, to earn her keep. Or so the warden, a large woman swathed in dark purple velveteen from neck to ankle, informed her in stentorian tones. Not that anyone asked Jinnie's opinion on the matter. It was as if she didn't exist; didn't have ears, brain or tongue in her head to express views of her own. What hope did she have of getting a government to listen to her voice, vote or no vote, if she couldn't even get a word in edgewise with two old women?

This thought, inspired by her long conversations with Edward, drove her to speak up. 'Here, 'owd on! Have I no say in the matter?' Jinnie began, only to have her arm grasped so fiercely by the purple dragon, she wouldn't have been surprised if the woman had clapped her in leg irons. The next minute Mrs Ashton had pressed a threepenny bit in her hand, told her to be a good girl and she would be well taken care of, and sailed out through the door. The sound of it clanging shut behind her would, Jinnie was certain, stay with her forever.

Billy Quinn never gave up. Like a dog with a bone, once he'd got his teeth into something, he kept them there, tearing and gnawing away until he'd got to the core of it. So it was with the matter of Jinnie. For weeks now he'd been searching for her, had all his mates keep an eye out for her but, mystifyingly, there hadn't been even a hint of a sighting. No one had the first idea where she might be hiding. But he knew she couldn't hide forever. Not from him. And now, at last, his luck had changed.

His chat with Sadie had been quite enlightening. She'd certainly come to rue the day she'd decided to interfere with Billy Quinn's domestic arrangements. The last he'd heard of her, she'd taken her two black eyes and broken ribs back to Bolton, where she'd be well advised to stay.

Now Len Jackson had got word on the street that Jinnie had been spotted going into the Ebenezer Mission. Taken there only yesterday by a well-dressed woman. Some do-gooder no doubt.

'Is he reliable, this source of yours?'

'S'far as I know. Want me to go and knock on t'door and ask?'

Billy growled his displeasure by way of reply and said he'd see to the matter personally. He was looking forward to seeing the expression on young Jinnie's face when he found her.

Bella was quite unaware of Jinnie's changed circumstances. Once the girl had settled comfortably into her new surroundings, Bella herself had quickly become absorbed back into her normal routine. In fact, she'd hardly set foot inside the house on Seedley Park Road during the last day or two. It didn't trouble her that Jinnie hadn't been in evidence the previous evening because she knew Edward had gone into Manchester on some errand for their father, and rather assumed that Jinnie had gone with him.

This afternoon, as on many another, she was busy catching up on her 'ladies'. She'd witnessed the direst poverty as usual, had advised on varicose veins, prolapsed wombs and the dangers of septicaemia, as well as extracting promises of better behaviour from several drunkard husbands, and had treated the usual assortment of sore throats, bad coughs and the ubiquitous head lice. Bella was inwardly convinced that all these everyday ills were worsened, if not actually caused, by prolific child bearing; by the burden of the large numbers of children that seemed to crowd every house; by them wearing the poor mothers down to the point of starvation, exhaustion, bad health and even death. If there was indeed some way to prevent such disasters, she would certainly like to hear of it.

She again visited Mrs Stobbs and was comforted to find young Lizzie on the mend, almost restored to her old cheerful self. Bella was delighted.

'I said that tonic would do the trick.' Mrs Stobbs beamed. 'Now, 'ow about that other little matter what I mentioned t'other day? Hasta found out what's what?'

'Not yet, I'm afraid. But I'll keep trying, I promise.' Bella wondered whether to take a chance with their old family doctor, though had little hope he would be prepared to talk to her, an unmarried woman, so kept putting the moment off.

The problem went clean out of her head when she arrived back home later that afternoon to find the house in turmoil. Bella heard the din the moment she entered the hall and found Mrs Dyson and Tilly unashamedly eavesdropping outside the parlour door.

'What on earth's going on here?' The pair had the good sense not to answer but to scurry back to the kitchen before they were given their marching orders.

This time it was Edward who was railing at his mother while Emily sat weeping and thrashing about like a woman demented. Simeon stood helplessly looking on, saying nothing as usual. He hurried over to Bella the moment he saw her come in.

'Don't get involved,' he warned, drawing her to one side. 'Something to do with that waif and stray you picked up. She's gone, and Edward is upset. He seems to be blaming Mother for not keeping a better eye on her.'

'Jinnie gone? Oh, no, where?'

'Nay, don't ask me, I'm just the master in this house. I know nowt, and I recommend that line of action to you too. Least said, soonest mended, eh? We did what we could for her, after all. Now she's gone back to her own sort.'

'Her own sort? And what *sort* would that be exactly, Father?' Bella felt outraged by his nonchalant attitude. Perhaps she didn't know her father after all.

'Na then, don't get on your high horse with me, lass. I fed and watered her, took her in off the street, and what thanks did I get? None.'

'It's not long since you were accusing me of helping her only for the sake of her gratitude.'

'*I swear I am not responsible for whatever has become of that girl!*' Emily inaccurately cried, wringing her hands with a nice dramatic flourish. 'I merely took her out for a walk in the fresh air, for the benefit of her health, that's all.'

Bella grasped her mother's hands in an effort to calm her. 'Where? Where did you walk, Mother? What exactly happened? Did Jinnie run off? When did she go?' She could almost see the battle taking place in Emily's head over whether to reveal all or fabricate a tale that might suit better. 'It's vital we learn the truth or she may be in danger from those who put her in hospital in the first place.'

She heard Edward's gasp at the very moment she recognised her error in almost blurting out the truth and hastened to rectify her mistake. 'I mean, there are those who'd not be averse to putting the blame for the accident on Jinnie, instead of the other way about. They may well be prosecuted for allowing the horse to run riot in the streets.' It sounded a feeble explanation but seemed to be accepted nonetheless.

Edward stood before his mother, his distress evident in every line of his tense body, in the clenching of his bony, boyish fists. 'Bella's right. Besides which where would she go? Surely not back to the squalor she came from. Tell us the truth, Mother. I expect no less of you.'

Tears ran down Emily's puffy cheeks. 'I did it for you, my

darling boy. She's no good for you. A trollop. No better than she should be, I'll be bound.'

'That's pure prejudice, Mother, and you know it. Not everyone without money is a thief or a harlot. Besides, I'll be the best judge of what's good for me. You've picked and chosen my friends for me long enough, mostly to no avail. It's time I had some say of my own. Where did you take her? I *insist* that you tell me.'

It was the first time in his entire life that Edward had stood up to his mother, and Bella watched with sympathy as Emily's face registered shock, and then her shoulders drooped and her whole body deflated like a punctured balloon.

'Oh, very well then. I found this marvellous place.' Just as if she had chanced upon it quite by accident. 'I thought it the perfect solution.'

'What place?' He wasn't letting her off the hook, not yet.

She put one hand to her brow. 'Oh, my head, my poor head. Why are you all so cross with me? I found her a place at the Mission, if you must know. It's a God-fearing place where she'll be properly cared for and led into the paths of righteousness.' Emily fell back in her chair, both hands now clutched to her head in a desperate appeal for mercy, her voice falling to a pitiful whimper. 'I did it for the best. It's where she belongs.'

Simeon turned on his son in a fury. 'Now see what you've done, you great daft lump! You've upset your mother good and proper and she was only doing her best for the lass. You ought to be horsewhipped, great bully that you are.'

'*You're* the bully, not me. It was no doubt all your idea to get rid of her. You're *glad* that Jinnie's gone. Both of you are. Well, *I* liked her, even if you didn't.'

Simeon seemed to swell to twice his normal size as he took a threatening step towards his son, huge fists clenched. 'Take that back, you jumped up, lily-livered excuse for a . . .'

'*Stop it!*' Bella rushed to intervene between father and son, as she'd had reason to do many times in the past. 'It's no use quarrelling between ourselves. I brought her here, so Jinnie is my responsibility. I'm the one to sort this out.'

'She's not *your* responsibility,' Edward shouted above the tears and accusations, in a voice quite unlike his own. 'She's *mine!* Jinnie and I love each other and I mean to make her my wife.' At which point Emily let out a terrible scream and fainted clean away.

Chapter Five

By the time Edward and Bella reached the Ebenezer Mission, the warden informed them in stiff official tones that nine o'clock was far too late to wake anyone. 'There was a young man here earlier asking after the very same girl but I told him the same as I shall tell you, she is asleep and cannot be disturbed. Mind you, he was most demanding, insisted he would be back first thing in the morning. Proper ruffian he looked too.' She sniffed her disapproval as she crossed well-muscled arms over her ample, purple-clad bosom, pointedly expressing her ability to see off such hangers-on with ease, should it become necessary.

Bella, concerned by this news, asked if he had given any name.

The warden shook her head. 'Friend or relative. He didn't say and I didn't care to ask. How these gels get involved with such villains I shall never understand if I live to be a hundred, but it's none of my business. He was wasting his time and I told him as much.'

Edward, by contrast, possessed excellent manners and was clearly a gentleman. It took him no time at all to exercise his charm on the warden and Jinnie was brought from her bed, still rubbing the sleep from her eyes. The moment she saw Edward, she flew into his arms with a cry of delight.

Bella hid a smile as she thought how her mother would react to this obvious show of affection. Much to her relief, there was no sign of either parent when they returned home later that night, so Bella helped Jinnie into bed and left her

to finish her sleep. There'd be time enough to talk tomorrow.

'I niver 'eard owt so daft in me life. *Me, married?* To Edward?'
Jinnie stared at Bella, disbelief on her pinched elfin face.

'I'm sorry, I thought he'd already asked you. I've spoiled it
for you, haven't I?'

Nay, ye've spoiled nowt. I'm not fit to lick his boots. He's a
proper gent and me, I'm – I'm . . .' Lost for words to describe her
own shortcomings, Jinnie fell to the usual Lancashire epithets.
'I'm nowt. Less than nowt.'

Bella chuckled. 'Oh, I wouldn't go so far as to say that. You
have some rather remarkable qualities. Determination for one
thing. Stubbornness. Courage.'

'Bloody-minded more like.'

'That too.' Jinnie gave a half smile and Bella came to sit
beside her on the sofa. It was past midday and Emily still had
not risen so Bella was taking the opportunity to initiate a little
heart-to-heart. The two girls had lifted the green paper blind to
let in whatever sunlight was available, and so that they could see
out on to the soot-encrusted houses opposite.

'Edward's utterly smitten. He adores you. I rather thought
you felt the same way about him?'

Jinnie looked forlorn. 'What can you do when clogs let
watter in?'

'Pardon?'

'Yer can't help gettin' wet. And I can't help loving him.'

'Oh, I see.' Bella was laughing out loud now. 'You have such
wonderful sayings. I'd never think of them in a million years.'

'What's so funny?' challenged Jinnie, upper lip curling in
that too-familiar snarl, and Bella hastily assured her that she'd
meant no offence and although the girl flinched away, hugged
her determinedly. Jinnie's shoulders felt bone-thin and rigid in
her grasp.

'There, that's to prove we're friends.'

'Eeh, I should niver have come here. I'm that sorry to have caused all this rumpus.'

'Don't apologise, I'm glad you came. I needed a friend. In fact, I've always longed for a sister. A sister-in-law would be every bit as good.'

Jinnie's dark brown eyes opened wide with appeal. 'But you must see that I couldn't ever marry your Edward. You know I couldn't.'

'Whyever not?'

'Because of what I did, of why you took me to that hospital. Edward thinks I had a terrible accident with a horse, fer God's sake. But we knows different. That nurse said I'd mucked mesel' up inside and I'd probably niver 'ave another. She seemed to think it were a blessing. So did I, at the time. Now – now it's anything but. Edward deserves a decent wife, childer of his own to carry on the family name. So how could I marry him? Oh, but you're right in one respect,' she gasped. 'I do love him. I think the world of him but theer's nowt I can do about it.'

It was the longest speech Bella had heard the poor girl make and pity swelled in her heart to witness the anguish in those bewitching eyes, revealing the pain Jinnie felt. Bella took hold of her hand. It still felt too fragile and trustingly childlike clasped between her own. She weighed her words carefully before she spoke. 'Why don't you tell him the truth? Why don't you explain to Edward all about your "accident"?'

Jinnie was vigorously shaking her head, eyes growing ever wider and darker if were that possible, revealing her terror. 'Nay, how could I do that wi'out ... telling him everything?'

'Perhaps you should. Tell him everything, I mean. Edward isn't an ogre. He isn't a snob like Mother, though she's more hot air and temperament than real malice. And even she would accept you, given time, because of Edward.'

'Sun shine out of his backside, does it? Aye, I thought so.' Jinnie's lips twitched and Bella burst into fresh laughter.

'You'd be so good for him. Good for us all. You make me laugh. You could make him laugh, make him happy at last. Edward is far too serious, always trying to please, striving to be the son his parents expect. He was just the same at school. Always far too quiet and retiring for his own good. Withdrawn almost, at times. He's always felt such a failure, like a square peg in a round hole. Perhaps you can help him to grow into himself and be a person in his own right, instead of what my parents expect him to be.'

There was a long silence while Jinnie appeared to consider all of this. Then she shook her head. 'Nay, I'd bring him nowt but disappointment and trouble, like yer mam says.'

'Isn't it what Edward says that matters? He's the one you'd be marrying, not my mother. If he asks you, and I'm sure that he will, at least tell him the truth about yourself. Give him the chance to decide.'

'He'd never speak to me again.'

Bella sighed. 'That's the risk you'd take, of course, but at least you'd know, wouldn't you?'

'Aye.' Jinnie became thoughtful. 'I'd know wheer I stood then right enough. Reet in t' muck midden.' And the pair of them started rolling about on the sofa while Bella mopped tears from their eyes, though whether they were caused by joy or sadness, she couldn't have said, not for certain.

The very next evening Edward took Jinnie out for supper, clearly intending to propose. Simeon and Bella hovered in the front parlour, peeping out through the lace curtains to watch the pair depart. Jinnie looking utterly charming in a borrowed green linen dress that hung in soft pleats about her slender figure, a close-fitting cap atop her now carefully washed and shining curls.

'I hope that lad knows what he's letting himself in for.'

'I'm sure he does, Pa. He loves her, and Jinnie is really very sweet. She'll do him no end of good. See how proudly she walks by his side, just as if she's been waiting for this moment all her life.' Tears thickened in her throat to see the couple's evident happiness and for a moment Bella envied them.

'I just wish I knew a bit more about her.'

'What is there to know? Stop worrying.' And kissing her father on his whiskered cheek, she pushed him gently in the direction of the door. 'Go on. Get on with your paperwork, or read the *Manchester Chronicle*, whatever it is you do in that study of yours. Everything will work out, you'll see.'

'I hope you're right,' was all Simeon said, looking anxious. 'But we'll soon find out either way, I dare say.'

They found out the following morning when Edward stood before his parents, the one ashen-faced, the other beetroot red with fury, and calmly informed them that he had indeed asked Jinnie to marry him and that she had accepted. Furthermore, since he was of age, there was nothing they could do about the matter.

'I have no wish for my wedding to be a hole-in-the-corner affair,' he continued, standing firm. 'You wanted me to wed, Mother, so, ever the obedient son, I mean to do so.'

As Emily made little choking noises, Simeon patted his wife's heaving shoulders and faced his son with barely contained anger. 'I've never heard owt so daft in all me life. Apart from owt else, the lass is young. Barely sixteen. I'll not have you throw away everything we've worked for all our lives. A good future for you in t'mill. A place in society. All you could rightly expect from life for some young chit . . .'

'All *you* expected of me,' Edward corrected Simeon, but his face too was pale and drawn with tension.

It was clear to Bella that the question of Jinnie's age had never entered her brother's head and she went to give his arm a comforting squeeze. 'Pa does have a point. She's little more than a child and you've known her only a few short weeks. Why don't you allow more time to get to know each other a little better?'

'Aye, that's the ticket,' Simeon agreed, snatching at the possibility of a postponement at least. 'You both need time to know your own minds.'

'I don't *need time*. I know my own mind well enough.' Edward's pale, lean face took on a hunted expression and Bella's heart ached for him.

'I'm sure you do,' she hastily put in, throwing her father a fierce glance to silence him. 'But this is all new to Jinnie. She needs time to adjust, to grow up a little. At sixteen she doesn't even know who she *is* yet, let alone what she wants from life. It's our duty and responsibility to help her to find employment, get strong and healthy, make her way in the world.'

'You mean, in *our* world.'

'That's not entirely what I meant but it's true that you and Jinnie do come from hugely different backgrounds. Get engaged if you must, but the wedding should wait until she's older. Two years would be about right.'

'*Two years!*'

Ignoring his protest Bella pressed on. 'If Mother would agree, we could let her make a home with us, see that she is safe and well. It could be by way of a trial, or experiment: to give Jinnie time to mature a little as well as to make sure that you are both compatible. Marriage is for life after all.'

'Quite so.' This from Emily who appeared strangely calm. While Simeon stood in his favourite position by the empty grate, hands behind his back, rocking on his heels as if at any moment he might catapult across the room and punch his son on the chin, Emily surprised them all by agreeing without protest to what she might have been expected to consider an outrageous suggestion. Perhaps because she believed two years would be ample time for her son to grow tired of this capricious notion.

Edward, however, was not appeased. 'I think it would be presumptuous. I don't need any – experiment to know that I'm in love with Jinnie and want her for my wife. What's more, she has admitted to loving me, so I don't give a brass farthing if she isn't middle-class.'

Emily's eyes seemed not to be entirely focused as she confronted her son. 'Sneer all you like but a middle-class life-style is the one she would have to lead as your wife. She would have standards to maintain, social engagements, a diary of charitable functions to fulfil, a house to run. And you expect this – this *street urchin* – to be equal to such tasks?'

Edward gritted his teeth, clearly attempting to hang on to his patience. 'Those are tasks that you have chosen to undertake, Mother. Jinnie can make up her own mind.'

'They are *duties!* Your father isn't just some tomfool overlooker, he's the mill manager no less, with a position, nay status, to maintain. *You are off your head* if you imagine I will *ever* accept that girl, a trollop with a man for every day of the week I shouldn't wonder, as *my* daughter-in-law. The very idea is monstrous!' Emily's calm was deserting her now.

'Nevertheless I will not give her up, Mother. I mean to marry Jinnie without delay.' Whereupon Emily completely lost control and let out a great wail of distress as if the very idea were too dreadful to bear.

Bella hastily intervened. 'I'm sure she isn't like that at all, Mother. She's really very sweet and can't help being poor as a church mouse.' Emily simply wailed all the louder.

'Na then, na then. Let's all try to keep calm, shall we?' Simeon pronounced in his most pompous tones, looking about him in flustered desperation as if praying for deliverance when in fact no one seemed even to be listening to him.

Emily was certainly beyond listening to anyone. 'I want that girl out of my house *this instant!*'

'If she goes, then I go with her,' Edward shouted back.

'Happen it would be best if we set the subject to one side for a bit,' Simeon suggested, attempting once more to calm things, muffling Emily's wails with a large white handker-chief as he fussed about her. 'What d'you say to that, eh?

We'll all sleep on it for a day or two. Take a breather, as it were.'

'Two years isn't very long, Edward. Besides, it will take Mother at least that time to plan the perfect wedding for you,' Bella soothed, throwing a teasing smile in Emily's direction to soften the words. It was not returned.

Edward's expression was bleak as he watched his mother's obvious distress, but Bella could see that he was weakening. 'Two years! It seems like a lifetime.'

'It'll fly by. Till then you could walk out together, court in the time-honoured way. Don't you think Jinnie deserves that much at least?'

Edward cast his sister a sheepish smile. 'I suppose I was denying her a bit of courting and I do want Jinnie to have the best wedding that money can buy. A proper bridal gown and everything.' He was clearly warming to the scheme so that he didn't recognise the glazed expression that still lingered in his mother's eyes as he dropped a kiss on to her brow. 'Two years then. But we marry the minute Jinnie reaches eighteen, not a day later. She has no family of any sort so you can stand in for her till then, Ma, and be the mother she badly needs.'

'You want me to be that trollop's *mother*?' Emily spluttered. It was the last straw. Anyone would have thought he'd asked her to dance naked in St Peter's Square, so shocked was she by the suggestion. But it was clear there was to be no further argument. The matter, so far as Edward was concerned, was settled.

His half-demented mother was carried to her bed and tucked in with a hot water bottle. Bella administered a sleeping draught while Simeon declared she'd be as right as ninepence in the morning, before escaping to his study.

Not when she learns that all her fears are well founded, Bella ruefully admitted to herself.

On her own way up to bed, she peeped in on Jinnie and

found her sleeping as soundly as a child, which was what she still was in a way: an irresistible combination of emotional vulnerability coupled with a worldly wisdom beyond her years. She seemed so frail and tiny in the huge bed, arms flung back upon the pillows, the violet bruises beneath the closed lids seeming even more marked in the dim light cast from Bella's lamp.

'Mother would not hesitate to throw you out on the streets if she knew about the abortion,' she told the sleeping girl. Bella couldn't even be certain how Edward would react if he learned the truth about the 'accident'. Yet it couldn't be kept from him indefinitely, not if he truly meant to marry her. He was conservative enough to want a traditional family life, something which it seemed Jinnie could never provide.

'You must tell him in the morning,' Bella whispered, before quietly slipping out of the room and softly closing the door.

Whether or not Jinnie would have summoned the courage to reveal the truth about herself the next morning was not put to the test. Sometime during the night Bella awoke to find her father shaking her by the shoulder in obvious agitation.

'It's your mother, lass. She's not well. Not well at all. She's taken a bad turn in the night. I've sent for the doctor.'

It seemed that when Simeon had finally gone to his bed, after a stiff whisky or two in the quiet of his study, Emily had again started ranting and railing about her inconsiderate son. She'd complained bitterly about Edward's utter selfishness and the lure of evil women, and eventually got herself into such a lather of distress that she'd fallen back on to the pillows jabbering nonsense, her twitching body suddenly gripped by a seizure.

Emily Ashton had apparently suffered a stroke. The doctor who issued this damning diagnosis was not their usual family practitioner but his new partner, Dr Nathaniel Lisle, and for that reason alone Simeon refused to accept it.

'Utter poppycock!' was his immediate reaction. 'My wife is as fit as a flea and always has been.' Then he turned upon his son, standing in bemusement by the bed in his dressing gown and carpet slippers. 'This is all your fault, you and your damned notions of fancy weddings to some guttersnipe you know nowt about. Look what a pickle you've got us all in.'

Edward recoiled as if he'd been struck. He was already beside himself with guilt and, no matter how much Bella assured him that the seizure could well have happened anyway, refused to be comforted. It was only when he found Jinnie on the front doorstep, attempting to sneak away, that he pulled himself together sufficiently to beg her not to leave him, for how could they be blamed for falling in love?

'I need you more than ever now, Jinnie.'

'But you'd be better off wi'out me,' She told him though her tears. 'I've brought nowt but trouble, like your ma says.'

'Stuff and nonsense! I mean to buy you an engagement ring and marry you just as soon as you're old enough. Bella thinks we should wait till you're eighteen and I'm not against the idea, now that I've had time to think on it. Can you wait that long? We could walk out together meanwhile, get to know each other better. I'll take such good care of you, dear Jinnie. Do please say that you will? How could I face life without you beside me?'

'You don't ever have to try,' Jinnie said, and the pair clung together, kissing away the tears as they held each other tight in a warm embrace. In spite of his mother's stroke, not for one moment was Edward prepared to risk losing his love.

Over the days following, the nature of Emily's plight became all too apparent. She lay in bed quite unable to move, hands curled into furious fists, mouth twisted in a macabre leer, above which blazed a pair of eyes dark with anger.

Not knowing how to put things right, Simeon sat day after day in his study, head in hands, refusing even to go to the mill. Anxious-looking clerks hovered in the hall but he refused to receive any of them. His life had fallen apart. It took all of Bella's tact and persuasion to convince him to carry on.

'Where would any of us be if the mill were to fail and you

were blamed for it? You have to go to work, Pa, if only to see that the others are doing what they're paid to do. Mother won't even notice you are gone, since you now have to sleep in the dressing room.'

'She may need me.'

'I shall be there to see to her.' With sinking heart, Bella thought this could well prove to be her lot in life from now on. Though she and her mother had never been close, it was more than she could bear to see Emily like this. Bella abandoned her regular afternoon calls and instead devoted herself entirely to the invalid's care, bathing her, feeding her with sips of beef tea, chatting to her or reading aloud snippets of news from the *Manchester Guardian* in the hope of engaging the interest of this wreck of a woman who lay prone and twisted in the great brass bed. The prospect of the years stretching ahead spent caring for her stricken mother filled her with dismay, coupled with a very real sense of guilt that it should. Dear God, she would go mad. 'Besides, we can't afford for you to lose your job. Who would pay for Mother's care then? She's going to need a great deal in the future, even when she starts on the road to recovery which I'm sure she'll do soon.'

It was this last, desperate plea which finally registered and the very next morning Simeon put on his three-piece worsted suit, attached his stiffest white collar to his blue striped shirt, added his blackest tie and hat, and left the house on the stroke of five-thirty, umbrella in hand.

Edward, too, went to the mill as usual. Dr Lisle called regularly every morning and, little by little, the daily routine of the house returned to normal, save for the fact that Bella's calls on Mrs Stobbs, Violet and her other 'ladies' must now cease. She regretted this hugely since the hushed atmosphere which emanated from the sick room was so depressing she would have welcomed any respite with open arms.

Bella was also concerned about Jinnie's continued avoidance

of the subject of the 'accident'. She'd finally admitted that she hadn't yet got around to explaining it all to Edward.

'He were – was – that excited when he asked me to marry him, I just couldn't spoil it for him. For either of us, if I'm honest. Then he told me about how we're to be engaged for two years afore we wed, so there's plenty of time, eh? It don't seem quite the right moment to tell him now, do it? He's troubles enough on his plate.'

'But you must tell him soon. You can't agree to marry Edward without telling him the truth, and the longer you leave it, the more painful it will be for you both. It's my fault in the first place for making up the tale. Would you like me to explain?'

Jinnie was adamant that she would do it herself, even pleaded with Bella to say nothing. 'I'll tell him. I will. Soon as maybe.'

Yet even these worries were overridden by deeper concerns about Bella's own situation when it became clear that her mother's condition showed little sign or hope of improvement.

Caring for the poor and needy was one thing but, for all she was more fond of her mother than she'd perhaps realised, being chained to her sick bed without hope of remission was another matter altogether. There had to be a better solution if Bella were not to forfeit her youth and freedom entirely. She set about finding it with renewed determination, resolving to discuss the matter with her mother's physician at the very first opportunity.

Chapter Six

Dr Lisle was a thin, wiry, bespectacled man who had clearly devoted himself to medicine since, at well past forty, he was still single. Thin strands of fading hair were carefully stuck down over a polished pate, though he wore a bushy moustache above his narrow top lip as if to prove he had once been endowed with a fine head of black hair. From either side of his small neat head protruded a pair of well-shaped ears. But none of this troubled Bella in the least, for though he was somewhat pedantic and formal in his approach, he possessed a cheerful enough aspect and an optimistic outlook that would be welcome in any sick room. His least endearing feature was the slightly fishy odour which seemed ever to cling to his clothes. This was caused by the fact that he occupied two rooms above Mr Solomon's fish shop and, clean as the premises undoubtedly were, there was no escaping the aroma which rose to the rooms above.

He appeared actively to court Bella's approval by frequently mentioning his work with the deserving poor, admitting to having given treatment on numerous occasions without any hope of being paid. 'It is a sad fact of life that those who need it the most can afford it the least.'

Bella listened with some amusement to all of this but guessed that her father would receive a large bill for the care of his wife on this occasion, though she supposed Dr Lisle was at least assiduous in giving value for money. Yet she still hadn't plucked up the courage to mention the subject of most concern to her.

As Christmas and New Year passed, the little doctor

continued to visit on a daily basis. Eventually, she remarked upon it. 'Perhaps you don't need to come quite so often now, Doctor, though a nurse perhaps, would be beneficial.'

He smiled cheerily at her. 'I'm sure you can give much better care to your dear mother than any nurse.'

'That's not necessarily the case, but even if it were true, in all honesty the task of caring for her is a hard one. I could do with a break now and then.' Emily seemed to be adept at ringing her bell at night just when Bella had finally drifted off to sleep, and everyone else in the house appeared to be either constantly absent or stone deaf.

Dr Lisle tut-tutted sympathetically. 'Of course it naturally falls entirely upon you, as the unmarried daughter.'

Bella attempted to smile through gritted teeth. 'I would simply like a nurse to help me.'

'Of course, of course, my dear.' But the following day he did not bring a nurse, only an invitation to supper. 'As single people with similar interests, perhaps you and I could provide some respite to each other from the caring work we both undertake so unstintingly. A little socialising would be good for us both. I thought that tomorrow, being Saturday, we could take a stroll around the Penny Bazaar. I know young ladies like to shop,' he teased, eyes twinkling. 'Perhaps finishing with tea at the Lyons House on the corner of Princess Street, or supper in my rooms if you prefer. Mrs Solomon could do us a nice bit of hake, I am sure.'

Bella felt a surge of panic. This wasn't what she'd intended at all. Her benevolent view of him now quite gone, the very idea of spending an entire afternoon or evening with Dr Nathaniel Lisle filled her with horror. But how to refuse without causing offence? 'It's kind of you to offer but I couldn't possibly leave Mother. Perhaps some other time, when she is feeling more herself.'

'Of course. I beg your pardon for intruding. I shall ask again later.'

Bella sincerely hoped that he would not.

She felt a complete coward. Taking supper with the doctor, surely an obliging enough little man, might well have given her the opportunity she'd once craved to ask some pertinent questions and find the solutions Mrs Stobbs, for one, so eagerly sought. How was poor Mrs Stobbs managing without her? She must be well on with her latest pregnancy by this time. Bella was filled with guilt that she hadn't been to see her, or any of her 'ladies', for weeks now. Nor had she done anything about the Marie Stopes book which Mrs Dyson had mentioned. Sadly, her mother's ill health had driven all such concerns, if not exactly out of mind, certainly out of her daily routine.

Dr Lisle's persistent attentions did, however, remind her of another matter on her conscience. She went to her brother and asked if Jinnie had spoken to him yet.

'About what?'

Bella's heart plummeted. She was wishing more and more that she'd never made up that tale of the runaway horse. This mythical accident was turning into a nightmare to haunt her. Yet what else could she have done? Mother would never have taken Jinnie into the house if she'd known the truth. 'There's something she wants to tell you.'

Edward's expression brightened. 'Has she decided that she'd rather marry me now, and not wait for two years?'

Bella sighed. 'You must ask her that yourself. I'm sure she will explain everything to you, in her own good time.'

Jinnie could hardly believe her good fortune. In her pocket jingled twelve shillings and sixpence, evidence of a proper week's work for the first time in her life. Up until now she'd never earned more than five bob, doing a bit of washing or charring here and there. Quinn had always been at pains to explain that she wasn't really employable, being one of the undeserving poor, and therefore entirely dependent upon his generosity to keep body and soul together.

It was Saturday and the mill had shut its gates for the weekend. She, along with hundreds of other girls, had joined the exultant exodus, free to do as she pleased till six o'clock on Monday morning. The clatter of clogs on the setts, competing loudly with the chatter and happy laughter, not forgetting the blare of the mill hooter, seemed to bounce off stone walls and wet pavements, filling the damp air with an atmosphere which, to Jinnie at least, seemed the very essence of joy.

They piled on to tramcars, jostling and joking, planning to spend the afternoon in the Flat Iron market, perhaps treating themselves to a toasted tea cake at the Broadway Café, then take in a flick or go to a dance at the Empress Ballroom on Church Street. The men would look forward to the Saturday match, a new packet of Woodbines or a threepenny bet on the two-thirty, and, win or lose, finish off with a bit of forgetfulness in the local pub. Simple, ordinary pleasures which Jinnie had been denied for so long.

Now she was one of the crowd. She had a job, albeit one spent filing or running errands in the mill office at the beck and call of the terrifying Miss Tadcaster. But it was a start. She also had regular meals every single night of the week. Even a bath, should she feel the need of one.

Then there was Edward.

Jinnie's insides melted just thinking about him. He was the dearest, sweetest man she'd ever met, and so determined they should wed, the excitement was at times almost too much for her to bear. It made her feel sick with a funny sort of fear. What if she wasn't good enough for him? What if he got bored by her stupidity and ignorance, or she embarrassed him by picking up the wrong knife or making a daft remark? And then there was the thorny question of children. Edward hadn't yet brought the subject up, being a shy man and them being new to this courting lark, but it was bound to be mentioned eventually. What should she say? Should she explain what she'd got Sadie to do? It was all right Bella telling her to be honest and truthful but one thing led to another. If she told him the truth about that dreadful night, then she'd have to explain how she came to be in that condition in the first place, which led to all sorts of complications.

Jinnie grasped the coins in her pocket and smiled to herself. Oh, but she'd worry about all that when the time came. For now she was on cloud nine. She was in love, just like Vilma Banky with Rudolph Valentino in that film *The Son of the Sheik*.

It was as she swung around the corner into Unwin Street that she ran into him, full tilt. One minute her life was perfect with a glint of sunshine on the horizon, the next it was all slipping away from her and she was drenched in fear.

'Hello, Jinnie girl. Long time no see.'

Billy Quinn. He was lounging against the wall as if he'd known she would come, if he waited long enough. Happen he did know. Happen he'd been following her for days, just waiting for Saturday when the mill closed early. A cold nub of fear churned in her stomach. If she'd waited an hour or two longer, till Edward had finished some accounts he was working on, she could've walked home with him. But she'd wanted to be one of the girls and now look what a pickle she'd got herself into as a result.

'Hello, Quinn,' she said, praying the nervousness inside wasn't revealing itself in her voice.

'Ye look well. In fact, I cannot recall ever seeing ye look better. Is it the new job that agrees with ye, or the company ye keep these days? Quite the swell, eh?'

Jinnie decided she'd no option but to brazen it out. She even managed the semblance of a smile. 'I'm doin' gradely weel, thanks. And yersel'?'

'Middlin', as you Lankys say.' He had on his Saturday suit, a houndstooth check jacket and waistcoat over matching trousers, a white cotton muffler tucked into the collar. On his head he wore a slouch cap, tilted cheekily to one side, and the inevitable cigarette was drooping from the corner of those full lips. Jinnie had forgotten how very good-looking he was and for a moment her stomach clenched, remembering those nights when he'd instructed her in what he termed 'the arts of satisfaction'. Billy Quinn never made the mistake of mentioning love. 'It took me a while to work out where you'd gone. Haven't seen you about for weeks.'

'I've been ill.' Jinnie could have kicked herself for owning up even to this much, in case he should start questioning what had caused the illness. But as he blithely continued, saying how sorry he'd been to hear of her loss, it soon became all too clear that it was too late to worry. He knew already. He must've got it out of Sadie. Jinnie didn't care to consider how and felt even sicker at what this meant for her own future.

'I'm wondering why ye didn't think to come to me first,' he mildly remarked, and Jinnie mumbled something about not wanting to trouble him but Quinn only laughed – a harsh grating sound that held not a scrap of humour in it. ''T'would've been no trouble. No trouble at all. If'n ye'd explained how yer were worried over having a babby, don't ye think I would've taken care of you better than daft Sadie? 'Tis a pity ye had such little faith in me that ye couldn't mention such an important matter to me first. And now these secrets are meking even more trouble, are they not? 'Tis a terrible mess ye've brought upon yerself.'

Jinnie was shaking her head, the sickness now making her feel giddy and light-headed in her fear, quite unable to think straight. She longed to turn and run as fast as her skinny legs could carry her but knew they'd be nowhere near fast enough for the job, not to escape Billy Quinn. There wasn't a person born could run that fast.

As if to remind her of this fact he grasped her arm and twisted it up her back. 'Ye weren't t'inking of running off again, were ye now?'

Jinnie could hardly draw breath, let alone speak. One more tweak of her arm and she was sure it would come right out of its socket. She shook her head and with a little chuckle he released it. Jinnie gave a cry of pain as it fell to her side which only made him laugh all the more. Knocking her back against the wall, he pushed one knee between her legs, rubbing it up hard against her groin. 'We've had some fun, you and me. And I don't easily let go of what's rightly mine. Don't ye realise how much I'd miss ye, Jinnie lass? How much I'd need ye.'

She began to whimper. 'Let me go, Quinn. You don't need me. I'm worth nowt. There's plenty of women who'd give their right arm to be with you.'

'Aye, but I don't want plenty of women. I want you, me little treasure, and I've got yer right arm already, have I not?' Taking hold of it again he tucked the arm, now blue with bruises, into his own in a parody of friendly companionship. 'I'll tell ye what I'll do, I swear me lips are permanently sealed. This new chap of yours will niver hear a word about your little difficulty from me if . . .' He paused, smiled his handsome, devil-may-care smile. 'Ye do have a new chap, d'you not? Is that not the way of it, Jinnie? I know ye well, so don't t'ink to tell me any porkies.' And Jinnie could do nothing but nod in a dazed sort of way. 'Well then, we don't want to spoil such a promising future for ye both, now do we? I'm sure we can work out some way fer ye to repay my generosity, if'n we put our heads together. Why don't we go and have a bite of dinner and see what we come up with? What d'you say, girl?'

With her arm grasped so tightly within his and the fear so tight in her belly, Jinnie had little choice but to go along with his plan and agree.

By the end of January, Bella despaired of ever returning to anything like a normal routine. She felt sick to her stomach with the constant smell of camphorated oil and liniment, with emptying chamber pots and lifting her mother on and off them. Fortunately, or unfortunately, depending upon your point of view, Emily had partly regained the power of speech though she had not, as yet, agreed to demonstrate this skill to the doctor. Nevertheless she would constantly whine to Bella to fetch Edward, who she complained rarely visited her.

'H-have been – g-good m-mither, not?' she'd complain, the words often slurred or jumbled. 'Why dushhe defy me?'

'Don't worry about it, Mother. All you have to do is to get well.' But Emily, as was her wont, showed no sign of patience and on one occasion threw such a tantrum of rage, screaming and yelling and foaming at the mouth, that Tilly was sent running to the mill to fetch Edward upon the instant. He came at once and sat by her bed for hours, holding his mother's hand while she simpered with love for him.

Bella was nauseated by this display and described the distressing scene to the doctor when he arrived promptly at ten o'clock the next morning, as was his custom. 'I feared for her sanity, yet the rage left her the moment Edward arrived.'

He stood holding Emily's limp wrist while he counted her pulse. Like many of his profession he still seemed able to carry on a conversation at the same time. 'Unfortunate indeed and, as you say, most distressing, but at least her son came when needed. Most commendable. She is well blessed. And you, my dear, are fortunate to have such a brother who is ready and willing to give up his work and offer the care your mother undoubtedly needs.' The usually mild tone was coloured by the slightest hint of acid.

Surprised, Bella still felt bound to agree. 'I don't deny it but Edward can't make a habit of coming home in the middle of the day. He must work, as must Father. Jinnie does what she can but she too has taken a job at the mill, as she is eager to pay her way. On the other hand, I cannot be with Mother around the clock.'

'Whyever not? You showed no sign of needing respite the other day, when I invited you out for supper.'

So that was the way the land lay. Bella sighed, swallowing a natural inclination to retaliate. 'Are you sure you can't find a nurse to help me?'

'Is our patient eating properly?' Ignoring the question he spoke over her mother's head, as if Emily were deaf as well as paralysed.

'Why don't you ask her? She can speak for herself now.'

'Fooling yourself that your dear mother doesn't need your full-time care will not ease your conscience indefinitely, Miss Ashton,' he coldly remarked as he tucked the limp wrist beneath the covers, smoothing down the sheet before proceeding to peer into the eyes of his patient.

Emily glared back at him in mute fury while Bella sighed her frustration. 'Speak to the good doctor, Mother. You know that you can, if you try.' The patient, however, remained obstinately silent and Dr Lisle's expression revealed his disbelief that she was even capable of it.

'You fancy yourself as some sort of medical authority, do you, Miss Ashton?'

Bella wasn't sure whether he mocked her or not but she answered with all due seriousness. 'I wouldn't presume to class myself as a professional since I have no qualifications of any kind, but I do what I can to help those in need. There are many women out there who perhaps need me more than my mother.' She jerked her head in the direction of the street. 'I do what I can to help because people trust me.'

'Ah, a lady of charitable good works. Of course, of course.' Nodding and smiling rather dismissively, the next instant he was shaking his head as he frowned at the thermometer. 'Dear me,' he tutted. 'Temperature normal but I had hoped we would be out of bed by this time. You *are* giving your poor dear mother the massages I mentioned?'

'Every two hours,' Bella agreed, smarting at having her most earnest endeavours so casually dismissed, as if she were not truly sincere in her work. 'I have the aching arms to prove it.'

'Splendid, splendid. I'm sure we'll see some benefit soon.' Leaning closer, he addressed his patient in ringing tones. 'We'll have you up out of this bed for one hour every morning,

Mrs Ashton. We'll enjoy that, won't we? Do us the world of good.'

Emily made a spluttering sound, very like fury, deep in her throat.

As he stepped away from the bed to collect his bag, Bella stubbornly returned to her own concerns. 'The women in these parts are in need of whatever help they can get, since their doctors give little enough attention to female problems.'

Dr Lisle raised a pair of mildly enquiring eyebrows. 'You have some criticism of the medical profession, Miss Ashton?'

'I merely criticise priorities which seem to be rooted in the Dark Ages.'

'For instance?'

Casting an anxious glance at her mother, Bella led him smartly from the room and briskly closed the door. In truth, she felt rather caught out since he'd already admitted to working for nothing on occasion for those in greatest need, and she could hardly blame him for the behaviour of his less altruistic colleagues. Even so, Dr Lisle seemed determined to find fault and demand from her a devotion which surely ranked far beyond the call of duty.

Out on the landing, Bella hesitated only a fraction before making up her mind to grasp the nettle. Adopting a pleasantly professional tone, she calmly announced, 'Birth control. So many women I meet are desperate to learn more about it. Their health, in many cases, depends upon it yet who will explain to them the facts? Certainly not their doctors who seem to imagine women would be committing some crime against humanity by using any kind of preventative measure. The only true crime is against the women themselves, keeping them in unnecessary ignorance so that husbands may enjoy their "rights" at the cost of a wife's health, even her life.' She stopped, mainly through lack of breath.

Dr Lisle was staring at her as if she had grown two heads. It took several moments for him to find his voice. 'The general view is that these matters should best be decided on moral rather than medical grounds.'

'How ill must a woman be to procure the help she so desperately needs? I have witnessed prolapsed wombs, procured miscarriages, fevers, stillbirths, frequent haemorrhaging and dreadful pain, not to mention exhaustion and varicose veins by the score. You may dismiss me as a lady of charitable good causes if you wish but I have seen more real distress than most young women my age.'

Clearly embarrassed at the mention of such personal female matters, Doctor Lisle's palid cheeks turned a dull red as he closed his eyes and held up one hand in a peremptory fashion, as if to ward off further disclosures or perhaps to remind her of the presence of their patient, separated from them by only a door. 'I can see you have strong feelings on the subject but this is neither the time nor place for such a debate.'

Tossing her head so that the red-gold curls bounced more wildly than ever, Bella preceded him down the stairs, a flounce in her step as she descended. 'And I see that you take the usual masculine view that a single woman should continue in the fanciful notion that babies are found under a bush, or perhaps that they come from nightly prayer, though clearly praying for the opposite will do nothing to help such as poor Mrs Stobbs.'

'Mrs Stobbs?' He sounded out of breath in his efforts to keep pace with her.

'A patient of mine who ...'

'*Patient*, Miss Ashton? I thought you said you had no qualifications.' His voice was irritatingly smug.

'I mean friend, client, a woman in desperate need of help.' Bella pulled open the front door with a flourish, furious at her slip, and stood back to allow him to pass.

Dr Lisle smiled at her, gracious as ever. 'Abstinence is the most moral victory of all, Miss Ashton. And extremely effective. I will say that you are surprisingly vehement on this – *harrum* –

rather delicate matter for one who has clearly chosen to remain, as I have myself, on the shelf.' And before she had time to frame any sort of cutting reply to this, he bade her a polite good day, collected his hat, and departed.

Bella flew back upstairs in a storm of anger, pausing at the top to draw breath and calm herself. Perhaps a walk in the fresh air might calm her shattered nerves but first she really must peep in on Mother, just to check she'd suffered no ill effects from this unprofessional squabble conducted over her prostrate figure.

Bella pushed open the bedroom door only a fraction, wary of disturbing Emily if she were sleeping. The bed was empty. Stunned, Bella stepped into the room, gazing about her in cold panic. Had she fallen out of bed? Had she somehow become trapped beneath the bedclothes? There was no sign of her, and then Bella heard the tap running in the adjoining bathroom. Moving quietly forward she could see Emily standing at the sink. Bella felt as if someone had slapped her in the face. *Her mother could not only move, she could get out of bed and walk to the bathroom unaided for a glass of water!*

Very quietly, without making a sound, Bella slipped out and softly closed the door behind her.

The very next day, all sense of guilt now gone, she engaged a night nurse to sit with her mother.

Chapter Seven

The afternoon was a dull cloudy grey with a few spots of rain on the wind but Bella pulled on a warm coat, wrapped a scarf around her neck and set out, striding along the street with a lift to her step and a happy tilt to her chin.

A day nurse had also been engaged and at last she was free to pursue her own interests. She felt like a child let out of detention. If Mother imagined that she could win the argument against her newly rebellious son by playing the invalid, how wrong she was. Bella had seen the light of conviction in her brother's eye. He would not give Jinnie up, not for anyone, certainly not a manipulating old woman.

But Bella was regretting her own outburst of temper with Dr Lisle. She'd handled it all wrong and gained not a jot of information as a result. If she was to be of any value to her 'ladies', she must aquire some degree of diplomacy and put the matter right without delay. The little doctor meant well, in his narrow-minded way, and he too had been taken in by Emily. Even if Mother had indeed suffered a slight stroke, she'd made it out to be something far worse than it actually was. In Bella's opinion, it would do her no harm at all to be left to stew in her own juice for a while.

Today, Bella meant to call on Mr Solomon the fishmonger, to see how his wife was after her latest confinement and casually enquire if Dr Lisle was at home in his rooms on the top floor. If she got to see him, then she would apologise, unreservedly, and ask him point-blank to at least visit Mrs Stobbs.

There was the usual queue of shawl-shrouded women with their clutch of bare-legged children in the shop, hoping for a pair of kippers or maybe a nice bit of haddock that would cost next-to-nothing and would feed a family of ten. Mrs Solomon herself, a frail, birdlike woman who looked as if a breath of wind might blow her away despite her probably having more regular sustenance than the women queuing downstairs, sat up in bed wreathed in smiles as she clutched her sixth daughter to her breast.

'Am I not the luckiest woman?' she cried, as Bella slipped quietly into the room. 'See. Is she not exquisite? Not the boy Eli wanted for the business, admittedly but he took one look at her and said at least she is healthy. Next time we will have a boy, yes?'

'*Next time!* Aren't you tired of trying?' Bella gently enquired, whilst agreeing that the baby appeared well. 'Having six young children to look after, as well as helping your husband in the shop, must be exhausting. Tell him it's time to stop; that he must make do with a girl to follow him in the business.'

Mrs Solomon seemed appalled at the very idea. 'Many husbands would be angry at such persistent failure on their wife's part, but not Eli. He gives me another chance. He is a saint. That's what he is, a saint.' And Bella was forced to agree that Mr Solomon did indeed exhibit exemplary patience. But then he didn't have to bear each child, did he? she longed to add, though managed not to.

Bella made Mrs Solomon a mug of tea and a fish paste sandwich, since the blessed man himself never had time for such menial tasks. On learning that Dr Lisle was not at home she settled for a note, pushed under his door, and, after seeing that mother and child were both comfortable, left the little woman to her joy. Bella went back downstairs where the 'saint' was arguing over the price of mackerel with a grey-faced woman who, judging by the number of babies in the bassinet she pushed, was in more desperate need of it than he.

'I'm off now, Mr Solomon,' Bella called to him and, as she slipped unthanked out of the door, heard him say, 'Take it or leave it, Mrs Blundell, it's all the same to me.'

She made several more calls after that, most of them far more depressing than the eternally optimistic fishmonger's wife, including Mrs Stobbs who, to her own heartily expressed relief, had lost the latest child she'd been carrying. Bella didn't enquire too closely how that had come about but issued a warning that she should still pay a visit to her doctor.

'What for?'

'To make sure everything is in order, that whatever should have come away has done so, otherwise you could get blood poisoning.' Unsurprisingly, Mrs Stobbs refused point blank even to consider discussing her private functions with any doctor, partly through embarrassment but also because of her natural distrust of 'official interference'. Her-friend-Gladys had checked her out, purged her, and there was an end of the matter.

More important, so far as Mrs Stobbs was concerned, was an answer to her question about how to prevent any further accidents and Bella promised to give the matter more serious attention.

She next called on Mrs Heap to offer condolences over the loss of her youngest to scarlet fever. Out of eight pregnancies, she had only two surviving children and, since her husband had also gone to his maker, there would be no more. It was generally considered that Mrs Heap had witnessed her husband's departure from this world with some relief, since he was known to have a fondness for the bottle. In an effort to feed her small family, she'd opened up her front parlour and taken up baking which had proved a greater success than most ventures of its kind. Parlour shops would frequently open up overnight, more out of desperation than hope, and just as quickly close. Mrs Heap's was different. She produced the tastiest pies and pastries in all of Liverpool Street and was well loved by all, particularly the local children who called her Aunt Edie and were often treated to a currant bun or ginger biscuit. Smiling, she handed a bag of pastries to Bella, refusing absolutely to take a penny in payment for them.

'You've done plenty for me and mine in the past,' she insisted, patting her visitor's hand.

Bella thanked her and decided to share them with her favourite client, who she'd deliberately left till last.

'Will you call in on Sally Clarke when ye have a minute? She had her latest the other week and her husband is itching to get at her again.'

'I'll pop in on my way home this afternoon. Promise.'

Violet Howarth was a large, amiable woman who seemed to be found most days with her big red hands plunged in hot soapy water. But then, as she said herself, with a houseful of brats to keep clean, how else would she spend her time?

This afternoon was no different. Bella found her leaning over the wash tub in the back yard she shared with her neighbours in Jacob's Court, her substantial backside quivering with the effort of scrubbing a stubborn shirt collar on the rubbing board. She glanced up at Bella's approach, and her round face broke into a huge grin.

'Hey up, 'ere's a cup of tea and two biscuits walking down me yard.' This was Violet's way of saying she was glad of the interruption.

'I've brought you an Eccles cake, for a treat,' Bella said, holding out the paper packet with a smile.

'Eeh, well, tha's doubly welcome then. I were just thinking o' purring t'kettle on. Our Dan'll be reet sorry to have missed yer. He's only this minute gone on shift. I'd berrer rinse these through fost, then we'll 'ave a natter.'

Bella looked up to consider the glowering winter sky, heavy with the threat of rain, then back at the woman who, despite the shawl pinned about her substantial chest, had a dewdrop on the end of her nose and whose bare wet arms were raw with cold. 'It's time you did stop. The heavens are about to open. Why are you doing your washing in the yard anyway, instead of in your nice warm kitchen?'

Violet drew out a large red-checked handkerchief from her capacious pocket and blew musically upon it. ''Cause I've just cleaned up in theer and I were hoping not to fill it wi' steam and watter again. But yer right, I'll 'ave to put mesen through t'mangle an' all, if I stop out 'ere much longer.' And she let out a great cackle of laughter.

Whenever she laughed, which was often, great rolls of flesh would shake and wobble, performing a ritual dance of delight to accompany the raucous sound. For whatever else you might accuse Violet of – a certain brashness; a loud and cutting sense of humour coupled with a casual bluntness that frequently wounded more tender feelings than her own; an undeniable fondness for her food along with other delights of the flesh – taking life too seriously wasn't a fault you could ever level against her.

'Isn't it always raining in Manchester?' Bella teased as she helped to carry the dripping washing back inside.

'Nay, that's a wicked lie med up by a chap 'oo come up from t'south and caught a fish in his turn-ups. Manchester's a grand spot. Capital of the north.'

Both women ate two Eccles cakes each, licking up every flake of crisp sugary pastry, every squashy currant. Not a word was exchanged between them during the repast as complete concentration was required to appreciate each delicious morsel fully. When her plate was clean of the last crumb, Violet heaved a great sigh of pleasure and regret as she sank back in her chair. 'Eeh, that were reet gradely. Pour us some tea, lass. It'll be strong enough to stand a spoon in if we leave it to mash much longer.'

Bella filled the two pint mugs which stood waiting on the table and passed one to her friend, enquiring after the health of her large family as she did so.

Violet ran swiftly through them all, from little Joe, the baby of the family at two, who was having trouble walking because of a faulty hip; the six-year-old twins, Emma and Hannah; then Pete and Georgie, always up to some prank or other; and Kate, the eldest girl at fifteen, who was causing her mother much grief over some boy she'd taken up with. Finally there was Ernest who'd found himself rushed into a hasty marriage at nineteen, and Dan, the eldest and most sensible at twenty-four. He it was who brought in the highest wages and made all the decisions, acting more like the head of the family rather than the eldest son in lieu of a father who, in Violet's own words was, 'A feckless lump, good fer nowt but one thing. All animal passion and no brains, 'ceptin what he keeps in his trousers.'

Bella fought not to giggle on hearing the inoffensive and overburdened Mr Howarth so described. Though it was true that for a man not known to drink, being a strong Methodist and teetotal, Cyril Howarth had certainly 'done his duty'. He'd now been diagnosed with emphysema and was unable to hold down a job. Violet treated this tragedy with her usual degree of black humour and made sure everyone knew he still had his 'faculties'. She'd been heard to complain for years that if she could have found a way to stop her numerous children from coming, she would certainly have done so. There had been several others who now resided in the local cemetery and were visited every week, without fail.

'I niver wanted a large family and if I could find some daft cluck to tek em off me hands, I would. But 'oo else would put up wi' em but me, eh?'

Bella always smiled at these remarks for it was clear to all who knew her that Violet worshipped the ground her children walked upon. Her house was spotless, if Spartan so far as furniture was concerned, and if the children's clothes were an odd assortment and practically threadbare, they were at least carefully darned with not a 'bobby's winder' – that is, hole in a stocking – to be seen. Despite her husband never earning more than twenty-six shillings a week throughout a lifetime of labouring on the docks, the stockpot had always been packed with good vegetables, grown on Uncle Albert's allotment. From time to time it was enriched with the scraggy remains of an old hen or a bit of mutton. Now she depended upon her older children to keep it filled but, despite all the family's difficulties, Violet was often heard to declare that no one in her house would ever go hungry, and she'd suffer no long faces neither.

'Anyroad,' she said now, finishing her tale along with the thick brown steaming tea, 'I reckon I've fettled it. I've found a way to stem the tide.' And chortling merrily she gave Bella a huge wink. 'Not that I should be talking about such matters to a young lady such as yersel, but I've been and got summat that seems to be doin' the trick nicely.'

'What trick? Stem what tide? You're talking in riddles, Violet.'

She leaned forward, picked up the tea pot and weighed it in her hand. 'There's happen enough for one.' Bella shook her head so Violet half refilled her own mug with the brown sludge. 'I'm talking about childer. What dusta think I'm talking of?'

'Childer. Lord, you don't mean . . . ?'

'Aye, I do. I've worked out how to stop 'em comin' at last, though happen a bit late in the day as some might say. Or at least I've found a new doctor 'oo's worked it out and is willing to let me in on the secret.'

Bella gazed at her friend now with eager attention, leaning forward in her seat. 'You're saying that a doctor has told you what to do? A doctor who – who gave you some-thing?'

'Aye. You could happen say so.'

'Tell me. I want to know. *Need* to know.'

Violet's eyes were like twinkling currants buried in folds of flesh but her mouth firmed into a narrow line of disapproval. Her round cheeks were flushed rose pink, though more likely from her efforts at the wash tub than with embarrassment. It took a lot to embarrass Violet. 'And why should I tell you, a single lass, or were last time I looked?'

Bella chuckled, not offended by Violet's assumption that her enquiry had been made for personal reasons. 'You know me better than that. I mean, I've been asked by certain of my patients – clients,' she corrected herself, 'for help in that direction. And, of course, being unmarried as you rightly say, I'm ignorant of such matters.'

'So you should be. Ignorance is bliss, isn't that what they say?'

Bella regarded the older woman with her direct, hazel-eyed, gaze. 'Do you believe that to be true?'

The slightest of pauses, then the fleshy jowls shook vigorously. 'Not for a minute. It were ignorance what got me in lumber in't fost place.'

'There you are then, and there are so many of my ladies who are desperate for help and look to me to supply it. Couldn't you give me a hint?'

Violet considered the question with all due seriousness for a long moment. 'Yer a funiosity, you. Tha calls yon women yer patients but they're not at all. Dusta know what thee should do? Go for training as a nurse.'

Bella looked startled. 'How did you know that I once had a fancy to be a nurse?'

'I'm physic.'

'Psychic.'

'That too. Are you gonna put kettle on again or just throw long words at me? Never mind, I'll do it mesel'.' Violet heaved herself to her feet and swung the great black iron kettle back over the fire in the huge Lancashire range that almost filled one wall of the tiny kitchen. She spent most of every Tuesday morning scrubbing and blackleading it yet every night, when she retired to the bed which she shared with her husband and youngest children, the cockroaches would still creep out from under the grate, much to Violet's despair.

Bella said, 'I used to wish I'd been old enough to serve in the war but I was only a child when it ended. From time to time since I've often thought about nursing, though I knew Mother wouldn't have approved so I kept putting it off. It never seemed to be the right moment to fight that particular battle and then I got too involved with my "ladies" to have time to think about it. I certainly couldn't leave home now.' She explained about her mother's stroke and Violet quietly took her seat again, expressing genuine sympathy over the news.

'Oh, she's improving but it wouldn't be appropriate for me to leave home at the moment.' Bella felt no desire to reveal her mother's masquerade, or explain the politics of her domestic life, so merely shrugged her dreams away as if they were of no account. 'Anyway, it's here in Salford that I seem to do the most good. How could I leave all my "ladies" who depend on me, to go off and be a nurse in some hospital or other that has any number of other nurses. No, I'll stay here and help them as best I can.'

Violet thoughtfully rubbed a reddened hand over her sagging jowls. 'Suit thesel'. But if you want to know owt about owt, as they say round 'ere, tha'll have to ask Dr Sydney. I'm saying n'more.'

The very next day Bella visited a bookshop in St Anne's Square where she purchased a copy each of both *Married Love* and *Wise Parenthood*, reading them from cover to cover to absorb every detail. While there was still a great deal which she didn't fully understand, the whole puzzle was becoming much clearer, and the answer now seemed obvious.

She must set up her own Mothers' Clinic, just as Marie Stopes and others had done.

There was, however, one huge problem. She was not, as Dr Lisle and now Violet had reminded her, a qualified nurse and in order to offer safe treatment, it was essential for the women to be tended by a professional. What she needed was a doctor, or nurse, as committed to saving the lives of exhausted mothers and their weakened infants as was she. Wasting no time, Bella set out the following evening to speak to Violet's Dr Sydney, taking a seat in the waiting room along with dozens of others to wait for the end of surgery, despite the risk of catching some dread disease from the coughs and sneezes of the unfortunates around her.

At last, after a wait of an hour and a quarter, the last patient of the day left and she was finally shown into the doctor's private sanctum. Here she pulled up short as she took in the tall, angular figure seated beside a large cluttered desk. Mousy brown hair cut short into the neck, a rather disreputable cardigan, shabby trousers and heavy working man's boots. Were it not for the stethoscope strung about the neck, Bella might have thought she was confronting an engineer or a labourer rather than a doctor. Except for one thing.

'You're a woman!'

'So my mother was led to believe. Though I think she had hopes of a more petite, feminine daughter than the ragamuffin she got landed with. My father, bless his heart, was a realist and on its becoming clear that there would be no further offspring, named me for the son he'd really wanted. Sydney Palmer, at your service.' She held out a hand that was surprisingly well-shaped and elegant. 'I believe you wish to speak to me on some matter?'

The woman's face was serene and smiling, bearing an open aspect that simply emanated friendliness, and Bella quickly introduced herself, anxious to get to the issue which had become so all-consuming. She explained her plan as rapidly and concisely as she could, finishing on a gasp of relief, 'And you're a woman doctor. Perfect!'

'You should curb this habit of yours for stating the obvious.' This was not said with any sign of rancour or ill feeling, rather with a tinge of amusement in the husky voice. 'This clinic you want to set up – who would fund it?'

Bella had spent most of the previous night sitting up in bed asking herself the very same question and, she hoped, coming up with some sort of an answer. 'We would need to hold a meeting to which the public would of course be invited – nay, positively encouraged – to come. Perhaps we could also persuade some local dignitaries or Members of Parliament who are sympathetic to the cause.'

Dr Sydney held up one elegant hand to stem her enthusiasm. 'You do realise how controversial the subject of birth control is? I hand it out only with care, and there are few other doctors as willing to take the risk. Marie Stopes' books provoked a huge debate which shows no signs of abating. Even those in power are divided upon the moral issues involved.'

'I know, but surely there must be some who would support us? All we have to do then is to drum up local press interest and there we are.'

'Becoming involved in opening a Mothers' Clinic could well be the kind of reckless undertaking on my part which would at best lead to ridicule from professional colleagues, at worst bring about the end of my career. I need to ask myself if I'm prepared to take that risk.'

Bella read the genuine concern in Dr Sydney's frank gaze and the blaze of hope inside her quietly drained away. 'I do see that it's a great deal to ask. Perhaps too much.' She got up and walked to the door. 'I should have realised what it was I was asking of you. Of course you couldn't possibly take such a risk.'

'On the contrary, I'd be thrilled to help. Sit down again, Bella. Let's thrash out the details here and now.'

These fears proved to be well founded as it soon became clear that the setting up of a Mothers' Clinic was not going to be quite as straightforward as Bella had hoped. Almost from the outset Dr Syd, as she insisted on being called, received a storm of angry letters from colleagues who'd heard of the planned clinic on the professional grapevine, many claiming that contraception caused sterility while others said it led to nervous breakdowns or even the asylum. One even accused them both of being 'painted women of the worst kind'. A description less appropriate for Dr Syd would have been hard to find, and caused them some amusement as they sat drawing up their plans one evening.

Bella tossed that particular letter on to the fire. 'Which is where such hysteria belongs.'

'We'd better check the rest carefully, just to make sure the objections aren't valid or won't lead to serious repercussions. The ignorance of doctors is our biggest stumbling block,' Dr Syd insisted. 'Their fears of sterility are scientifically groundless but contraception isn't even on the syllabus during all our long years of medical study. I consider that to be appalling. Negligent, in fact.' She could become quite heated on the subject but Bella was glad to see how much she cared.

They were interrupted by a sharp rap on the door which Bella opened upon a tight-faced Dr Lisle. He strode into the surgery as if he had every right to be there, his cold expression entirely matching the fishy smell which emanated from his clothing.

'Professional duty dictates that I should come and plead with you personally to think again about this foolish undertaking you are about to embark upon.' He then proceeded to lecture them for a full twenty minutes on how they were advocating a sad lack of restraint which would lead to excessive sexual indulgence; how practising artificial prevention would result in the perpetrators becoming degenerate and their eventual offspring effeminate. 'It is the responsibility of the husband to consult his doctor about the duties and risks of matrimony, and thereafter to use whatever personal restraint seems appropriate.'

Bella was outraged. 'The women's *husbands*? Doesn't that just prove our point? Who bothers to give advice to the women themselves? Nobody. The man is always considered to be in charge, even of his own wife's body.'

The little doctor adopted a tone of voice one might use with a child as he solemnly continued, 'Only working men are meant to benefit from state health care, ineffectual though it might seem at time. We cannot waste costly resources on women's troubles. How could they ever afford to pay the necessary subscriptions?'

'And because they can't afford to pay, they get no help at all? Is that the way of it? It makes my blood boil.'

Dr Syd placed a restraining hand on her friend's arm. 'Sadly, obstetrics and gynaecology are further subjects in which many doctors have little or no experience. Changes are in the air, Bella, but coming far too slowly. I, for one, would be quite happy to play my own small part in speeding up the process. It's a pity others don't feel the same degree of compassion.'

A flush of anger crept up Dr Lisle's neck and darkened his cheeks. 'I do what I can but I think you overstate the cause for concern. A woman has only to signal when her husband may approach for sexual favours, during the safe time in her cycle, perhaps by displaying a ribbon, worn in her hair or round her neck.'

Bella almost choked while Dr Syd mildly enquired, 'Did you have any particular colour in mind? Perhaps pink would be most appropriate.'

'I do not see this as a laughing matter,' the good doctor tartly responded, and stalked off into the night in high dudgeon while both women collapsed in a fit of giggles. Though, in truth, it wasn't funny at all.

The following morning the seriousness of their situation was illustrated all too clearly when Dr Syd arrived at the surgery to find scarlet paint had been daubed all over the door and windows.

Chapter Eight

'You were right about the dangers. Are you sure you want to go on with this?' Bella softly asked as the pair of them stood contemplating the damage.

'Even more so.'

'There are obviously others far more determined to stop us than pompous Dr Lisle. In this morning's *Guardian* it says the Public Morals Committee, whoever they might be, have gone so far as to say that easy access to contraceptives "produces poorer hereditary stock". You could indeed be drummed out of the profession.'

'There are always those seeking an excuse to do that. No, I'm willing to take the risk. Let's say I have my own reasons for fighting this cause. I feel fortunate to have three healthy children of my own and the knowledge of how to keep it that way. My elder sister died in childbirth although she'd been warned not to get pregnant again after a difficult labour in which her first child died. Yet no one told her how to prevent it happening whilst still maintaining a happy marriage.' Dr Syd stared at the scarlet paint splattered all over the surgery windows and door, eyes filling with a rush of tears. 'It's one of the reasons I became a doctor in the first place. We just have to make sure that we win.' She transferred her gaze to Bella, who quietly nodded.

'Oh, we'll win. Make no mistake about that.' She felt honoured to be granted this insight into Dr Syd's motives for she seemed a very private sort of person. Somewhere in her late-thirties, the doctor had served in the war but Bella had learned nothing about her family until this moment, since they only ever met at the surgery. 'The clinic is going to be a huge success and many lives will be saved as a result. It will be a fitting tribute to your sister.'

Dr Syd blinked. 'Thank you. What about you? You too will be vilified, an unmarried woman without even medical qualifications.'

Bella smiled. 'Maybe I'll rectify one or other of those valid objections, in time. I wouldn't mind a family of my own one day. Of a manageable size, of course, and properly spaced out.' She gave a wry smile. 'Meanwhile, whatever I have to deal with can't be anywhere near as bad as the suffering I witness day after day. We will prevail. Nasty letters, attacks on our property or persons, will only harden my resolve to win through.'

'We'll need a nurse. I think I know of the very person.'

'Excellent.'

Nurse Shaw was asked to call at the surgery, was interviewed by Dr Syd and hired on the spot. With renewed determination, Bella took it upon herself as the lay member of the team to write letters begging for donations to everyone she could think of. Unfortunately, most recipients either refused point-blank to help, or ignored her request completely. Finding a venue for the public meeting proved to be another stumbling block. No one was willing to run the risk of trouble. Finally she wrote to Marie Stopes herself who offered what support she could by suggesting some interested persons who lived in the area. By this means a local magistrate's wife stepped in to help and a date was arranged for a meeting to be held at Pendelton Town Hall.

Every newspaper editor in the two cities of Manchester and Salford was given notice of the meeting and there was nothing more to be done then but pray.

The meeting took place on 3 March 1928 with over 200 people, mainly women, attending. A committee of four was elected, comprising Bella as Organising Secretary; Mrs Lawton, the magistrate's wife, as Honorary Treasurer; plus Dr Syd and

Nurse Shaw. Unfortunately, though it was plainly evident that such a clinic would be popular, those attending did not have the wherewithal to fund it. Not a single newspaper sent a reporter to cover the event and only four pounds was collected in coppers at the door, which was nowhere near enough to rent suitable premises and launch the clinic. Undaunted, Bella persisted, asked around and finally persuaded Mrs Heap to rent them the two rooms over her cook shop.

'Call me Aunt Edie,' she said in her friendly way. 'Everyone else does. I'm no longer troubled by such matters, but I'm only too happy to help other married women who suffer as I did. Right drunken layabout my 'usband were. A drench o' cold water would've done him good at times.'

The good lady even went so far as to help Bella and her team of helpers scrub out the entire premises with carbolic soap. Jinnie gladly volunteered to lend a hand, too, though Bella expressed some concern that she didn't overexert herself as she'd seemed somewhat tired and withdrawn lately, not quite her usual ebullient self.

The clinic opened quietly and without fuss and a few women came, hesitantly at first, creeping up the stairs like pioneers into a strange land. They kept their heads carefully covered by shawl or scarf, unwilling to risk anyone recognising them, in particular their husbands who would consider any form of artificial interference as undermining their masculine pride and virility. But then the trickle became a flow and within a week a couple of dozen women had been seen for their first appointments. Those who were able to pay the shilling fee gladly did so, while women who couldn't were treated for nothing.

Encouraged by this good response, Bella called a second meeting, this time to be held in the Co-operative Rooms. If they were going to survive beyond a month or two, they desperately needed more money. Again the place was packed to the doors, this time not only with valiant supporters but a whole pack of protesters as well. These made such a disturbance in the street outside that it brought out a rash of newspaper reporters from both cities, curious to know what was going on.

Within days the local press was bursting with articles, many of them sympathetic though some expressed self-righteous outrage at the very idea. The *Catholic Herald* was particularly vociferous, using emotive phrases such as 'thwarting natural law', 'defeating God's plans' and 'indulging in sin', even speaking of 'vicious practices'.

The result, however, so far as the new Mother's Clinic was concerned, was astonishing. Money started to roll in. The Anti-Birth Control League of Protesters had done more to publicise the new clinic than Bella and her able volunteers could ever have hoped to do. Within a month they'd opened a bank account and deposited several hundred pounds. They were up and running.

It was one evening as Bella was locking up the clinic and making her way out through Edith Heap's shop that she came across Dan Howarth, Violet's eldest son. He was queuing up for his supper, he told her, indicating the rack of hot meat and potato pies, and would she like to share it with him? Since the delicious aroma seeping up the stairs had been making her hungry for some hours, how could she resist? Bella accepted the hot pie with gratitude and they walked together along Liverpool Street, unashamedly eating.

'Oh, this is good. You've no idea how hungry I was. I've been so busy at the clinic I think I must've forgotten to eat lunch.'

Dan laughed as he watched her brush the last crumb from her lips. They were rather nice lips and his gaze lingered upon them for several seconds. 'I reckon I can tell, since you've wolfed that down in double quick time. Shall I go and get you another?'

'No, no, that would be far too greedy, and there's really no need. I feel much better now. Almost human again. Thanks.'

'Don't mention it.' There was a slight pause as they walked along, Dan quickly finishing his own pie. Even the way she spoke indicated the yawning chasm between them. What Bella called lunch, he knew as dinner. She certainly didn't look the sort to eat hot pies. He carefully wiped his mouth, then cleared his throat before politely remarking, 'You're kept pretty busy then, in that clinic. How's it doing?'

'Oh, fine. Fine.' For the first time in her life Bella suddenly felt embarrassed and shy. She wasn't too sure it would be appropriate to discuss the work of the clinic, or even its aims, with a single male. She didn't, in any case, know Dan all that well since he was usually at work when she called on his mother. Perhaps he's suffering from a similar affliction Bella decided as silence fell upon them both as they progressed along the street.

'How about a drink to wash the pie down?' Dan hesitated outside the Ship, wondering what he could say to persuade her to agree. 'Or happen you're in a hurry to get home afore it gets dark?' Blast! Now he'd given her an excuse to refuse.

'No, no. A drink would be lovely. I've never been in a pub before.'

'Never? By heck,' he said with a grin, 'then it's time we changed that. I'm fond of a pint meself. But don't tell me dad. He's teetotal.'

Bella was laughing now as he led her to the quietest corner of the lounge bar that he could find. 'I believe your mother has mentioned the fact once or twice.'

Dan cast her a sideways grin. 'I dare say she's told you all sorts of stuff about us. You may safely believe about half of it. You have to have a good sense of humour to live wi' my mam.'

'I can imagine. Oh, I always take Violet with a large pinch of salt.'

He brought her a glass of port and lemon which seemed to Dan a lady's sort of drink, and a pint of best bitter for himself. Though he hastened to assure her that he was no more than a moderate drinker. 'Not like some round here.'

'I'd noticed.'

They sat for an hour or more over their drinks and Bella soon forgot her shyness, as she enjoyed talking with him. Born and brought up in the rough and tumble of Salford, the image he presented was of a strong, clean, sound sort of chap who could make his mark without throwing his weight about. With his powerful physique, square-jawed face, broad nose and fair hair cut close to the head, he might have been taken for a pugilist were it not for the gentleness of his blue-grey eyes and open friendly smile.

'Happen we could do this again some time,' he said, as they parted at the end of the street.

'I'd like that,' Bella agreed and, as she walked away, keenly aware of those eyes following her, realised that she meant it.

Bella found that she loved working at the clinic. She brought in a box of toys to keep the children amused while their mothers waited to be seen by the doctor. She set two or three chairs against the wall but the rest of the women waited happily enough on the stairs, gossiping to each other to pass the time.

The first task was for them to be seen by an experienced helper. Bella drafted in a couple of married women for this job. They would fill in a case card with a patient's medical history and discuss any particular difficulties. Sometimes this took quite a while but no one was allowed to feel under pressure or hurried in any way. After that the woman would go in to see Dr Syd for a consultation and full medical examination. Patients who hadn't already been too badly damaged by child bearing were then left with Nurse Shaw to be fitted with an appliance, and given the necessary instruction. After the doctor had checked that all was well and any fears were mollified it was Bella's job to hand out a printed card with the woman's next appointment on it as well as to arrange a suitable time for a home visit.

The clinic was only open a few hours each week, from 9.30 to noon on a Tuesday morning and 7.00 to 9.30 p.m. on a Thursday evening, but whenever she wasn't occupied doing home visits, she would pop in, perhaps to do some paperwork, send out further requests for donations, or simply to tidy up or do a spot of cleaning. Also, Dr Syd would often ask her to write to other clinics, already operational, for advice on some problem or other, so her correspondence load was heavy. Not that she minded in the least. Bella wanted the clinic to be a success and meant to do everything in her power to ensure that it was. She wrote again to Dr Stopes to keep her informed of their progress and was delighted to receive an encouraging letter in response. And as she worked she would think about how the clinic, and Jinnie of course, had changed her life completely.

She was a little concerned about Jinnie who'd taken to going out on her own quite a lot recently. Which was strange, considering how carefully she had kept within doors when she'd first arrived. Perhaps she visited old friends or even met up with Edward at some secret rendezvous, as lovers do. On the other hand perhaps, like herself, Jinnie was glad of any excuse to escape the depressing atmosphere of Seedley Park Road. Bella vowed to speak to her on the matter, make sure that there were no problems, bar the obvious one of Emily's animosity.

Bella had been tempted on numerous occasions to unmask her mother's illness for the sham it truly was but had resisted, on the grounds that it was Dr Lisle's responsibility to decide what was best for the welfare of his patient, and not hers. Hadn't he told her so a dozen times? Besides, her mother must be both clever and exceedingly determined if she was prepared to suffer such miserable confinement in order to fool everyone, even her own doctor, so any attempt to foil her little scheme could have unknown repercussions, another tantrum, perhaps even a genuine stroke, and Bella had no wish to be the one to cause it.

When she wasn't at the clinic, she spent practically all her spare time calling on patients to check that they were coping and experiencing no problems. Hygiene was of paramount importance and she used a good deal of the clinic's funds on purchasing soap and doling it out to those in need. Sometimes she found that a woman had stopped using the essential barrier cream contraceptaline because of cost, resorting to ineffective Vaseline instead. Or the pessary had been lost and the patient was afraid to return for another.

Having persuaded Mrs Blundell to attend the clinic Bella called on her one day to check her progress, only to be confronted by an irate husband filling the doorstep with his powerful bulk so that she was prevented from entering, despite his wife's pleas that she be allowed in.

'I'll not have her getting up to mischief while I'm at work,' he roared, waving a huge fist in Bella's face. 'I threw the bloody thing on t' fire.'

A voice called out from behind him in the lobby. 'Daft bugger! I told him I weren't playin' away, but would he bleedin' listen?'

'Don't argue with me, woman.'

Bella tried desperately to intervene and calm tempers down. 'I'm sure Mrs Blundell would never do any such thing. The help we give her at the clinic is for *your* sake as much as hers, so that you and she can enjoy a happy marriage without fear of the consequences.'

'Pull the other leg and see if that's got bells on!'

Bella spent an hour or more attempting to persuade him otherwise, with half the street privy to the noisy argument, but was forced to admit defeat when he practically pushed her backwards into the gutter, yelling that she'd turned his wife into a whore and he wouldn't stand for it.

Within weeks of this incident Mrs Blundell popped in to

Aunt Edie's cook shop and sadly confessed she'd fallen yet again. Bella chanced to be in the shop at the time, having a chat before going upstairs to open the clinic.

'Nay, lass, I'm that sorry,' Aunt Edie said, putting an extra currant tea cake in the bag as if by way of consolation. 'What'll yer do?'

'I don't know which way to turn, but I don't blame you, lass. Tha did thee best to help.'

Bella said. 'Come up and see Dr Syd anyway. She can at least give you proper care during your pregnancy.'

'Aye, happen I'll do that.'

But if poor Mrs Blundell could be counted as a failure, which wouldn't strictly speaking be true since it wasn't the method which had failed, the clinic certainly had plenty of successes, Mrs Stobbs among them. The moment she'd heard about the new clinic, she'd been one of the first to trek up those stairs and had been a devoted advocate of birth-control ever since, so far with excellent results. Even her husband was happy.

'Education is the answer,' was Dr Syd's endless cry and both she and Bella, who had become firm friends, set out to provide just that, with Nurse Shaw's able assistance.

Bella got into the habit of visiting Dr Syd at her rooms after surgery every Monday to thrash out the problems of the clinic for the week ahead. They needed to reach more patients, to gain better publicity in the press and encourage the medical community to take more of an interest.

'Ten years ago, when I was tending our boys in the trenches, I never thought I'd be fighting another war, one of politics and prejudice. Yet you've only to walk down Broad Street or North Street and see the number of children with legs bent by rickets, nothing but rags on their backs since their decent clothes are in pawn and often not even a pair of boots to their feet, to know that society is failing vast swathes of people and creating even more of an underclass. Is it any wonder they fall to drink or gambling, for all they can't afford it? Anything to alleviate their miserable lives.'

'At least we're attempting to better their lot to some extent,' Bella assured her. Perhaps she never would understand the true meaning of poverty, not unless she actually experienced it for herself which, thank God, was unlikely to happen.

On two or three occasions Bella found Dan Howarth waiting for her in the shop when the session was over and her heart would give a strange leap of pleasure at sight of him. Not that she let him see what she felt, for Bella had no wish to give him any unrealistic hopes. She told herself firmly that she'd enough to deal with, being fully occupied with running the clinic. Even so, they would often enjoy a quiet supper together, a drink in the the Ship or the Old Railway, or simply a walk in the evening air.

'I reckon it's a bit of a cheek for me to be asking you out, daughter of a mill manager, when I'm no more'n a dock labourer,' he said one night.

'Heavens, don't be silly. We're good friends, aren't we?'

'Aye, that's it. Just good friends.' Dan's sideways glance spoke volumes that he'd like them to be much more but Bella was waving to Mrs Blundell across the street, so didn't notice.

For all she gave little indication of it, she came to enjoy his company and looked forward to the time they spent together. Sometimes, as she stood at the window gazing out over the soot-encrusted streets of Salford, she found herself watching for him, telling herself it was only because he was such entertaining company, constantly regaling her with tales of his mates with whom he worked down at the docks. Bella began to ask herself where this friendship might be leading, where she wanted it to lead, but found no ready answers.

One Sunday afternoon they walked all the way to Dawney's Hill. It smelled of fresh green grass and spring sunshine and Bella felt deliciously happy as they sat watching the children run about, the wind tugging at their kites. Dan told her how he used to come here with his dad when he was a boy.

'I suppose one day I'll have childer of me own, and I'll fetch them out here wi' a kite or fishing rod.'

'I suppose you will.'

'Though I must say, I'm not in any hurry. I've enough childer round me feet every day of the week, all creating mayhem one way or another.'

'It must be lovely, though, to be part of a big, happy family.'

Dan snorted his disdain at the very idea. 'Allus needing summat. Lot of responsibility.' He cleared his throat, picked a few daisies and began to form them into a chain in an abstracted sort of way. 'How about you? I dare say you fancy being wed, one day like.'

Bella rolled on to her stomach, feeling oddly shy as she casually plucked a daisy and handed it to him. 'I'd like a family of my own certainly, though whether that's a good reason to consider marriage, I'm not sure. My husband would have to be someone very special, and I'd need to love him very much.'

For a long moment they gazed at each other in silence, fingers touching as they both held on to the flower. Then Bella took her hand away, cheeks softly flushed as she gave a shy smile. Her mind seemed to have gone a complete blank and she could think of nothing to say.

'A lass like you must have a fair number of suitors.'

'Suitors? What a lovely old-fashioned word. No, I have no suitors, much to my mother's despair. I shall end up an old maid on the shelf, no doubt.'

'Nay, I can't see that happening, not a likely lass such as yoursen.'

Bella watched the children with the kites for a moment, then picked another daisy, twirling it between her fingers as she smiled softly to herself. 'You're so gallant, Dan, but I'm no beauty, and I'm not – how shall I put it – very biddable.'

He grinned down at her. 'Stop fishing for compliments. You know well enough how attractive you are. But, no, you're right, no one could accuse you of being biddable.'

She cast him a quick glance from beneath her lashes. 'How about you? Is there a queue of likely lasses waiting breathlessly for your proposal?'

'Nay. Chaps like me can't afford the luxury of marriage too soon. Unless they're daft enough to jump the gun.' He returned his attention to the daisy chain as if it were an important engineering feat, or some great work of art he was producing. 'My wages are needed at home anyroad, fer the little 'uns, more's the pity, so any lass with hopes to be my wife would have to be prepared to wait a long while for the privilege, while I saved up.' And it could never be with the likes of you, he thought wistfully, forcing himself to face reality.

'Maybe a girl would be happy to wait for a fine upstanding bloke such as yourself.'

'Aye,' he said consideringly, again gazing into her face with keen attention. 'And mebbe some women would take more saving up for than others.'

'Perhaps they'd be more worth the effort.'

'Happen.' The silence this time seemed palpable, as if something vibrated in the air between them. 'And happen she'd grow old and grey and bored with the whole daft notion afore I'd managed to save up enough even to buy her a ring.'

Dan placed the daisy chain on Bella's head. It hung upon her wild tawny curls like a silver crown. Leaning closer he adjusted it slightly, smiling directly into her eyes so that she felt a sudden tightening in her chest. Bella caught her breath as she thought for one glorious moment that he was going to kiss her, that above all else, she wanted him to kiss her. Sensing his shyness, she made a desperate effort to encourage him. 'Maybe she wouldn't care about a silly old ring. She could always use one of her own after all.'

His smile instantly faded, his tone of voice becoming harsh

and grating. 'If she were to be a wife o' mine, she'd have to wear *my* ring.'

'Oh, yes, of course. I'm sorry, I didn't mean to . . .'

He sat up, the moment of intimacy over, his voice taking on a bitter note. 'Happen some girls like to flirt. They enjoy making fun of a chap, slumming it like, for a bit of a lark.'

Bella stared at him, shocked and deeply sorry that she'd hurt him. 'Is that what you think I'm doing? Flirting? Having a bit of a lark?'

'I think ye'll happen salve yer conscience by working round here for a while afore going off and marrying a nice steady chap wi' a good job. A bloke like me, on the other hand, is thankful for work of any sort, even if it is casual.'

The silence now was uncomfortable as she pictured him waiting patiently each morning at the docks in the hope of getting taken on for a day's work while she sat in middle-class comfort enjoying a good breakfast cooked by Mrs Dyson. Though what Bella could do about it, she didn't quite know. When she finally spoke, it was in a false, breezy manner as if trying to recapture their earlier happy mood. 'Look at those little lads over there, off to the river with their fishing lines and buckets. They seem to be having fun. Did your dad teach you to fish as well?'

'Aye, so what?'

'I just thought, maybe next time we come here, we could bring rods and you could teach me. I wouldn't mind having a go. Or we could go down by the canal if you prefer.'

He looked at her for a long moment, wondering again if she wasn't making fun of him. But she looked so sincere, so warmly genuine, that he regretted his outburst and was suddenly anxious to return to that warm, magical moment with the daisy chain. Perhaps, if he could see her again, he might get the chance. 'Aye, all right. Not that there are many fish in the cut, and them that you do catch has a bad cough.'

And then they were laughing and joking again, as so often when she was with Dan. Bella rather thought that, despite their differences, in the months ahead he could indeed become a good friend. Quite special in fact.

Chapter Nine

The heady excitement of Saturday afternoon had been a dream too good to last, Jinnie could see that now. Quinn's demands were quite straightforward. All she had to do was to take bets off the girls and women at the mill. Even if it meant their pledging the rags off their own children's backs, she had to get them hooked. It was well known that mill operatives were restless and unproductive on big race days and that owners were on their guard to stamp out any sign of betting on their premises for that reason alone, if no other. Gambling was bad for business because it meant loss of profits. Women were considered to be particularly vulnerable and, in the management's view, had to be protected as they set a bad example to their children.

But who would protect Jinnie?

Weary of terrible Miss Tadcaster's iron rule and bullied by Quinn, she'd moved into the weaving shed where she would be in daily contact with the other women and therefore of more use to him. She was now being taught how to operate a loom. Weaving was a top job and at any other time in her life she would have been delighted, thrilled to be given the chance of a proper future. But there was a snag.

Becoming accepted by these women was not going to be easy. In their eyes she was the lowest of the low who was now aping her betters. They called her 'a forward little bitch', 'a jumped-up 'un', and more pungently, 'common as muck'. Whatever differences Jinnie imagined might exist between the middle and working classes, she was aware of far more serious divisions within the lower class itself. And since she wasn't considered fit to belong to any class at all, she had no illusions about the difficulties she faced.

At first the women refused to show her how to 'kiss' the shuttle and she'd struggle to thread it any way but the right one, or how to scutch the cotton fibres from the loom without breathing all the dust into her lungs. They left her loom perilously idle whenever a thread broke, and nobody 'spoke' to her because they said she didn't know how to mee-maw, the usual language of the weaving shed.

But Jinnie didn't give up. If she didn't know, she would ask and find the answer somehow. She was desperate to learn and finally they recognised this desire and began to respect her for it. They were also longing to have a bet.

Jinnie's task was to collect the stake money from her clients, handing out betting slips when the foreman or tackler wasn't looking, then to deliver the bets to Len Jackson or Harold Cunliffe during her dinner break. They in turn put the bets in what was called the 'clock bag' which had a timer on it that snapped shut at the start of the race to prevent fraud. Len, or Harold, would then take the bag to Billy Quinn, and he would not be pleased if she didn't have plenty of bets in it for him.

'Nay, I can't afford a flutter today, lass,' a woman might protest, in which event Jinnie was instructed to offer Quinn's tip of the day, maybe on a horse running at Hurst Park or a greyhound expected to do well at the Salford Albion. Hopefully the woman would be sorely tempted by the prospect of a surefire winner and take the risk, even if it put her in hock with the money lender or pawnbroker. Much as common sense might dictate otherwise, the lure of a sub-stantial win could ease the grind of making ends meet for weeks to come. Besides, the odd bet here and there added a spice of interest and hope to an otherwise miserable existence. On race days there would be a feeling of buoyancy in the air, as if it were a holiday, and housewives could be found standing on their doorsteps poring over the racing papers, comparing odds.

To Jinnie's profound relief, most women never got involved to this extent. Many enjoyed a bit of a flutter, often as little as a penny, at most threepence on an each-way bet. They were never as extravagant as their husbands who might place as much as a shilling, but there was the odd one who got in over their head and, though Billy Quinn welcomed commitment, he didn't allow debts. All transactions were strictly cash.

'You help me to get rich, Jinnie girl, and I'll not stand in yer way with this whey-faced fella of yours. Ye'd do that fer me, would ye not? Fer old times' sake. Then I'll buy meself a fine house on the Polygon and become a benefactor of the community, like Tommy Lill, allus ready to give a handout to those in need. Wouldn't that be grand?'

The prospect of Billy Quinn turning into the kind of bookmaker who was willing to help out his customers if they were in need of a loan to pay for a doctor or a burial perhaps, or had lost their job and fallen on hard times, was beyond even Jinnie's imaginings.

'Whatever you say, Quinn.'

''Course, if'n ye decided to come home where ye belong, I'd mebbe be willing to take ye back.'

'I'd rather die than share your bed ever again.' For a moment she thought she'd gone too far but then he put back his head and roared with laughter. She could see the hairs in his nostrils and for once his handsome image deserted him, leaving only a cruel parody of good looks.

'Ye'd rather die, would ye? Well, that can allus be arranged.' He grasped hold of her chin, pinching it tightly between finger and thumb. Jinnie could smell the foulness of stale whisky on his breath as his face moved closer to hers. 'Ye'd not want your fella learning the truth about yer past, now would ye, me lovely?' And, releasing her, he strolled away, laughing like a drain.

Jinnie felt as if she were walking a tightrope. If she obeyed

Quinn to the letter, as she must if she wasn't to end up a bag of broken bones like poor Sadie, she'd be betraying her new friends. On the other hand, if she didn't drum up enough business to please him, she could lose everything she'd gained, including Edward.

And Edward had become of paramount importance to her.

Sunday was now their only day together. The day usually began with chapel in the morning. They always sat in the special pew, once with Emily in a wheelchair carrying her own hymn and prayer books and wearing her best hat following some slight altercation to persuade Bella to wear hers. After chapel there'd be Mrs Dyson's roast beef and Yorkshire. These days Emily would remain in her room and be spoon-fed later by Bella or Tilly, after which Simeon would snore in his chair for half an hour or so before setting out again for the chapel to act as Superintendent at the Sunday School. It was at this time that Jinnie and Edward would take the opportunity to sneak away and enjoy a walk along the canal bank or a tram ride into the city centre where they'd walk along Deansgate or King's Street, doing a bit of window gazing and dreaming of their future together as lovers do.

Today, Jinnie had made up her mind to tell Edward everything. It was the only way to get Billy Quinn off her back once and for all.

It was hot and sunny, being late-June, and they meant to enjoy a picnic in Seedley Park. On her arm she carried a basket, filled with more good food for one single meal than she used to see in a fortnight. Later they'd sit down to supper at a table groaning with food, as they did every evening. Edward's family would eat it without even noticing, all the while talking about politics, the state of world trade, who was to marry whom and other doings of their friends and neighbours. Jinnie felt as if one minute she was living a dream, the next a nightmare, though which one might turn into reality she couldn't be sure. It all depended upon how Edward reacted to what she had to say today. The thought took some of the edge off her happiness but it couldn't destroy it entirely, because she loved him so much.

Surely he could forgive her anything, since he was clearly mad about her. The way he held her arm so firmly in his and gazed so lovingly into her eyes whenever they walked out together made Jinnie feel sure the curtains would be twitching all along the street. Even here in the west of Salford they weren't above a bit of gossip and she was living in his house, after all.

'We should be more discreet,' she whispered, seeing at least one movement in a window opposite.

'Fiddlesticks! Let the world know that I love you. Shall I shout it to the heavens?'

Horrified, in case he did exactly as he threatened, Jinnie hurried him up the long street, desperate to reach the park before he embarrassed them both. In a strange way, Edward was far more unpredictable than Billy Quinn. Not that she intended even to think of *him* today, not on her day off. Being a Sunday there was no racing, no bets to be placed, not for her anyway as the mill was closed until Monday. For once she was entirely free.

They were minutes from home, yet it felt as if they were in another world. The park was a pleasant oasis of green in the heart of the city. There was a fountain, a duck pond and a walk known as the Flower Path, and if the weather turned inclement, they could go inside the Buile Hill Museum to see the stuffed animals and birds in their cases. They scampered like giggling children over the manicured lawns and found a private corner behind some neatly clipped laurel bushes where Jinnie spread the cloth and set out the sandwiches. Edward grabbed her from behind, holding her tight in his arms and making her squeal in surprise before whirling her about and kissing her with a thoroughness that left her breathless. Sometimes she felt on fire whenever he touched her; at other times like now, she felt close to panic, almost as if eyes were watching them from behind every tree.

'Give over, you wicked man. You'll have me over in a minute if you don't behave.' But she wasn't really angry. She never could remain cross with Edward for more than a minute and when he started kissing her again, she made no protest at all. Long before this second kiss was over they'd both fallen to the sweet-smelling grass and rolled down the hill to lie in a tumbled, giggling heap at the bottom. Jinnie, for one, could have stayed there for ever. Eventually he did release her and she stood up and made him dust all the grass seeds from her neck, scolding him gently about green stains on her new Sunday frock. It was a pretty pink print with a velvet collar, the nicest frock she'd ever owned in all her life. In fact, the only *new* frock she'd ever possessed. Jinnie was thrilled to bits with it.

Edward went to buy a jug of hot tea for twopence from the tea rooms just by the Museum, then they sat and munched on their lettuce and potted beef sandwiches while Jinnie tried to think of a way to bring up the subject of the 'accident', without appearing too obvious. It wasn't easy, and she was unused to diplomacy. She'd asked him once if he'd mind her calling him Eddie, as Edward seemed such a formal, grand sort of name. He'd looked surprised, as if the idea had never entered his head.

'Don't you like it?'

'Of course I do. It's a smart, proper sort of name.'

'Well, why change it then? Don't you like me being smart and proper? Do you want me to change too?'

'I didn't say that. I just thought happen a shorter name would be – oh, I don't know, easier to say. More comfortable like. It were a daft idea. Forget it.' She'd never made such a suggestion again, careful to remember how new was their relationship, and what a wide gap lay between them that must somehow be bridged. 'Are you glad I come to live wi' you?' she asked now. 'I mean, came to live with your family.'

'Of course I'm glad. What a question. You've changed my life, Jinnie.' He rolled over on to his stomach so he could gaze up at her adoringly. 'When d'you think you'll be ready to say yes? You know it's what I want most in all the world, for us to be wed.'

He asked her the same question every time they went out together. Jinnie smiled and tickled his nose with a feathered grass stem. 'When I'm eighteen. Wasn't that the agreement?'

Edward groaned. 'Oh, Jinnie, don't be so cruel. I can't possibly wait that long.' Then he was pulling her down beside him and kissing her again, with more fervour this time and, oh, how could she stop him when his lips were so warm and demanding? She wanted him so much that she could make no protest at all, not even if Billy Quinn himself were standing right behind them, taking it all in. Jinnie pressed her body close against his, pushing her fingers through his softly curling hair and forgot all about Quinn as Edward's hand crept ever nearer to her breast and she strained towards him so that he couldn't help but cup it entirely. She heard him groan, deep in his throat. Was she being a tease? she wondered. But Jinnie couldn't help herself if she was. She wanted Edward so much that it hurt. By the time they broke free they were both breathless, pink-cheeked, and Jinnie's mouth all bruised and swollen from his kisses.

'Oh, God, just to look at you like that with your eyes all big and trusting makes me go weak-kneed. You look like we've been to bed already, my love, instead of needing desperately to do so. How will I bear to wait for two whole years?'

Jinnie sat up quickly and primly tugged her dress down over her knees, since it had slid right up to her pale thighs. 'Would you like an apple?'

Edward gave another groan, accompanied by a throaty chuckle this time. 'Now you sound like Eve. Will I be damned, like Adam, if I accept it?' And Jinnie giggled, not fully understanding what he was saying, nor expecting to, since he was so much cleverer than she.

After tea they strolled, to all outward appearances entirely prim and proper, through the sunken rose gardens, past the tennis courts and bowling green. Yet fingers kept clasping, thigh brushed against thigh, his arm even strayed about her waist once or twice and Jinnie had to hiss gently for him to remove it. It wouldn't be right to kiss and canoodle in public. You never knew who might be watching. Eventually, the afternoon grew late and they set off to walk the short distance home, anxious not to miss evening chapel or Simeon would never forgive them.

Jinnie had that sensation of panic again, like butterflies beating in her stomach; their magical time alone together nearly over and she still hadn't found a way to tell him.

It was as they turned the corner to walk the last few yards home that they were joined by Bella. Her voice hailed them from behind and they both paused to wait for her to run and join them.

'Where have you two dear people been?' she asked, linking her arms with theirs, her eyes on Jinnie's flushed face. 'Or is that a secret?'

'Not at all. We've enjoyed a delicious picnic in the park.' Edward and Jinnie exchanged smiles as if indeed sharing a secret but for once Bella didn't notice as she was too busy relating her own happy day, filled not with good works for once, but a fishing expedition.

'I caught two fish, would you believe? But they were small, so Dan made me throw them back.'

'Sounds a sensible chap. I bet he helped you to catch them in the first place.'

'Of course he did. Said I couldn't catch a cold on a wet Monday.' And they all went into the house laughing, wondering what delights Mrs Dyson would have made them for supper. As the door banged shut and the sound of their happy voices faded, a man less than fifty yards behind them turned up his coat collar, lit another cigarette and, turning on his heel, strolled away. Not only did he now know where Jinnie lived but with whom. Most interesting.

Simeon was waiting for Bella and, for once, was not his usual benevolent self. He was striding back and forth in the green-shaded parlour, cigar in hand and rage glowering on his face. 'In here this minute, Isabella, I wish to speak with you,' he announced the moment she set foot in the hall. Edward cast her a surprised but sympathetic glance as he and Jinnie hurried upstairs to wash their hands before supper. Bella went into the parlour and quietly closed the doors.

'Good evening, Pa, and how are you on this lovely June evening? I'm sorry I missed chapel this afternoon but it was far too nice to . . .'

Simeon interrupted her. 'Much as it pains me to bring the subject up, I've been speaking with Dr Lisle. As sidesman of a neighbouring chapel, he came to a meeting we were holding after the afternoon service to discuss this Mothers' Clinic of yours. He had much to say about the matter, not least your involvement with it, the full details of which would have been better coming from you direct.'

Bella showed her surprise. 'But you were well aware that I'd opened a clinic. I informed you in advance of my intention to do so. I also told you about the public meeting. Besides, you must have seen reports in the press.'

'Happen I was so taken up with the health of your dear mother that the full significance of what you were about had not properly registered.'

'Or perhaps, since it was women's business, you didn't properly listen?'

Simeon jabbed the air with his cigar. 'The whole meeting was of the opinion that any woman will be brought safely through childbirth if she and her husband continue to live in faith and love and growing holiness, and that with a little more natural self-restraint the numbers of children could easily be reduced.'

'That seems to me to be a rather optimistic and decidedly unrealistic viewpoint.'

'Are you saying that you don't trust in the Lord?'

Bella closed her eyes for a brief second, to give herself time to gather breath and patience. 'No, I'm not saying that at all. I'm merely pointing out that if two people love each other enough to marry, it is surely unrealistic to expect them not to engage in love making. Abstention could damage a marriage, could it not?'

'And what would you know about the matter, miss?' Simeon sharply responded, his neck flushed with anger, as if she'd touched a nerve.

Bella did not blush. She met the fury of her parent's gaze with equanimity. 'I hope that I understand something of life, Father, else how do I come to be here?'

Shocked by her response and momentarily lost for words, Simeon puffed out his reddening cheeks, then clenched his teeth furiously on his cigar and strode to the window in an attempt to disguise his embarrassment. He decided on a different tack. 'Dr Lisle suggests that you deliberately attempted to keep the true import of your work from me. What you are doing is peddling pornography. You are actively promoting a sin against morality and, even worse, against the Will of God. Now that I understand fully what it is you are up to, I insist that you stop. At once.'

'I beg your pardon?' Bella felt herself grow quite still. She couldn't believe that her ever-tolerant, mild-mannered father had turned into this narrow-minded bigot.

'I will not have my own daughter involved with encouraging licentious behaviour. You must cease your impertinent preaching of sexual impropriety to the masses.'

'Impertinent ... Utter tosh! I teach nothing of the sort.'

Simeon now appeared to be turning purple before her very eyes. 'You deny that instructing the young that unchastity can be safe is not a sin? *How dare you?* I never thought to hear a daughter of mine attempt to thwart the law of propriety in such a manner. You are taking advantage of your mother's ill health to run wild and *I will not have it*.'

'I am of age, Father. I can do as I please.'

'Not in *my* house.'

'Then I'd best leave your house.'

'Don't you dare answer back to me, miss.'

Never, in all her life, had her father spoken to her in such a way and Bella strove to hold on to her own temper. Certain that Dr Lisle had twisted the truth out of a peevish desire for revenge born out of her rejection of him, she attempted to put the matter right in as calm a manner as she could muster. She walked over to her mother's chair and sat down. 'Pa, I think you have got hold of the wrong end of the stick entirely. We are not, in any way, teaching birth control to the unmarried, nor turning any woman into a prostitute.'

'Do not use that word in my . . .'

'I'm sorry but I must call a spade a spade. Our purpose is to help those overburdened wives and mothers who already have more children than they can cope with.' For all her voice was cool, even serene, the clenched fists in her lap told a different story. 'And to prevent the very same sort of disaster happening to their own married daughters. Yearly pregnancies, any more than frequent miscarriages and stillbirths, should not be accepted as the norm. The result is weakened offspring, even damaged children who are handicapped in some way, as well as an unhealthy mother who cannot possibly manage. It's not right and must be stopped.'

'*Not by you, miss!*'

'Why not by me? Because I am your daughter, Simeon Ashton, manager of a fine cotton mill and person of standing in the community? Doesn't that make me even more responsible since I have the time, intelligence and wherewithal to help?'

'Welfare clinics have already been established for the poor, and that is quite sufficient. If something more needed to be done, don't you think the government would have dealt with the matter?'

She was on her feet again, unable to sit still. 'No, actually, I don't. Working to alleviate poverty doesn't win votes, does it?'

Simeon rocked backwards on his heels, smoothing his moustache in an attempt to maintain his temper. 'I've always thought of meself as a liberal-thinking, tolerant man who wants to provide for his family, but in my opinion it isn't the job of a woman to interfere in matters more suitably left to her betters. If there are differences between folk, the class system as you call it, they must be there for a purpose. I see no help for it. There are some folk incapable of organising their own lives.'

'Because they've never been given the opportunity or the education to enable them to do so!' Bella could feel her own control slipping, her patience being swamped by a red hot rage that matched Simeon's own. 'Who really cares whether the likes of a Mrs Stobbs or Mrs Blundell has one too many children and it kills her? Certainly not the government. The Conservatives exercise conventionally narrow-minded and misguided objections to birth control and the Socialists believe, again misguidedly, that having the poor produce more and more children will somehow provide them with the fodder to fight against the established order. Nobody, beyond women such as Marie Stopes, Mary Stocks and her ilk, seems to appreciate that the promotion of birth control is essential in creating a just and healthy society. Absolutely essential.'

Simeon ground out his cigar and strode, stiff-backed, to the door. Here he paused, hand grasping the polished brass knob, and turned a bland, expressionless face to his daughter. 'You will close your clinic tomorrow. First thing in the morning. Then we'll say no more on the subject.'

Needless to say Bella did not close the clinic the next or on any other morning. She did, however, pay a call upon Dr Nathaniel

Lisle at his surgery and told him, as bluntly as she dared, to keep his nose out of her affairs in future. 'I would be obliged if you did not attempt to stir up trouble between myself and my father by feeding him emotive and inaccurate arguments against birth control. Your task is to tend to my mother who, I believe, is fitter than she admits, rather than to interfere in how I spend my time.'

'It may suit your conscience to believe your mother to be better than she actually is but as the unmarried daughter of the house, the duty of her care is entirely in your hands. You should be at her side night and day, not playing at politics and misguided good works.'

Bella did not demean herself with further argument but stormed out through the waiting room, scattering leaflets advertising her Mothers' Clinic to his patients as she went.

Chapter Ten

Dr Syd's advice was to take it on the chin. Jinnie assured Bella that she was indeed doing something worthwhile and even Edward offered his support, saying that their father was always quick to lose his temper if he felt his good name was under attack. The result was that father and daughter were barely on speaking terms. It was a sad and depressing state of affairs but Bella grew determined not to give in. She refused, absolutely, to close her precious clinic.

In retaliation Simeon decided that his prospective daughter-in-law was the one who now deserved his care and attention and there came a veritable stream of obliging helpers to the house. A girl to cut and dress Jinnie's hair, a dressmaker, bootmaker, milliner, and anyone else who had the faintest idea how to make a silk purse out of a sow's ear, as he jokingly put it. Jinnie accepted it all with surprising equanimity, even submitting herself to weekly elocution lessons where she recited endless little ditties about Susie selling sea shells or ragged rascals running around rocks. The two shillings an hour appeared to be wasted, however, as she continued to recite the poems in a resounding Lancashire accent.

Bella watched and listened to all these activities and improvements with wry amusement and considerable pleasure, despite finding herself more and more left out in the cold. One evening Simeon invited both Jinnie and Edward to accompany him to the theatre but Bella was not included in the party. He merely cast his most disapproving glare in her direction and said that he assumed she would be far too busy with her 'patients' to spare the time for such trivialities.

'I shall sit with Mother,' Bella tartly responded, determined not to react to this show of disfavour.

Emily, however, seemed less than grateful for the extra attention and, whatever Bella did for her, she objected to it. When Bella brought her supper, she said the soup was cold. When Bella read from *Wuthering Heights*, she asked for *Jane Eyre* instead. If Bella tucked in her sheets or drew up her shawl, Emily would try to slap her hand away. Yet if she did not, she would complain of a draught on her neck.

'This en-engagement – is – all your – f-fault,' Emily informed her, dragging out the words with painful difficulty.

Bella never made any comment about this irritating habit which came and went at will. She simply went along with the masquerade. 'I know, I know. I brought Jinnie here but not for a minute do I regret doing so. I love her dearly, as does Edward, and he is surely free to marry her if he so wishes.'

'I've heard all about your licentious behaviour. Utterly shocking.'

'Licentious? Oh, for goodness' sake, Mother, don't *you* start. What I do at the clinic is important to me. Why can't anyone care about how *I* feel? I surely deserve my freedom too.'

'Why? I never had any. Why should you be allowed to do as you please?' Emily peevishly responded in ringing tones, revealing the bitter jealousy she harboured against her more liberated daughter.

'Because there are too many women needing help.'

'Let them suffer. I had to watch your father curb his natural instincts because we could not afford children in the early days of our marriage, why should not others too?' And then, as if realising she had perhaps revealed too much, or else remembering her own supposedly precarious state of health, Emily sank back dramatically upon her pillows, fluttered a hand to her throat and let out a tremulous sigh. 'You behave in this way only to vex me. It's time you were m-mirrored.'

'Mirrored?'

'Mirrored. Dr Lisle — w-wed you timorrer.'

'Oh, God, you mean *married*! You want me to marry Dr Lisle? I think not, Mother. I doubt he's my type.' Bella almost laughed out loud at the very idea and later that day when Dr Lisle himself appeared, offering again, in his simpering, condescending manner, to escort her to the theatre should she wish to go, Bella almost got a fit of the giggles. With commendable restraint she thanked him for his kind offer and said she really had a great deal of paperwork to do.

He looked peeved, as if she didn't properly appreciate the great honour he did her. Bella merely smiled and sailed out of the room, saying she would leave him with his patient as, with no qualifications herself, she was quite obviously unsuitable to assist in medical matters. It was an unkind remark she later came to regret.

Invited to speak at a women's meeting being held at the Congregational School Hall, Bella decided to put the case for her Mothers Clinic with vigour. Not for a moment would she allow the Dr Lisles of this world to damage her cause.

She went alone and on foot, untroubled as ever by the thought of walking through the tangled web of narrow streets. They were never empty, always something going on. This evening was no exception. Overexcited dogs bounded after her while bowlegged children looked up from their game of marbles or top and whip to watch her walk by, giving them all a cheery wave. Bored men lounging on street corners fell momentarily silent, though one or two doffed their caps as they recognised the familiar sight of her upright young figure striding past.

The knife grinder was standing on one corner, a queue

of women idly gossiping while they waited patiently to have their knives sharpened. Others, still wearing their mill aprons, known as 'brats', sat on their kitchen stools gossiping and crocheting at ever-open doors on this warm summer evening, their mouths moving in the usual mee-maw with no sound as they conducted their conversations in complete privacy over the heads of unsuspecting children, a skill they'd acquired in the mill. Bella smiled and nodded as she passed by, stopping to exchange a word here and there with one or other of them.

One woman, Sally Clarke, ran after her to grasp Bella by the arm. 'Hey up, luv. Eeh, I'm reet glad to see thee. I've been wanting to come to that clinic only I dursn't.'

Bella smiled encouragingly at her. She'd been a regular visitor to Mrs Clarke's house ever since Aunt Edie had tipped her off that the woman needed help after her last confinement. 'There's nothing to be afraid of, Sally. Why don't you pop in next Tuesday morning?'

'Me 'usband'd kill me if he ever found out. Tha knows how High Church he is fer all he's not a Catholic. Doctor sez if I has any more childer I'm done fer, so Reg asked our vicar if there were owt as he could do like, and he told him that abstinence were bad fer his health and contraception against the laws of decency, so Reg sez we're not to use owt. Goes against his scruples, he sez.'

'Scruples?' Bella was incensed. 'What about your health? Doesn't he care about that?'

'Aye, well, theer's no answer to that one, is there?' Sally glanced back over her shoulder, nervous that her husband might even now be listening, and then hurried on with her explanation. 'I wondered like, if I sent one o' me older childer, if you'd happen give her summat fer me? In a plain packet?'

Bella sadly shook her head. 'You have to be properly examined, Sally. You have to come yourself.'

'*Sally!*' A door banged somewhere in the nether regions of the house and an angry voice wafted out along with the sour-sweet aroma of unwashed clothes and urine. Panic lit the woman's eyes as she peered fearfully into the gloom of the lobby. 'I'll send our Mavis,' she hissed, then rushed back inside leaving Bella facing a half-naked infant who sat bare-bottomed on the doorstep, sucking his thumb.

Bella arrived early at the hall. From the outset she could sense antagonism in the air. The audience was middle-class and hostile. They were there to air their own views, not listen to hers. Nevertheless, she managed to remain collected and patient throughout the ordeal of the next hour or more and, she hoped, give little sign of her inner nervousness. Spurred on by Sally's plight, she did not shirk this golden opportunity to press home the failure of any Church – Catholic, Anglican or Nonconformist – to give sound advice to desperate women on the subject of family limitation.

One matron rose to her feet and announced that she herself had four children and agreed that childbirth was both agonising and highly dangerous. 'Nevertheless, having lost two sons in the Great War, I'm grateful that I had a large family. And since the working classes lose even more offspring to disease and malnourishment, it is surely necessary for them to have numerous children.' Whereupon she sat down to rousing applause.

Bella responded by informing her audience that her battle was equally against poverty and ill health, both of which were caused as much by overpopulation as economic factors, and that it did the middle classes no credit simply to sit back and do nothing to help prevent these evils. 'Many would be glad to confine their families to four, if only they knew how. Why leave these poor women in ignorance of information that the better educated have possessed for some time? That's nothing short of prejudice and neglect of the worst possible kind.' The result was uproar.

People were on their feet shouting for her to leave. There

were even cries for her to be arrested and put into prison. One overexcited woman screamed that she was guilty of murdering innocents.

'I believe you are confusing contraception with abortion,' Bella responded, lifting her voice as best she could above the din.

Throughout she held her cool, even striding from the platform into their midst, ready to continue the discussion with all comers. She stood hatless, as was her wont, surrounded by a raucous and self-opinionated group of women, none of whom seemed prepared to hold silent long enough to listen to any reasoned argument.

When she finally emerged into the humid warmth of a summer night, it was to find the usual group of protesters on the doorstep of the hall. Their demonstration seemed even noisier than usual, joined as they were by the women from the meeting. Eggs and flour were hurled at her, splattering her costume, and Bella felt suddenly bone weary. She hadn't expected this to be easy but it disturbed her to be so treated by other women. Surely they should understand, even if everyone else – the government, the Church, ignorant husbands, the medical profession itself – refused to alter their obdurate attitude?

One particularly large missile hit the side of her head and she stumbled and half fell, would have done so had not arms reached out to support her. 'Oh, thank you.' The arms that held her were young, male and taut with muscles beneath rolled up shirt sleeves. She could see a pair of corduroy trousers held fast by a wide leather belt, a canvas bag slung across his back, hob-nailed boots, seeming to indicate that the man was on his way home from work. She glanced up to offer a smile of gratitude and met a pair of piercing blue eyes that regarded her with blatant approval from beneath a slouch cap tilted back at a rakish angle over floppy brown hair. High cheek bones, a long straight nose and a wide mouth, slightly lifted at one corner in a devil-may-care sort of smile, all conspired to present the most handsome face Bella had ever encountered in her life.

Her mind seemed to go numb and for a moment she could think of nothing to say. She could only look deeply into those eyes which served to remind her, forcibly, that pioneer of sorts she may be but Isabella Ashton was also a young woman. The power of the muscles beneath her hand, the strength of his hold upon her, even the warm perspiring closeness of his body, left her feeling slightly breathless. She attempted to release herself from his grip but only half succeeded for he kept an arm protectively about her as she began to brush herself down.

'Thank you, I'm fine now. A slight accident, that's all.' Bella knew she should move away from that encircling arm but somehow felt reluctant to do so. It must be for reasons of safety, she told herself, for he was not her sort of man at all. Far too rough-looking, the greyness of his chin indicating he was in dire need of a shave.

'Accident my left foot! Those witches were out to get you.'

She let out a shrill laugh, hearing it ring high-pitched and hollow, fervently wishing he would remove his hand from where it now rested on her middle back. Bella could feel the heat of it burning through the thin cotton jacket she wore. 'Don't be too hard on them. They have every right to their opinion.'

'But not to knock ye down when you express yer own. Will ye let me buy you a good Irish whiskey, to steady yer nerves?'

Bella could think of nothing she'd like better but politely declined. She thought it might not be quite appropriate to be seen entering a public house with this man, though she was sure he was entirely respectable. He was holding out one hand for her to take. It was perfectly clean, well-shaped and with tidily trimmed finger nails. 'Billy Quinn, at yer service.'

'Pleased to meet you, Mr Quinn. Isabella Ashton.' And she gave him her own hand which he held for far too long before letting it go with obvious reluctance. The impression of his fingers against hers remained with her for some moments afterwards.

'Are ye any better now? I could feel yer shaking. Ach, they are indeed witches, the whole blame lot of 'em. Come on, I'm tekking you for a pick-me-up, no protests allowed.'

'Thanks, Quinn, but I'll see to Miss Ashton.' Dan Howarth materialised out of the crowd before them. And Bella hadn't even known that he was there.

She frowned in surprise while noticing how her rescuer bristled and his hand clenched into a fist behind her back. 'And who d'you think ye are? Her guardian angel?'

'Something of the sort, Quinn. She certainly needs no help from the likes of you.'

Quinn fingered the buckle of his wide leather belt as he regarded Dan out of narrowed eyes. 'And does she have any say in this, I wonder?'

Dan ignored him. 'Come on, Bella. I'm taking you home.'

Quinn was tugging on the leather thong, as if threatening to loosen the belt. Heart in mouth, Bella recognised the aggression mounting between the two men, could feel the air almost crackle with it. She liked Dan a lot and was heartily relieved to see him now for all she'd already been safely rescued, yet for some reason the two men seemed to be only seconds away from a brawl. If that buckle were ever swung in anger, as was commonly done in these parts, she was concerned that Dan might come off the worst, despite his impressive physique.

She smiled into those devastating blue eyes. 'It's all right, Mr Quinn. Dan Howarth is a friend of mine. I'm quite happy to go with him.' Allowing no opportunity for Bella even to thank her saviour for picking her up off the pavement, Dan commandeered her arm and began to thrust his way through the throng of curious onlookers.

In truth, she was grateful for his opportune arrival, unexpected as it was. There was something about Billy Quinn which she'd found strangely disturbing, almost an animal magnetism about him, though there'd undeniably been chemistry between them. She glanced back to see that he still stood where they'd left him, thumbs hooked into the leather belt at his waist, cap pushed back on his head now and a smile she didn't care to investigate too closely on his handsome face. But she couldn't help hoping she might meet up with him again. In happier circumstances, of course.

'Lord, Violet, I thought they were going to lynch me,' Bella said later, as she sat in the comforting safety of her friend's kitchen with a glass of stout in her hand. She would have preferred to share Violet's pot of tea but Dan had bought a jug from the selling-out shop, on the basis that she was in dire need of its strength. Bella didn't argue. She sipped the unfamiliar bitter liquid and hoped it would indeed calm her frayed nerves and stop her hands from shaking. 'I've never been so petrified in all my life.'

'Ignorant buggers,' Violet announced, and took a long slurp from her own mug of hot, sweet tea in disgust. 'You shouldn't have gone on yer own, that's the trouble. You should've tekken Dr Syd with you.'

'Dr Syd has her own role to play. She has medical quali-fications which I don't have. This is my role: to educate, to inform, to raise funds. I can't go crying to her for help every five minutes.'

'I'll come with you next time,' Dan announced. 'With the likes of Billy Quinn in the vicinity, God knows what might have happened if I hadn't arrived on the scene.'

She was about to ask how Dan had chanced to be there at all that evening when Violet interrupted, her face a picture of outrage. 'Billy Quinn? That good-fer-nothing young whip-persnapper! He wants his nose knocking out of joint, does Billy Quinn.'

'Why, what's wrong with him? Who is Billy Quinn? He

seemed a very helpful young man. I'd've fallen and been trampled underfoot had it not been for his help.'

'He's a bookmaker, that's what Billy Quinn is. And a Roman Catholic.' Which was almost as bad in Violet's eyes. 'He's trouble, that's what Billy Quinn is. Aye, nowt but trouble,' she repeated, as if to emphasise the fact.

Bella smiled, having a sudden image of the handsome Quinn and feeling her cheeks grow warm as a result. 'I thought everyone liked a bit of a flutter, and for all street betting is illegal, it's common practice in these parts, isn't it? Bit of a lark.'

'Not at our chapel, it in't.' Violet sniffed her disapproval and Bella hastily apologised. She'd forgotten what a strong Methodist her friend was.

'He let Harold Cunliffe languish in t'clink fer three months 'cause he were too mean to pay his fine. Nasty piece of work is Billy Quinn.'

'Perhaps he wasn't allowed to pay his fine, or would've implicated himself if he had,' Bella reasonably pointed out, trying not to pull a face as she took another sip of the thick brown stout.

'You can be sure,' Dan informed her, 'that any favours Billy Quinn does help him more'n anyone else. You'd best stay clear of him in future.'

'I see. Well, I'll remember that. Thank you.'

Bella wasn't blind to the fact that Dan was fond of her, and that he must have turned up this evening because he thought he might be needed. Nor did she mind. She liked Dan Howarth, liked him a lot. She enjoyed his attention and greatly valued his friendship, but it didn't seem to be going anywhere. He always seemed to hold back and still hadn't even kissed her. Bella's disappointment over this was such that at times she wondered if he ever would. Certainly she wasn't going to make the running. Their walks recently had often been at her suggestion and she'd pretty well pushed him into taking her fishing that time; now she wondered if perhaps he'd sensed the tension between herself and this Billy Quinn and was a little jealous of it. She certainly had no wish for Dan Howarth to set himself up as her protector, and decided it was best to make that clear. 'I doubt that I shall need defending, glad though I was of your help this evening. I'm sure that was an isolated incident.'

'Just as you like,' he said, frowning into his mug.

So Bella paid no heed to Dan's opinions on a possible rival, and Violet's comments she dismissed as quite natural, if somewhat bigoted, religious rivalry.

When she went to the clinic the following Thursday morning it was to find a very anxious Mrs Heap standing behind her counter, wringing her hands and declaring that she'd been unable to do anything to prevent it.

'Prevent what? What are you trying to tell me?'

'They just marched in here, bold as brass, and took every last stick.'

'Every stick of what? I'm afraid I haven't a clue what you're talking about, Edie.'

'All the stuff in the clinic – desk, chairs, the whole caboodle. Them chaps come in here and took the whole lot away. Then they sent all the women home, telled them, and me, that the clinic'd been shut down.'

'Shut down?'

'Aye. Closed. Finished. Kaput!'

Bella's first thought was that this had been done by the protesters, and then she decided to look closer to home. Storming through the front door and confronting her father in his study, she demanded to know if he was the one responsible. Simeon readily confessed to having sent some of the men from the mill to close the clinic down. 'I made my views on the matter perfectly clear. There's nowt more to be said.'

'Indeed? Then I'll not waste my breath on you.' And Bella stormed out just as quickly, leaving every door open to the four winds as she went. Simeon roared his rage as papers swirled from his desk and flew all over the floor.

'Come back here this minute, miss!'

She paid him no heed. Bella did not stop until she'd regained the sanctity of the clinic's now empty rooms above Edith Heap's cook shop. Dr Syd and Nurse Shaw were already fully occupied picking up whatever packets and boxes were salvageable, and attempting to sort loose papers and patient notes back into their proper files.

Bella grabbed a piece of cardboard and penned a large notice which clearly stated that the Mother's Clinic would be open tonight as usual, for consultations and treatment. 'We'll show them.'

Thankfully word got round and the usual queue of women was soon straggling up the stairs. There was a slight delay before they could open the doors, not only because of all the clearing up they had to do but because they were inundated with offers of help. Curtains were provided in place of the screens which had been removed, in order to create the necessary privacy for the women to be examined. The greengrocer brought some orange boxes to hold the supplies which had been so carelessly tossed about. Mrs Solomon donated a small wooden table and two chairs which she insisted she'd no real need of. Mrs Heap, anxious to do her bit, provided a hot supper of pie and peas for the willing workers. And all of this from people who had nothing.

'The folk of Salford might have less than nowt, as they say round here, but they're ready enough to share it,' Mrs Blundell agreed, wielding a hammer with gusto as she tacked up curtains, stomach bulging ripely beneath her pendulous breasts.

Bella could only weep with gratitude, humbled by their generosity, and didn't in the least mind walking home later than usual that night. On finding herself once more confronting an irate father who stood waiting for her in the hall, she might well have wept out of sheer frustration had she not been so consumed by anger herself.

Dr Lisle hovered close by and Bella knew, without even asking, that the little doctor had come specifically to inform Simeon that she'd disobeyed him. She was proved entirely correct.

'So you've opened it again?'

'Yes.'

'Against my wishes.'

'It isn't your wishes I have to consider, Father. It's what is right and proper for the women of Salford.'

She might well have found further arguments to press her case but was given no opportunity to do so. At that precise moment the leaded window shattered as a brick flew into the hall, missing her by inches. Glass was sent everywhere, lodging in her hair and sticking into her clothes, one shard piercing her cheek so that Bella cried out with the shock and pain of it as blood ran. Dr Lisle, she noticed, hastily backed into a corner of the hall, thereby avoiding the worst of the damage, while her father was as equally covered in flecks of broken glass as herself.

'Hell's teeth! What ignoramus has done this? See what you've brought upon us. *How dare you!* As if I haven't enough on me plate with your dear mother sick.'

Jinnie ran down the stairs to comfort her, dark eyes wide with fear, swiftly followed by Edward but Bella waved their concern away. 'These ignoramuses, as you call them, are merely registering the same blind prejudice as yourself, Father.'

'Utter rubbish! Well, I'll not have it. I'll not be attacked in me own home because of a daughter who has lost all her morals. Out.'

'I beg your pardon?'

'*Out!* I want you out of this house this minute.'

Bella gave a half laugh, more from disbelief than amusement. 'To go where? It's nearly eleven o'clock at night.'

'You should've thought of that before you reopened that

damned clinic and started this caper in the first place.' So saying, he flung open the door, grasped Bella by the arm and flung her out into the street. Her foot skidded on the wet pavement and she fell awkwardly, twisting her ankle. She heard Jinnie's cry of horror, Edward's protest, but when she lifted her head on a cry of agony, it was to find that the door had shut fast. Even as she called out to her father, she heard the lock turn and the bolts being drawn.

Chapter Eleven

Bella sat in Violet's kitchen with her head in her hands, closer to despair than she'd ever been in her life. What was to become of her? Everything had gone wrong. If it weren't for her dear friends she'd be sleeping rough on the streets with not a penny to her name. She felt fortunate to have them. When she'd picked herself up from that pavement, all Bella could think of to do was to come here, to Violet, and her friend had opened her arms and gathered Bella close to her ample bosom.

'We're not used to visitors from your end of town,' Violet had drily commented. 'You'll happen find us a bit rough, a bit lacking in the social graces department.'

'I find the atmosphere here warm and comforting after the frigid one in Seedley Park Road.'

Violet had tended her wounds and welcomed Bella into the heart of the family as if she had every right to be there. As if she belonged.

'That's our Vi,' her husband had calmly remarked when he'd encountered a stranger at his breakfast table the following morning, and heard Bella's explanation and apology for the intrusion. Cyril Howarth had calmly asked for a second slice of bread and dripping and told Bella she was welcome to stop on as long as she needed. 'One more's neither here nor there, though where tha'll sleep is a mystery. Vi'll sort that out.' As she did most things, Bella guessed. Cynil was a mild-mannered little man who all his working life had tipped up his weekly wage packet without protest in return for a bit of baccy money. Now that he was unemployed, he happily continued to refer all major decisions to his wife as the normal way of going about things. 'Tek us as yer finds us,' was his only other comment, evidently referring to the mayhem of children milling around, all seemingly half dressed as they searched for socks, shoes or snap tin, yelling for a jam butty or rushing off saying they hadn't time even for a slurp of tea.

He didn't look in the least like the sex fiend Violet had so graphically described, though his eyes certainly filled with love every time he glanced in his wife's direction. Rather as Dan's did when he looked in Bella's.

She couldn't help wondering how that particular friendship might survive, living at such close quarters. Would Dan quickly grow disillusioned, once he saw her on a daily basis, or would it develop into something deeper? Bella couldn't even make up her mind what she wanted to happen, being too caught up with the near disaster over the clinic even to consider personal feelings at the moment.

Those first few days were difficult, however, despite the warm welcome she received. As she sat down to her first meal with the Howarth family she was presented with a dish of tripe, lightly simmered in milk with onions, a delicacy few Lancastrians could resist. But Bella felt her stomach lurch. She'd never developed a fancy for it despite Simeon's efforts to persuade her to eat it over the years.

'I'm sorry but I don't care for tripe.' She sensed Dan's curious gaze upon her and avoided meeting it. Violet looked stricken as well she might since, being cheap, the family largely lived off offal, pig's trotters or sheep's head. 'Don't worry, I'm not very hungry, a little bread and butter will do well enough instead.' Even so, seeing how little of the loaf remained to be placed before her, Bella's sense of guilt quadrupled.

'She can have a slice of mine,' Dan said, handing one over. 'We can't expect a young lady of Miss Isabella's standing to eat tripe, Mother. What were you thinking of?'

At which comment, Bella lost her appetite altogether.

No one, it seemed, had the first idea where Bella had gone, or where she was now. She had apparently vanished off the face of the earth and Edward vowed to do everything in his power to resolve the problem, find his sister, bring her home and effect a reconciliation.

He made several valiant attempts to persuade Simeon to allow Bella back into the house. He'd tried and failed on the night in question and, despite further efforts since, had been given short shrift. After his fourth plea for some sign of forgiveness, if not repentance for his father's action against her, he recognised the futility of his efforts. The very mention of her name was banned and Edward judiciously decided that in order to maintain peace in the household he must wait a while. For the moment, his father remained obdurate.

'It's a terrible thing to disown a daughter but she's gone beyond the pale this time, lad.' He had cast her off and was done with her.

For all that the cause Bella was involved in was quite radical, even shocking in its way, Edward found this attitude of his father's hard to understand. For Simeon to find fault with his favourite child, let alone reject her, was unheard of. Hadn't he always protected Bella – overprotected at times? But then recently every facet of Edward's world had been turned upside down.

Over the years he'd grown accustomed to being in constant conflict with his father but had never been in the habit of criticising his mother. Now he did so, privately at least. Not only had she objected to his wish to marry Jinnie, she neither noticed nor cared that her only daughter was missing from home. Emily was always cloyingly grateful for his rare visits to the sick-room and he did his best on these occasions to keep the conversation light, never discussing his future plans.

More often than not, however, his mother would suggest that it was time Jinnie went home, back to where she belonged, at which point he would beat a hasty retreat.

If only Jinnie would agree to marry him now, instead of waiting. He'd thought, when Bella had mentioned she had something to tell him, that this might be what it was. However, Jinnie seemed to agree that he needed time to be absolutely certain before committing himself. Absolute nonsense in Edward's view. He adored Jinnie and couldn't envision life without her. And he was certain that once the deed was done, family life would settle back into a normal routine and everyone would be happy again. Edward hated discord and ill feeling of any kind.

Following his sister's eviction from the house it proved to be Jinnie now who was treated as the favourite child. Simeon lavished even more attention upon her, spoiling her outrageously, pandering to her every whim, many of which Jinnie had never even thought of until he made the suggestion.

Would she care for a trip into town or perhaps dinner out? A new gown or hat? A trip to Bell Vue perhaps? Or the Opera House in London? A weekend in Paris? Nothing was too good for her, nor too much trouble.

'I've said no to the lot. Not because I'm not grateful, but can he afford such fripperies? He'd be bankrupt in a week,' Jinnie remarked to Edward, who laughed with wry amusement.

'I doubt it.'

'Anyroad, he's turning me from a slattern into a flapper.' But Edward assured her that she'd never been the former and certainly wasn't the latter.

The very next Sunday Jinnie and Edward were sitting on top of a tramcar, heading home after spending an afternoon listening to the band in Albert Square, when she decided the moment had come. If she didn't tell Edward the truth about herself soon, then she'd never be free of Quinn. Never. She should be grateful he'd asked no more of her than to take a few bets but who knew what he might do in the future? She didn't trust him an inch and had to find some way to break free

Surely Edward loved her enough to forgive the terrible things that had happened in her past, for they'd been no fault of hers. Didn't everyone in the poorer areas of Salford have similar troubles? She'd been no more than a frightened child when Billy Quinn had taken her to his bed, too terrified to refuse him. Still was terrified of him.

'There's something I've been wanting to talk to you about, Edward.'

'Is it about when we are to marry?'

Jinnie couldn't help but smile softly at him. He reminded her of a little boy with his nose pressed to the window of a sweet shop, longing to taste the wares. 'Can't you wait even a little while?' she teased. 'Just to be absolutely certain that we are suited.'

'I could wait for ever,' he recklessly and inaccurately assured her. 'And of course we're suited. I adore you Jinnie.'

'Oh, and I adore you but – why did you choose me? I mean, you know nowt about me. You know nowt about wh I lived afore we met, 'ceptin' that I come from t'roug streets; nor where I were born, not that I rightly know I'd no job, no family, nothing but the clothes I st in, so how can you love me? Why did you want me?'

'I love you because you're *you*.'

Jinnie felt her heart contract with love for hi I'd Edward had ever said such lovely things to her. done summat terrible?'

'How could you possibly have?' He nuzz neck and Jinnie had to push him away, to m behave. Cheeks flushed, she looked so delig that he kissed her again.

'Stop it, folk are looking. What if I'd told you lies or summat?'

'I don't believe you could ever tell a lie, darling Jinnie.'

He smiled into her eyes and Jinnie experienced that familiar melting sensation deep inside, followed by a clench of pain somewhere she shouldn't. Oh, but she loved him that much, Jinnie felt she might die if she lost him. She reminded herself that it'd been Bella who'd made up the tale of the accident with a runaway cart horse, not herself. She'd been too ill to care. Though it was true she'd had ample opportunity to put the matter right since. She tried again. 'Well, not a lie exactly. What I'm trying to say is, how could you possibly still love me if I had – done summat terrible, I mean.'

'What sort of *terrible thing* can a sixteen-year-old girl as lovely as you possibly do?' He was laughing at her now, tweaking her pert nose then kissing it, right there on the top of the tram. 'Anyway, I don't care about your life before you met me. That's over.' It was all exactly what Jinnie had most longed to hear and her heart soared with fresh hope. But before she could get another word in and finish what she'd started, he began to spoil it. 'I love you because you are special, different, not like the other girls always up to mischief in those rough streets. No better than they ought to be.'

After a moment's pause for breath, she said, 'What if I were same as the other girls, the ones allus up to mischief, would you still love me then?' She was gazing at him with pleading eyes but he didn't seem to notice because he was busily kiss her cheek before the conductor came upstairs for ages.

stand ver let me hear you speak of yourself in this way your lo not like the other girls. You're *my* girl. You have fingertips. s, beauty. That much is clear in every line of in your sweet, delicious body, in your fragile

Jinnie closed her eyes, weak with love for him. 'Give o'er. You sound like you're drunk.'

'I feel drunk. Drunk with love. You make me so happy, Jinnie. Don't ever talk of my not loving you again.'

How could she tell him how wicked she'd been after that? But she remained thoughtfully silent for the rest of the journey.

'Same again next Sunday?' Edward pleaded as they alighted at the corner of Liverpool Street and Jinnie could only nod, bemused and oddly excited, brown eyes glittering with raw emotion.

If she'd failed to tell him the truth about her past, what did it signify? He loved her and would hear no word said against her, not even from her own lips. She was perfectly certain that nothing and no one could destroy their love. Not ever.

Edward was waiting for Bella in the pie shop after the clinic closed the very next Thursday evening, and begged her to come and talk to their father. 'He's looking for you to meet him halfway and will be only too happy to take you back. He already regrets his outburst of temper.'

'He hasn't said as much, though, has he?'

'Not in so many words but he does feel it, I can tell. He's miserable as hell and hardly leaves his study.'

Bella pressed her mouth into a tight line, apparently unconvinced. 'He knows where to find me if he wants me. You did. He can leave a message any time at the clinic, or with Aunt Edie here,' indicating Mrs Heap whose ears were flapping along with a good many other interested spectators' as she slid pies into waiting basins. Then Bella grinned up at her brother. 'Have you any money with you? Buy me a pie. I'm fair clemmed, as Violet would say.'

'You're just as stubborn as he is,' Edward railed, slamming

some coins down on the counter. Bella bit into the hot pastry, hazel eyes bright with mischief.

'Maybe that's where I get it from.'

Taking her by the elbow, he marched her out into the street where they might talk within greater privacy. 'Is this what you're living on? Pies.'

'I'm living on charity.'

'With Violet Howarth? Pa would never think to look for you there. And he'd not come here either.'

'If this is a battle of wits he's on to a loser, because I won't give in. Ever. The clinic stays and I'll fight anyone who tries to close it.'

'You would too, you daft idiot. You were always the spirited one in the family. I remember you socking me one on a number of occasions when we were children. There were times at school when I could've done with your strong right arm.'

Bella chuckled as she made a parody of punching him then tucked her arm into his. They walked for some time in affectionate but gloomy silence, each acknowledging the impossibility of either her or their father ever backing down. 'Do you know something? I'm happy here. I feel I'm doing something useful. But I miss you. Jinnie too.'

'And we miss you. I admire your gumption, sis, but we'd both like you to come home.'

'I can't ever do that. I've certainly no intention of abandoning what I passionately believe in, just to please Father. It's far too important. Has Jinnie spoken to you yet? Has she told you . . .'

'Told me what? You've asked me that before. What is this?' He held her away from him, a frown puckering his brow.

'Nothing. I just thought . . . Nothing. I'm probably worrying unnecessarily.' Bella fondly patted his cheek. 'Go on with you, soft lad. Go home and be a better son than I've been a daughter. Tell Mother I'm fine and I'll pop in and see her one afternoon while Pa's at the mill. Is she up and about yet?'

Edward shook his head, his expression doleful. 'I doubt she ever will be. And it's all my fault she had that damned stroke. I shouldn't have gone charging in like a bull in a china shop with my decision to marry Jinnie.'

'Well, perhaps your ardour should have been tempered just a little. But don't worry, Mother's state of health is not your responsibility. These things happen. It isn't your fault and I'm sure she's not half as bad as she makes out.'

Bella was sorely tempted to tell him the truth, that it was all a pantomime to bring him to heel, but decided against it. Family emotions were stretched to breaking point as it was, heaven knew what might happen if Emily's little charade were ever discovered. It could destroy the mother-and-son relationship for all time. Much better she be left to come out of her sulks in her own good time. 'Don't fret. She'll make a miraculous recovery one day, I guarantee it.'

'Ever the optimist.' Edward poured the contents of his pocket, little more than five shillings in coppers and silver coins, into her hand. 'I'll get you some more. I can do that for you at least, even if Father won't. What a family, eh?'

'Bless you. Yes, what a family!'

A few days later Bella returned from a visit to Sally Clarke to find a note propped up against the mantel-clock. The compassion in Violet's eyes told her it was from Seedley Park Road, even before she recognised the handwriting.

Bella picked it up with a sense of foreboding. It had not been a good day. Her visit had been entirely unsuccessful. Only once had she persuaded the woman to come to the clinic and every time she'd called at the house since, Bella could never get to speak to Sally without her husband being present. Today had been no different. Reg Clarke had been adamant that his wife would use no artificial means that went against his religion and might be seriously detrimental to his own health.

'We will leave the matter in God's hands,' he'd told Bella, showing her firmly to the door.

It was, she felt, like beating her head against the proverbial brick wall.

Now she opened the letter and was horrified to discover that her father had stopped her allowance. Afraid of being a burden to her kind hosts, she barely touched the substantial meal set before her. How dare she take food from out of their children's mouths? It wouldn't be right. She did what she could to help Violet around the house but, with no money coming in, how could she pay her way? Bella decided that she must find employment, and soon.

Dr Syd expressed concern on being brought up to date with events and instantly suggested that the clinic pay Bella a wage. She refused. 'That's not why I opened it, to make money for myself. Anyway, it isn't possible. The clinic barely has enough to survive. I have some savings to call on. Besides, I mean to speak to Mother. She may be willing to help. Falling that, I shall sign on. Isn't that what everyone else does?'

'You could always find yourself a husband,' Dr Syd suggested, lips twisting into a wry smile. 'That's usually the answer for a penniless female.'

'No, thanks.'

'You surprise me. I heard you were walking out with Dr Lisle.'

'Heavens, whoever gave you that idea?'

'He did. He's quite convinced you would make a perfect pair.'

'Drat the man! All he does is adopt the moral high ground and preach at me. I swear there'd be murder done if I were ever alone with him for more than five seconds.'

Bella's 'ladies' at the clinic were equally sympathetic but no more able to solve her financial problems than their own. Aunt

Edie said baking for a living was hot, tiring work and very poorly paid. Mrs Solomon admitted they didn't have any vacancies for an assistant in their fish shop, largely because they rarely had much fish to sell and even fewer customers. 'Those who pay regular anyroad. We get by,' she said. An oft-repeated phrase. Mrs Stobbs was unfit for work of any kind, even if she could get it, what with her numerous children and her health problems, and Mrs Blundell said that she worked a punishing shift system in the mill, which she wouldn't recommend to anyone.

'Not to a lass such as theesen. Though that Jinnie's different. She's used to roughing it and has her old friends around to mek her feel at 'ome'

'Old friends?'

Mrs Blundell folded her arms across her billowing bosom, leaned against the door jamb and settled in for a long natter. 'Aye. She hobnobs every dinnertime wi' that Len Jackson and Harold Cunliffe. Right pair o' loose bobbins them two. Never seem to do a hand's turn, but harmless enough, I dare say, in their way.'

Bella frowned but asked no further questions. What Jinnie did was really no concern of hers. Though perhaps it was of Edward's, a voice in the back of her head quietly commented.

When Harold Cunliffe came to Jinnie with a suggestion to cheat Billy Quinn, she refused to have anything to do with it. 'Nay, if you value yer life so cheaply, that's up to you. I want to live a bit longer.'

Harold pointed out that Quinn had left him rotting in jail for three months during which time his wife had been taken into the sanatorium, his children sent to an Orphans' Home and his youngest child had died of malnutrition. 'Otherwise known as starvation. By the time I come out I'd no job, no family, and not even a house to call me own. He's left me wi' nowt, and I'm not the first he's treated so badly. For all he's put me back on the payroll as his runner, I can't forgive him for what he did. It's time someone stood up to Billy Quinn. I thought happen you'd feel the same.'

'Oh, I do, I do, but . . .'

'Thee's too much of a coward? Like everyone else round 'ere, you want to save yer own skin.'

'Is that a crime?'

'It is if it leaves such as Quinn on the rampage. Like a loose canon he is. One of these days he'll blow somebody's bleedin' head off.' Harold leaned closer, eager now to share his plan. 'We could get our own back on him if we joined forces, Jinnie lass. Make money out of him, instead of him makin' a fat profit out of us. He owes me that much at least. All we have to do is fiddle the clock bag by not shutting it till after the first race. Then you run and put on a last-minute bet. He doesn't get the result through quickly, so he takes bets till the start of the second race. We'd clean up, I tell you.'

Jinnie listened to the plan with mounting trepidation. 'How would you get the result, though, before he does?'

'There are ways. Are you in then?'

'I've enough to do keeping tabs on all these bets. I'm up to me ears in work.' She wisely opted for self-preservation. She collected the bets and handed them over to Harold, exactly as she was told to do by Quinn. No risks. No trouble. What Harold did with them after that was his affair.

The following week Mrs Blundell won twelve pounds and made sure everybody in the weaving shed knew about it. 'By heck, I'm rich. Here, lass, it's all due to you.' And she gave Jinnie a sovereign.

Jinnie stared at the coin in wonder. She'd never held so much money in her hand before in her entire life. Nervous of having the coin about her person and afraid of anyone finding it, she tucked it in the back of a dressing-table drawer when she got home that night and said nothing to anyone about it. The less Edward knew about her working as a bookie's runner, the better.

A week or two later Mrs Blundell won again, twenty pounds this time, her pendulous breasts shaking with joy as she trundled through the weaving shed, yelling to everyone about her good fortune. 'Hearken t'this, I've come up trumps agin! Berra watch which horse I puts me money on in future, eh?' This time she gave Jinnie two sovereigns. 'Thee's a reet lucky star fer me, lass. Buy yoursel' summat nice.'

Jinnie gazed at the money with eyes grown big and round with wonder. 'How did you do it, Mrs Blundell?' It didn't seem possible to win once, let alone twice in just a few weeks. She could hardly believe it.

Neither, it seemed, could Billy Quinn.

He was waiting for her at the end of her shift, as she'd half feared he might be, lounging against the wall in his familiar arrogant manner. Jinnie recognised the curl of blue smoke from the end of his cigarette long before she reached him. No one else had so much money to spend on fags as Billy Quinn. She felt a chill of cold fear settle in her stomach.

'What's going on?'

'I beg your pardon?'

'Don't practise yer fancy new way of talkin' to me, girl. This punter of yours, how come she won twice? Is there something ye should be telling me, Jinnie?'

'What can there be to tell? I've no idea which horse will win, have I? I just do what you tells me, give them the tip like you say I has to, then I collects the money and hands it over to Harold and he puts it in the clock bag.' A memory stirred, of Harold's plan to fiddle the clock bag, and she suddenly saw how it came about that Mrs Blundell had won twice. It could all be done very easily, even without her connivance. Jinnie could feel herself flushing, just as if she were indeed the guilty party, and realised with a quickening of fear that Quinn had seen the betraying blush too. The blue eyes narrowed with suspicion. Pinching the fag end between finger and thumb, he tossed it aside.

'You and Harold wouldn't have a little racket going, would ye?'

'Racket? No, 'course we don't. What sort of racket could that be? I know nowt about any racket.' However hard she tried, Jinnie couldn't keep the guilt out of her voice. She could kill Harold Cunliffe for getting her in this mess, as if she didn't have problems enough already. 'I'm going to miss me tram, Quinn, I have to go.'

He struck her with the flat of his hand, jerking her head back so hard that she heard her neck crack. She felt a trickle of blood run from her nose and into her mouth. Then he slammed her up against the entry wall, making her cry out as the back of her head met solid stone. Quinn pressed the length of his hard body against hers, one hand circling her throat, trapping her so that she could scarcely breathe, let alone move.

'Ye know what I'd do if ye were ever daft enough to cheat on me, don't you, girl?' Jinnie couldn't even move sufficiently to nod. 'I'd cut out yer lying tongue, so I would. Then put you through the mincer, just as if you were a pound of beef.' He smiled and the effect was chilling. 'And ye can tell Harold Cunliffe he'll get the same treatment, if'n he tries anything. No, on second thoughts, don't bother. I'll have a quiet word with Harold meself, so I will.' Having made this decision, he released her and stepped back. Jinnie almost fainted from relief.

'There, I'm not so terrible, am I? Now get off home, Jinnie me love, afore I change me mind. Go *now!*' he yelled, and she wasted no time in doing so, not even pausing to catch her breath until she'd jumped on to a passing car.

The minute Jinnie arrived back in Seedley Park Road, she quickly secreted the two sovereigns in the back of the drawer beside the first, shaking with fear as she did so. If Quinn had looked in her pockets he'd have found them for sure, and she'd have been mincemeat there and then. At least she was safe now, and had some privacy here to hide her money. No one would ever find it.

It was a couple of days later that a man's body was dragged from the canal. It was identified as that of Harold Cunliffe, presumed to have taken his own life through drowning after losing his wife and children.

Jinnie listened in stunned silence to the report as Edward read it out from the morning paper. Her heart froze with fear but she urged herself not to panic. All she had to do, she told herself sternly, was exactly what Quinn had told her. Hadn't she always known those were the rules? Harold had understood them too, until desperation had driven him to abandon caution. On no account must she make the same mistake.

Chapter Twelve

Attendance at the clinic was increasing week by week with a regular supply of new clients, as well as repeat cases. Bella kept careful records and discovered that the first 100 or so patients had previously sustained between them over 500 pregnancies. One woman alone had endured eighteen, including four dead infants, three miscarriages and three children described as imbeciles. Another with four living children had lost an equal number of stillborn babies, plus suffering several miscarriages. It was a sorry state of affairs and similar pitiful stories regularly reduced her to tears.

Bella's regulars were more hardened and would readily stand on their doorsteps in their crossover pinnies, to 'do a bit of campin'' as they called it. There was nothing they liked better than to exchange titbits of gossip. They'd clip their children round the ears for 'marlickin' abaout', complain over being bone weary and powfagged after a long day at the mill, usually followed by several more hours' cleaning and cooking at home for their large families, and yet find the energy to have a good chin-wag well into the late evening.

After they'd moaned about their respective families, they'd turn their attention to the latest lovers walking arm in arm up the street for an evening out. 'He must be a fresh catched 'un,' they'd say, if a girl had a new boy friend. Or if the couple seemed plain, or ill matched, or were considered odd in some way, one wit would drily remark: 'Weel, they won't spoil a pair.'

Gossiping on the stairs at the clinic was also a favourite occupation. Speculation about who might have 'fallen' as a result of not following the careful routine set down by Dr Syd was of enormous fascination to all. They would bemoan the dozens of marriages damaged by the wife's fear of showing affection. 'Can you blame 'em,' Aunt Edie would point out, 'when it'd mean another kid?'

Mrs Blundell, having recently been delivered of a surprisingly healthy boy, jiggled the baby in her arms as he suckled at one floppy breast and told of a sailor's wife who went into hiding whenever her husband's ship was in port. 'In the end he stopped comin' back down Ship Canal altogether. He were last heard of wi' a Chinese woman in Hong Kong.'

'Eeh, some 'usbands'd use any excuse to tek on a fancy woman.'

'Aye, what can you do wi' em, eh?'

Several rude suggestions were made, all in silent mee-maw, which caused great hilarity and a good deal of frustration to those further up the stairs who were hoping to glean some titillating piece of information.

'Eeh,' said Mrs Stobbs, anxious to outdo this terrible tale, 'I know of one woman who spent years in a TB sanatorium and got put in t' family way every time her husband come to see her. She told him to give o'er comin' in the end, so he stopped at home to look after all t'childer.'

No one quite knew whether to believe this story or not but it certainly chilled the blood.

By the time they'd reached the top of the stairs and were settling themselves on the line of chairs to await their turn to see the nurse, they were back to their favourite topic of who, amongst their friends and neighbours, had recently fallen. Mrs Blundell made herself comfortable by switching the baby to the other breast and casually remarked, 'Hasta heard? Sally Clarke's been caught again.'

'Caught?' Bella looked up from a card she was writing at

her desk, thinking she meant the police had picked Sally up for some crime.

'Aye. Daft bugger should've got off at Deansgate but went through to London Road instead.'

Even more bemused Bella said, 'I still don't understand.'

'Nay, lass, don't be so gormless. She's up the spout!'

'Oh, dear God, no. Not again. But the doctor said the next baby would kill her.'

'Aye, well. That obviously didn't worry Reg Clarke. 'Course, he can easy get another wife, can't he?' And as they all exchanged looks of dread, there wasn't one woman present who didn't cross herself with fear, and make a private vow to be even more vigilant with the help they received at the Mothers' Clinic.

Bella went at once to see Sally but, standing in the filthy kitchen and seeing the bemused expression on her worn, tired face over the panic she'd created, and the way she kept half glancing across at her husband where he sat reading the Bible in the only comfortable chair in the room, Bella knew in her heart that the case had been hopeless from the start.

'I offered to help,' she explained to Dan, pouring out all her guilt and anxiety over the matter. 'I argued the toss with him for ages but he wouldn't hear of it. He said his wife needed help from no one, thank you very much. Wouldn't even allow her to come and see Dr Syd for a check up now she's expecting again. Preached to me a whole load of stuff from *Genesis* or *Revelations* or some such. I could've hit him!' Whereupon she promptly burst into tears.

'Nay, nay, don't tek on. Thee can't win 'em all.' Dan gathered her into his great arms, giving her shoulder awkward little pats. 'Come on, you're overtired, that's all it is.'

'I could have saved her. I could!'

'No, Bella love. You can't save everyone. Some folk are born losers. You've been working too hard, that's your trouble. You know what I'm going to do? Take you to the fair.'

She stared up into his smiling face, laughing as she wiped the tears from her eyes. 'You're what?'

'The fair at Charlestown. You deserve a day out. We both do.'

As soon as Violet heard of the plan she agreed whole-heartedly. 'Eeh, aye, that'll do thee both good. I'll pack up some butties fer thee.'

There didn't seem any reason to object and so, with packets of sandwiches and slices of Violet's best ginger parkin in their pockets, Bella and Dan set off, walking the length of Liverpool Street and up Cross Lane.

They could hear the music long before they reached the fair, *Orpheus in the Underworld* and the famous Strauss waltzes. In no time they were riding the garishly painted hobby horses, squealing like children on the Scenic Railway and trying their hand on the coconut shy, three balls for sixpence.

'Oh, you're right. This has cheered me up no end,' Bella agreed, tucking in to a dish of black peas as they stood listening entranced to the barrel organ, laughing at the mechanical conductor wagging his stick in time to the music. Afterwards they bought dishes of ice cream from Salvatores', cart, the best in the district. Then Bella tried her hand on the hoopla stall, wanting to win a nice pot jug for Violet. Instead she was handed a goldfish in a jar. 'What on earth shall I do with this?' she laughed.

'Give it to our Pete. He'll love it.'

They had to try the candy floss, of course, which stuck all over Bella's lips, and a drink of dark, herb-flavoured sarsaparilla. As darkness fell and lamps were lit, the scene changed, as if they weren't in the middle of Salford at all, a city as shabbily familiar as a pair of old slippers. It was as if they were in a new and magical kingdom where even the sound of ships' hooters down at Salford Quays didn't spoil the effect. The night seemed to embrace them, shrouding the shabbiness of the dusty fairground in mystery.

'I really appreciate your taking me in, an orphan from the storm.'

Dan chuckled and, as they strolled through the crowds, caught her hand in his. She didn't protest but left it there and his heart lifted. 'Ma says you're doing a grand job at that clinic. I know she'd love to help you but doesn't want to push her nose in where it's not wanted.'

'It's wanted all right. We need all the support we can get. Violet's just the sort of woman we need to chat with the younger ones, offer them some motherly advice while they wait for their check up. I'll speak to her about it.'

'Grand! I'm proud to be your friend, Bella.' A slight pause. 'I'd like to be more than a friend, s'matter of fact.'

'Dan Howarth, what are you suggesting?' she teased.

A betraying flush of crimson suffused his neck. 'I'm asking you to walk out with me, to be my girl.'

'Are you now? Well, I'd need to give that my most careful consideration.'

They circumnavigated a roundabout of blue and scarlet cocks and hens while children scrambled eagerly aboard and he looked down into her lovely face, flushed with happiness, bright hazel eyes so full of laughter and fun. He ached to snatch her up into his arms and kiss her till she throbbed with the same passion that pulsated through him. He made a half move to do so, his heart thudding as he saw what appeared to be a spark of interest in her eyes. But then he checked himself. What was he thinking of? It was no doubt only kindness. Bella was nothing if not kind. And practical of course. So full of this job she was doing at the clinic that she barely noticed him, not as a chap to walk out with.

'Are you going to kiss me, you great daft lump, or must I do it for you?' Then, to his astonished delight, she reached up, put her arms about his neck and pulled his head down to hers.

Her lips were sweet and soft, deliciously warm against his. He felt as if something were exploding inside his head and he wanted to do more than kiss her, ached to make her a part of him forever. Shame washed over him. What was he thinking of, showing no respect, and to a well-brought-up girl like Bella? He put her firmly from him.

'I'm sorry. I shouldn't've done that.'

'I don't believe *you* did anything.' She was laughing up at him and Dan felt suddenly confused, not quite sure whether the kiss had pleased her or not. 'Might it have a future then, this "walking-out"? We'd be "doin' a bit of coortin'", would we?'

'Arta making fun of me?'

Bella was instantly contrite. 'No, of course I'm not.'

He considered her in all seriousness, her lovely face a picture of innocence. Now what did she mean by that? Having him on, surely. Nothing Bella liked better than to have a bit of fun with him. She'd never see him as a likely candidate for a husband. Why the hell should she? She could have her pick of admirers. Despite this spat with her dad, she was still miles above him. Miles and bleedin' miles. Used to fancy frocks and good food on the table, not clogs and beef dripping. 'What could a chap like me have to offer a lass like you?' he said, unable to disguise his bitterness.

'I suppose there'd be a bit of love, would there? If you were seriously offering for me, that is?' Her eyes were now wide and questioning.

'Tha knows what I'm talking about. Money. Brass. I've nowt to offer a lass like you. Mebbe never will have.' He felt flustered and unsure of himself, thrown off balance by her teasing.

Bella let out a heavy sigh, then put her hands to her hair as if she meant to tear it out. It was wild and curling and tawny-coloured and Dan longed to run his own fingers through the silky waves. 'I'm sure we've had this conversation before but I'll say it again, Dan Howarth. If I were *truly* in love with someone, it wouldn't matter a jot what they earned. It's *who* a person is that counts, not what they do for a living.'

'That's easy said.'

'But it's *true*.'

He saw what might have been sincerity in the steadiness of her gaze but he was too far gone in self-pity to respond to it. He should never have asked, never have suggested such a daft thing in the first place. 'You may think so now. But when the first childer started coming, it'd be a different story then, wouldn't it?'

'Which is where my clinic comes in. A woman needn't have children at all until she's ready for them.'

'Aye, but the clinic would have to close once we were wed, wouldn't it?' Dan knew, the instant the words popped out of his mouth, that he'd made a bad mistake.

Bella stopped in her tracks to stand and stare at him. 'Have to close? *Why* would it have to close?'

He strove to justify himself. 'Because you'd be married. Everyone knows a woman can't work at a proper job, not once she's wed. Not unless she has to, or her husband meks her. I'd niver do that to a wife o' mine. Besides, they say it takes bread out of a chap's mouth when a woman works.'

'Well, I think that's a silly rule, to make women give up a perfectly good job just because they've got married. And who says they'd be taking away work from a man? I certainly wouldn't be, would I? Not at the clinic.'

Dan longed to retract but didn't know how. His own misery had led him down this path and he wished he could retrace his steps. He made a stab at it. 'Aye, well, I grant you that, but happen you wouldn't have time to work, not if we were wed. You'd have the house to see to, dinner to mek, the childer ...'

'Dear God, I've heard enough.' Bella turned on her heel and marched away, and though he instantly ran after her, she studiously ignored him, yelling that he was as pig-headed as all the other men she knew.

He grabbed her arm, dragged her to a halt. 'Why am I pig-headed, just because I'd want me wife to stop at home while I went out to work to look after her? What the hell's wrong wi' that?'

'Everything. It turns me into a chattel. And I'll not be anyone's *possession*.' Snatching herself free, she strode away. 'And I won't close the clinic for anybody, not even you, Dan Howarth.'

'All right, all right. I never wanted you to. I'm sorry. Keep yer clinic then.' But it was too late. She'd been swallowed up by the crowds, by the darkness, and although he searched every inch of the fairground he failed to find any sign of her. The magic of the evening had evaporated and he was alone in a mucky old field, swearing loudly and comprehensively at himself for having just ruined a perfectly good evening through his own blind stupidity.

Bella walked no more than twenty yards before regretting her outburst. Their conversation had just been getting interesting when she'd ruined it. It had been foolish to lose her temper, and all because Dan wanted to look after her if she had a family to care for. What was so wrong with that? And whose children would they be after all? Hers and Dan's? She felt her heart start to race in a strange, uneven rhythm. Oh, Lord, what had she done?

'Damnation!' If she wasn't careful she'd turn into a carbon copy of her mother. Stupidly prejudiced, wanting all her own way and never listening to any other opinion but her own.

But was it so surprising that she'd not properly taken in what he was trying to tell her, in his clumsy, self-effacing way? In all their times together, Dan had never even kissed her. Even now that she'd made the first move he'd soon backed away, and she saw that he'd been afraid. Yet he must like her even to be hinting at something of this nature between them;

had shyly admitted as much and confessed to feeling nervous over the differences between them. Heavens, and she'd made those differences a hundred times worse! He'd never want to kiss her again now, let alone find the courage to ask her out again, for fear of rejection. She'd just made herself even more unapproachable.

Tears were sliding down her cheeks and Bella was almost sobbing as she turned on her heel, her one thought being to find Dan and apologise for her behaviour.

A figure stepped out in front of her. 'What's this, a damsel in distress? Well, would ye believe it! We've bumped into each other before, have we not, Miss Ashton? Obviously we're destined to meet whenever you're in need of a sympathetic shoulder to cry on. Try mine, 'tis broad enough. Remember me? Billy Quinn. At your service.'

It was a dangerous moment. Without question Bella could sense the danger in the air, taste it in her mouth, and discovered to her shame that it excited her. Mother would suffer yet another fit, a genuine one this time, if she even guessed her only daughter was standing in a fairground with a man of this sort. He hadn't even taken off his cap in a proper show of respect. But then, he wasn't at all the kind of man even the rebellious Bella would normally look twice at, for all his good looks. And yet – perhaps because of them – he possessed an undoubted attraction, like forbidden fruit, and she instinctively knew that unlike Dan, Billy Quinn wouldn't be in the least concerned about the difference in their backgrounds. He'd be glad enough to kiss her any day of the week. She could see it even now in the glitter of those marvellous blue eyes. In that instant, this fact alone made him utterly irresistible.

'I-I was on my way home,' she said, hating herself for the stutter.

'Then I'll escort you. A woman such as yerself shouldn't

be walking abroad at this time of night, and whoever let ye go off on yer own is a rat. Isn't that the truth!' He took her arm in a proprietorial way and, although Bella inwardly berated herself for not resisting, she allowed him to lead her from the fairground, aware of the pressure of his hand upon her elbow, the swing of his body as he walked beside her. He was clearly the kind of man used to taking charge and she couldn't find it in herself to argue.

He didn't ask her why she'd been upset, or who she'd been with at the fair, and she didn't tell him. She glanced back once, with the half hope that Dan might again materialise out of the darkness, but there was no sign of him.

They spoke not one word down the length of Cross Lane and most of Liverpool Street. It was only when she stopped at the corner of Jacob's Court that Quinn looked down at her with a slight frown.

'I didn't think you lived here.'

'How do you know where I live?'

'I don't,' he calmly corrected himself. 'I assumed that a woman like yerself would live somewhere better. Posher.' His gaze flickered over her, clearly admiring what he saw and some pulse in Bella's stomach fluttered with pleasure that he should find her as attractive as she found him.

'You know nothing about me.'

'Indeed I don't. But I'd like to. Can I see you again, Bella?' And before she had time to consider the consequences, she'd agreed to meet him the following Sunday evening in the Hare and Hounds on Broad Street.

Dan was waiting for her at the door, full of apologies for their quarrel. 'I was as much to blame as you,' she admitted as they went into the house together, each anxious to give the impression that everything was fine.

'Eeh, asta had a nice time?' Violet asked, setting a mug of tea before them both the minute they walked into her kitchen. There never seemed to be a moment in the day when she couldn't lay her hands on a pot of tea, and if she noticed any awkwardness between them Violet was shrewd enough not to comment on it.

'Lovers' tiff,' she informed Cyril as she climbed into bed beside her husband.

'They're getting on well then?' he drily remarked.

It wasn't until Bella was curled up beside the children, drifting off to sleep, that she remembered Quinn had used the shortened form of her name. And she hadn't even realised she'd given it to him.

Billy Quinn spent Sunday afternoon on the canal bank with his cronies as usual, taking part in their favourite occupation: gambling. He held a school there regular, putting a few of his best mates 'on crow' to keep a watch out for any rozzers idling by. Not that Billy Quinn had too many fears in that direction. He usually got wind in good time of any likely prowlers from the local nick, and several bobbies were ready enough to turn a blind eye in return for a useful tip now and then.

He enjoyed his afternoons by the canal. They might almost be in the country were it not for the dusty grass well flattened by lovers, soot-tinged dandelions and glimpses of coal tips between the bridges. A few yards further along he could see a group of men playing pitch and toss. On the far bank a whippet race was in progress, a lively crowd of onlookers eyeing up the dogs and judging where to place their bets. He was doing good business as a result. Len Jackson was busily collecting money, handing out tickets and chatting folk up as he persuaded them to lay down more than they'd intended. Quinn had carefully stationed himself beneath one of the canal bridges, the blackened brickwork scrawled with rude messages forming a secure backdrop to the game of chance he was conducting.

'Find the Lady' was his chosen game for today, and no matter how carefully the punters might watch his clever, flying fingers, they never chose the right card, not unless Quinn wanted them to. Now and then he'd allow them to win, in order to keep up their interest and draw them deeper into the game. Once they were hooked, he took them for every penny.

His mind, however, wasn't entirely on his work this afternoon. While he went through the motions, flicking, tossing, shuffling, running through the patter, his mind was turning over plans. Assessing, rejecting and finally devising a scheme in his wily brain that might serve his purpose nicely.

Billy Quinn knew exactly what he wanted. Status. By this he meant power and respect. He needed to be a person of note in the community. Tales of bookies acting as philanthropists were rife in the streets of Salford and although that particular cap didn't fit him well, he meant to try it on. But only when he had the wherewithal to afford to do so. It took money to buy power and status. A lot of money. And before he started lending it out piecemeal to the feckless, useless masses, he meant to set himself up in style. A good house in the Polygon, a motor car to drive about town, flash suits, cigars ... he could see it all.

He wasn't looking for the kind of power that came with the old-style Scuttlers, the rough sort who held sway over their particular gang and swung belt buckles and clogs in street fights. He'd done a bit of that, of course, in his time, but Billy Quinn craved the kind of power that carried respectability with it. Of a sort. The kind of status that brought people who otherwise wouldn't have given him the time of day to come knocking on his door, asking for favours, donations and contributions to their various good causes. Billy Quinn meant to buy his place in the community, once he'd bought himself the life-style he coveted.

He coveted Jinnie Cook, had always enjoyed her. There was an innocence about that doe-eyed, elfin-faced child which excited him. Although their coupling had become more or less routine, a physical necessity, it provided its own degree of pleasure. The fact that she'd refused to come back permanently still galled him. Maybe he'd take his revenge one day. Silly little tart.

But was it enough? Were his needs changing?

Jinnie Cook had led him to a much richer prize, one that would serve his purpose better. As luck would have it, she'd led him to a woman who could assist him in his quest for respectability and status far more than Jinnie herself ever could. This woman was not only class but a comely piece as well, no doubt about that. The light in her eyes had quite warmed the cockles of his heart. He was pleased with how well he'd managed 'accidentally' to bump into her. Not for a moment had she any idea that he'd been keeping an eye on her ever since that day he'd followed Jinnie and her lover from Seedley Park. Oh, indeed, he'd set his sights on a different woman now. Isabella Ashton was the one he meant to have.

He was late. Bella waited outside the public house, afraid to go in alone yet feeling painfully conspicuous as various groups of shabbily dressed men eyed her with open curiosity as they went inside or hung around the door. Stomach churning, she asked herself for the hundredth time what the hell she was doing here. She should go now, escape while she could, before he arrived.

'I didn't think ye'd come. Like to slum it, do ye?' Quinn was standing before her, a smile of arrogant satisfaction on his handsome face.

Bella swallowed, hating the thrill of excitement almost akin to fear that beat within. 'Why shouldn't I?' She lifted her chin in defiance yet meekly allowed him to lead her inside and without demur accepted the gill of dark brown stout he brought her.

Afterwards he took her to the Salford Hippodrome to see a troupe of wrestlers. Bella had never experienced anything of the sort before: the smoky atmosphere; the clamour of rowdy enthusiasm that was almost tangible; the stifling warmth of so many none-too-clean bodies packed closely together. The wrestling, however, came as a surprise — more like circus acrobatics than serious sport. She watched, fascinated, even found herself shouting out along with the rest of the spectators. Quinn, she noticed, would often be approached by men in caps and mufflers, discussions would take place, money quietly change hands and tension would mount. She could sense it in him, along with his relief when the right man won. His profits for the evening were such, he bragged, that he could afford to take her out to supper to celebrate.

'Is it fixed?' she dared ask as they sat eating oysters after the performance.

'Not a question ye should ever ask of a bookie.' He glowered at her, as if the question had offended him.

Bella hastened to rectify her slip, feeding him an oyster by way of apology. 'Then I won't.'

'Didn't take you for a sensible girl. Wrestling is a new sport. I hope it catches on since I reckon I could do well out of it. Billy Quinn is going places, girl, make no mistake about that. Folk of your class wouldn't appreciate the importance of making one's own way in the world, of being at no other man's beck and call, 'cause you're too used to being the ones in charge.'

Bella laughed. 'Of course I appreciate it. I understand perfectly.'

'Amuses ye, does it, that I have ambition?' The soft Irish brogue had turned harsh, grating.

'No, of course not. I admire ambition in a man.'

Their eyes met and held. 'There's plenty I admire about you too.'

After that his natural animosity seemed to dissolve and, as they ate, he told her about his family in Ireland, and about how he came to be in Salford following the many jobs, disasters and misfortunes he'd endured on the way. Bella listened, fascinated by this insight into a different world. Sometimes his fingers would brush hers as they both reached for bread, or he would pause in his tale to consider her carefully, his face unsmiling, and she would find herself blushing like a schoolgirl.

When he walked her home Bella ached for him to hold her hand or put his arm about her waist. He did neither. Instead of taking her to Violet's front door he led her instead down the back entry. 'I'm more used to back doors,' he told her by way of explanation. 'And if yer going to be my girl, 'tis well ye get used to it.'

Bella laughed in disbelief. 'Who said I was going to be your girl?'

'I do.'

'Oh, and what you says goes, does it?'

'Usually. Are you going to be the first to prove otherwise?'

'I might,' she said, affronted by his arrogance even while it excited her. She'd never met anyone quite so self-assured. 'You certainly have a very high opinion of yourself.'

'Mebbe because I deserve to? Ye'll get used to it. Ye'll be like all the rest, eating out of me hand in no time.' And giving a ripple of soft laughter, he pulled her into his arms and kissed her.

She went to him hungrily, opening her mouth to him, letting his tongue caress hers, and the burst of emotion inside her was tumultuous. He half lifted her against the damp wall, fumbling expertly with her clothing, his calloused hand rough and cold against her bare breast but she didn't stop him. She couldn't. She wanted him to caress her, to hurt her, to devour her, and Bella thought she might die of ecstasy if he didn't take her there and then. But it was he who broke away first.

They were both breathing fast, eyes wide and dark with desire. 'Ye'd best get some of that stuff ye give out at your clinic afore we go any further, girl. I doubt I can keep me hands off ye fer too long.'

Chapter Thirteen

It was the following evening and Jinnie experienced the usual burst of alarm to find Quinn waiting for her in the back entry on her way home from work. She longed with a passion that was almost crippling to be rid of him. If only she'd managed to summon up the courage to talk to Edward. If only she were strong and brave like Bella.

To be given a taste of a new life only to be trapped by Quinn again . . . she could weep, she really could, at the injustice of it. And all because Bella had been forced into that stupid lie in order to gain her family's approval. For the first time in her miserable life Jinnie felt that she had some sort of security and a future, one she was fiercely determined to hang on to. She'd learned years ago to stand her own corner, to fight for what she needed to stay alive. Near-starvation had driven her to hunt for food in rubbish bins and she'd flattened any other kid who'd got in her way. Despite her diminutive size Jinnie had learned, along with most in these streets, how to use her clogs as a weapon, her fists too if need be. But never against Billy Quinn. That was one battle she could never win.

Now he was calmly and quietly explaining that he needed proof that she was still trustworthy, that she hadn't been in league with Harold Cunliffe and trying to cheat him.

'Don't I prove that every day by collecting the bets for you?' Jinnie kept well back in the shadows of the entry, anxious that neither Edward nor Simeon, if they emerged from the mill, should catch sight of Quinn and her hobnobbing together.

'And don't I require loads of assurance? I needs to be sure of your undivided loyalty, me pretty one.'

'It was you, wasn't it, what done poor Harold in?'

Quinn laid one finger to the side of his nose and smiled his most chilling smile. 'Ask no questions and I'll tell ye no lies. Jest you listen to what old Quinn tells ye, girl, and you'll be right as ninepence.'

Jinnie rather thought she might never be right again, not unless she slit his miserable throat with her own fair hand. The thought made her shake with an emotion that took her by surprise. Seeing her tremble, Quinn chuckled. 'Don't fret, 'tis nothin' ye can't handle. I want you to set up a Draw Club.'

'What the hell's a Draw Club when it's at 'ome?'

The object, apparently, was for her to find fifteen to twenty women who were willing to pay sixpence a week to be members of the draw, which operated like a savings club. 'Then you gives everyone a number and write these on slips of paper. Each week a number is drawn and that person wins whatever's in the pot. Some will be lucky and get their winnings in the first few weeks, the others will have to wait longer. It's a way of encouraging you women to save.'

Struggling to understand, Jinnie thought it all sounded very complicated. 'So, what're trying to tell me, that yer turning soft in yer old age?'

'A philanthropist, m'lovely. Isn't that grand!'

She was highly suspicious and struggled to find the catch. 'And what do you get out of it?'

'There now, don't ye know me too well? Wouldn't it be grand if I didn't have me living to earn, like many another?' Quinn grinned at her. 'I takes a commission o'course. One penny in every shilling.'

'That's highway bleedin' robbery!'

'It's no worse than what they'd pay the moneylender.'

Jinnie knew this to be true, knew that some charged more.

'Hey up, but you aren't lending them any money. It's their *own* money.'

'So it is, me lovely, so it is.' He leaned closer and Jinnie shrank back further against the wall as he issued a dire warning in low ominous tones that she'd best not miss collecting a single week's payment from the women. 'Or ye'll be in dead lumber, so ye will. Tell 'em they has to pay, otherwise I'll stew ye for me dinner.' He seemed to find this thought amusing.

A wave of sickness hit her. Here was the snag, a great big net to catch her in. 'How can *I* mek 'em pay? That'd be a nightmare, to collect sixpence off 'em week after week.' Jinnie knew well enough the trouble the rent man had.

'Aw, they'd pay right enough. Wouldn't they be sorry to have any accident befall their sweet Jinnie? And if'n they don't pay, they don't get a draw.'

Vainly she pointed out the difficulty of keeping up the interest of the ones who'd been given an early draw and must continue to pay up for the remaining weeks. 'I'd have to keep books, records, natter at 'em ivery blame week to pay.' It would be a nightmare.

'It'll keep ye out of mischief, to be sure. Just don't forget that ye must pay me my commission, regular, whether they pays up or not.'

'*What?*'

He cast her a questioning look out of dangerously hooded, narrowed eyes; a look which spelled out a warning, that reminded her of the very vulnerable situation she was in. 'Is there something I'm not making quite clear? Something ye don't understand?'

Jinnie swallowed, managed a tremulous smile. 'No. No, Billy. I think I've got it right in me head now. I understand. A Draw Club it is.'

'That's good. Get on with it then, and see ye make it work. If'n ye know what's good fer ye.'

Jinnie experienced an unexpected surge of rebellion. She'd fallen on her feet when she'd been rescued by Bella from that hospital. Now she risked losing all that she'd gained: the excellent food that at last was putting flesh on her bones and making her grow healthy and strong, steady employment, the lovely frocks that Simeon kept buying her. And Edward's love. It was this last and most telling thought which decided her. 'To hell with it! No, I won't do your dirty work. Go jump in the bleedin' canal yourself, why don't you? See if I care.' And jerking her chin in the air she stalked proudly away from him.

It was a moment before he moved and then, as always, his reaction was swift and lethal. He had her arm in a punishing grip and she wasn't going anywhere, not without his say-so. Quinn's mouth came to within an inch of her own, and the menace in his voice seemed to pulsate through her. 'That's a terrible cruel thing to be saying to a chap who has done as much fer ye as I have.'

Fury gave her the power to shake him off and Jinnie stood before him, arms akimbo, recklessly shouting at the top of her voice, hoping the whole world might hear. 'You've done *nowt* but what suits your own nasty purpose. I don't want yer damn' money.'

Quinn raised his eye brows in a parody of surprise. 'Ye might not want it but ye surely need it. Ye can't depend on that chap of yours always to provide for you. What'll happen when he hears about the babby you killed, eh? What'll he think of his sweet little Jinnie then?'

Despair numbed her and all the fight drained from her. Jinnie couldn't think what to do. Why was she even risking an argument? Billy Quinn had her trapped like a scared rabbit, no matter which way she turned. Yet if she didn't fight, and win, wouldn't he keep on squeezing her, more and more, till she was nothing but a wrung-out dish mop?

'I'm goin' home right now to tell Edward everything. I'd rather lose him through his knowing the truth than be in thrall to a nasty bit of tripe like you for the rest of me livelong days. Do yer worst, I don't give a damn.' Tossing her head, she turned on her heel and strode away, frantically urging herself not to run. Quinn's voice drifted after her, sounding clear and sharp in her ears, despite its soft Irish tones.

'Do you give a damn what happens to Bella?'

She was back before him in seconds, her young face pinched tight with fury. 'What did you say? What the hell do you know about Bella? You've niver even met her.'

'Oh, but I have, m'lovely. I've more than met her. Haven't I taken her out fer supper, and didn't I give her a kiss not fifty yards from this spot? Aye, and wasn't it grand? I reckon she enjoyed it, so I do.'

Jinnie slapped him, right across the face. Until she saw her hand swing across she wouldn't have known that she had it in her. But there it was, she'd struck Billy Quinn. Now she waited, breathless with terror, to see what he would do next. He'd done something nasty to Sadie, who'd never been seen again, and tossed poor Harold in the canal. Jinnie dreaded to imagine what might befall herself as a result of this latest dangerous act of folly.

But Quinn was chortling with glee. He threw back his handsome head and actually laughed at her. ''Tis like a flea batting an elephant. Ye'll not hurt me that way, girl. Ye'll not hurt me at all, no matter what ye does.'

Then, leaning close, he hissed his parting words directly into her face, so close that flecks of spittle spattered her cheeks. 'If ye don't want Bella to have problems keeping those good looks of hers, ye'll do as yer told.' The stink of tobacco and whiskey from his breath remained with her long after he'd strolled away, hands in pockets, whistling softly.

'How could you have been so daft as to go out with Billy Quinn?' Bella was locking the clinic doors when Jinnie burst up the stairs like a tornado.

Bella was tired and ready to call it a day. The last thing she wanted right now was an argument. Sighing with resignation, she unlocked the door and the two girls went back inside so that Jinnie could unleash the torrent of rage boiling up in her without entertaining all the customers in the shop below.

'Who told you I'd been out with Billy Quinn?'

'He did, o'course. And took great pleasure in so doing.'

'You know him well, do you?'

'That's rich, that is. Know him well? I'll say I bleedin' know him well, and if you've any sense you'll mek it your business not to.'

Bella put down her bag and considered her little protégée with interest. Was this an example of jealousy? It looked very like it. 'I don't think it's quite fair for you to come storming in here preaching about who I should see and who I shouldn't. I'll not have it. Are you as friendly with Billy Quinn as you are with Len Jackson? Oh, don't look surprised, I've heard about your little dinnertime get togethers, though I warrant Edward hasn't. But then, you make a habit of keeping secrets from Edward, don't you, Jinnie?'

'What d'you mean by that?' The shocked expression on her face revealed she'd been thrown momentarily off her stride, hearing Bella knew about meetings she'd thought to be secret.

'I think you know what I'm referring to. You've agreed to marry Edward when you're eighteen and yet you still haven't told him that you may not be able to give him children. Don't you think that's rather unfair?'

Jinnie had the grace to flush, though whether from anger, embarrassment or guilt wasn't clear. 'It weren't me what fabricated that tale about the runaway horse.'

Bella had the grace to look sheepish. 'No, that was my fault entirely, I admit it. Though done from the best of motives. Would you like me to explain it all to him? I don't mind.'

Jinnie flew across the room, fists clenched as if she were coming out fighting in a round of boxing. 'Don't try to twist it all round. I've not come here to talk about me. I can sort out me own problems. I've come to warn you off Billy Quinn. He's a dangerous man to tek up with.'

Bella could feel her own anger growing. She'd certainly no intention of being dictated to by a young girl who was apparently cheating on her fiancé, Bella's own brother. 'Quite frankly, I don't consider it any of your business who I choose to take up with. Perhaps Mother's right and you really are a trollop with a man for every day of the week.' It was an unkind remark, unworthy of her, but somehow the fire that Billy Quinn had lit in her that night couldn't easily be extinguished.

Jinnie regarded Bella for a long moment in stunned silence. 'So, it's gloves off, is it? Right, if it's fighting talk you want, I'll give it to you.' She explained then, in graphic and unstinting detail, how it was that she'd come to know Billy Quinn. She was utterly remorseless in the telling of her tale, leaving Bella white-faced and clinging to the edge of the table by the end of it.

'I don't believe a word of it. He wouldn't do all of that – not – not to a child, and that's all you were when he met you, no more than a child.'

'I were twelve. Children grow up fast round here. I certainly did. They start half-time at the mill at thirteen 'cause its summat to be a weaver. Top dogs, they are. Not that you'd understand, but slum scum like me don't get tekken on at t'mill. Not a bookie's girl. Bottom of the heap, that's where they put me, along wi' beggars, petty thieves and harlots. Even with the decent start you've given me, I've still had to fight me way in. They didn't talk to me at the mill fer weeks. Back then, Billy Quinn med sure I were unemployable. That way he kept a better hold on me.'

Bella's weakened knees had driven her to sink into a chair but still she couldn't find it in her to equate the picture of the man Jinnie painted with the one she knew. He'd twice come to her aid, been entirely polite and considerate, and used no foul language. He could have done with her what he willed yet he'd behaved like a gentleman and stopped, for all he'd admitted he could hardly keep his hands off her. How could they possibly be one and the same? But then she didn't want to believe it. It was far too dreadful, too shaming. Her own behaviour in particular. Bella could find no words to express what she felt.

'He hasn't – hasn't done owt serious to thee, has he?' Jinnie's anger seemed to run out of steam as, watching these thoughts flit across her friend's face, she grew suddenly anxious.

Bella managed to shake her head and, sighing with relief, Jinnie put her skinny arms about her and gave her a warm hug. 'Thank God fer that! Well, you weren't to know what he were like,' she added magnanimously, smoothing Bella's tawny curls back from her hot face. 'Anyroad, now that you do know, berrer you don't see him again. Like I say, once Billy Quinn gets his claws into someone, he never lets go. Believe me, I know what I'm talking about. Stay well clear of him in future, luv.'

Bella buried her face in the crook of Jinnie's shoulder and kept silent, still too numbed by this new information to take it all in, let alone respond.

'Right?' Jinnie persisted.

'Right,' came the muffled response, but even as Bella made the promise, her body betrayed her with a clench of aching muscles, indicating all too clearly her desperate need of him.

It was one bright Sunday in October that Sally Clarke was delivered of her latest child, a girl. The baby lived for less than a hour before quietly departing with much less fuss than her arrival. Not long afterwards her mother likewise succumbed to the inevitable and followed her.

Every curtain in the street was drawn as a mark of respect. The women who had crossed themselves that it thankfully wasn't them when they'd heard of Sal 'gettin' caught' again, now stood weeping in a sorry bunch around her door. Aunt Edie brought a dish of hotpot for the bereaved children. Violet marched in and gathered up all the stained sheets and soiled bedding and took them away to be bleached, scrubbed, darned, mended and returned a day or two later in pristine condition. One by one the women trooped into Sally Clarke's front parlour which smelled of dust and mothballs from lack of use, overlaid with the scent of hot candle wax, and stood silently by her coffin, softly remarking on how peaceful she looked now all life's troubles had been taken from her. Every mirror had been draped in black, the paper blinds pulled down, a fan of paper laid neatly in the empty grate.

'No one to harass you now, lass,' Mrs Blundell murmured, patting the cold dead hand with a surprisingly gentle touch. 'God bless.'

At the clinic Violet proved to be a resounding success. Dr Syd, assisted by Nurse Shaw, worked tirelessly in an attempt to serve the needs of the community but both agreed that they'd never have got through the volume of work in those first months without the assistance of helpers, in particular Bella's stalwart friend.

Violet Howarth was popular with the other women because she was one of them. She'd patiently sit and listen to a client's worries and tales of woe, advising, comforting, mopping up tears, even clutching a desperate woman to her ample bosom in a comfortable motherly fashion, and of course making endless pots of tea.

'Na then, na then. Doan't tek on,' she'd say. 'We'll soon put thee right here,' as if the Mothers' Clinic had all the answers to life's ills.

The first question was always, 'Where did you hear of us?' and the answer was nearly always the same. 'At the protest meeting.' Or, 'We were told in church not to come.'

Sometimes a woman would already be pregnant and they'd be unable to help. Violet or Bella would then urge the client to visit an ante-natal clinic but this was not always easy to accomplish. Many women were refused medical help until after they'd passed the seventh month, so as to avoid any danger of a doctor becoming involved in a miscarriage which might well have been procured. For the same reason ante-natal clinics did not advertise their times of opening.

'It's a scandal,' Bella would cry. 'How can we get these women the health care they so desperately need if medical assistance is constantly denied them?'

'We can only tackle one problem at a time,' Dr Syd would warn, softening her harsh words with a smile. 'Educating the medical profession into providing a good health service for women in general is going to take much longer.'

The death of Sally Clarke, who had paid one visit to the Mothers' Clinic and still got pregnant, was seized upon by many as proof that Bella's claims about the safety of the contraception they offered were false. This was an effort on the part of the religious press to discourage women to come to the clinic for advice. In response Bella sat down and wrote long articles for all the local papers, explaining that the methods only worked if the woman concerned used the appliance properly which many, Sally Clarke included, had not.

Bella welcomed the extra work. Ever since the confrontration with Jinnie she'd been doing her best to avoid Billy Quinn, not even to think about him. Jinnie was right. He was no good for her, for anyone. Even if he hadn't done any of those things Jinnie had accused him of, it was best if she kept him out of her life, despite the fact that her less disciplined flesh took quite the opposite view.

She also sent off a screed of letters, to ante-natal clinics, doctors and church ministers, to the Prime Minister and even to the Bishop of Manchester. None of the replies were of any use, save for one from an 'interested doctor' who declined at this stage to give his name but confessed that he would like his students to be allowed the opportunity to investigate further the work she was doing, if this could be achieved with discretion. After a short and carefully worded correspondence this enlightened doctor did indeed permit his students to attend the clinic on a regular basis. They were smuggled in after dusk, so they were in no danger of being seen by any other member of their profession. They proved to be both enthusiastic and beneficial to the clinic as well as eager to learn.

'Well done,' Dr Syd said, grateful for the extra pairs of hands.

'It's a start,' Bella agreed, and strove ever harder to visit patients more regularly, which wasn't easy considering her work schedule and the fact that the very poor were constantly changing addresses. 'One day all women will get the birth-control and ante-natal care they need. As of right,' she predicted.

Bella was always pleased if she found Dan waiting for her in the shop after a session. This happened less frequently than had once been the case and was largely, she guessed, out of duty or because Violet had sent him, rather than a result of the friendship they'd once enjoyed. She deeply regretted their quarrel and, to a degree, its aftermath. She'd once longed for Dan to touch her, to kiss her and hold her close. Now Bella experienced only a deep sense of shame and guilt whenever she was with him. Perhaps she'd offended him by her gentle teasing, pricked that fragile bubble of pride. Perhaps if she hadn't met Quinn at that moment of intense vulnerability it might all have been different. As it was, an awkwardness had sprung up between them and she could find no way to bridge the widening gap. There was no talk now of their 'walking-out' or 'doin' a bit of coortin'.' Even so, she still felt a lingering fondness towards him, as if whatever there might have been between them was still there, unresolved, unexplored.

She longed to put matters right between them, to recapture those magical moments they'd once enjoyed together, and one evening, as he walked her home from the clinic, she decided to try. 'That question you asked me ... at the fair ...'

'Forget it, I weren't thinking straight,' he told her, hands thrust deep in his pockets, shoulders hunched and eyes cast down rather than seeking to meet her gaze.

'You aren't wanting an answer then, to your question?' Surely, if he truly cared for her, he'd be eager to repeat it. He wouldn't let a silly quarrel, or the difference in their backgrounds, stand in the way if he truly loved her, would he?

'Nay, I reckon I got me answer. I hear you walked home wi' Billy Quinn instead, despite my telling you to steer well clear of him.'

Bella was astounded, instantly followed by a flash of annoyance that he should imagine he had any say over what she did or who she spoke to. 'Have you been spying on me?'

He didn't deny it. 'It's not difficult to know what's goin' on round 'ere. This is a close-knit community. Kick one and they all limp.'

'For goodness' sake, Dan, it was all perfectly innocent. Quinn saw that I was alone and upset after our silly quarrel. He walked me home and there was an end to it.'

He jerked to a halt and turned to face her, his usually gentle face clouded with sullen anger. 'That weren't the end though, were it? You were seen comin' out of the Hare and Hounds wi' him the very next night.'

'How do you know that?' Bella experienced a chill of discomfort, remembering other occasions when Dan had just happened to be around when there was trouble or she'd needed company, the riot after the meeting, for instance, and the times he'd visited the clinic. 'For God's sake, you haven't been following me, have you?'

He ignored the question this time. 'If it's a bit o' slummin' yer after with the likes of Billy Quinn, then no wonder thee can laugh at my daft proposal. I must 'ave sounded a right sentimental Charlie.'

'I didn't laugh at you. I was just teasing, having a bit of fun, and you never gave me a chance to answer. I . . .'

'Oh, aye, thee enjoys a good chuckle at my expense. Well, I know when I'm licked, Isabella Ashton. Don't worry, I'll not stand in your way. You can do what you damn' well please in future.'

In a strange sort of way it was Bella now who felt rebuffed and rejected, and more hurt than she'd expected. She wanted Dan to fight for her, to say he still wanted her to be his girl, that she belonged to him, not Billy Quinn, and he meant to have her. But he'd given up with scarcely a tussle, before they'd even begun. And all because she'd offended his acute sensitivities. Where was his sense of humour? Where was this love he'd professed to feel? Perhaps he was too wrapped up in his own sense of inadequacy really to care for her at all. Quinn's supreme sense of confidence, arrogance even, that he could have anything he wanted in life, seemed an attractive contrast to the huge chip Dan seemed determined to carry on his shoulder, at whatever cost to their future.

They walked home in aggrieved silence that evening, as they did on many another following, neither able to breach the chasm that now yawned between them. Bella certainly had no intention of ever mentioning the subject again.

Chapter Fourteen

Violet came to her one Thursday evening and whispered that there was a gentleman wanting to see her. 'He's outside. Aunt Edie wouldn't let him in.'

Bella felt her heart thump. If it wasn't Dan, and Violet wouldn't have referred to her own son in such a manner, then who could it be? Despite her efforts to avoid him, she'd caught a glimpse of Quinn once or twice, lounging about the streets. Surely he hadn't followed her to the clinic? Should she confront him, tell him to leave her alone once and for all? She felt a stir of that treacherous excitement. Could she trust herself to do that? 'Thanks, Violet. Will you take over for me here?'

'Aye, 'course. Hello, Maggie. Tha looks like tha's lost a shilling and fun' ha'penny. Doan't look so glum. We're blessed miracle workers here.'

'I hope you are. I could do wi' a flamin' miracle.'

The rest of this conversation was lost as Bella hurried away. She ran down the stairs, her mind in confusion. Did she want Quinn to be there or not? She was quite out of breath by the time she flew out on to the street, though not simply from rushing.

'Good evening, Miss Ashton.'

It wasn't Quinn at all, it was Dr Lisle, looking even more smug and self-satisfied than usual. Her concern turned at once to the student working upstairs. The young man's career could be ruined before it had begun if Dr Lisle became aware of his presence.

'What can I do for you, Doctor?'

'I thought it was perhaps time I inspected this clinic of yours.'

'*Inspected?*'

'Perhaps visit would be a more appropriate word.'

'Perhaps it would.' Gathering her wits, Bella held out a hand as if inviting him to walk a little way with her, summoning all her charm into a brilliant smile. 'Unfortunately the clinic is desperately busy tonight and I've no wish to embarrass the ladies waiting on the stairs. Perhaps another day, when we have more time to answer your questions?' At any other time she would have been proud to show it off but if he went into the clinic now, he would see more than she'd bargained for. Dr Syd would never forgive her if the young student's presence were discovered.

The little doctor seemed more than happy to oblige, puffing out his chest in a self-congratulatory fashion as they progressed along the street, taking her elbow with a proprietorial air. 'I did wish to have a quiet word with you, my dear, to warn you that opposition to your clinic is growing. Sending out those letters calling for an improvement in ante-natal care was unwise. It smacks of criticism of your betters.'

'My betters?'

'The medical profession as a whole. You are no more than an amateur after all.' He smiled condescendingly at her.

'Dr Syd isn't an amateur.'

'True, but she is a woman. Medicine is not really a suitable career for a woman.'

'I beg your pardon? She has been to university, to medical school and qualified as a doctor.'

He gave what she could only describe as a grimace of displeasure. 'Nevertheless, a career can never be as important to a woman as it would be to a man with a family to support. Once she marries she will naturally leave, as is usually the case.'

'Dr Syd is already married and has a family.'

He cleared his throat, looking momentarily confused.

'Nevertheless, generally speaking, I think you will find me correct in my supposition, my dear. Your very able nurse, Mary Shaw – is that her name? – could never consider marriage. In her case, being only a nurse, it would most certainly be against the rules of her profession, and quite right too.'

Bella ground her teeth with frustration. Why was it that every time the man opened his mouth, she wanted to take issue with the words that came out of it?

'You too, my dear, would be far better off married than meddling in matters which are beyond you. I believe I have mentioned something of the sort before?'

Holding on to her determination at least to keep his prying nose out of her affairs, she attempted to smile through gritted teeth. 'I believe you have.'

'I should be happy to apply for the post myself, since it is vacant.'

Bella jerked to a halt and stared at him in disbelief. 'I don't think I quite understand?'

Nathaniel Lisle smoothed the strands of hair over his balding head as he blithely continued, 'Then perhaps you will allow me to make it quite clear? I believe you to be in dire need of a husband. I should be happy to fill the role and offer you my protection. I think it's time you settled down and had some children of your own, my dear Miss Ashton, or may I call you Isabella?'

Stunned, Bella could do no more than gaze at him in stupefied wonder while he smiled fondly at her, as if it were perfectly normal to propose in the middle of the street and he'd just provided her with the answer to all life's problems. 'I am not asking for an answer this evening, my dear. I shall call upon you again, in a day or so when you have had time seriously to consider the benefits. In the meantime, you promised that you would, at some opportune moment, do me the great honour of taking supper with me. I have taken the liberty of making the arrangements. Mrs Solomon has prepared a nice bit of Finnan haddock for us this evening, as a treat.'

'Finnan haddock? This evening? But . . .'

'I hope you will not refuse me a second time.' He had halted by the fishmonger's door, smiling down at her in happy anticipation of her acceptance.

Drat the man, how on earth was she to deal with this? He had caught her entirely unawares. Confused, Bella glanced about in panic, seeking escape. She was perfectly free to decline and walk away from him, to take the risk that he wouldn't follow her back to the clinic. It would certainly be the best course of action in the circumstances. She was about to do so when, out of the corner of her eye, she recognised a familiar figure hovering a few yards away. Quinn. Why was it that wherever she looked, he was so often there, almost as if he were watching her every move? He'd seen her, was coming over. Oh, dear lord, what should she do now? Bella could feel herself going hot and cold all over. She really couldn't risk taking Dr Lisle into the clinic because of the student doctor. Nor, because of her own appalling weakness whenever she was with Quinn, had she any wish to be waylaid by him. Not just yet, till she'd got him out of her system. Was it possible for her to escape unmolested from them both?

She glanced up at Dr Lisle, so patiently awaiting her decision, and felt a rush of sympathy for him. Heavens, surely she could fend off one well-meant proposal without causing offence. Let him down lightly as it were. Didn't she know what it was to suffer unrequited love? After her own disappointment over Dan, she couldn't find it in her heart to be too brutal with the man, irritating though he undoubtedly was. Quinn was the real danger, plus her own weakness whenever he was around. There was surely none at all in showing a little consideration towards foolish Dr Lisle. Perhaps in befriending him, Bella thought, she might even succeed in putting an end to his campaign against her.

Quinn was almost upon them. She really must make up her

mind. 'How can I resist Mrs Solomon's best haddock?' Had it been hemlock she would have accepted.

The haddock was beautifully cooked and running with butter but, seated in Dr Lisle's claustrophobic room on the top floor of the fish shop, eating off a table draped in a green chenille bob-fringed cloth and surrounded by dusty medical tomes, Bella found she had no appetite. Her mind was on Quinn down in the street; on his taut muscled body, his handsome devil-may-care face, on the fact that he was waiting for her, perhaps to challenge her over why she'd been avoiding him. How could she deny it? It was true. The very idea that he'd ever slept with Jinnie when she was little more than a child revolted her. She could not deal with it, despite her years working in the poorer streets of Salford which had, she'd always believed, broadened her mind considerably.

Finally abandoning any pretence of eating, Bella apologised and watched dispassionately as Dr Lisle wolfed down her leavings, 'So as not to offend dear Mrs Solomon's feelings, which would never do after she's gone to all this trouble.'

'I'm sorry. Perhaps if I'd had more warning . . .'

Dr Lisle interrupted. 'I do believe a surprise invitation is much more pleasing, though, don't you?' He sat back replete, dabbing his mouth with the corner of his napkin. 'Perhaps we should celebrate.'

'Celebrate? But I haven't given you an answer yet.' Bella was horror-struck. What was she even doing here, becoming embroiled in Dr Lisle's fantasies?

'And I hope you won't. You mustn't feel it incumbent upon you to make any hasty decision this evening. Think upon my offer, my dear. I am sure you will find that accepting it would be to our mutual advantage. You are clearly a young lady with energy and robust good health, and I like that. As I pointed out, I can provide you with the stability you sorely need in your life.

Now, if we hurry, we could catch the last show at the Cromwell Picture House. Come along, my dear, let me fetch your coat.' It was as if he had satisfactorily concluded a business deal.

Seconds later they were clattering down the stairs, making their way out through the usual queue of women waiting in the fish shop, and Bella again determined to make her escape. But as they burst through the late shoppers seeking a bargain, out on to the pavement, there he was again, Billy Quinn, watching her from his adopted station across the road. Slipping her hand under Dr Lisle's arm, Bella smiled up into his face. 'Let's hurry then. We don't want to miss the big picture.'

The cinema smelled of unwashed bodies, cigarette smoke and the all-pervading stench of the neighbouring gas works. The film itself did not hold her attention and, tired after her stint at the clinic, Bella found herself slipping into a doze, grateful for the relative warmth and fug of the darkness, lulled by the melodious piano music.

She suddenly jerked awake, wondering if a more lively rendition of music had disturbed her before becoming aware of a hand upon her knee which had somehow found its way beneath her skirt. It was smoothing and rubbing with persistently increasing pressure, each movement bringing the hand a little further up her stocking-clad leg. Bella sat frozen with horror, wondering what on earth she should do. Her first reaction was to scream but she realised hysteria was not the answer. How long, during her snooze, had this been going on? Dr Lisle must have thought she enjoyed it. The hand slid a little further up her leg, too far for Bella's comfort. She kicked him, right on the shin.

'Oh, I do beg your pardon,' she whispered, in freezing tones. 'I was simply moving to a more comfortable position.' But if she'd hoped that the ploy would work and he'd take the hint to desist, she was instantly disappointed. Instead he slid one arm about her shoulders and within seconds the other hand had once more shamelessly crept beneath her skirt and was making no bones about its destination.

Bella jumped to her feet, red-faced with fury. 'You despicable little man! Take your filthy hands off me.'

'My dear, I thought this was the sort of thing you enjoyed.'

'Despicable toad! I'd like to . . .' What it was she would like to do to him he was never to discover for, shushed and shouted down by her neighbours more interested in watching the film, despite many of them chuckling and giggling at her maidenly outrage, Bella scrambled her way along the row, pushing past knees, falling over feet, until she'd reached the aisle where she fled outside. Once gaining the pavement she almost fell into Billy Quinn's arms. They seemed a reasonably safe haven after her experience with Nathaniel Lisle.

'And that's the truth of it,' he finished. 'I never laid a finger on the girl until she was fifteen, I swear to God. And only then at her instigation.'

They were sitting on a wall down by the Quays, rays of moonlight fingering the wide expanse of water, illuminating a partly laden coal barge. Bella looked about her at the criss-cross lines of derricks and cranes forming an intricate pattern against the deepening blue of the sky; the dark bulwarks of a cotton warehouse; the arch of a footbridge and a string of recently docked timber boats waiting their turn to be unloaded at first light. The ethereal beauty of the industrial scene almost made her want to reach out and clutch it to her breast. It seemed to pulsate through her fingers, along her arms and grasp her by the heart, making her breathless to be a part of this land, this north country of hers, with a passion she had never before experienced. She felt young and vulnerable and yet vibrantly alive, full of power, capable of anything.

She'd put the accusation of child molestation to Quinn and he had answered without hesitation, without any protests, freely admitting that he and Jinnie had indeed been lovers. 'But not until she was old enough to know what she was doing, for all she was a forward little madam.'

'But didn't you realise you could be accused of taking advantage of her?'

He gave a dismissive shrug. 'Can I help it if she had a fancy fer me from the start? 'Twas no more than a young girl's crush but she wouldn't let me alone. I swear if she'd told me about the babby, I'd've wed her, so I would. You do believe me, do you not, Bella?'

He turned those piercing blue eyes full upon her and Bella felt her insides turn to water. What was it about this man which attracted her so compellingly? 'I'm trying to.'

'Aw, it'd break me heart in two if ye didn't. More than anything in the world I want you to think well of me.'

She considered him in all seriousness, aware of the rapid beating of her heart. 'And why is that, Quinn?'

'Aren't you and I meant for each other? Ye can feel it too, can ye not? Don't deny it fer 'tis writ clear as day in yer lovely face.' He reached for her then, knowing that if he didn't make his move soon, he'd lose all chance of winning her. If that little bitch had told on him then it behoved him as a good Irishman who'd certainly kissed the blarney stone to put his own case well, and he was almost certain that Bella had swallowed his explanation hook, line and sinker. All he had to do now was give her no chance to question him too closely.

'Aint ye the loveliest little colleen I ever set eyes upon? Ye know how I feel about ye, Bella. How much I want ye.'

Even before she felt the flutter of his breath upon her cheek some primeval instinct told her that he was going to kiss her, and that she wouldn't resist. When his mouth closed over hers Bella gave herself up to it, not minding in the least that it tasted of Player's Weights. The burning need in her was far too strong for her to concern herself with such trifles, with anything but her own physical need. Another hand now was upon her knee, smoothing her leg with an urgency that robbed her of breath, of every thought in her head. This time she was making no protest at all when it sought, and found, its target.

Bella believed every word he told her, every variation of the tale he devised, every invention, every bare-faced lie. Mainly because she wanted to. And when he pushed her down along the top of the wall so that he could better explore this burgeoning passion between them, she only urged him on, pulling him closer, pressing the hand, that persistent source of delight, ever closer. Giving a little whimper of pleasure she slid her arms about his neck and gave herself up to a need which consumed her utterly and yet needed so much more.

Billy Quinn was disappointed at not having achieved his goal that night at the Quay. For all the pleasure Miss Isabella Ashton clearly found in him, so far and no further was the order of the day. Still, he would enjoy the challenge of pursuing her and her ultimate surrender, when it came as it surely must, would be all the sweeter for his exemplary patience. Not that patience came easily to him. The incident had left him a bit crabby, a mite frustrated, you might say. But there was always an alternative.

He made a regular habit of waylaying Jinnie after the mill had loosed on a Saturday, just to check that everything was running smoothly. This afternoon he announced he had another proposition for her.

She sighed with resignation. 'What is it this time? I'm having the devil of a job with this Draw Club. I spend half me time chasing 'em up for payment.'

'Yer looking mighty pretty today, girl. Going up in the world suits ye, so it does.' He chucked her under the chin. 'Time enough for explanations later. There's another little matter I wanted to have a word with you about. Ye've been talking to our mutual friend, I believe.'

'Mutual friend?'

'Miss Isabella Ashton.' Even as the urge to run flew into

Jinnie's mind, he was taking her arm, starting to lead her through the maze of streets.

'Don't fret, girl, I'll forgive you for spilling the beans about our colourful past, though it comes at a price. Now yer not going to be difficult again, are ye? Ye know how I hates to hit yer, so be a sensible girl and don't provoke me or I might regret me kind generosity.'

Fear curdled like sour bile in her stomach and Jinnie whimpered a silent prayer for deliverance, desperately glancing about to right and left, hoping someone, anyone, would come to her aid. No one did and she knew only too well that salvation, were it to come at all, could only be brought about by her own hands. I just have to do as he says, she repeated to herself, over and over, then he'll let me go and I'll be free to go home again, to Edward.

He led her to his new abode: a two-up-and-two-down dingy back-to-back in one of the many courts off Liverpool Street. Thrusting her into a stinking kitchen, Jinnie was confronted with a pot sink piled high with pans and dishes congealed with stale food. Flies buzzed about and on the floor where a pool of milk had been spilled a rat scuttered away, disturbed at his feasting by their entrance. Quinn closed the door and shot the bolt across. Jinnie's heart plummeted, knowing she was trapped and there was nothing she could do about it. He ordered her to make him a bacon butty and while she set about frying and buttering, she could feel his eyes watching her every move as he smoked a Player's Weight cigarette.

Thinking of how she could be spending this lovely sunny afternoon, Jinnie felt like weeping. But she didn't weep. She grimly cooked his meal, made him a mug of tea and sat quietly by as he consumed it, his attention now entirely taken up with reading the *Chronicle*. As he ate, she summoned all her fighting spirit and soon it was as if flames were licking the backs of her eyes, as if the entire room had taken on a haze of fiery red, so filled with rage was she. Finally it burst from her in a torrent of words. 'Well, I can't sit here all bleedin' day. Are you ever going to tell me what all this is about?'

Quinn folded up his paper with painstaking care and set it carefully to one side. 'It's good to see ye so eager. Well, pin back yer lug holes and I'll tell you what I have in mind. I wants ye to go "on crow" fer me.'

'Eh?'

'All I'm askin' is for ye to make yourself useful, to help keep watch for the rozzers while I run me regular school by the cut every Sunday afternoon. Now that I'm a man short, ye understand. Simple, is it not? I'll even pay you. How does thirty bob grab ye? No reason why ye shouldn't benefit from my increasing good fortune. I'm a fool to meself but feeling generous with ye today.'

Jinnie was devastated. This meant he wanted her to give up Sundays now, as well as Saturdays. Her one free day with Edward. What possible excuse could she give if she suddenly stopped being available to go on their regular Sunday afternoon walks and picnics? He already objected to her mysterious errands on a Saturday afternoon as well as the odd evening during the week when she was forced to work for Quinn. He'd be accusing her of having a lover if she went on in this fashion. And Quinn would be happy enough to prove the fact, if it suited him.

'Nay, I don't think so. I've enough on me plate, ta very much.' She got up to go. Quinn smiled, gestured to her to sit down again. Jinnie obeyed.

'Ye'll meet me by the canal next Sunday, and ivery one after that. Ye'll have no difficulty in finding me, since there'll be quite a crowd. Two o'clock sharp. There's a good girl.'

Jinnie knew when she was beaten. 'Aye. Right. I'll see what I can do.'

'Ye'll do splendid, I'm sure. Don't ye always?'

She thought, now that he'd given her these fresh orders, that he would let her go and again Jinnie got to her feet, ready to leave. But she was wrong.

He put back his handsome head, wiped the crumbs from his mouth and chuckled softly. Then he jerked his head in the direction of the stairs and fear gripped her so fiercely she couldn't move. Still laughing, Quinn grasped her by the scruff of her neck and pushed her up the stairs, thrust her into a bedroom that smelled of damp and green mould and shut fast the door. Jinnie felt as if she'd walked into the jaws of hell.

'Don't stand there quaking in yer fancy shoes, Jinnie girl. Ye know me needs and how I like to be kept happy. Haven't I been patient long enough? Ye owe me this one, Jinnie girl.'

If it crossed her mind to protest, it was no more than a fleeting, desperate thought, quickly swamped by memories of Harold and Sadie. If she didn't want to be the next victim nursing broken bones or dragged from the canal, then she'd be wise to do as he said. Only a fool crossed Billy Quinn. Jinnie said not a word as she slid out of her smart grey work frock, letting it fall to the stained linoleum floor. Quinn's eyebrows lifted in appreciation as she stood before him in her crêpe-de-Chine cami-knickers. Seeing the excitement mounting in him she uttered not a sound as he pushed her back on to the filthy sheets, though he tore the fine fabric as he ripped them from her.

'Ye'll do as I say, girl, or rue the day. Ye wouldn't want to spoil things with that lovely man of yours, now would ye?'

Jinnie knew Quinn would take great pleasure in telling Edward everything. He'd sicken that lovely, innocent young man, not only with the unvarnished truth but by supplying a version much embellished by his own sick fantasies. He'd tell of the nasty things she used to let him do to her, making it seem as if she'd wanted him to do them. Edward would then call off their wedding and Emily would have the excuse she'd always longed for to throw Jinnie out of the house.

Assuming Quinn hadn't already chucked her in the cut and saved them all the trouble.

He entered her, as he always did, with brutal force and, well trained in the art of survival Jinnie swallowed her whimpers of pain, bit down hard on her lower lip, closed her eyes and lifted her mind into some far-distant place, waiting patiently for it all to be over as she had done so many times before. She knew that she'd no control over how he used her body but she could at least keep her spirit free. She could tolerate his abuse of her because she'd developed, through the years of her adolescence, the kind of toughness needed to withstand it. Wasn't she an expert?

Yet this time it was different. This time, when his grunting, sweating body heaved and pounded endlessly upon her, bruising her pale skin, Jinnie experienced a deep sense of revulsion. She felt nauseated by the acrid stink of tobacco and whiskey on his breath, loathed the liberties his hands took with her. He was so unlike Edward, so much the opposite of everything she had come to love, that she could barely keep these emotions hidden. Yet she also knew that to allow Quinn even a glimpse of the deep fear and hatred she felt for him could well be the death of her.

Inside, deep in her heart, she believed herself to be pure. Edward was the one she loved and nothing Billy Quinn could ever do to her would eradicate that. She would protect those precious feelings, and her beloved Edward, no matter what the cost to herself.

Finally, Quinn's body shuddered with orgasm and slumped heavily upon her. Jinnie sent up a silent prayer of thanks that at least his seed could do her no further harm. She waited until she heard the familiar sound of his snores then struggled back into her clothes, hating the feeling that she was dirtying these precious garments by putting them back on after what Quinn had done to her.

As she crept out of the house and hurried back towards Seedley Park Road, Jinnie knew, as Quinn had intended her to know, that she was not free of him, and never would be. Not while he lived and breathed.

Chapter Fifteen

Bella barely slept that night, receiving odd glances from Violet at the breakfast table and studiously avoiding any contact with Dan. Still unable to find a job, she walked to the clinic, and engrossed herself in paperwork and letter writing, getting through the morning somehow, her mind in turmoil. Who should she believe, Jinnie or Quinn? Who did she *want* to believe? Even fifteen was too young. But if he had made mistakes in the past, couldn't he change? Couldn't she change him?

On Saturday morning she called on Reg Clarke to check on how Sally's children were doing, taking them a few old clothes and odd items of food and groceries. His eyes lit up at the sight of the parcel in her hand and he eagerly allowed her inside, explaining he was bearing his loss as well as could be expected but couldn't cope with looking after a family on top of his work at the factory. Bella offered to find him a child minder but he said the vicar was asking someone he thought might help. Bella handed over the groceries, watching with sad resignation as he carefully stored the few items into his empty cupboard, wondering if the children would even get a taste. Sally had always made them both a pot of tea. Reg merely sat down in his chair by the fire while she examined the four children.

She heated water and bathed them all without assistance, combed their hair free of nits as best she could, put cream on their sore bottoms and dressed them in the clothes she had brought. Then she fed them on bread and jam and milk, advised Reg not to let them crawl about on the floor unless he gave it a good scrub first and finally took her leave, promising to call on the children from time to time, whenever she could manage it.

The visit had taken longer than she'd thought. Since it was Saturday she abandoned all idea of further work for the day and headed for Pendleton Co-operative where she intended to purchase some new boots, her own looking decidedly shabby after the hard wear they'd been given recently. Quite by chance, she ran into her colleague, Dr Syd, who wanted to know where she'd vanished to the previous evening. By the time Bella had finished the tale, Dr Syd looked ready to land a punch on the little doctor's nose personally.

'You realise he'll be even more of an enemy now?'

Bella looked into her friend's concerned face and knew that she was right. 'What was I supposed to do? The toad thinks that just because I'm involved with a women's clinic, I'm some sort of tart. I could easily have killed him on the spot.'

Dr Syd giggled. 'I think I would have. You were absolutely right to speak your mind and leave. But I reckon we'll have to deal with the back-draught.'

'You can't take everyone's battle on your shoulders.' The voice was that of Nurse Shaw and Bella swung around, realising for the first time that Dr Syd wasn't alone.

'Mary, I didn't realise you were here too. Must be a day for shopping.' By her side was a young man and Bella cast him a quick glance of enquiry, smiling politely as she waited to be introduced. He was smartly dressed in blazer and slacks. Two young girls, one of about ten, the other little more than seven or eight, were hanging on to his hands. The man was frowning, as if displeased by something, perhaps being ignored.

The young nurse flushed slightly and beckoned him forward. 'I forgot to introduce my brother Tom and his daughters – my nieces Sarah and Alice.'

'I'm very pleased to meet you.' Bella held out her hand which he shook limply, still managing to scowl as if she'd offended him in some way. What a very unpleasant brother he must be,

Bella thought, smiling as charmingly as she could. 'We rarely have time to compare notes about family at the clinic. Are you visiting or do you live close by?'

Before he had time to answer, Dr Syd explained that Tom's wife had recently died and he therefore now shared a house with his sister.

'That seemed the most sensible arrangement,' Mary Shaw agreed.

Poor man, to be widowed so young. No wonder he looked so miserable. 'I'm happy to have made your acquaintance.' When Tom did not respond Bella turned back to Dr Syd and their previous topic. 'As you say, Dr Lisle is sure to cause even more trouble now. I swear I'll swing for that man one day.'

'We have to find some way to control him.'

'Don't worry, we'll think of something. We always do.' And waving to the two little girls, Bella went into the shop and switched her attention to boots. After that she bought a few items of groceries for Violet, waiting patiently as sugar was weighed into neat blue bags, the butter patted and the ox tongue carefully sliced and wrapped in greaseproof paper. Having a few coppers' change, she bought some metal tokens for milk then treated herself to a toasted tea cake and a queen bun in a nearby café.

Feeling suitably fortified, Bella dropped her parcels off, brushing aside Violet's thanks, and made her way to Seedley Park Road to call upon her mother. She went more out of a sense of duty than in any real hope that Emily would help her cause, though there would be nothing lost by trying. She found her mother still in bed, still playing the invalid, the curtains still drawn against any threat of sunlight penetrating her sanctuary; the pallor of her skin indicating that this masquerade was probably doing more real harm to her health than her son's love life.

Bella adopted a jovial tone. 'And how are we today, Mother? Feeling a little better, I trust.'

Emily tightened her lips and muttered something about unfeeling daughters who neglected their parents.

'You should really get about more. It's glorious out – a golden autumn day. It would do you no end of good. Would you like me to enquire about an invalid carriage for you, then I could push you about?'

'I wouldn't be seen dead out with you. Not after the way you've brought shame upon us all,' she announced in crisp, sharp tones with not a sign of stumbling or hesitation.

'Indeed, I am sorry to have caused you and Pa any distress but there it is. One must do what seems right.' Bella sat by the big brass bed for the better part of an hour and spoke about her work, describing the trials and tribulations of her various clients, the valiant efforts of Dr Syd and Nurse Shaw, their battles with the Church and the more conservative members of the medical profession as well as the constant quest for money. Apart from an occasional acid comment about women behaving with more decorum in her day, Emily sat stony-faced throughout, saying nothing. 'I don't suppose you'd be prepared to make a small donation, Mother, for the sake of women less fortunate than yourself?' Bella finished.

Emily would not.

'What about me, your erring daughter? My own savings are running desperately low though I'm trying, so far with little success, to find paid employment. And I really should find some place of my own to rent. I can't prevail upon Violet's hospitality indefinitely. I don't suppose you'd . . .'

'Never!' Emily interrupted.

Sighing, Bella kissed the flaccid cheek, announced her intention of paying a brief call in the kitchen before returning home, and left the room with a profound sense of relief. Mrs Dyson and Tilly's welcome at least was warm and genuine. They sat Bella at the table, plied her with tea and gossip as they used to do, and then listened avidly to her news.

'How's Pa?' Bella gently enquired when she'd run out of

gossip, more concerned to hear the answer to this tentative question than she cared to admit.

Mrs Dyson shook her head, pursing her mouth in that particular way she had when she didn't much care for what she was about to say. 'Not the gentleman he was, that's for sure. Hit him hard, it did, you leaving home like that.'

'And whose fault was that?'

'Aye, well, that's not fer me to judge but I don't know where he would've been without that young lass to comfort him. He's at least warmed to her, for all him and Mr Edward are still at daggers drawn.'

'So he is still in favour of their marrying?'

'Oh, aye, but he keeps his feelings on the subject close to his chest, as it were, since yer ma is no nearer to accepting it and shows no sign of improvement. That too is a great source of sadness to him.'

'I could flatten her, I really could, for putting him through such misery,' Bella burst out, and then flushed at their surprised expressions which clearly condemned this open show of hostility.

'The poor lady can't help what God has cast upon her.'

'No, no, of course she can't,' Bella hastily put in and wondered again about the wisdom of keeping her own counsel over Emily's charade.

As Bella was leaving, Mrs Dyson tucked a home-made pork pie into a brown paper bag for her, handing it over with a broad wink. 'They'll never miss it. I can't give you any money for yer scheme, love, but it's just to let you know not everyone's agin you in this house.'

It was as she crossed the hall that the front door opened and Simeon himself walked in. Bella was shocked. He seemed thinner, his face almost haggard, his eyes bleak and unfocused, at least until they lighted upon her and then the familiar blaze of anger lit their hazel depths and all colour drained from his usually ruddy cheeks.

'Oh, it's you.'

'I've been visiting Mother.'

'So you should.'

'She seems – about the same.'

'Aye. Nowt's changed round here.'

'No, I don't suppose it has.'

Having made this pronouncement he strode past her into his study and slammed shut the door.

'He seemed so unfriendly, Violet. Like a stranger to me.'

'He's hurting, lass, that's all it is. He's wanting thee to beg his forgiveness and be his little girl again.' Violet comfortably disposed her rolls of flesh in the battered fireside chair, and settling a basin of potatoes between her fat knees began to pare away long strands of peel with a sharp knife.

Bella, sitting hunched on the three-legged stool beside her, fought down a rush of emotion and frowned. 'But I'm not his little girl any more and I couldn't possibly go back home. There'd be nothing but friction and squabbling from morning till night, not to mention Mother's silent condemnation. According to Edward, who at least comes to see me regularly, Father is apparently on first name terms now with Dr Lisle. It's Nathaniel thinks this, Nathaniel thinks that. Dreadful little man! They seem to have adopted a stance of comrades-in-arms, much good may it do the pair of them.'

'Tha should have landed t'doctor a fourpenny one, right in his weddin' tackle,' Violet remarked in her droll way. 'That'd've cooled his ardour reet enough.'

Bella giggled. 'I dare say it would. Well, they may win one or two battles but I'll win the war, right?'

Violet made no comment to this but continued to peel potatoes and, without glancing in Bella's direction, idly remarked, 'I were wondering about you and our Dan. Whether it were all off like.'

'All off?'

'Aye. I thowt you two had clicked. Our Dan certainly thinks well o' thee, lass. I were reet sure tha'd be gerrin spliced. What's gone wrong? Has it turned into cold porridge? Or is it that shoes haven't come and clogs won't do?'

Bella took a moment to interpret Violet's picturesque philosophies and then shook her head. 'No, it's nothing to do with class. I'm not looking for anyone grand so clogs would do well enough. But cold porridge!' She pulled a face. 'Perhaps you're right. Perhaps it has gone off the boil a bit, though it would be fairer to say that it never reached the boil. What do you think I should do about it, Violet?' She glanced appealingly at the older woman, waiting anxiously for her response.

'Doan't try to warm porridge up. It's niver t'same.' Then pausing, knife held firmly between fingers and thumb, she looked directly into Bella's eyes and said, 'Bide thee time. Thee might find that what seems like a tastier dish leaves a nasty taste in yer mouth, then mebbe tha could fettle a new one wi' my lad and bubble it up nicely. Tha niver knows, eh?' And she placidly continued peeling potatoes.

Bella sat stunned, astonished at how astute Violet was in her homespun wisdom. Had she guessed about Bella's secret passion for Billy Quinn and how it shamed her to admit it, even to herself? Or was she simply on a fishing expedition, hoping to get to the bottom of whatever troubled her lodger? Bella decided it might be prudent to change the subject and hurried on to express her concern over the way she was imposing on the good nature of the Howarth family by not finding a job or a place of her own to rent. 'I really must do something about that.'

'I reckon you're busy enough, what with all the clinic work tha's doing. How would thee have time for owt else?'

Bella admitted that this was a problem, one that needed to be resolved. 'Perhaps I could find a part-time job, serving on the market or something.'

Violet roared with laughter. 'Eeh, aye, I can just see thee weighing out tripe, or slicing up black puddings wi' them dainty fingers o'youm. Nay, I doan't mean to mock, lass, and tha mun do what thee thinks reet, but doan't traipse about all day lookin' fer work round 'ere because tha'd be wasting thee time. Theer aren't s'many jobs about these days and it's gerrin' worse, no matter what them in government might say.'

Finding work in Salford was indeed proving difficult, if not impossible, and after two more weeks of 'traipsing about', as Violet called it, Bella cast her net farther afield and found a part-time job in Kendal Milne on Deansgate, on the glove counter. The hours were long but they were willing for her to work a three-day week: Wednesdays, Fridays, and of course Saturdays, their busiest day. This left her sufficient time for the clinic and, for all she had a long journey to work on the tram for three days, it would be a great relief to have some money in her pocket and be able to pay her way in the household. Violet said little but was clearly relieved, Bella could tell. Unfortunately, the job meant that she would have less time for her home visits. But then, you couldn't have everything.

Jinnie's Draw Club was experiencing severe difficulties. After a euphoric start with Mrs Blundell, still apparently on a lucky streak, winning the first week's draw, by the fifth week interest was beginning to wane, except in those still waiting for their number to come up. This was, of course, exactly as Jinnie had predicted. Persuading the winners to continue to stump up sixpence every week became increasingly difficult as time went by, sometimes impossible when they rightly claimed they had no money left at all. Jinnie tried to be understanding but since Quinn gave her no quarter, she couldn't be too sympathetic to their plight.

'But you can't have spent it all,' she'd say. 'What've done you wi' it?'

'Ate regular. Bought some clogs for our Cissie and a suit for our Bob. What d'you think I spent it on, a bloody cruise?' would come the swift rejoinder. Rarely had the money been frittered away, but even used wisely it left the woman concerned with a debt she somehow had to repay and she'd do her best to gain extra time to settle it, which didn't figure in Quinn's scheme of things.

'Stand no nonsense,' he kept repeating as Jinnie handed over the regular weekly interest which he insisted upon, whether her clients had paid up or not. He never had any suggestion as to how she could force money out of them that they did not possess.

'Blood out of a stone,' Jinnie said.

'Squeeze 'em harder, m'pretty one,' was his unfeeling reply.

Nor was it her only problem. Edward was growing increasingly impatient with her excuses. Time after time Jinnie was forced to decline his invitation to a walk on Sunday afternoons, for no good reason that he could see. She would claim to be visiting a friend from the mill or an elderly relative of her mother's that she'd just discovered, or she'd complain that she wasn't feeling well and needed to rest. Then Jinnie would have the difficulty of creeping out of the house when he wasn't looking. The constant subterfuge was forcing a wedge between them, one she would find impossible to dislodge unless she could break free of Billy Quinn.

This particular Sunday was wet so there hadn't been quite such a problem. Edward hadn't even suggested a walk, though neither had he suggested that they play backgammon in the parlour as he might once have. A distance was growing between them which Jinnie found frightening, for she loved him as much as ever and longed for a chance for them to be together.

'This is the last time,' she told Quinn as she stood shivering on the canal bank in the pouring rain and took her instructions for the afternoon.

'And why would that be, little one?'

'I'm gonna tell him tomorrow, the whole sorry tale from start to finish, and tek me chances that he'll forgive me.'

Quinn put back his handsome head and laughed, white teeth glistening, the lock of hair on his brow slick with rain. He took off his cap, flicked back the quiff and replaced the cap at a more appropriate angle. 'Aye, ye do that, and I'll expect you back home first thing the next morning.'

Back home with Billy Quinn? Jinnie's spirit quailed at the prospect. And there remained the worry over Bella. Was she still seeing Quinn on the quiet, or had she acquired a bit more sense? You could never tell with Bella, she kept things close to her chest. There must be some way to break free, she thought, desperation closing in as she felt hemmed in on all sides. 'What good am I doing here? You can find any number of chaps willing and able to watch out for you, and glad of the money you pay. Why does it have to be me?'

'Because you lost me Harold, and he was a good man to have around, so he was.'

'You lost him yersel' with yer nasty ways,' Jinnie shouted right back. 'Like I said, for all I know you might have murdered the poor beggar.'

The last time she'd queried Harold's supposed suicide, he'd found her suspicions amusing. Now Quinn's assumed benevolence vanished in an instant and he struck out at her with his fist, knocking her back against the parapet of the bridge, bruising her chin with the blow. 'I've warned ye to keep a civil tongue in yer head and do as yer told. Is that too hard for ye to understand?'

'No! No, I do understand. I do, Quinn.' Jinnie was quaking with terror, berating herself for being stupid enough to complain. Always a mistake.

Despite the bad weather it was a busy afternoon. There must have been 2 or 300 shabbily dressed men gathered along the towpath, rain dripping from the nebs of their caps, white cotton mufflers their only concession to the Sabbath. There was a lively game of pitch and toss going on between a local group of colliers, known as a croft, who competed fiercely every week, tossing old clog irons at the mott. Whippet racing, pigeon fancying and the ubiquitous ferrets were all in evidence that day, along with the usual variety of dice and card games and the favourite 'crown and anchor' cliques, as well as more cruel sports such as cockfighting which took place in carefully selected spots, well away from disapproving eyes.

Jinnie's task, as always, was to be 'on crow'. This involved her taking up position on the fringes of the crowd, keeping an eye out for the 'slops', a common nickname for the police. She was fully aware that it wasn't always easy to spot them since they had a knack of mingling with the other punters, dressed in plain clothes. Quinn never seemed too worried about such a possibility since he had his mates in the force who were ready enough to turn a blind eye. Besides, there'd been no hint of a raid today and bookmakers were rarely caught, being almost immune from prosecution like the punters. Jinnie found herself a spot under a horse chestnut tree, where she could shelter from the biting wind and yet have a good view of the activities going on around her. The scene was lively and not uninteresting but she was tired and cold, wishing she could be home in Seedley Park Road with Edward in the cosy parlour.

An hour or so later the rain finally stopped and she ventured out from under the tree to shake the drops from her hair and lift her face to the warm sun. A horse and cart ambled across the bridge, followed a few moments later by a small furniture van. She leaned on the broken fence to watch it go by. A great weariness weighed down her eyelids and she began to day-dream that it was carrying furniture to their own house, hers and Edward's. Since it was Sunday, they'd have been to church together and she would have cooked them a lovely dinner of Yorkshire pudding followed by roast beef and apple pie. After that they'd take a walk on the canal bank before going back home together where they'd make love in their own front parlour without any fear of interruption. The dream was so blissfully real that the activities on the towpath faded from sight and she could see only Edward's dear face smiling down at her.

'Come on, miss. You come along wi' me. We don't want no fuss and bother.' It was then that she heard the shouts and Jinnie came to with a start to find it wasn't Edward's face looming above her at all, but one topped by a police helmet. Men were running about in every direction. Whistles were blowing, police chasing them every which way. Scuffles and fights were breaking out and at least one man lay prone on the bank. Another fell into the cut and a policeman jumped in to fish him out.

'Where yer teking me?' Jinnie cried out in alarm as the policeman grasped her by the arm, though not unkindly.

Seconds later she found herself being thrust aboard the furniture van, along with five or six others, variously described as loafers, wastrels and feckless lumps by their captors.

'I had a winning hand,' whined one complaining voice.

'See how yer luck holds out when you come face to face with the magistrate,' commented the constable with dry good humour as he thrust Len Jackson on board after her.

Jinnie fell to her knees in the back of the van which had carried her imaginary furniture to her dream house, and burst into tears.

Chapter Sixteen

Jinnie was charged with 'loitering for the purposes of betting' and bound over to appear before the magistrate. She'd probably get a ten-pound fine or fifty-one days. In their way the police were being generous for, satisfied with a few arrests of this nature on their books, they weren't too troubled that the bookie had slipped from the scene with the speed of greased lightning, lost in the hundreds of fleeing punters. For Quinn this represented success. For Jinnie the day had turned into a disaster. She didn't possess such a large sum, had no hope that Quinn would save her as he should, so had an unacceptable choice to make. Either she asked Edward to pay the fine, or she did the time.

As it turned out the choice was made for her. She was brought from the police cells within an hour of being incarcerated. Someone must have informed on her as Simeon himself stood at the desk with an expression like thunder on his face. Without a word he led her outside where his motor stood waiting at the kerb, Sam in the driving seat. In response to an irritable flap of his hand, Jinnie climbed aboard and in complete silence they drove back to Seedley Park Road.

'Right, are you going to tell us what that daft nonsense was all about, or is this the usual way you repay a person's generosity?'

Sitting facing her fiancé and future father-in-law in the gloomy parlour Jinnie rather thought she would have preferred the magistrates' court, or even Strangeways, to the condemnation and disappointment she read in their eyes.

She swallowed carefully, cleared her throat and began to speak. 'I didn't have any choice . . .'

'No choice?' Simeon roared. 'Don't try to make more of a fool of me, lass, than you have already. There's always a choice.'

Tears were rolling down her cheeks and she could do nothing to stop them. 'It's true,' she sobbed. 'That's why I haven't been able to spend Sunday afternoons with you these last weeks, Edward.' She gazed pleadingly at him, begging him to intervene, to hold her in his arms and assure her that all would be well, but he sat mute and rigid in his mother's chair, his face set like granite.

Simeon took off his spectacles and began to polish them vigorously on a large pocket handkerchief. 'Going off with your fancy man, was that the way of it?'

'*No!* Billy Quinn made me do it.'

'Oh, aye? And if Billy Quinn, whoever he might be, were to tell you to jump in the cut and drown yourself, you'd do that too, would you?'

Jinnie jerked her head in what might pass for a nod. 'Yes. If Quinn told me to jump in, aye, I would. Otherwise he might throw me in hissel', or worse. I reckon he's done that already with a friend of mine, though I can't prove it.'

There was a small silence as the two men digested this startling information. After a moment Edward said, 'So why didn't you tell us you were being threatened by this man, Jinnie? We could have helped you stand up to him.'

She gazed bleakly into Edward's kind eyes, marvelling at the innocence in that boyish face for all there was evidence of hurt. How could she begin to explain her predicament without revealing everything? Even revealing half of it would be to forfeit his love for ever, she was sure. Telling Edward the truth about her so-called 'accident' with the mythical horse would have been hard enough. To explain all of that in front of his father as well was more than Jinnie could bear to contemplate, yet she could see no other way. She must explain what Quinn used to do to her as a young girl, though she certainly had no intention of revealing what he still did on Saturday afternoons before race meetings in that smelly bedroom of his.

Her hesitation was causing Simeon to grow red in the face with temper. 'Well, answer him. Is this Billy Quinn your fancy man, or isn't he?'

She almost shouted back her response. '*No!* I've told you, I'd no choice.'

Edward held up a hand, calming them both. 'Then you must tell us everything, Jinnie. Why won't you? How did you get involved with this Quinn in the first place, and what hold does the man have over you to make you do something illegal?'

'Aye. Let's have the truth now. No fairy stories.'

So she told them. She gave a confused picture of the betting, the Draw Club, the possible fate of Harold, followed by a brief description of her relationship with Quinn when he first found her, close to starvation at twelve, finishing with exactly what Sadie had done to her, and why. Her voice was bleak, cold and matter-of-fact. When she was done, Jinnie sat back and waited for the sky to fall.

The only sound in the room was the pendulous ticking of the mantel-clock. After a few moments it began to whirr and wind itself up preparatory to striking the hours. Jinnie counted eight slow chimes before an awesome hush once again enfolded them.

'Dear God!' The voice that finally broke the silence was Edward's, the tone one of shocked disbelief. Jinnie risked a glance at his ashen face, her own awash with tears.

'I were no more'n a kid when he took me in,' she stoutly defended herself. 'How could I stand up to him, a grown man? He's not one to cross in't Billy Quinn. I tried to tell you on the tram that time, then lost me nerve. I were afeared of owning up to the fact that I might not be able to give thee any childer; in case you didn't want to wed me once you knew the truth. I'm – I'm right sorry.'

Two pairs of eyes considered her in stunned silence. Knowing the strength of Simeon's morals, of how he had reacted to his own daughter becoming involved in a birth-control clinic, Jinnie didn't hold out much hope. Nevertheless, she could have sworn there was a slight thaw in the atmosphere, a touch more sympathy in their joint gaze as they considered what options a twelve-year-old, half-starved orphan might find in the streets of Salford.

Then Edward was on his knees before her, his arms folding her to the solid comfort of his chest, his hand smoothing her hair, wiping the tears from her hot cheeks. 'My love. My little love. Don't cry, my darling. Don't cry. It doesn't matter. Nothing matters. I love you still. I shall always love you.' Then turning to Simeon he informed his father that first thing in the morning he intended to call the banns. They would be wed within the month. 'And Billy Quinn will never be allowed to hurt you again. Not ever.'

And Jinnie finally let go of all the pent emotion she'd bottled up inside and wept on Edward's shoulder. It felt so good, such a relief. Quinn could demand nothing from her now that Edward knew the truth, if not quite the whole truth. Though what he didn't know wouldn't hurt him, not any more. Not once they were wed. Quinn would be forced to leave her alone then, wouldn't he? And Bella too. They'd both of them be safe.

It was as if a weight had been lifted. Everyone was happy and laughing, teasing and making jokes. Life became fun again and even the blind was lifted in the front parlour to let in some late-autumn sunshine.

Preparations for the wedding were hastily made and would certainly have foundered completely had it not been for the steadfast support of Mrs Dyson and Tilly. They set to with a will to scrub and clean the entire house from attics to cellars and finally spent a whole week baking from dawn till dusk, determined to present a wedding breakfast fit for a queen, let alone a Salford waif. Edward, equally determined that his marriage not be a hole-in-the-corner affair, personally wrote and addressed over 150 invitations and waited, grim-faced, for the replies. Each morning he would rifle through the post on the tray in the hall and go off to his office sick with disappointment but tense with resolve. If not a single soul turned up to celebrate his nuptials, he would never regret marrying Jinnie Cook. Never.

There were a few polite refusals; the remainder of the Ashtons' so-called friends and acquaintances chose to ignore the invitation completely. For a while it even looked as if Emily would likewise not attend, even in a 'specially purchased invalid carriage. It would shame her to be seen so incapacitated, she said. She felt ill whenever she was moved. She complained of feeling giddy and light-headed, decidedly off colour. Her usually robust appetite diminished and she began to leave food untouched on her plate and was frequently observed suffering bouts of furiously silent tears.

Bella expressed her own reservations to Edward about his plans, attempting to ascertain whether his love would be firm enough to withstand the opprobrium the couple would undoubtedly suffer in consequence of Jinnie's arrest. She pointed out that there was no guarantee that her past history wouldn't be discovered eventually. Edward declared himself perfectly immune to anyone's opinion of Jinnie but his own.

'Good for you. I simply want you to appreciate that it isn't going to be an easy day, let alone an easy future for either of you,' Bella astutely commented. 'What with Father not speaking to me, and Mother certain to throw a tantrum or suffer some affliction or other at the eleventh hour, we'll all need to tread warily.'

'I think you do Ma a disservice. I've explained everything to her and she made no comment whatsoever which, if I may say so, was generous of her.'

Bella chuckled. 'Sounds more like a smouldering volcano to me.'

The volcano erupted, exactly as predicted, the morning before the big day. Tilly, who took Emily her breakfast up as usual, was heard to scream and the tray she was carrying came crashing to the floor. It sounded, Edward told Bella the moment she came rushing over from Jacob's Court, as if the sky had indeed fallen in, or the bedroom chandelier at the very least. Poor Mother, it appeared, had apparently suffered a further seizure and been found on the rug, having fallen out of bed.

Dr Lisle was naturally sent for at once. He prodded, poked and peered at his patient, tut-tutted and clucked like some fussy old hen (Bella's description), ordered milk sops, a fire in the bedroom and complete bed rest. On no account must Emily be moved, nor given any sort of shock as she would certainly not survive it. It was, he declared, the scandal of the hasty wedding which had affected her heart.

'No, only her temper,' Bella drily commented, earning herself a chill glance of reproof. It was the first time she'd spoken to Dr Lisle since their trip to the Picture House, yet still he offered no sort of apology for his infamous behaviour.

'And she will, of course, Miss Ashton, require constant and careful nursing.'

Bella did not need to ask who he had in mind for the post. 'Perhaps,' she artfully suggested, 'if Mother is as bad as you say, she should be in hospital benefiting from qualified medical care. Perhaps *I* am not up to the task.' Privately she began to wonder about Dr Nathaniel Lisle's own skills as a physician if one female patient could hoodwink him so easily, first over a stroke which was either fabricated or at best nothing like so bad as her mother made out, and now the discovery of a supposedly weak heart. The timing of both was suspiciously convenient.

'Indeed that will not be necessary so do not imagine you can escape your duty in that manner,' he tartly informed her.

Bella bit down hard on her lower lip and managed to refrain

from comment, knowing any attempt at further argument would be fruitless. When Dr Lisle had gone she persuaded Edward and a stony-faced Simeon to go to work as usual, since there was no reason why they should risk losing their jobs too. After that, Bella got Tilly to make up a fire in the bedroom while she herself tried to tempt her mother with a little bread soaked in warm milk, as directed. The patient's lips remained clamped shut.

'Will there be anything else, miss?' Tilly asked, still tearful from shock.

'No, thank you, Tilly. I'm most grateful for your help. Go and have your own breakfast now, and a nice cup of strong, sweet tea.'

When the bedroom door had closed for the last time Bella drew a chair up to the bed and sat calmly upon it, folded her hands upon her lap and began to address the still figure lying prone beneath the bedclothes. 'This may come as a surprise to you, Mother, but though you may fool the doctor, I am well aware that there is nothing whatsoever the matter with you.' She paused, watching for any reaction, but apart from a sharpening of interest in the icy glare there was none.

'You see, I happened to return to your bedroom on one occasion. I forget quite why, but when I ventured further into the room I found, to my surprise, an empty bed and discovered you to be in the bathroom where you had presumably walked unaided. Your back was towards the door so you didn't see me but it was a most enlightening experience. As a result, I confess my sympathy has been somewhat clouded by this knowledge which, so far, I've managed to keep to myself.'

Emily's eyes were now riveted upon her face, blazing like hot coals against the pallor of cheeks hollowed from lack of sustenance. Her mouth opened slightly then closed again, rather like a stranded fish seeking air. Not a sound came out.

Bella continued in the same, calm tone. 'Tomorrow is an important day for Edward. He is to marry the girl he loves. Whether Jinnie would be your choice or even mine, though I happen to be rather fond of her, is quite beside the point. She is Edward's choice. He wants Jinnie for his wife and I for one rejoice in his happiness. I shall make sure that I am present at my brother's wedding in order to wish them both a long and happy life together. And today, Mother, is to be a very important day for you. Today you are to make a miraculous recovery.'

Now a sound did come from the bed: spluttering, strangulated, outraged noises which bore no relation to any words Bella knew or cared to translate.

'Indeed, spurred on by your great desire to attend the imminent nuptials of your darling son, you will rise from your bed, take an excellent luncheon served at a table by the window here in your room, in order to renew your much-depleted strength, and after a short afternoon nap you will *walk*, with suitable assistance for the sake of appearances, downstairs to the parlour and take tea. Tomorrow, Mother dear, you will be seated in the front pew to witness your only son "gerrin' spliced", as dear Violet would say.'

Emily's outrage finally boiled over. '*Never!*'

'Oh, I think you will discover that already you are beginning to feel much better; that this wasn't a second seizure at all but a reversal of the first, and that in fact your heart is quite sound.' Bella got to her feet and quietly replaced the chair in the window embrasure. 'Because should you suffer a further "relapse", shall we say, then I will be forced to give a full and detailed account of the true nature of your "illness" which I'm sure we both appreciate would alienate Edward and drive him even further from your side.

'Whatever you hoped to achieve by this foolish ploy, you have failed utterly. I would go so far as to warn you, Mother, that if you don't suffer a suitably swift and complete recovery, you could well end your days mouldering in this room visited by no one but Tilly.'

* * *

The wedding ceremony was duly reported in the *Manchester Guardian*, the article remarking that there were less than a dozen guests at the marriage of Edward Robert Ashton, son of the manager of Collins Mill, and his bride Jane Cook, known as Jinnie to her friends.

The groom's sister, Miss Isabella Ashton, well known for her work at a Mothers' Clinic in one of the poorer districts of the city, attended the bride. Mr Daniel Howarth acted as best man. Other guests included Miss Ashton's colleague Dr Sydney Palmer and Mr and Mrs Cyril Howarth, together with a handful of neighbours. The family retainers occupied a back pew. The blushing bride, given away by Mr Simeon Ashton himself, looked fragile and pretty in cream satin with a bandeau of bud roses about her forehead and carrying a spray of orchids. All present expressed astonished delight at how brave it was of Mrs Emily Ashton, who has suffered a long and debilitating illness, to venture outdoors on this, the very first day out of the sick room following her amazing recovery. After a hearty wedding breakfast, the happy couple departed by train for a honeymoon in Colwyn Bay.

In the weeks following the wedding Bella felt decidedly unsettled. Ever since their meeting by the docks when she'd accepted Quinn's explanation of his relationship with Jinnie, they'd continued to meet almost every week. She did not discuss the matter any further with Jinnie who remained in ignorance of their liaison. It was Bella's secret which she kept entirely to herself, partly out of a sense of disloyalty to her friend who'd warned her off Quinn but also because she had no wish to have her own belief in him challenged.

Even so, Bella knew he was wrong for her, that the relationship could lead to trouble. She would occasionally attempt to free herself of her obsession and deliberately not go to an appointed meeting. But the very next Sunday evening on the dot of seven she could usually be seen hurrying to Dawney's Hill, impatient not to be late in case he didn't wait for her. Rain or shine, that was where they met. Bella refused absolutely to go to his house on Bromley Street, for all his attempts at persuasion. Being outside in the cold or the wet meant that nothing too intimate could take place between them. It was Bella's only form of protection, a safety net against her own weakness, provided by the uncertainties of the Manchester weather.

Even so, the dangers of their relationship were only too real. The power of his hands upon her over-sensitised skin, his demanding mouth warm upon hers, the very sight of him striding along the road towards her, would turn her limbs to liquid fire and leave her helpless with desire. She set few barriers beyond that of ultimate surrender for all she longed to do so, and there were times when Bella thought she'd go mad in her efforts not to give in to that need.

And always there was the guilt.

He was not the man for her. She knew this. Every waking hour she scolded herself for her shameful behaviour. Yet how could she resist? Billy Quinn had awakened in her an appetite that was new and dangerously exciting; one she felt quite unable to quench.

She continued to live with Violet and her rumbustious family but her welcome, she ruefully admitted, was perhaps wearing a little thin. Violet was as warm and friendly as ever, Cyril Howarth of course made no comment upon the situation and the children dashed in and out of the overcrowded house, too caught up in their own lives to care one way or the other.

But despite an attempt to patch up the quarrel between herself and Dan, relations remained difficult. He seemed to be in a constant sulk and rarely spent more than half an hour in the house if she were there, save during meal times when he would take any opportunity to snipe at her.

'Don't forget, Bella doesn't care for tripe or pig's trotters,' he'd remind Violet, 'her never needing to acquire such a lowbrow taste.' And on another occasion, 'Don't expect Bella to eat that brawn yer making, Mother. She's used to grander fare.'

Bella told him not to be ridiculous, that she'd been eating the stuff for years and loved it. It was only tripe she didn't care for, much to her father's despair as it was his favourite dish. 'Do you care for jellied eels?'

'Nay,' put in Violet. 'Tha'd think his face had dropped a stitch if I were to put owt o' that sort afore him.'

'There you are then!' Bella laughed in triumph as Dan scowled.

He took his revenge when he came upon her with her sleeves rolled up, arms covered in blacking as she helped Violet clean the range. 'By heck, this is a turn up for the books – Miss Isabella Ashton getting her hands mucky.'

The final straw came when he returned home early after his shift to find Bella in the steamy kitchen, elbow-deep in soap suds, scrubbing his father's socks on the rubbing board. 'What are you trying to prove, acting as skivvy fer us lot? We don't need thy help to do flippin' washing. Mother, what're thinking of, letting Miss Ashton demean herself in such a way?'

Violet gave him what could only be described as an old-fashioned look. 'I've asked her to do nowt, lad. I couldn't get gooin' this morning. Ah'd both feet in one clog and t'lass offered to help. What's up with thee? Tha's allus chunnering over summat these days. Stop showin' thee monkey and leave lass alone.'

'I'm not in a temper. She's the one creating problems here, not me.'

'Drat you! I've had enough of this.' Bella flung the socks back in the wash tub, sending soapy water flying all over Violet's shiny steel fender. 'Might we have a word in private? Outside, if you don't mind.'

'Nay, it's chuckin' it doawn,' Violet protested but Bella paid no heed.

Standing facing him in a wet back yard, rain soaking

whatever parts of her she'd managed to keep dry during a long morning's washing, Bella said, 'Why are you behaving like this, Dan? I used to think you and I were friends. Now, nothing I say is right. What exactly is it that I've done to deserve this sort of constant backbiting?'

'If you don't know, then I see no reason why I should bother explaining.' He half turned from her but she snatched at his arm, pulling him round to face her.

'No, I'm not letting you escape so easily. I want you to tell me what's wrong. Do you want me to leave, is that it? Is it a nuisance, having me present in your house?'

'*Present in your house*? Hearken to the way you talk. Doesn't that just show you don't belong in Jacob's Court?'

'For God's sake, you're not still obsessed with my so called middle-class status? What the hell does it matter? It shouldn't, not between friends.'

'Aye, but we're not friends, are we? You blows hot and cold, you, like the wind.'

'What are you talking about?'

'Tha knows *who* I'm talking of. *Billy Quinn*.'

Bella felt as if the blood had drained from her face and then rushed back in again, making her feel hot and uncomfortable despite the rain. 'So you know about him.'

'Aye. I know.'

'Well, he's just a friend, like you, and it's none of your damned business what other friends I have. Is there some rule that says a person can have only one friend?'

Dan laughed, and it wasn't kindly meant. 'You're one of them lasses what likes to do a bit of slumming with whoever happens to be handy like, and when you've had yer laugh, yer bit of fun, you walk away; like you could walk out of here any time you fancy and go back home to your posh house and to hell wi' the lot of us.' He prodded his broad chest with the heel of one thumb. 'But I can't walk out. I live here.' Whereupon he marched back indoors, leaving her to stand alone in the rain, steaming with fury and frustration.

Yet in a way Bella had to concede that for all it was none of Dan Howarth's business who she saw as a friend, in other respects he'd made a valid point. She could indeed return to the comfort of her middle-class home, any time she chose to do so. The fact that she didn't was because it would mean she'd either have to tolerate her family's disapproval or give up the Mothers' Clinic altogether. A price she wasn't prepared to pay. So either she suffered the back-draught of Dan's temper, or she found a place of her own to live.

Chapter Seventeen

In view of the strained relationship between herself and Dan, Bella at once began to look for a house of her own. She soon realised, though, that it wasn't going to be easy to find one that was clean and decent, in a respectable neighbourhood and at a rent she could afford.

Her only income was what she earned herself, working three days a week on the glove counter at Kendal Milne, and she certainly had no intention of asking her father for any help. In the end she gave up looking in the better streets and settled for a tiny two-bedroomed cottage in a row only slightly more salubrious than Jacob's Court. But it was at least close to the clinic. It was also nearer to the cattle market which was unfortunate as the early-morning lowing of cows being brought to the pens, not to mention the smell that seemed to permeate the entire neighbourhood, would be something she must learn to tolerate. But then, was it any worse than the sulphurous stink of the gas works?

Violet rolled up her sleeves, flexed her substantial muscles and set to with a will to help Bella scrub and scour the hovel clean from top to toe. Cyril gave it a wash of distemper, 'to keep down the bugs', and the older children pegged Bella a rag rug out of their scrap box.

Simeon grudgingly agreed to her taking a few pieces of furniture from her own room at Seedley Park Road, including her bed, which were brought round on a cart by a cheerful Sam who readily lent a hand to help her settle in. Mrs Dyson included two pairs of curtains that had lain neglected in a drawer for years, and of course a basket of food, just to start her off.

'By heck, tha'll be as snug as a bug in 'ere, lass,' Violet remarked with satisfaction as she surveyed the finished result, 'though happen a kitchen table and a horse-hair sofa wouldn't go amiss downstairs. Have a scout round the market. It's surprising what thee finds theer.'

'I will. Thanks, Violet. I appreciate all you've done.'

Her friend's bright eyes filled suddenly with tears and, pulling a large handkerchief from the capacious pocket of her pinny, she resoundingly blew her nose upon it. 'Eeh, I'll miss thee, lass. I've enjoyed our little chin-wags and you helping around the house, putting in your fourpen'north.'

Bella attempted to give Violet an affectionate squeeze, though it wasn't easy to stretch her arms even halfway round her friend's girth. 'I shall still pop round for a chat, don't you worry. And don't forget we'll meet regularly at the clinic too.'

''Course we will. Tara then, chuck. I'd best be off and see to me own hungry crew.'

When they had all gone, Bella closed the door and walked back into the empty kitchen, feeling strangely vulnerable and alone. Violet had lit a fire in the grate and on an upturned orange box were the plates of sandwiches and cakes sent by Mrs D, though Bella's appetite had suddenly deserted her and she didn't feel in the least hungry. A few daisies and buttercups from Tilly stood in a jam jar on the mantelshelf, and it must have been Sam who'd filled her coal scuttle and chopped her some kindling. The thoughtfulness of these kind friends, in stark contrast to the support her own family had signally failed to offer, brought a gush of tears to her eyes. Drat them, they could have helped, but wouldn't. Drat Dan for being so pigheaded. Drat them all. Not even Jinnie had come round to help or even wish her well.

Life seemed suddenly far from easy. And to make matters even more uncomfortable, she still couldn't get Billy Quinn out of her mind. What would happen when he learned she had moved to a place of her own? Her heart gave a tiny jump of alarm as Bella realised she could have made herself even more vulnerable to his charms by doing so. She wouldn't tell him. There was no reason for him to know where she lived. She must stand by her pledge not to allow the relationship to develop any further, no matter how much the weakness of her flesh may crave otherwise.

It was at this moment that she heard footsteps hurrying up the yard and suddenly there was Jinnie's bright face at the kitchen window and the bang of the back door as she bustled in. She flung herself down in the only chair in the room, quite out of breath.

'Hello. Eeh, I know I should've been here earlier, luv, to help you get sorted out but Emily took one of her turns and has kept me on the run for days. I'm fair wore out. By heck, but these needs t'patience of a saint to deal with that madam. How did you manage for so long?'

Bella was laughing, delighted to see her friend and not in the least concerned about her mother's apparent relapse, the timing, as always, impeccable. Bella had come to realise over these last months that despite Emily's aspirational, some might say snobbish, approach to life, there was much more to her than that. While she clung to Edward with a tenacity that drove her to the limits of self-sacrifice in order to keep him at her side, she was in fact jealous of Bella's achievements and freedom. Consequently she would do anything she could to deflect attention away from either of her children, in order to focus all eyes upon herself. Reading between the lines of comments made by both parents, Bella suspected this desperate need for attention had something to do with the cracks in their marriage. Though Simeon wasn't willing to admit it, moral restraint had perhaps taken its toll upon them both. Bella understood all of this now and had learned not to blame herself for her mother's behaviour.

'Oh, I can't tell you how glad I am that you came. It's so

good to see you. But I'm sorry if Ma's being a nuisance.'

Jinnie's eyes lit with wicked laughter. 'Aw, don't worry, I can cope well enough. I think she's warming to me, the old besom.'

Bella chuckled. 'You'll have her eating out of your hand in no time, just like Father and Edward.'

'Aye, happen I will an' all.' Noticing the plate of sandwiches and another of flapjack biscuits reposing grandly on a paper doily on the upturned orange box, she raised her eyebrows. 'Mrs Dyson?' And when Bella smilingly nodded, saying she'd been about to have a bite herself, Jinnie produced a bottle of wine from inside her coat.

'I nicked this from Father-in-law's cellar. At least, Edward did. He'll be along later by the way, soon as he can escape Mother's clutches, meanwhile we're to get on with celebrating your new home, he says.'

Bella sank to her knees on the rag rug, overcome with emotion. 'I thought you weren't coming. I thought nobody in my family cared.'

Jinnie looked at her askance. 'How could you think such a thing? Nay, we love you, our Bella. Don't ever think different.'

Suddenly realising she was ravenously hungry, Bella snatched up a sandwich and bit it into it. 'Best cooked ham. What joy! Help yourself, Jinnie.' And as she held out the plate a thought struck her and she began to laugh. 'Do you realise that you and I have changed places? You're the young lady now, living in the fine double-fronted Accrington brick, and I'm the one in the slums.'

Jinnie's dark eyes opened wide with surprise, then she glanced about at the undoubtedly poor, if neat, surroundings, and let out a shout of laughter. 'Well, ah'll go ter the foot of our stairs, I reckon we have.'

They were both laughing then, merry bubbles of glee, helped along by the generous glasses of wine they were drinking. But as they laughed and joked, teased and made fun of each other, Bella wondered when she might taste such fare again, or how she was going to manage in future with precious little money coming in. Life would certainly be precarious but at least she'd be responsible for herself, for better or worse. 'And how's married life?' she finally got round to asking, deliberately turning attention away from her own worries.

Jinnie's dark brown eyes seemed to melt with the warmth of her love. 'Eeh, it's grand. I can't tell you how happy I am, our Bella. You don't mind me calling you that, do you? Only you are now, aren't you? And it's so good fer me to have a family of me own again, I like to do it.'

'Of course I don't mind. I'm honoured. I love having a sister too.'

'We'll allus be there fer each other, won't we?'

'Absolutely.'

'Well, the best of this marriage lark is that I'm finally free of Billy-bloody-Quinn. You must be pleased to be free of him too?' Jinnie bit into a sandwich, eyes shining, enjoying the taste of Mrs Dyson's best cooked ham so much she didn't notice the slight hesitation before Bella answered.

'Yes,' she said. 'Of course I am.'

The idea of living on her own was at first daunting but, as in all the houses in the neighbourhood, Bella's front door would stand open from dawn to dusk so that anybody could walk in, as they frequently did. Neighbours would ask to borrow a pinch of sugar or cup of milk to get them through the day, knowing that she would never refuse them even though she'd rather go hungry than ask for help in return.

Violet would frequently breeze in and comfortably dispose herself in the only chair to have a bit of a 'chin-wag' and offer her opinion on the kitchen table that Bella had acquired or the latest bit of gossip from the clinic. Aunt Edie would pop by every Monday evening with a few Eccles cakes or a bit of currant seed cake, 'just to keep yer strength up, luv', and could easily be persuaded to stop long enough for a cuppa and to share one with her. Even the tough-talking Mrs Blundell had been known to drop by, just to see how she was fettling.

Bella found this all rather comforting and began to feel accepted, as if she were one of them now and the gulf between them was shrinking. Except that the wall between herself and Dan remained as solid as ever.

He never came to her house which saddened and depressed her far more than she cared to admit. Deep in the secret depths of her heart, Bella grieved for the loss of his friendship. And all because he thought the gap between them too wide. What utter nonsense! It didn't trouble his mother or Bella's other friends, so why should it bother Dan? It didn't surprise her that he disapproved of her friendship with Billy Quinn for all he'd done nothing to prevent it. Why hadn't this love he supposedly felt for her allowed him to overcome his prejudice? Because he didn't really love her at all? Because he cared about his own pride more? Bella didn't know, couldn't understand this evident sense of inferiority he suffered from.

Sometimes as she watched the children flying their kites out on Dawney's Hill she'd be reminded of their walks together and would think sadly of their fractured friendship. She studiously avoided the gloomy expressions of sadness and sidelong glances of disapproval she saw in his eyes whenever she called on Violet. Though more often than not, he'd reach for his cap and walk out of the door the moment she arrived.

But if ever she began to feel too sorry for him, Bella sternly berated herself to pay no attention to his hurt looks and childish sulks. Dan Howarth had been given ample opportunity to ask her out again but had never done so. So blow him! If he didn't care for her, no more did she care a jot about him. She was happy, wasn't she? Of course she was. She must be. Didn't she have her work at the clinic, as well as all her friends? Didn't she have Jinnie and Edward, Violet and Cyril and their family to call on whenever she felt in need of a bit of company?

And if sometimes she sat in her little house worrying over

where her liaison with Quinn might lead, Bella would tilt her chin, summon up her rebellious spirit and congratulate herself on at least being free to live her life exactly as she pleased. What went on between herself and Billy Quinn was her own business and nobody else's, certainly not Dan Howarth's.

Quinn never came to the house either, of course. Bella had made it clear, in no uncertain terms, that she valued her privacy and didn't want him coming round. Ever! He wasn't pleased by her decision but appeared to accept it. What she didn't tell him was that he was the last person she wanted in her home because how would she ever trust herself to resist him if he did come?

By November, however, as the days grew colder, she began to notice a slight shift in his attitude. He grew increasingly demanding, less patient, constantly reminding her that he was no young lad and she no chit of a girl.

'It's damned cold out here on Dawney's Hill. Why don't we go to my house? Isn't this the daftest place to meet when at home I've a good fire going and a warm bed to offer?'

'That's the reason I won't go.'

Again that laconic smile, which had a chilling effect upon his clear blue eyes, making them glitter like ice. 'And I'm still waiting for that invitation to tea. I reckon it's mean and unfriendly of ye not to ask. Will I come round tomorrow and ye can give me the guided tour?'

'No!'

His irritability suddenly spilled over into anger at her refusal. 'Hell's teeth, Bella. Why won't you get something from that damned clinic of yours?'

'Because it's for married women to plan their families, not for single girls to take their pleasure.'

'Are you saying that 'tis wrong to give pleasure? You think sex is a sin?'

'N-no, of course not. It's p-perfectly normal and healthy.' Bella could have kicked herself for the stutter but that was the effect he had upon her.

'Well then, isn't it time that ye set aside yer maidenly blushes and let us make love like two mature adults?'

She felt caught, trapped by her own desires, longing to succumb to his demands and yet anxious to hold on to her scruples. It was a conflict Bella felt quite unable to deal with and, following this discussion, she avoided seeing him for several weeks before again, driven by a need she could neither deny nor admit to, she finally hurried back to their place of rendezvous.

As on many previous occasions following one of their quarrels he wasn't there waiting for her so she visited each of his favourite haunts, one by one. She hovered at the door of the Railway, then on to the Hare and Hounds in the hope of catching sight of him. She went to the greyhound track, walked along the canal towpath, searched anywhere he could possibly be, and in the end found and went to him like a homing pigeon.

He didn't ask how she was, or where she had been. He stood and gazed at her for a long, silent moment, that familiar smile of arrogant satisfaction curving those full lips, his sleepy-eyed gaze quietly assessing her. Then he grasped her by the arm, told whoever he was with that he had business to attend to, and marched her smartly away.

She knew what to expect for this show of independence. As on many previous occasions he led her down some filthy back entry and made love to her with casual disdain. Sometimes it might be up against a tree in the park, behind the band stand or under a canal bridge. He really didn't care so long as he made her cry out with her need for him. These were the only times he never asked for more than she was willing to give. As punishment for her neglect of him he would take her to the brink, making Bella beg for more before releasing her and calmly walking away with a smug snarl of satisfaction on his handsome face, leaving her raw and shaking with emotion, guilt and shame.

✳   ✳   ✳

Their strange, on-off relationship continued in a madcap, roller-coaster ride of sensation. Whenever they met she would go to him without hesitation, fall into his arms, offering her mouth hungrily to his. Only when her passion was temporarily sated would she manage to let him go, flushed with embarrassment for revealing the rawness of her need.

'When can I see you, Quinn? Tonight?' She always felt giddy and light-headed just looking at him, as wickedly hand-some as ever.

Revelling in the effect he had upon her, he would laugh softly, deep in his throat. 'Why don't ye come round to my place on Bromley Street? It's no more'n a step away.' He gave a sideways jerk of his head and the lock of hair flopped down over his brow. Bella had great difficulty in restraining herself from reaching up and smoothing it back into place.

'I can't. You know I can't.' There was the familiar tightness in her breast as she struggled to hold herself in check.

Quinn shrugged, thrust his hands into his pockets and, turning on his heel, began to stroll away, whistling softly.

'*Quinn!*' she called after him, devastated by his indifference.

'Think about it, Isabella. Let me know when yer ready to stop playing games.' Then he turned the corner into Liverpool Street and vanished from view. Bella stood rooted to the spot, watching him go, longing to run after him. Yet she did not. She held fast to her principles and let him go.

Billy Quinn's anger was mounting. He hadn't expected it to be this difficult to win over Isabella Ashton. The woman was surely the most obstinate he'd ever met. No other had ever held out against him so long. The worst of it was that he genuinely did fancy her. He itched to get her into his bed. There was no question of anything permanent between them, of course, like love or such sentimental twaddle but he wanted her all the same.

He no longer had Jinnie to keep him amused, now that she was wed and studiously avoiding him. Though he hadn't given up all hope in that direction. Matters could very easily turn in his favour again one fine day. Not least because young Jinnie would do anything to prevent that milksop of a husband from being taught the lesson he deserved for causing Quinn such inconvenience.

In the meantime, the tarts he made regular use of didn't fulfil him half as well as Bella Ashton would. But what could he do to persuade the dratted woman to succumb? He'd used every ploy he could think of, every art of sensual persuasion of which he was capable to make her need him, yet still she resisted. What possible trick could he try next? He wondered at times why he wasted so much time and effort on trying.

Not that he was considering giving up. Oh, dear, no. Perhaps the time for tricks and persuasion was over. Mebbe he'd been too soft with her, and it was time he showed her who was the boss. If ever he made up his mind to have her, what could she do? She might try to hold him off but it'd be like trying to stop the tide. He deserved to have her, did he not, if only for his exemplary patience. And make no mistake, he would. Who else had the gall to stand up to him? No one in Salford, that was for sure. Only his pappy when he'd been a boy in Ireland. Hadn't he taken the strap to young Billy more often than he cared to recall? No wonder he'd run away. But those days were long past. Quinn was in control now.

And wasn't he running out of patience with the damn' woman? He'd give her a few weeks more to come to her senses. But if he had to take what was due to him by force, it would be a day that would make her regret her obstinacy, so it would. He'd make sure of it. Isabella Ashton had to be shown that, as always, Billy Quinn was the one in charge.

Chapter Eighteen

In January 1929 the Prince of Wales toured the mining communities of North Wales, expressing his concern at their living conditions and poor pay. In May the Tories regained office but although the Labour Party might have gained fewer votes, they held more seats, aided by the 'flapper vote' now that women could vote at twenty-one. The balance of power lay in the hands of Lloyd George who wasted no time in exercising it. By early-June, Baldwin had been forced to resign and Labour took office for the second time in history. They even appointed a woman as Minister of Labour, the first ever to sit in Cabinet.

Throughout that long summer in Salford, though jobs remained hard to come by, Labour's popularity soared and it seemed that the workers' troubles would soon be over.

In Seedley Park Road Edward and Jinnie were settling happily to married life. Edward bought her a blue taffeta dress and took her to the Empress Ballroom and to tea dances at the Midland Hotel in Manchester, often purchasing her a buttonhole of violets or freesias from the flower sellers on Salford Market. On Saturday afternoons they would call at a shop on Bury New Road which seemed to be stocked from floor to ceiling with braids, buttons, rickrack, lace trimmings and ribbons of every hue. Jinnie would agonise for an age over which to buy while Edward would sit on a bentwood chair set by the counter specifically for this purpose and patiently wait for her to choose.

The following week she would spend a happy afternoon

brightening up some hat or frock, ready to wear for the next dance or for one of their regular trips to the Ambassador Cinema. Edward always insisted on paying for the best seats, sometimes as much as half-a-crown, for all Jinnie protested that if they went early in the afternoon and not be so fussy, they could get in for sixpence. They saw Mary Pickford in *My Best Girl*; Buster Keaton in *The General* and a new Disney cartoon, *Steamboat Willy*, which delighted them both.

By October, Manchester folk were expressing sympathy for their comrades in America who'd been made unemployed because their rich employers had lost a fortune on the Stock Exchange crash. Hearing of these catastrophic events from the safety of the opposite side of a great ocean lulled many into a false sense of security.

'Just goes to show that for all street betting might be illegal, it's a good deal safer than speculating with shares,' said some.

'Thank goodness it won't affect us,' those comfortably ensconced in good jobs declared.

Simeon wasn't so sure. There were strong links between the cotton-producing states of America and Lancashire where it was woven into fine damask and calico. He watched the concern on the face of his employer, Josiah Collins, and wondered.

Emily's recovery continued apace. She certainly seemed well enough to hold court in her parlour each day and instruct her new daughter-in-law in the mysteries of housewifery. Far from resenting this intrusion, Jinnie gave every appearance of welcoming Emily's advice and was always willing to fetch her wrap, should she feel a draught; call for a tea tray or bring her a cup of Ovaltine. She would wind up the gramophone or clean the brasses; read an episode of *The Adventures of Huckleberry Finn* or darn stockings; hold a skein of wool out for hours on end as her mother-in-law wound it, or thread needles as she sewed. The young bride seemed eager to learn all she could and, when she wasn't going out with her new husband, was quite content to confine herself safely indoors for hours on end. Consequently a surprising rapport developed between the two ladies.

'What a blessing she is,' Simeon would be heard to declare, several times a day.

'She's certainly far more biddable than Isabella,' Emily would agree.

A favourite child indeed.

Bella called upon her parents regularly every other Sunday afternoon although relations with her father continued strained and with Emily had sunk to a new low now that her daughter had fallen so low as to take a house in the 'slums'.

Not that Bella had the time or even the energy to worry too much about her parents' disappointment in her. She continued to work at Kendal Milne, catching an early tramcar three mornings a week to Deansgate and back again late each evening while resenting every moment that took her from her beloved clinic and the care of her 'ladies'. Each day was filled from dawn till dusk with activity and work of some sort and at times she felt bone weary, close to exhaustion.

And still she went on seeing Billy Quinn.

In addition, a string of crises sprang up at the clinic. Eli Solomon, having given his wife another 'chance', had been presented with yet another daughter and was considering divorce, much to his poor wife's shock and dismay. It took all of Bella's charm to talk him out of the notion and remind him that he was really quite fond of all his girls. In the end, though largely from economic considerations since the legal bills would be crippling, he gave the marriage a stay of execution.

Bella went to see the second Mrs Clarke, a young girl of nineteen who'd come to mind Reg's children and ended up as his wife because he was unable to live without his nightly comforts. Bella hoped to persuade her to be more sensible than poor Sally. Instead, she was given a lecture on how a good Christian wife must not be a stumbling-block to her husband's eternal salvation. In vain did Bella plead that the good Lord wouldn't want the same terrible fate to befall his new wife as his first.

Reg Clarke simply insisted that the outcome was pre-ordained.

Bella, contemplating the tangle and tragedy that the need for sex engendered, gazed thoughtfully upon the creams, appliances and instruction leaflets stocked at her clinic and wondered how much longer she could restrain Quinn, or even herself. Would she ever be tempted to break the golden rule? She prayed not.

Before she found a solution to these problems a second patient got pregnant, which of course was made much of in the local press. Bella called upon the woman concerned, noted the open tin of Nestle's sweetened milk standing on the statutory newspaper-shrouded table, the pitiful crust of bread beside it and the dish of beef dripping, and was unsurprised when the woman couldn't rightly remember where she'd put the appliance that had been given her, together with careful instructions on its use.

'I'm not blaming the clinic,' she protested.

The local churches, however, were only too ready to cast blame. Bella was classed as an 'impertinent, middle-class busy-body', and charged with turning Christian marriage into 'legalised prostitution'. Hostile articles were again featured in the pages of the Roman Catholic press, using emotive words such as . . . 'powers of evil' . . . 'filthy things' . . . 'unsavoury subjects' and 'defiling the minds of the people'. The only result was to bring ever more clients flocking to the clinic and they were forced to extend their opening hours.

Late into the night, when she should have been catching up on her rest, Bella spent hours writing letters in response to this criticism, and in seeking out new supporters. Her days were filled with her work at Kendal Milne and her evenings and days off with house calls and clinic work, plus the planning and holding of regular meetings as she strove to raise money to keep the clinic afloat. Far from resenting this, Bella welcomed the work, drove herself ever harder, anything to banish the images that disturbed her sleep and haunted her thoughts in any idle moment of her day.

Would she succumb to Quinn's charms or should she, as Jinnie had long ago advised her to do, drive him from her life completely?

'You can't go on in this road for much longer,' Violet protested, anxiously watching the exhaustion grow worse as Bella attempted to squeeze in more and more work. Dr Syd agreed.

'It's damaging your health and where would we be if you were taken ill?'

In the end she was. Bella caught a chill which confined her to bed for the better part of two weeks. It was Jinnie who called each day to nurse her, bringing steaming basins of Mrs Dyson's broth and little pots of calves' foot jelly, turning Bella into a reluctant patient. On the tenth day when Jinnie came it was to find her dressed and preparing to go out on her rounds. The two girls had one of their fiery quarrels which finally resulted in an uneasy truce when Bella agreed to put off her return for a day or two longer but refused, absolutely, to return to her bed.

'Sit by this fire then, and don't set a foot outside that door. By heck,' Jinnie said, 'you're even more stubborn than Emily.'

Early one evening, just before Bella was due to leave for the clinic, she realised that the footsteps marching in through her front door were not those of Jinnie, Violet, or the persistently cheerful Aunt Edie. These were heavier, with a slow and measured tread. Even as her heart jumped with recognition at the familiar sound he was there before her, standing in her kitchen doorway. For an instant she felt almost flattered that he'd come. Not having seen her for so long because of her illness, he must have missed her and deliberately sought her out. But then the sight of that laconic smile on his handsome face brought with it a wash of confused emotion. Disturbed about where this unexpected visit might lead, shame of where she might *want* it to lead was mixed with that delicious cocktail of danger and excitement. But it was anger at his intrusion which Bella chose to use as her salvation.

'How dare you walk in unannounced?' she challenged him, as if no one else would ever do such a thing without a written invitation. She stood, hands clenched, cheeks blazing with anger while Quinn simply laughed, tossed his cap on the table and told her to put the kettle on.

'I'll do no such thing.' She was gathering her composure now, was almost certain that the fire in her cheeks was subsiding. He strolled into the sanctuary of her small kitchen as if he owned the place, thumbs hooked into his leather belt, pacing about like a panther on the prowl. ''Tis a fine place that ye have here, so why so coy about showing it off?'

Bella stood paralysed with foreboding, uncertain what to do next. 'You've no right to come here. I told you never to come to my house unless I asked you to, which I haven't, so far as I am aware. Get out!'

'That's not a very friendly welcome, to be sure.'

'It isn't meant to be. I mean it, Quinn. I want you to leave. This minute.' A tiny thrill of excitement was pulsing somewhere deep inside her but Bella ignored it, holding open the door to indicate she meant what she said. Quinn made a parody of puckering his brow, as if giving the matter due consideration, then softly chuckled.

'Why don't ye stop pretending that ye can't wait for me to skin the clothes off yer back? Haven't ye been panting fer it ever since ye clapped eyes on me? Admit it now, m'lovely. Can't I see it even now in those bright hazel eyes of yours? Sure and aren't they the loveliest in all of Salford.'

Bella could feel herself drawn by the desire she read so plainly in the deeply hooded gaze riveted upon her. She could feel her limbs start to tremble and weaken, her will-power fading away. Summoning all her strength, she tilted her chin with characteristic obstinacy. 'You won't get round me that way, not with all your smarmy flattery and soft Irish words. I want you out of this house, Quinn. *Now!*'

Snaking out one hand, he grasped her by the collar and pulled her to him. 'I'll do as I damned well please. Have ye not learned that yet?' His mouth claimed hers and for a moment, despite her better judgement, Bella became lost to everything but the sensations exploding and ricocheting inside her. It wasn't pleasure that she experienced, merely a desperate urgency, a desire for him to appease whatever this need was that burned within her. Dear heaven, how she wanted him.

While one hand moved to encircle her throat, the other slid under her blouse to fondle her warm breast. He wasn't gentle with her. The rough skin of his hand grazed the softness of her skin; his mouth against hers was hard and brutal, the unshaved stubble on his chin rubbing her face raw, and yet when the kiss ended she whimpered with regret.

Quinn lifted his brows in mocking surprise and chuckled with quiet satisfaction as he ran the tip of one finger over her moist lips. 'So, 'tis more yer wanting, is it? And isn't it about time ye admitted ye can resist me no longer?'

'N-no. I'm sorry, I never meant – n-never intended to encourage you.' Damnation! why was she stammering, like some stupid schoolgirl? Bella half turned away, thrusting him aside. 'I think you'd better leave now, Quinn, before this goes any further.'

The gesture infuriated him, inflaming his temper, and he grasped hold of a fistful of her hair, slamming her against the table, jarring the edge of it against her back and making her squeal with surprised pain. 'I'll go when I want to go and not a moment before. Is that clear, m'lovely? I'll not have some woman telling me what I can and cannot do.'

'For God's sake, what's got into you? Let go of me this minute. I'll make my own decisions in my own house, thank you very much.'

He began to laugh then and this was no soft Irish chuckle; this was a deep-throated, harsh sound that bubbled up from the depths of his dark soul, curling his lip into a cruel sardonic twist. 'Now wherever did ye get that daft notion from? Ye'll do what *I* sez, if'n ye know what's good fer ye. *I'm* the one in control and don't ye ever forget it. Now get up them stairs afore I drag ye up by the hair.' He tightened his grip in order to emphasise his point, making her wince with pain. 'I've had enough of this coyness of yours. 'Tis time to stop playing games and behave like the pair of adults we surely are.'

Bella was shaking now, though whether from rage or fear she couldn't have rightly said. She felt trapped, intensely vulnerable and entirely defenceless. He'd released the hair now, only to circle her neck, caressing it with a false tenderness, the tone of his voice taunting, the cruel light in his bright blue eyes holding not a shred of pity. Why had she imagined that the notorious Billy Quinn would ever respect her privacy? What sort of naïve fool was she? Don't children who play with matches always get burned?

'Come to think of it, though, we can manage well enough here, can we not?' he was saying, lifting her skirt even as he spoke, pushing his hand between her legs.

Bella was instantly reminded of the odious doctor and felt defiled. In spite of the intimacy she'd allowed Quinn in the past, now his touch became an insult to her good name and reputation.

Yet pure terror held her in his thrall.

Unable either to move or speak, Bella gazed into those steel-blue eyes, stupefied, rigid with self-loathing, wishing herself anywhere but in this impossible situation. Why hadn't she listened to Jinnie? Why hadn't she taken note of her friend's warning and shown more sense? She longed for Quinn to go, to leave her in peace, all passion in her quite dead. Bella could almost wonder, in that moment, what on earth she had ever seen in his facile charms. He was a different man now, a monster unmasked, and herself a naïve fool to have been taken in by soft words and flattering love making. She must have been out of her mind.

Furious with herself as much as him, Bella came to her senses and began to fight. She slapped his hand away, kicked him in the shins, hearing his cry of pain with a sense of satisfaction. But he only found her puny attempt at retaliation amusing. She was rewarded with another slavering kiss, with the stench of his tobacco-tainted breath as he roared with laughter. 'Go home, Quinn, damn you! You're being ridiculous.'

His rage ran completely out of control then and he struck her across the face with the knuckles of one hand, making her cry out as she fell back across the table. 'So, 'tis ridiculous I am now, is it? And did ye get something from that clinic o' yours, like I told ye to?'

Bella could taste blood on her swollen tongue but was desperately trying to remain calm and not panic. That way she hoped to persuade him to come to his senses and leave. 'No, of course I didn't. I've already explained, birth control is available for married women only. It wouldn't be right or proper for me to use it. For any single woman to make use of the clinic's facilities. Stop wishing for the moon.' She gave a half laugh and again attempted to push him away. It was a mistake.

'More fool ye then.' And with a vicious shove Quinn thrust her down on to the rag rug, ripping open her blouse as he straddled her. He pinned her down, using the pressure of one arm held across her throat, while clumsy fingers fumbled with the ribbons on her camisole. Finally losing patience, he tore them apart with his bare hands and reached greedily for her breasts. Seeing the naked lust in his blue eyes Bella lost all control and screamed as loud as she could. He silenced her with a blow.

'Ye realise at last that I mean business, don't ye, m'lovely? Are ye going to beg for mercy? Aw, now, wouldn't I jest love to see that? Miss High-and bleedin'-Mighty begging for her virginity. For ye are still a virgin, are ye not? Isn't that what this maidenly reluctance is all about? Not like our Jinnie. Oh, dear me, no.'

He was unhooking and dragging off the leather belt at his waist, unbuttoning his trousers, and Bella was crying, her hands flying everywhere, desperately seeking some purchase, turning her into a termagant of fury and terror as she begged and pleaded for him to leave her alone. But he wasn't listening. He was too far gone in his own excitement.

It was then that the door flew open.

It all happened so quickly that Bella didn't have time to think. One minute she was fighting a hopeless battle against what felt like a dozen pairs of hands and a huge pressing weight on top of her, the next a sound like a roar filled her head and somehow Quinn had been ripped from her and was flying across the room. He landed with a crash against the back door, his head meeting solid oak with a terrible crack.

'Are you all right?' The voice came out of nowhere. Then Dan's face swam into focus, his arms came about her and she went into them on a gasp of heartfelt relief.

They sat at the kitchen table and sipped their mugs of sweet tea as if it were the most normal thing in the world for Bella to be in a dressing gown at this hour of the day. As if it were of no account that she'd almost been raped by Quinn and Dan had stepped in at just the right moment to rescue her.

Neither of them spoke for a long time, each reluctant to face the inevitable. Eventually she thought to ask how it was that he'd happened to be there, just when he was most needed.

It was a moment or two before he answered, and then with a sheepish half smile. 'Aren't I always?'

They smiled shyly into each other's eyes. 'You certainly used to be.'

'The truth is that I'm never very far from your door. I come over regular and hang around for a bit, just to check that you're all right. At other times I follow Quinn. I like to know what the bastard's up to, pardon my French, because I'd an idea he might try summat daft and I was proved right, wasn't I? I saw him come here. I wouldn't have done owt only I heard your scream.'

Bella couldn't find anything to say to this. She merely gave a small nod of acknowledgement. At length, knowing she should show proper gratitude for his opportune arrival and the way Dan had manhandled Quinn out of her front door, she said, 'I've behaved like an idiot, haven't I? Perhaps I felt the need for some excitement in my life, after Seedley Park Road where everything was always so predictable, so dull. Father always petting and humouring me, wanting me to be the perfect little lady. Mother constantly complaining and having hysterics whenever I set foot out of the door. I felt weighted down by their expectations and demands, needing a release, some small rebellion to prove I could manage my own life. Except that it got a bit out of hand. I've been an utter fool, haven't I?' She smiled ruefully up at him and Dan's mouth twisted into a wry smile.

'I'm glad you said that and not me. You'd 'ave clocked me one if I'd risked saying it.'

'Maybe, but I'm right, aren't I? Go on, admit it.'

'Nay, I daresn't. Let's just say that I'm glad to be of service. Glad you're safe and sound. I wouldn't have liked owt to happen to thee.'

His gaze was so intense that Bella was finding it difficult to meet it, so filled with shame was she at her own behaviour. She really didn't deserve a friend like Dan.

She longed to tell him how often she had thought of him, how much she'd missed him; how much she'd once enjoyed his company and the fun they'd had together, while Quinn had only troubled and disturbed her. She wanted to ask if she might see him again, if perhaps one day he might even want to kiss her again. 'More tea?' she suggested and he shook his head, got slowly to his feet.

'Nay. I'm swimming in the stuff. I'd best be off.' He put

the words immediately into action and Bella was forced to do the same and follow him to the door.

'You'll come again, though? Now that you know where I live. Properly this time, not hiding in the shadows.' She was almost holding her breath, waiting for his answer.

'Happen.'

'I'll take that for a yes, shall I?'

Another slight pause as he considered the matter. 'Aye, I reckon tha can tek that for a certainty.' Then he flicked on his cap, politely doffed it to her, and quietly took his leave.

1930

Chapter Nineteen

As the decade drew to a close and a new one dawned, the feeling of optimism in the two cities of Manchester and Salford became superseded by one of mounting unease. Within a few months it became apparent that the careless Twenties were over, and the Hungry Thirties had begun.

This was brought forcibly to the notice of the occupants of Seedley Park Road one Friday afternoon in early summer. Jinnie, having given up her job when she married, now discovered that her comfortable life as a loving wife without a care in the world was over. It ended with the arrival home of Edward from the mill one evening when he starkly announced that he'd lost his job. The mill owner, Mr Josiah Collins, realising it was the only way that his business might survive, had put the operatives on short time. Edward's services, along with those of the other clerks and office boys, were dispensed with, as the redoubtable Miss Tadcaster would now run the entire office single-handed. She was, however, expected to do so on reduced pay, as was the manager. Overnight Simeon found that his weekly wage had been halved.

Emily, unable to take in the full import of this catastrophe, sat buttering her second scone and complained bitterly about her husband's employer who had always, in her humble opinion, been a vindictive piece of goods.

'How will you manage?' the more streetwise Jinnie wanted to know. 'How will *we* manage, Edward, if you don't have a job at all?'

He reached over to stroke her silken curls. 'I shall find another, my sweet, fear not. I have qualifications.'

'Of course, I was forgetting. But we'll have to make savings, won't we, since Mr Ashton is also earning less? Will Mrs Dyson or Tilly lose their job too? I should hate that to happen but if it were necessary I'd do the work Tilly usually does, Mrs Ashton, if you take on the cooking.'

Emily looked askance, eyebrows raised in surprise that Jinnie should even entertain such a notion. 'Heavens, what a very gloomy outlook you have on life, child. I suppose that comes of living in the slums.'

Jinnie looked around at each member of this new family that she'd joined, seeking some sign they understood the terrible calamity which had unexpectedly befallen them. Simeon was frowning, though more from annoyance than any real sense of foreboding. Edward was already reaching for the *Manchester Evening News* and taking out a pencil, preparatory to making applications for likely jobs. Emily rang the bell and ordered more tea.

Following the trauma of that visit from Quinn, Bella took to keeping her front door not only closed but firmly locked. Her neighbours took great offence; even her 'ladies' objected to having to knock and 'hang about on t' doorstep' whenever they called, until she explained that she'd been having a few problems with a certain unwelcome intruder. They knew at once to whom she referred so Bella described the whole sorry episode. She tried not to go too deeply into why Quinn should choose to attack her, since she'd no wish to disclose all her shameful secrets. Yet something in the knowing quality of their studiously bland expressions made her suspect they guessed much of it.

Mrs Blundell said she'd thought Billy Quinn were up to

summat when she'd spotted him hovering about one day. 'I told him to bugger off. Fat lot of good that did! I should've called t'police. Nasty piece of work he is, for all his pretty looks.'

Aunt Edie brought Bella a ginger parkin and Mrs Solomon said that Dan happening along at just the right moment served only to show how things always turned out for the best. He came out of the tale a hero.

'Now you can be friends again, like you used to be.'

It seemed that Bella's 'ladies' knew more about her affairs than they were letting on. In a way this increased her sense of shame, yet their reaction to her was entirely non-judgemental, as if accepting that a few wild oats must be sown in every young woman's life.

Violet's condemnatory silence on the matter, however, was even worse than an 'I told you so'.

'All right, I should have listened to you,' Bella wearily admitted. Her friend merely buttoned her mouth still tighter.

But the episode dinted Bella's confidence badly. Where once the thought of Billy Quinn had excited her, now she felt wary, even frightened of him. Whenever she ventured out, if only to the corner shop for a loaf of bread, she found herself constantly glancing over her shoulder and jumping at every shadow, as if she were being followed, and not by the benevolent Dan. She took another week off work to recover fully. And as if this weren't bad enough, by the time she was finally well enough to go out and about normally again, she'd lost the job at Kendal Milne.

Dr Syd insisted that instead of seeking another, she give her full attention in future to the work of the clinic and to visiting the mothers in their homes. 'It's vital that someone keeps a regular check on them, else how will we persuade them to come in for their check-ups?'

At any other time Bella might have protested but she was so shaken by the incident that she readily agreed. The clinic would be her sole concern, for the moment at least.

✻ ✻ ✻

In spite of Edward's qualifications, his years of experience and his optimism, he did not simply walk into another job. Every day for a month or more he combed the *Manchester Guardian*, the *Evening Chronicle* and any other paper he could lay his hands on. Even if he was fortunate enough to find a suitable position actually being advertised, which was in itself rare, whenever he telephoned it was only to be told that the post had already been filled.

'I'll find work soon, love,' he told an anxious Jinnie. 'Don't worry.' And at first she didn't. She believed in him utterly. They'd been married little more than a year, were a young couple deeply in love with every faith in a good future together. Besides which, being short of money was not unusual for Jinnie and certainly the Ashtons' idea of poverty bore no relation to her own definition of the state. Food still appeared regularly upon the table. Emily still took afternoon tea once a week at the Midland Hotel. She went shopping on King Street and bought a new gown or hat should she desire one. Neither Mrs Dyson nor Tilly, nor even Sam the handyman/chauffeur, had been laid off, so what was there to worry about? If Mr Ashton did not earn quite what he had once done, they couldn't claim to be on the bread line.

For a while Edward even continued to take her each week to the Ambassador Picture House at Pendleton or the Odeon Café, though not so often as he once had, and gradually, as he became concerned about dipping too deeply into his savings, the trips ceased altogether. People began to talk of a slump and as the situation worsened, Edward sank into gloom. Once, Jinnie tried to cheer him up by bringing out one of the sovereigns she had secreted, suggesting they use it to award themselves a well-deserved afternoon treat.

'Where did you get that kind of money?' he asked, appalled that she should even make the suggestion. 'It's not your place, as my wife, to finance an outing.'

'What does it matter which of us pays?' Jinnie protested. 'It's money I saved while I was working.' She thought this answer perfectly reasonable and it could very nearly be true, so long as she didn't have to explain what kind of work. But Edward wouldn't hear of it.

'Absolutely not!'

'If it's just yer pride what's stoppin' you, that's stupid. A trip to the flicks to see Fatty Arbuckle would make us laugh, take us out of ourselves. Then we could go out for tea afterwards.'

'I said no, Jinnie. If I can't afford to take my own wife to the pictures, then I'm damned if I'll ask her for a handout.'

'You great pig-headed soft lump! Aw, what am I to do wi' you?' It was the closest they'd come to a quarrel and if Jinnie hadn't felt so swamped with love for him, and such a rush of pity for his foolish pride, it might well have degenerated into a proper one. Instead, they ended up going early to bed and making love.

'At least they haven't worked out a way to charge us for this, eh?' she teased. 'Not yet, anyroad.'

'I'll find work soon,' he assured her, as if repeating this declaration often enough would make it happen

But as the months of fruitless searching slipped by, Edward began to feel something akin to fear deep in his belly. He couldn't believe he hadn't yet found a job. Perhaps he'd been looking in the wrong places, ringing the wrong firms, but in his view unemployment did not happen to people of his ilk, only to those with no skills of any sort to offer, the feckless and the layabouts. He watched, appalled, as his savings became depleted to a dangerously low level and he was finally driven, along with his working-class counterparts, to walking the streets of both cities; to knocking on doors, calling on offices, to standing in line in a desperate quest to try every firm and factory which seemed likely to have work. And Edward discovered, like many another in Salford and Manchester and around the country, that qualifications and skills counted for nothing in a depressed job market. He could find no work because there was none to be found and, like his peers, was forced to go to the Labour Exchange and sign on. It was a humiliating experience.

For Jinnie, the worst part of seeing her husband suffer in this way was that she believed it was all her fault.

The fact that no friends had attended their wedding had been just the beginning. By marrying into the Ashton family she'd obviously turned them into social pariahs. None of their old friends would have anything to do with them now. They were virtually ignored by everybody. The stigma of being linked to someone who came from the lowest streets, a girl no better than a common thief or harlot and who might well have been either for all they knew, was too dreadful to contemplate. Consequently they had no further wish to be associated with the Ashton family, despite what amounted, in some cases, to years of unblemished friendship.

Simeon might object to Bella's lack of moral rectitude. Emily might frequently be heard to complain about her daughter degrading herself by going to live in squalor, bringing shame upon them all, but none of this made any impression upon Jinnie. She was entirely convinced that the reason her husband had been sacked and Simeon's wages reduced was because Edward had chosen to marry her, a street urchin, little better than a harlot. As a result, the sanctimonious mill owner had been only too glad of any excuse to be rid of the embarrassment of employing him.

If Jinnie had imagined that Emily would understand these sentiments, or her increasing sense of isolation, she was soon disenchanted. Relations between mother and daughter-in-law suffered something of a setback. Jinnie was again treated to the cold draught of Emily's displeasure. She began deeply to regret having given up her job as a weaver which she'd only agreed to do in order to please her mother-in-law. Even working short-time would have been better than nothing. It would have given her and Edward some disposable income of their own and a degree of self-respect. Jinnie knew that he worried what would happen when all his savings were gone. If he didn't find work soon, they would be dependent upon Simeon for every penny.

She decided that, with or without Edward's approval, she must seek work herself. She could hardly take in washing, not at Seedley Park Road, and the mill wasn't taking on any new hands but Jinnie was convinced there must be something she could do. They needed to have some money coming in. There must be work of some sort, somewhere. She only had to find it. When she'd found herself a decent, respectable job, it would be too late then for Edward to disapprove.

Following the change in their circumstances, Simeon's temper grew ever shorter, He would storm about the house seething with suppressed fury, making Mrs Dyson and Tilly run for cover whenever he approached while Emily beat her fists in despair, constantly reminding her husband how she had warned him against this very danger.

'We've been cast out! Ostracised! Let down by our children. Oh, what are we to do?'

In the end, driven to the limits of his patience by her complaints, Simeon turned on her, for once standing up to his wife. 'This has nowt to do with Jinnie, or even our Bella. It's the fault of Parliament, politics, world trade, and those stupid and greedy enough to invest in fantasy instead of new manufacturing methods.'

Emily burst into tears and ran from the room.

For the first time in his life Simeon did not rush after her, or offer any sort of palliative to her woes. He took off his spectacles and began to polish them vigorously on his pocket handkerchief. After a moment he put his head in his hands and permitted the swell of fear which had been growing inside like a cancer to swamp him. It beat in his head like a drum, flooded through his weary body in a hot tide of terror, and for several long moments he remained thus, overwhelmed by events.

He knew why he hadn't gone after Emily. Because there was yet more bad news that he still hadn't plucked up the courage to tell her.

Work at the mill was rapidly drying up. Each morning he opened the post with an increasing sense of foreboding as he found it comprised mainly bills and invoices, with no fresh orders coming in. The office telephone remained ominously silent and Mr Josiah was conspicuous by his absence, which must be a bad sign. It indicated to Simeon that his employer was either avoiding reality or feathering himself a nest somewhere else, in order to make his escape.

Simeon felt the kind of unrest an animal experiences when a storm is brewing. He was aware that the cotton boom was on the wane, that foreign competition was beginning to take its toll. During the war, unable to get supplies of cotton goods to India, their biggest customer, the Indians had taken to producing their own. Hadn't he warned Mr Josiah to expand their market before it was too late? Hadn't Simeon strongly recommended a hundred times since that they'd be better able to compete if he invested in new looms, but the owner had refused to act, or even to listen to his manager's advice.

It wasn't difficult to work out why his employer had taken this line. He was short of ready cash because he'd invested too much on the American Stock Exchange, presumably in the hope of making an instant fortune like many another greedy fool. If so, it was surely only a matter of time before there were further cutbacks. Mr Josiah could very well decide to save even more wages by sacking his manager and running the mill himself.

What in heaven's name would he do then? Simeon didn't dare to think. He knew there was little chance of his finding another mill to take him on. Too many had closed already and the rest were all on short-time, suffering in exactly the same way. And he certainly knew what to expect in the open market place.

Watching his son fall into that listlessness so painfully evident in the unemployed cut him to the heart.

He sank into his chair, still with his head in his hands, and almost sobbed out loud with the pain that gripped him. Despair weighed heavy and Simeon longed with all his heart for Isabella, his darling daughter, his favourite child. In that moment he needed her beside him, to offer comfort and love. Hadn't they always supported each other over the years? He'd always encouraged her in her philanthropic work, believing it was right and proper for people in their station of life to help those less fortunate than themselves, but she'd surely overstepped the mark. He'd expected her always to behave like a lady yet she'd gone beyond the bounds of propriety. If only she hadn't been so stubborn, so utterly outrageous ...

And if only he hadn't been so damned puritanical about that dratted clinic, a small voice in his head pointed out. But then how could he, a stalwart of the chapel, have condoned such outlandish, immoral behaviour? No, the fault was entirely hers for putting him into such a difficult position.

After a time Simeon replaced his spectacles, smoothed his whiskers and lit a cigar which he smoked in contemplative silence. The action soothed him and he began to feel calmer, more in control. Even Isabella must acknowledge that circumstances had now changed and if family problems compelled her to abandon her racketing life style, then the ill wind had blown some good at least. Simeon slid a sheet of paper from his bureau and began to write.

He sent a note instructing his daughter to come home at once. Tilly delivered it to Bella at the clinic. Her father informed her that since Edward and Jinnie were temporarily unemployed, her mother's health still uncertain and he himself on reduced wages, it behoved her to return home. They needed whatever contribution she could make to the household expenses. 'Your first responsibility is to your family, not to the Howarths or to the clinic. The wages you are paid by Kendal Milne, however inadequate, are now required here.'

Saddened to hear of her family's straitened circumstances Bella knew she could do nothing to help, even had she still worked at the store. Her family were not alone in their troubles. About half the husbands and sons of her 'ladies' were also on short-time or out of work and she took careful note how they coped with increasing poverty, digging ever deeper into their meagre resources. They would try anything rather than relinquish their pride and ask for official help.

The items they'd once prized so highly as proof of their status and respectability – a gramophone perhaps, the family piano, or a bicycle which a husband had used to take him to work, even a silver watch and chain left by a beloved parent – had long since been sold or pawned. Fenders and fire irons, jugs, mugs and ornaments, even a mantel-clock presented at a family wedding or anniversary, would go the same way. After that, women were reduced to pawning bundles of clothes: a Sunday suit or coat which would otherwise hang idle in the cupboard all week, or a husband's only decent pair of boots. Anything to bring in a few shillings to see them through to the next pitiful dole payment.

Bella admired their fortitude even while she wept for their distress. Not for a moment had she expected her own family to suffer in a similar fashion. She asked Tilly if it were indeed true.

The dark fear in the little housemaid's eyes answered the question even before the vigorous nod and the ready tears. 'Mrs D reckons her and me'll be out on our ear afore the month is out. Lord knows where I'll go, Miss Isabella. I've no 'ome but Seedley Park Road. I'll end up at the workhouse, I know I will.' And the poor girl burst into noisy sobs.

'I'm sure it won't come to that, Tilly,' Bella said, doing her best to console her. Despite the peremptory tone of the letter, she couldn't believe the situation to be half so bad as her father made out. No doubt he'd been egged on by her mother's usual hysterics. 'Tell Pa that I'm sorry. Truly sorry. Unfortunately, I have no paid employment either, except for the few shillings a week I get for working here at the clinic. A pittance by anybody's standards. It barely covers my food and keep.'

This only resulted in a fresh paroxysm of tears and Bella became anxious for Tilly to leave. 'I couldn't tell him that, miss. I couldn't. He'd be that cut up. Couldn't you do summat to help?'

Bella's throat tightened with emotion as she recalled the relationship she'd once enjoyed with her father. It broke her heart to be so at odds with him but he was asking the impossible. She couldn't give up the clinic and certainly not to find paid work to keep her mother in the manner to which she'd become accustomed. 'I'm sorry, Tilly. Times are hard for us all.'

She wrote a short note informing her father of these facts. She politely pointed out that he'd chosen to curtail her allowance the day he'd thrown her out and, in spite of her efforts to heal the breach between them since, neither their relationship nor her financial situation was in any way improved. Bella wrote that she was no longer employed by Kendal Milne but earned her living, such as it was, through her work at the clinic which she could not, and would not, give up. 'In the circumstances, I regret I can be of little help to you. Nevertheless I remain, as always, your loving daughter, Isabella.'

When Simeon read the letter, handed to him in his study by Tilly with some trepidation, he swore loudly and comprehensively. He flung several interrogative questions at her which only brought a flood of tears and finally ordered the quivering maid to leave. As she fled, he tore the letter into shreds and tossed it into the flickering flames of a paltry fire.

He was painfully aware that the entire household depended upon his income, modest though it now was, and looked to him for a solution to the family troubles. Yet he could not be held responsible for everyone. Whether Emily liked it or not, savings would have to be made. He would begin in the kitchen.

Chapter Twenty

Bella and Dan seemed to be back on their old good terms. They began by meeting up every Monday evening for a walk in the park or by the Irwell. She no longer showed any interest in going up Dawney's Hill. Afterwards, Dan would buy them each a fish supper for tenpence which they would eat with their fingers as they walked along the street, content to be together. Then their meetings increased to twice a week, three times, till she saw him most days at some point or other, even if it was only for him to walk her home from the clinic, and Bella was glad.

She was afraid now of walking home alone in the dark.

On one never to be forgotten evening as they reached her door, before she had time to guess his intention, Dan grasped her by the arms, almost lifting her off her feet, then pulled her against the breadth of his chest and kissed her. Finally! At last! Of his own free will. And it was surely worth waiting for. Dan's kiss, unlike Quinn's, managed to be both passionate and tender, gentle yet irresistibly seductive, and in a strange sort of way far more compelling, leaving her utterly breathless. After it was over he set her carefully back on her feet and they stood there on the doorstep, alone in the moonlight, with his arms wrapped around her and Bella snuggled close and warm against his chest.

'You like working at that clinic, don't you?' he said while Bella mumbled something incoherent by way of response. 'Happen one day though, other events in your life might be more important.'

She glanced up at him, her hair rumpled from his fingers,

eyes dazed by the depth of her emotion. 'Happen they will,' she teased, 'but I shall always want to be involved with the clinic. You must understand that.'

'I do.' Smiling softly, he pulled her tighter into his arms. 'So long as I'm right up there, at the top of your list, I'm happy.'

On fine Saturday afternoons, Edward and Jinnie would sometimes join them for a picnic and they'd laugh and giggle together, because they were young and in love.

'You know that Tilly and Sam have been given their notice?' Jinnie whispered as the two girls walked arm in arm along the Flower Path in Seedley Park.

'Oh, lord, I was afraid something of the sort might happen. Poor Tilly. Has she found another place yet?'

Jinnie shook her head, saying that the last anyone had seen of Tilly was when she caught the tramcar home to her grandmother in Irlams o' th' Height. 'I doubt she'll be welcomed, not unless she's a regular wage in her hand.'

'Poor girl. We can't let her end up in the workhouse. We must do something for her.'

'Save some of your sympathy for Edward. He still hasn't found a job and your pa isn't the man he was. There's summat else worrying him, I can tell. As for your mother – well, she point-blank refuses to enter the portals of the kitchen so Mrs Dyson stays, no matter what. I do Tilly's job, which suits me fine. It makes a change from winding wool and threading needles.' And the two girls were giggling again as if it were all no more than silly nonsense and not a serious state of affairs at all. But then Bella had suffered her fill of problems recently. She really felt it was time she had some fun, for surely this slump couldn't last. There'd be work enough for everyone come the spring, she was certain of it.

One bright Saturday afternoon in late-autumn, Dan and Bella caught the number 34 tram to Belle Vue, marvelling at the fireworks and the set battle pieces. This time they went alone, Jinnie and Edward saying that, cheap as it was, they couldn't afford such treats. Not until he'd found himself a job. Dan was still getting regular work down at Salford Quays and it seemed strange to Bella that he should suddenly be better placed than her brother, as if the world had indeed turned upside down. She started to protest that she could afford to pay her own way, thank you very much, but recognising the stubborn light of pride in Dan's eyes, managed to bite back the words just in time. She knew better now than to risk offending him by showing too much independence. Besides, they were young and in love. What did a tram fare matter anyway? That chip was still there, hard and fast upon his shoulder, and she'd no wish to cause offence or hurt him in any way.

Another time he took her to the Salford Hippodrome to see a *Christmas Spectacular*, otherwise known as a pantomime. Bella laughed at the Ugly Sisters till her sides ached and almost got hit with a custard pie as one skidded off stage. She'd never had so much fun in all her life which thus far had seemed to be made up almost entirely of duty and responsibility, of suffering opprobrium from her adored father as well as fending off Emily's imagined woes and crises. For all she regretted these difficulties with her family, it was good to be reminded that she was still a young woman with a zestful appetite for life.

Apart from her days out with Dan, her daily routine continued as busy as ever, if not more so. Bella marvelled at how well her colleague coped with a medical practice as well as the Mothers' Clinic. She truly was a treasure and there were no real problems now. Even the local press had gone quiet, perhaps because they could find nothing more to complain of at present as the whole operation seemed to be running quite smoothly.

In the weeks leading up to Christmas Bella realised she had counted her blessings too soon. Dr Syd became increasingly harassed with yet another round of 'flu victims as the clinic was locked in the grip of an epidemic. This put extra strain on all the staff as they felt duty bound to visit patients in their own homes, if only to check that all was well and they were receiving the care they needed.

The local papers had a field day, of course. *'Mothers' Clinic is unhygienic!'* screamed one. *'Don't get pregnant, get sick!'* yelled another and, as with all the other publicity which had been meant to harm them, the articles brought a fresh flood of eager disciples to their door. 'How will we cope?' cried the overworked Dr Syd, who looked far from spry herself.

'We will cope because we must,' answered Bella, aching in every limb, just as if someone had beaten her black and blue all over.

When Nurse Shaw herself took sick, there seemed to be no help for it but to consider the unthinkable. The clinic would have to close.

'Nay, tha can't do that,' Violet protested. 'What about all them women who aren't ill with the 'flu? They still need you. What about asking your Dr Lisle, see if he'll help?'

'Over my dead body!' Bella protested. 'And he isn't *my* Dr Lisle.'

'No, but he'd like to be,' joked the irrepressible Mrs Blundell.

Fortunately, Dr Syd remembered a student nurse who'd helped her in the past on a part-time basis and Bella went to see her. She was called Diana Crompton, was young, pretty, hard-working, and most important of all willing to volunteer for a few hours' duty during her free time from the hospital. The girl arrived at her first clinic the very next Tuesday morning on the dot of nine, as instructed. Once she was settled in and seemed to be coping well, working with smooth efficiency beside Dr Syd, Bella hurried off to begin her morning calls, leaving Violet and Mrs Blundell to counsel the new patients.

That same dinnertime Quinn strolled into the little pie shop at precisely the moment that the pretty young nurse came hurrying down the stairs, thereby managing accidentally to knock her flying.

'Aw, now aren't I the clumsy one? Will ye look at what I've done? Knocked all yer bag and papers on the floor, so I have. Let me help you pick them up. Are ye all right?'

'Yes, I think so.' The young nurse lifted her eyes to his, ready to assure him that she was fine, and he heard the slight intake of breath.

Quinn offered his most dazzling smile and knew with the certainty of experience even as he suggested that he owed her a drink at least, by way of recompense, that this girl would refuse him nothing. This girl would be putty in his clever hands. And wouldn't Isabella Ashton be sorry, then?

It was one Thursday evening in late-November that Bella spotted a shadowy figure standing beneath the gas lamp across the street. Not Dan this time but Billy Quinn. She'd recognise those hunched shoulders and that slouch cap anywhere, not to mention the thread of blue tobacco smoke. He glanced up at the window and Bella drew back quickly, heart pounding, not with desire but from her recollection of their last alarming encounter. She was not easily frightened yet Quinn's behaviour that night had shaken her to the core. As she watched, Bella heard Nurse Crompton call goodnight and clatter down the stairs. The next moment the girl walked across the road, straight into Billy Quinn's arms.

Bella agonised all the following week over whether she should speak to Diana Crompton. It surprised her that she didn't feel in the least bit jealous, only concerned for the young student nurse, and angry with Quinn. He mustn't be allowed to ruin this young girl's life as well. Hadn't he done enough damage to Bella's own, and to Jinnie's?

No more than eighteen or nineteen, she seemed pleasant and friendly, was gentle and trusting, probably because she came from a sheltered background, and possessed a warm heart entirely suited to nursing. In Quinn's terms, she was ripe for the plucking. Bella decided she would be doing Diana a favour if she could break things up between them before matters became too advanced. But it must be done with tact. The very worst scenario would be for Bella to blunder clumsily in, seeming to interfere in another's life and thus provoke a disastrous rebellion.

She could always dismiss Diana, save for the fact that the nurse was a volunteer, working for the clinic for no reward out of the goodness of her heart. And since her recovery from the 'flu, Nurse Shaw was now nursing her brother and nieces, who also had gone down with the illness. She wouldn't be back for another two weeks at least and then only on Tuesdays for a while, she'd told them, because of her other commitments. Besides, even if Bella insisted Nurse Crompton was no longer required, which would easily be recognised as a lie, it wouldn't necessarily prevent her from continuing to see Quinn. It might even make the situation worse as Bella would have no way then of protecting her.

Each day Bella meant to search him out at his favourite places in order to tackle him on the subject, to tell him to leave the girl alone. Yet each day she avoided the task. As keenly as she once used to rush to Quinn's side, now she wanted to avoid him at all costs. Unable to decide what to do, she called on Jinnie for advice. Her response was not encouraging as she reminded Bella of how little notice she herself had taken of well-meant intervention. Bella accepted the truth of this, and admitted that confrontation with the young nurse might not be the best approach.

'Besides, Quinn is the one causing the problem, the one still interfering in your life, albeit indirectly, so he's the one you should tackle,' Jinnie bluntly told her. 'But don't ask me to do it, I've enough on me plate. Besides, Edward wouldn't want me seeing Quinn again and I've no intention of taking the risk of losing what I have with my lovely husband.'

'What you're saying is that I've got myself into this mess, so I can get myself out of it.'

Jinnie's expression was bleak. 'Nay, luv, don't put it quite like that.'

'How else can I put it? It's true.'

'I would help thee if I could only . . . I can't. I really can't.' And unable to bear the disappointment in Bella's eyes, Jinnie turned and hurried away.

The very next Thursday evening, when Diana Crompton arrived at the clinic as usual, Bella could sense in her that same pent-up excitement she herself used to experience just before a meeting with Quinn. It alarmed her to observe another fall into the same trap.

'Nurse, I wonder if you could stay on late tonight? I have some paperwork to do and I really could do with your help.'

The girl looked stricken, her young face naked in its disappointment.

'You didn't have any other plans, did you?'

Diana seemed to shake herself mentally, gave a tremulous smile. 'Well . . .'

Bella gave her shoulder a conciliatory pat. 'Sorry, but what with the 'flu epidemic and Christmas coming, poor Dr Syd has had enough on her plate recently. It's desperately important that we catch up on these record cards or we're going to end up in a hopeless muddle.'

'Of course, I'll be glad to help.'

Quinn was again leaning against the lamp, head cocked to one side as he constantly cast sideways glances up at the window; waiting impatiently for his new love. Bella felt sick remembering how she had once ached with need before every meeting with him. Quinn, however, had very quickly found a replacement.

And then it dawned on her that he wasn't waiting for the young student nurse at all. He knew Bella often stood at this window, her favourite place to watch the world go by; that he'd seen her there the previous week watching for Dan, and was actually challenging her to come down and speak to him. Bella was suddenly quite certain that he'd only started seeing Nurse Crompton in order to take his revenge on her.

Her fear now curdled into a bitter anger. She hated Quinn for having put her in this impossible position and there was only one way out. Since she must save the poor girl from herself, Bella must take the risk and play the game through to the end.

She did not make the mistake of rushing across the road to meet him. Instead, she waited in the cook shop doorway, knowing he would come to her. The ploy clearly irritated him but he came nonetheless.

'So, ye've come to yer senses at last, have ye?'

She refused even to discuss the matter until they'd found a quiet corner in the Ship and Quinn had placed a glass of port and lemon before her. Bella told him then, in no uncertain terms, what she thought of his heartless treatment of the nurse and that she knew exactly why he was behaving in such a despicable manner. 'You're a cold-blooded, evil-minded cad and I won't allow you to get away with ruining a young girl's life, just to get your own back on me.'

'Flatter yerself, do ye not?'

'Are you trying to pretend that it's pure coincidence that, having failed to seduce me, you are now courting my nurse?'

'She's a pretty little thing.'

Bella screwed up her fists into tight, fierce balls, wishing she had the courage to plant one in the middle of his arrogant face. 'Why are you doing this?'

He took his time answering, lighting a dog end with a match he struck against the heel of his boot, drawing on it deeply. The smoke was blown out through his nostrils as he spoke. 'Well, as ye've rightly guessed, I'd much rather have yourself, Bella, than some eejit nurse. Aren't you and I the perfect pair? All ye have to do to save this little colleen from what ye clearly see as my terrible clutches, is to agree to come out with me again. That's not too much to ask, is it?'

'Not for the world would I *ever* agree to such a thing. It's over between us. I've come to my senses at last.'

Quinn got to his feet and in a leisurely, unhurried fashion, finished his beer in one long swallow then wiped the froth from his mouth with the back of his hand. 'Aw, I think ye'll change yer mind on that one, Bella m'lovely, when ye've had time to reconsider. After all, as ye say yerself, she's pretty, and we wouldn't want aught to spoil that fresh young beauty, would we now?'

Bella sat speechless with rage as he strolled calmly away, hands in pockets, whistling softly. By the time he'd reached the door she was on her feet. '*Quinn!*' she shouted to him above the noise and chatter. 'Don't you *dare* touch her. I'll not be bullied by you ever again, nor have you bully her. I'll see you in hell first.'

He didn't reply, barely paused long enough to listen, simply chuckled softly to himself, pulled open the door and continued on his way. The other drinkers all turned to gaze upon her in fascinated horror, appalled that a woman should elect even to enter a public house, let alone shout out at the top of her voice in such a brazen fashion. What was the world coming to?

Stubborn to the last, Bella sank back into her seat to finish her drink, which she felt in dire need of after her tantrum.

Unable to think of any other solution, Bella did speak to Diana Crompton and warned her off Quinn, with the same kind of bluntness Jinnie had used upon her. It seemed the only way. The girl went white to the lips then, pressing them firmly together, responded exactly as anticipated, stating very succinctly that it was her life and she would do exactly as she pleased with it. She even accused Bella of jealousy.

'Just don't ever say that I didn't warn you,' Bella told her with a sad shake of the head when all attempts at further persuasion failed.

Diana Crompton was madly in love, young and hot-headed, and had every intention, she informed Bella, of moving into Quinn's house on Bromley Street. Bella felt sickened at the thought of what might happen to this foolish young girl, and all because of her. Yet she'd no intention of allowing Billy Quinn to win. She refused the girl's notice, at first asking her to stay on at the clinic and finally insisting that she couldn't leave until they'd found a replacement. Diana must be saved, against her will if necessary.

In the end she went to see the girl's parents. Mr Crompton came at once to the clinic and gave his under-age daughter a thorough dressing down in front of everyone. She burst into noisy tears, confessed that despite being besotted by him, she was also nervous of going against Quinn's wishes in the slightest, whereupon she was promptly gathered safely into her father's arms. After this touching reunion, the girl was taken safely back home and Bella breathed a sigh of relief. At least she had succeeded in rescuing another victim from Quinn's wickedness.

He continued to linger under the lamp every Thursday evening, gazing up at the clinic from beneath the neb of his slouch cap. He was waiting, Bella realised, for her to come down and tell him that she'd changed her mind, that she would see him again after all. Courting the young nurse had been only the opening skirmish in this battle. He was letting her know that he could wreak much greater havoc on her life, should he choose to. Bella resolved not to flatter his vanity by allowing him to see she was concerned. She would waste no more of her energy on the likes of Billy Quinn. What more could he do? He had no hold over her whatsoever. In the weeks before Christmas she became far too busy to give him more than a passing thought.

Chapter Twenty-one

It had become a part of Bella's self-imposed duties in the community to raise money each year to provide treats for children most in need. In the summer they would be given a week's camping holiday at Lytham St Anne's or on a farm in North Wales. Much of the money for this was provided by local firms who also supplied the transport to take the children on their trip. In the winter the grind of daily life grew ever harder with the constant battle against the cold and damp, on top of the worry of where the next hot meal was coming from. Simeon had, for several years, sponsored the Christmas Breakfast, a treat greatly looked forward to and enjoyed. This always took place on Christmas Day at the chapel schoolroom, where a hundred or more children would be fed on bread and sausages. Bella had always relished sharing the task with him, readily going along to help.

It was Jinnie who brought her the news that this year it was not to go ahead. Simeon had stated that he couldn't afford it, nor was Mr Josiah prepared to make his usual contribution. Bella was not only hurt and disappointed by his decision, she was incensed. However hard up these men of business were, surely their difficulties couldn't be compared with the sufferings of the children, and Christmas was the time for children, wasn't it? She felt as if her father was taking it out on them because of a foolish estrangement from his own daughter. It was insupportable.

She determined to raise the money herself and after much badgering and hectoring of local firms, all declaring their poverty and that they were in imminent danger of closure, Bella managed to scrape together sufficient money to fund the Breakfast.

She asked Dan if he would help her to supervise it.

'Why me, for heavens' sake?'

'Because you're used to children, with all those brothers and sisters.'

'Nay, don't ask me. I'm sick o' childer. Our house is allus full to bursting with the little blighters. I like to get away from them on my days off, thanks very much. Ask Jinnie.'

'Spoilsport.' And she pulled a face at him but didn't take his comments too seriously. He was merely afraid of seeming soft in front of his mates. But he'd be there. She was perfectly sure, in her heart, that he wouldn't let her down.

Christmas Day came and Jinnie and Bella, together with Mrs Blundell and Violet, went along to the chapel early to start frying sausages and buttering bread. Moments later, Mrs Heap arrived with her eldest, both of them carrying a tray of mince tarts.

'I've been up half the night baking these beggars,' she cheerfully remarked, plump cheeks aglow with her efforts.

'Eeh, Aunt Edie. Tha deserves a gold clock,' Violet told her, taking the loaded tray from the poor woman's aching arms.

By eight o'clock a queue of children stretched halfway round the block. At half-past eight the Superintendent of the Sunday School arrived to let them in and nearly 200 faces, washed clean in honour of the day, lit up with pleasure at the sight before them. There were rows of trestle tables draped with white cotton cloths and decorated with sprigs of holly, a beautifully adorned tree on the platform, and best of all the wonderfully delicious aroma of frying sausages. Not a mouth didn't water at the thought of the feast ahead.

For a moment pandemonium threatened as children began to run about in every direction, pushing and shoving in their scramble to find a place. Bella stood helplessly flapping her arms, her voice lost in the din as she desperately tried to maintain order amidst a sea of battling children, fearful one of them might be trodden underfoot by the stampede. Miraculously, more because of the promise of good food than anything she did, every small bottom finally found a seat and every plate was filled. Soon there was the satisfying sound of chewing, though the chatter only abated by the very slightest degree.

In frighteningly quick time every crumb was gone, every plate was licked clean, the special treat of sarsaparilla had been relished to the last drop, and once more the clamour and hubbub rose by several decibels.

There seemed to be twice as many youngsters this year than ever before, probably because this was their best chance of getting fed today. Bella was wondering if it would be possible to organise so many children into some sort of game when the door opened and in strode Father Christmas, grinning from ear to ear above a cascade of flowing white whiskers. He wore a floppy hat and a home-made cotton jacket and baggy trousers which someone had attempted to dye red but had instead rendered a slightly streaky pink. He carried a sack over his shoulder and on his feet were huge black clogs. He looked superb. Even more surprisingly, he was closely followed by Edward, carrying yet more parcels.

'Na then, na then. What's all this racket about? We can't have none o' that nonsense here. Stand in line them as wants a present.' The voice was unmistakable. Dearest Dan. Oh, how she loved him. It came to her, like a small shock, that it was true. She did indeed love him. She'd loved him all along and it was only in this moment that she fully realised it.

'Quite right,' Edward was saying, in his most agreeable tones. 'We must have order before we can have the fun.'

Bless them both. Hadn't she known they wouldn't let her down?

She would never forget the look of wonder on the children's little faces as each one collected an apple, orange, a few precious nuts and one of Aunt Edie's mince pies. Pure delight.

Afterwards, when they'd all dashed home to show off their prize, Dan removed his beard, pulled Bella tightly into his arms and kissed her underneath a piece of mistletoe he just happened to have handy. She felt herself go weak right through to her toes. His kisses filled her with an aching need that was quite unlike anything she'd experienced before, linked as they were with the most delicious sensation of being cherished.

'*Marry me.*' The words, half whispered against her ear, were indistinct.

'What did you say?'

Dan grinned and tweaked her nose. 'Can I see you later? I'll ask you properly then.' She shook her head, the soft glow in her hazel eyes silently revealing her newly discovered love even as she explained how she was expected for Christmas lunch at Seedley Park Road.

'Difficult as it will be, I must go. Pa and I can't carry on indefinitely in this fashion, hardly speaking to each other. I must try, somehow, for a rapprochement. Besides, I owe it to Jinnie and Edward. They have enough to contend with being temporarily unemployed, without endless family squabbles.'

'Tomorrow then. Perhaps we'll have more time to talk then. Mam'll expect you for dinner anyroad.'

Bella nodded happily, unable to do anything to prevent the smile from spreading across her face. 'Tomorrow. We'll spend all of Boxing Day together. Happy Christmas, Dan.' And placing her hands one on either side of his dear face, Bella kissed him. Within seconds she was once more pressed hard against his chest and could hear Edward's voice, teasing them.

'Put my sister down, Dan, you don't know where she's been.'

But Dan wasn't listening. They stood in the empty hall, wrapped in each other's arms, oblivious to the 'ladies' tidying and gossiping and chuckling around them as the kiss went on and on. It was then that Bella felt a lurch of excitement in some secret place deep inside, reminding her of Violet's homespun wisdom, for a new dish was indeed being cooked up between them. And Bella knew it would taste nothing like cold porridge.

* * *

Christmas Dinner at Seedley Park Road was an awkward and dismal affair, more like a wake than a festive occasion. Even the holly wreath hanging on the mahogany front door only added to the funereal tone. It was true that there was a Christmas tree decked with candles in the hall, though these were only lit for a short time for fear of the branches catching fire. A seasonal log fire blazed in the parlour. Kisses and gifts were exchanged and they all sat down to dine as if they were a perfectly ordinary and loving family, bent on enjoying the festive season together.

Simeon carved the goose which Mrs Dyson had prepared with Jinnie's help and Sam served, dressed in a new satin waistcoat provided by Emily, since she considered his usual attire not to be in keeping with the glories of her dining room. Nobody mentioned Tilly and when Bella asked after her, the question was met with blank looks from both her parents. It seemed heartless after the years of service the little maid had put in. She'd worked for the Ashtons ever since she'd left school, when she took her first job with them as a scullery maid.

Edward said, 'She must be back from Irlam because I did hear that someone spotted her queuing at the workhouse for a basin of soup.'

Simeon's head jerked up and he glared at his son. 'I'll not suffer your implied criticisms at this table today of all days, thank you very much. I did what I could for her. Gave her a month's pay in lieu of notice. The girl was warned months ago to find herself another position.'

'But there aren't any other positions to be had,' Edward rightly pointed out. 'And I wasn't meaning it as a criticism, Father. It's just that when I heard of her plight, I thought it must be miserable to be hungry at Christmas. Poor Tilly.'

There was a small silence while everyone considered their laden plate. Emily briskly brought them to order by reminding them all that dear Mrs Dyson had spent hours slaving in the kitchen and the least they could do was to justify her efforts by enjoying every morsel. 'There is absolutely nothing we can do about Tilly right at this moment.'

'Perhaps over the next day or two, one of us could go to the workhouse and see if we can find her,' Bella suggested, feeling guilty that until today, poor Tilly's plight had quite slipped her mind. 'See if we can't do something to help.'

Simeon said, 'Will you go, Bella? I'll give you a Christmas box for her.' And for the first time in months, father and daughter looked upon each other with something close to understanding, rather than animosity.

'I'd be glad to,' she agreed, offering a soft smile and seeing a flicker very close to warmth in her father's eyes before he dropped his gaze and, snatching up his knife and fork, briskly instructed them all to eat as he'd paid a fortune for the goose. Exchanging a quick smile with Edward, Bella tucked in.

The Christmas pudding followed, flaming merrily in its drenching of brandy. After the substantial main course, eaten largely in silence, Bella was tempted to decline on the grounds she was too full to manage another crumb. Except that in his present grumpy mood Pa could very easily dismiss Mrs Dyson for incompetence if any food was left untouched, and Bella knew that she would have put enormous effort into the preparations, no doubt waiting patiently in Lipton's Grocers while the currants, raisins, sultanas, sugar, candied peel and cherries were weighed out on the big brass scales. They would then be packed into little blue bags, the corners carefully pressed and folded into place, and carried home in Mrs D's huge wicker basket. After this would come the painstaking washing, cleaning and drying of the fruit, the chopping of the candied peel, the crushing of the sugar loaf, the sieving of the flour, the mixing, the beating, and finally the hours and hours of steaming to produce this delicious treat.

'Another slice, Isabella?' Emily politely enquired of her daughter, clearly on her best behaviour today.

'Yes, please.'

Following dinner Father was soon snoring in his chair while Emily retired to her room for a short nap. Edward, Jinnie and Bella took a stroll around the park, 'In order to shake down this excellent food and make room for more,' as Edward expressed it. Certainly the fresh air was welcome after the stuffy oppressiveness of the house.

'I like that Dan of yours. Looks like you're pretty fond of him too,' he drily remarked and paused, as if challenging her to repudiate this statement. Bella neatly avoided answering by turning the conversation on to whether he'd managed to find work. She regretted the question almost at once as a shadow crossed Edward's face. 'Dan says he'll ask down at the docks, see if there's anything going, loading and such like.'

Bella bit back the comment on the tip of her tongue that loading wasn't at all what Edward was trained to do, and even managed a smile. 'Why, that's wonderful.'

Jinnie suddenly blurted out, 'I've found a job,' and oblivious to their exclamations of surprise, calmly announced that it was part-time, cleaning offices. 'It has to be done early morning before the staff come in. And it's only two hours a day but better than nothing, don't you think?'

'Why, that's splendid news,' Bella agreed, not daring to glance at Edward but all too aware of his bleak misery that his wife should find employment so easily while he remained on the dole. She prayed Dan's offer would pay off, though she did wonder what Emily's opinion would be of her privately educated son working as a labourer on the docks.

'It'll help tide us over,' he grudgingly agreed, and Bella hugged his arm, urging him to be patient, while she squeezed Jinnie's hand, offering what consolation and comfort she could to them both. 'Wait and see, the New Year will bring a new beginning and good fortune for us all. Is trade getting any

better at the mill? You might even get your old job back there
eventually.'

Edward shook his head. 'Some say it's left-wing reactionaries
who are destroying people's confidence and that's why orders are
poor. Yet I think the answer has more to do with the future
of India than anything we can do here. But let's not talk any
more about serious issues, not today,' he said, deliberately jovial.
'It's Christmas, the sun's shining. Let's enjoy the holiday, for
God's sake.'

Tea followed with Christmas cake, crumbly Lancashire
cheese and mince pies, and Bella thought she might not need
to eat again for a week. She couldn't help wondering what
Christmas fare would be found on the tables of her 'ladies': Mrs
Stobbs, Mrs Blundell, Mrs Heap and even the Howarths. After
tea Emily insisted on playing a few carols on her pianoforte and
they all attempted to sing in tune, Bella taking the blame as usual
whenever they found themselves out of time with her mother's
fumbled notes.

The chiming of eight o'clock brought Bella to her feet with
some relief and she went at once to ring the bell for Sam to fetch
her coat. 'I'd best be off home. I don't want to be too late.'

Simeon insisted they all take a glass of sherry by way of a
nightcap, which Bella didn't feel able to refuse. She wouldn't
have declined Edward's offer to walk her home either, had she
not seen the glance that passed swiftly between husband and
wife. The pair were clearly longing for some time alone after
the strain of the day, and she knew that Jinnie would have some
explaining to do over the new job. 'No need,' she insisted. I'll
be perfectly all right, as always.'

She kissed each of her family in turn, first Edward, then
Emily, and finally she approached her father. Apart from that
fleeting moment over their shared concern for Tilly, Simeon had
barely acknowledged her presence today but for all he remained
obstinate, Bella was equally determined to prove that it was not
her wish for them to be at odds.

'Goodnight and Merry Christmas, dearest Pa. I'm glad we can at least still enjoy a civilised meal together. I hope you will never forget that I love you.' Emily, unused to such open expressions of affection in recent years, jerked her head up from her needlework to frown at her daughter while Bella placed a gentle kiss on top of her father's head and waited hopefully for his response. None came. Simeon moved not an inch and finally Bella let out a weary sigh, collected her hat and made for the door.

It was only when he heard the parlour door click shut that Simeon lifted his haunted gaze to stare blankly after her.

In the hall Bella embraced Jinnie with genuine fondness. 'It's so lovely to see you happily settled with Edward but take care not to upset him over you working and him not. Give him time to get used to the idea. You mustn't risk trouble between you.'

'Oh, I won't, Bella, don't worry. We are happy. I adore him. If only he could find a job, though. It's a real worry, it is that.'

'Remember what I said. It'll be the New Year soon. A new beginning, a new future for you both.'

'More like a cob of coal for the first-footer, and a big bill from t' coal man.'

Bella was still giggling as she hurried down Liverpool Street. The sky was like soft ebony velvet pricked out with diamonds but there was a piercing cold nip to the clear air. If it hadn't exactly been a white Christmas there was certainly frost about. She tucked her scarf tighter about her neck and trotted along as fast as the icy pavement would allow, offering the compliments of the season to whoever she met along the way.

As she crossed streets and courts and scurried past back entries, Bella kept her chin down and her eyes straight ahead, not wishing to examine too closely the shadows that lurked within them. It was annoying that her bad experience with Billy Quinn had shattered some of her confidence. It was as if she had lost the freedom to move about her own district.

With no small sense of relief, she finally reached her own front door, quite out of breath but inwardly pleased with herself for having got through the day so well, and without anyone squabbling. She'd even managed to show her father that she still cared about him. Stubborn old fool. When would he ever come out of his sulks and accept that life was changing? Or that she was grown up and a modern girl now? She shivered as a draught of icy air chilled her and glanced back over her shoulder, as if she half expected to find someone standing there. The small court and the street beyond were both empty.

She pushed her key hurriedly into the lock and almost stumbled over a bundle left on her step. What on earth was this? She picked it up to peep inside, and nearly fell over with shock.

Chapter Twenty-two

Bella sat up most of that night in stunned disbelief. Why would someone leave a baby on her doorstep? It wasn't a new baby, probably about three or four months old, a girl, and though she seemed somewhat fretful, the shawl wrapped about the child was clean enough. Tucked inside was a feeding bottle, sadly empty. Perhaps this was the reason she'd been abandoned. There was no note pinned to the cotton night-gown, no means of identification.

Bella boiled some milk and water, added a pinch of sugar and fed the mixture to the baby, hoping for the best. She suckled hungrily, her small hands taking a firm grasp on the neck of the bottle. Afterwards she seemed to settle and was fast asleep in seconds, snuffling gently. Bella sat on in her kitchen chair with the child snuggled in her lap, a tumult of emotions playing havoc with professional common sense. So many questions jostled in her mind.

Had some poor woman reached the end of her tether and abandoned the child because she could no longer feed it? Could it be someone who used the clinic? The baby was perhaps living evidence of a 'failure'. It was clearly someone who knew her and believed she would be prepared to help. From what Bella could see, after a hasty examination, the child was well cared for, if somewhat small and underfed. The most important thing was to find the mother.

The next morning enquiries around the neighbours elicited no further details. No one had seen anyone approach Bella's front door, or heard a sound outside. But then everyone was too busy enjoying their own Christmas celebrations to notice.

Dr Syd declared the baby fit and healthy but agreed she was slightly malnourished. She handed Bella a diet sheet and a tin of baby food, along with a whole string of instructions of which Bella understood about a third, before ushering her out of the surgery.

'Is that it? What am I supposed to do now?'

Dr Syd chuckled. 'You seem to be managing fine. Just keep it up.'

'But I must find the child's mother. Isn't there an orphanage or some such? I mean, who usually deals with these sort of things?' Bella felt confused, overwhelmed by this turn of events.

Her colleague gently stroked the baby's cheek, tucked warmly in the folds of the shawl. 'You'd need to contact the Board of Guardians. Sorry, but it is Boxing Day. This is only supposed to be an emergency surgery and, as you can see, I have a full waiting room. After this lot, I'm going home to enjoy my own Christmas, belatedly.'

'Of course, I'm sorry. I wasn't thinking. I can manage perfectly well, at least over the holiday.'

On her way home she suddenly remembered that she'd very little food in the house, and a loaf of Aunt Edie's bread wouldn't go amiss. With luck, Boxing Day or no, she would have done a batch since the little shop rarely closed.

Bella collected a small loaf, together with half a dozen freshly baked mince pies, but the visit to the cook shop naturally took twice as long as normal. Not only because the other customers were reluctant to leave the warm, festive atmosphere but also because the baby had to be passed around, jiggled and tutted over, amid much speculation as to whom she might belong. Bella said that if anyone had any thoughts on the matter they could discuss them with her in private so as not to cause embarrassment for the woman, or girl, concerned.

'I'll ask around,' Mrs Blundell said, nodding wisely as she let the baby suckle on her grimy little finger. 'It's knowing 'oo to ask, that's the secret.'

'I shall leave the matter in your capable hands,' Bella declared, retrieving the child from this possibly life-threatening source of nourishment. 'But if I don't find the mother soon, I dare say I shall have to take her to the Board of Guardians.' This was greeted with much indrawing of breath, clearly indicating their opinion on this particular subject.

Once out of the shop, Bella hurried along Liverpool Street towards Jacob's Court, anxious not to be late, and although she caught a fleeting glimpse of a familiar figure in a slouch cap hovering on a street corner just ahead of her, by the time she reached the spot, he'd vanished. Bella put it down to her overactive imagination.

Violet was enchanted by the baby though utterly dumbfounded by her unexpected arrival.

'Before you ask,' her husband mildly remarked, from the cosiness of his chair by the kitchen range where he sat with his stockinged feet propped on the warm fender, 'the answer is no. We have enough to feed already. We want no more childer in this house.'

'Nay,' Violet said, rocking the baby up and down in her plump arms. 'I weren't going to ask thee, luv. This little 'un would be one too many even for me at my age, as she happen were fer her own mam. Poor lamb. But then this slump is putting the squeeze on everyone. What arta going to do with her?' addressing this question to Bella, as if she had all the answers.

'I don't know. I rather hoped you might advise me.'

They all sat down to a substantial meal of hotpot with lamb, instead of mutton, since it was Christmas. It tasted delicious, the potatoes all crisp on top and the juices from the meat making a rich gravy. The baby was a constant topic of conversation throughout the meal with much speculation as to her parentage and what Bella should do about her. The twins kept trying to persuade her to nibble a slice of carrot until Violet put a stop to their antics.

'Whatever thee does, doan't tek yon child to Ignatius House. I know them sisters are supposed to be charitable but, by heck, they show little indication of it. Hard as nails, the lot of 'em. They doan't know the proper meaning of love and affection. If a child wets its bed — and what child wouldn't, dumped in a huge monolith of a building wheer faceless women i' black cloaks glide about freezing corridors? — the poor mite gets the cold bath treatment. That's supposed to "cure" its bad manners. Heartless, they are. Nay, find a proper home for this little 'un. She deserves better.'

Bella glanced across at the baby, now sleeping peacefully in the Howarth children's old crib, then at all the kindly faces around this dinner table. Violet was right. The child did deserve to be loved and cared for in a proper family, not in an institution. Violet's family might be poor but they were rich in every other respect. Richer than Bella's own, for instance, certainly where love and affection was concerned.

Dan was stolidly eating his hotpot and Bella realised he'd said nothing, thus far, about the baby. Now she smiled at him. 'What do you think I should do with her, Dan?'

His fork paused on its journey, hovered, was set down on his plate again. 'I should think the answer is obvious. Find the mother. You can't afford to care for a child, Bella. Neither can we. The woman, whoever she is, must be made to accept her responsibility.'

'Made to?'

'Helped in some way then. But this baby has a mother somewhere. She needs to be found That's all I'm saying.'

It was, of course, sound advice but somehow Bella felt a nudge of disappointment in him. Throughout the day he never glanced at little Holly, as she was duly named, it being Christmas after all. While other members of the family took turns to nurse and feed her, Dan kept well away. Even Cyril took his share of burping and feeding, singing her a lullaby to send her off to sleep. It was as if Dan didn't want to know about the child. As if he didn't care what happened to her. But Bella dismissed this thought as unfair. Hadn't he only yesterday morning performed the role of Santa Claus for 200 children, just days after he'd stated that he didn't care for them and preferred to avoid the little blighters whenever possible?

'Na then,' Violet said, after the meal had been cleared away. 'Shift these', Father, and mend that fire. I'm going to have ten minutes' shuteye. We'll mind the babby, lass. Get theeselves out for a walk, pair of you. Fresh air'll bring a bit of colour to thee cheeks.'

Bella and Dan strolled along Liverpool Street arm in arm in the brilliant sunshine of a frosty afternoon, the silence between them lengthening. They passed the Rec, where they left the younger ones in the care of Ernest and George to watch the rugby, and continued on their way. They turned the corner into Bromley Street, a decision Bella instantly regretted as she found herself glancing over her shoulder every other second, half fearing Quinn might emerge from his house and start following her again.

They walked all the way to Brindleheath without speaking a word. At length, when they reached Dawney's Hill and Bella could see the children running about excitedly flying their new kites, she could bear it no more. 'Dan, is there something wrong?

'Not that I know of.'

Despite his words it was perfectly clear that something had changed between them. His tone was brusque; even the set of his shoulders seemed hunched and uncommunicative, repelling any invasion into this private world he was constructing about himself. Was it only her imagination yesterday, Bella wondered, or had he truly asked her to marry him? Hadn't he looked at her with extra warmth, with a deeper intensity in his loving gaze? Now he barely lifted his eyes from the pavement. He seemed to be withdrawing, exactly as he'd done once before, the shutters coming down, the bridge that spanned the gap between them disintegrating before her eyes. 'You said it was time we talked. What about? Was there something particular that you wished to say to me, Dan?'

A long pause and then again, 'Not that I know of.'

Bella's heart contracted with a fierce stab of disappointment. How could he do this to her? One minute it was all Christmas kisses and loving promises, the next being cold shouldered for no reason that she could fathom. She'd expected a serious proposal today. She'd found herself dreaming of life as Mrs Dan Howarth, and hadn't found the idea in the least unpleasant. Quite the opposite. Intoxicating, in fact. Bella loved the prospect of being with this man she loved so dearly, day and night. She wanted to bear and raise his children, to be there for him on their shared journey through life. But if he was having second thoughts, surely it was no more than his usual lack of confidence, this chip he carried on his shoulder. The mood would pass, if she ignored it.

Bella began to tell him, in her usually bright cheerful fashion, of Christmas Day with her family. She chattered on, making it all seem thoroughly entertaining and amusing, even her mother's rendition of 'Christians, Awake', in which she rarely struck the right note. She made much of the glass of sherry her father had finally produced for them, when it was almost time to leave. 'Though it was little more than half a glass. He's so *mean* these days,' and then went on to describe her concern over Tilly. 'I thought of going to the workhouse tomorrow, to try to find her. She might not actually be a resident or inmate or whatever you call them but Edward says she's been spotted queuing for soup. I'd like to find her, see that she's all right.'

'Aye, you find her. Then tek her home and feed her, and

find her a job, and look after her like you did Jinnie. Aye, why not? That's what you're good at, isn't it? Looking after other folk. Sorting out and interfering in their lives, you and your "ladies". Tha's time for everyone but them as matters most.'

Bella had stopped walking to stare at him and listen to this unexpected tirade, a frown puckering her brow. 'What was that little outburst supposed to mean?'

'Nowt.' He turned up his coat collar, shoved his hands deeper into his pockets and walked on, chin clamped down between hunched shoulders, leaving her where she stood in frozen dismay. Bella had to hurry to catch him up.

'I wish you'd tell me what's bothering you. You were fine yesterday. What has changed?'

'Nowt!'

'It must have. You're not usually this grumpy. I absolutely refuse to get into a silly squabble today, Dan. It's Christmas, for God's sake, and – and – damn it, I thought something special was happening between us, that you had something important to say to me about *us*.'

He strode on, glaring fixedly ahead, refusing to meet her gaze. 'It is. I did. Well, I might have had, anyroad.'

'Good. Well then, why don't you tell me?'

''Cause you'd not want to hear it.'

'Of course I would. I know I work too hard but I'm here with you now, aren't I? I'm listening.' She was scurrying beside his striding figure, laughing up at him, despite her scolding words. When still he did not respond, she dragged him to a halt. 'Very well then, Dan Howarth, if you won't say it, I will. The fact is, I love you, you great soft lump. There, that wasn't so painful, was it? *I love you!* I adore you. I rather hoped that you might feel the same. Happy Christmas.' And she flung her arms about his neck and kissed him; a full and loving kiss. His mouth instinctively responded, moving swift and hard against hers, his arms coming around her as he almost crushed her to him, so intense was the emotion between them.

When he released her sufficiently to allow her to breathe again, she pressed her cheek against his broad chest and sighed happily. 'Do I take that as confirmation of your proposal yesterday? It does mean what I think it means, doesn't it?'

His response was a long time in coming. Too long. 'Aye,' he said at last. 'I meant it right enough but everything's changed now.'

'Why? I still love you. You still love me. What can possibly have changed?'

All the light seemed to have faded from his face and his expression was stony. 'Just tell me that you don't intend to keep it?'

'I don't understand. Keep what?'

'Yon babby. I'd just like to know that you mean to find who it properly belongs to.'

'The baby . . . is that what this is all about?' Bella stared at him in disbelief. Could the arrival of one small baby make such a difference to his mood? Surely not, though she could think of no other reason. 'Heavens, you're surely not jealous?' She began to laugh but as his face tightened with displeasure she stopped at once, for it was all too clear that Dan did not share her amusement. 'Don't worry, I've already said that I intend to find the mother.'

Then he held her from him, looking deep into her eyes. 'There's nothing I want more than for us to be wed but I want things to be right for us, that's all, Bella. I don't want us to be scratting about for every penny. I want us to be happy.'

'Oh, we will be. We will be *very* happy.' And then he was kissing her again and everything was good between them, just as it should be, and would continue to be, Bella was sure of it.

Bella was not unduly concerned over Dan's strange mood. She knew him for a prickly character at the best of times — loving, caring, steady, always there when she needed him and with the promise of something wonderful developing between them, but not an easy man to know.

The warm glow of excitement which the prospect of married life with him had lit in her was tempered somewhat by his innate caution. But then you could never accuse him of being impulsive. Every decision was always carefully considered, measured and judged by its possible consequence. His one aim in life was to feel safe and secure, to be sure that he knew where the next meal was coming from, whereas Bella was usually one to jump in with both feet and worry about the possible outcome later.

Unlike her own sheltered existence, Dan Haworth had needed to work hard for his. Of course he wanted to provide well for her, for the sake of his pride and because security was desperately important to him. And was it any wonder? Life for the Howarth family had never been easy, and it was even harder for them just now with Mr Howarth unwell and so many children still living at home. But it would surely get better now that the family were growing up. Ernest had already left, he and his new wife and baby having gone to live with his in-laws. Soon the little house would begin to empty as they each in turn went off to marry, or to make their own lives in the greater world. Georgie was already talking of going into the Navy, and Kate was seriously walking out with her young man. Dan would then be largely free of his share of responsibility to his family, and able to start one of his own. Though she was sure the entire brood would continue to give a helping hand to their loving parents when needed.

Bella's thoughts moved on to the problem of the abandoned baby. Dan was entirely right in saying that she really must make every effort to find the mother. And if she didn't succeed? Much as it broke Bella's heart to think of Holly being so casually left on a doorstep, was she the right person to take on the care of an orphaned baby? In her present circumstances, could she even afford the luxury?

She lay awake much of the night worrying over the matter and by the next morning had quite made up her mind to take the child at once to the Board of Guardians. By the time she'd bathed, fed and changed her, and of course played with her on the rug, her resolution was fading. The bright blue eyes, so wide and alert and surely displaying a sharp intelligence, the sweet baby scent of her now that she was dressed in warm, clean clothes, the translucence of her eyelids, the miracle of each tiny finger and perfectly formed toe nail, were a joy to behold. In no time, it seemed, the morning was gone and it was almost dinnertime. Perhaps the visit to the Board of Guardians could wait a little while. Tilly was the higher priority.

Bella tucked the child warmly into the bassinet lent to her by Violet and bowled happily along Liverpool Street in the direction of the workhouse on Eccles New Road. Dinnertime should be a good time to catch Tilly if she was a regular visitor to the soup kitchen. Bella's intention was to hand over the envelope of money which constituted the maid's Christmas Box from Father, then make a start on her usual home visits, calling in at the Guardians' office on the way. There was nothing to be lost through a little delay.

It was as she turned the corner of Hodge Lane that a hand grasped her by the elbow and a familiar grating voice hissed in her ear, 'Were ye hurrying away from me, m'lovely?' Bella heard herself cry out in dismay, heart racing, as she realised she'd been right all along. Billy Quinn was following her.

She managed to wrench herself free and swung away from him, her voice, when she found it, coldly furious. 'Don't you dare creep up on me like that.' Bella half expected him to ask after the baby but he in fact ignored its presence completely, just as if she wasn't hanging on to the handle of the bassinet like a protective weapon wedged between them.

He apologised for having neglected her recently and while

Bella was still reeling from that bit of effrontery, blithely informed her that he'd had a stroke of good fortune, winning a substantial sum on the horses over Christmas. 'I've bought meself a fine house in Weaste, not quite the Polygon but I'm on me way. I'm going up in the world, so I am. I reckon ye can have no further objection to me now. Aren't I a man of substance at last, fit to be considered acceptable even by Miss High-and-Mighty-Ashton?'

Bella looked at him askance, eyebrows disappearing beneath the wild tawny curls tumbling across her brow. 'The fact that I have not behaved in the least bit "high and mightly" towards you is nearer to the truth, as well as ample evidence of my folly. It might have been better if I had been more, shall we say, circumspect.'

'And haven't we swallowed the big dictionary today?' Re-establishing his hold upon her arm he gave her a little shove to get her moving, starting to lead her back the way she had come. Bella tried to protest but it was impossible to shake off the punishing grip. Hindered as she was by the bassinet, she could do nothing but comply, though glancing desperately about, wishing for Dan somehow to spirit himself out of the cobbled setts over which they clattered. Sadly, Bella knew he would be back at work today, the holiday over; that he might not even call in on her this evening, since she'd avoided promising to immediately hand over baby Holly to the Board of Guardians. Wherever it was Billy Quinn was taking her, she had no option but to go.

Chapter Twenty-three

'So I think it would be best if ye did as I told ye to. Haven't I made it clear how good we are together? 'Tis long past time that ye stopped fighting me, girl, and gave in to the inevitable. Why don't ye admit that you and me, we're made for each other, so we are.' Quinn had taken her no further than his favourite stinking back entry so they could speak in some degree of privacy, chasing off a gang of nosy kids and pushing her up against a reeking pile of rubbish.

It was only then that he glanced down at the baby, put out a hand and stroked her cheek. Bella wanted to scream at him not to touch her but suddenly felt too afraid. She watched helplessly as he picked Holly up out of the bassinet and dangled her awkwardly in his long, pale hands. Bella was terrified that he might drop her. 'Put her down, Quinn. She's just a baby. Put her back in the pram.'

'And isn't she a fine little colleen? 'Tis a girl, is it then? I'd not object to ye bringing her to live with us. Couldn't ye give me a son next time?'

'Live with you? What the hell are you talking about?' He stood squarely before her, legs apart, one hand holding the child like a rabbit, the other at his waist, thumb hooked in the leather belt, eyes narrowed but seeming to pin Bella down where she half lay against the heap of rubbish. Yet still she fought him, with every ounce of courage she possessed. 'And how can there be a *next time*, when there hasn't been a first? For God's sake, Holly isn't your child. You and I never ... we never ...'

'And who would know that we didn't? 'Tis your word against mine.'

Bella felt all the blood drain from her face. His threatening stance, her fears for the baby and the stench from the rotting vegetables at her back almost made her faint. It was sheer will-power alone that kept her conscious. Holly gave a little whimpering protest at the discomfort she was experiencing and, in spite of Bella's fear, or perhaps because of it, she staggered to her feet and snatched the baby from him. She held the now sobbing infant against her shoulder, patting, smoothing and hushing her as best she could. As the baby's hiccuping sobs quietened, she heard Quinn's soft laughter.

'Sure and I'd need to get in a bit of practice at fatherhood, would I not? For now you'd best go home, pack yer things and I'll be round to collect them, yerself and the babby later this evening. We'll get someone to sit with the child while I take ye out this evening, to celebrate our reconciliation. How would that be?'

'Over my dead body!' Bella responded.

'That could be arranged,' came his soft reply. 'If ye insisted, though I doubt ye'd care for it in reality.'

Bella simply glared her defiance at him, then quietly slid the baby back into the bassinet, tucking the soft blankets up to her chin. Holly snuffled with contentment, blue eyes gazing adoringly up at her new mother. Bella jiggled the handle and told Quinn that she was indeed going home now, that if he ever bothered her again she'd call the police. Quinn simply laughed as if she had made some sort of joke.

'I'm not done with you yet, m'lovely. Pin back yer ears and listen well.' He began then, in his softly menacing style, to fill her in on the facts of life. 'Ye'll do as I say and move in with me this very night, otherwise I'll be forced to let the papers know how the philanthropic Miss Isabella Ashton, founder of the marvellous Mothers' Clinic, has taken a lover and given birth to an illegitimate child. Now wouldn't they be fascinated to learn such an interesting little gem? They'd start asking all sorts of awkward questions and there'd be plenty of folk about who'd be only too happy to add to the gossip and say how we were often seen together in the Hare and Hounds, at the wrestling and so on. 'Twould be a pity, would it not, if this grand clinic had to close because of its founder's immoral behaviour?'

Bella was staring at him in open horror, bemused and weak with fear at what she was hearing. Eventually she found her voice for all there was a tremor in it. 'Don't be ridiculous. Everyone knows I found her on my doorstep. We've all been trying to find Holly's mother. Besides, my friends aren't stupid, they know whether a woman has shown signs of carrying a child or not.'

A quick frown of doubt puckered his brow and Bella gained some grim satisfaction from having thrown him somewhat, seeing that he hadn't quite thought his plan through. But then his face cleared and he laughed, a harsh grating sound that cut through her complacency. 'Even if the child isn't ours, there's still evidence of intimacy between us, and there's always the question of improper use of clinic property.'

Bella gasped. 'Clinic property? If you mean what I think you mean, you know damn' well that isn't true. I'll admit I behaved like a fool but I refused you, and I refused to use anything from the clinic to satisfy your demands. It's a complete lie to say otherwise!'

'And who's to know that but you and me?'

'You think they'd take Billy Quinn's word against mine?' She flung the words at him in a typical gesture of rebellion. It was brave, perhaps even foolhardy, Bella realised, as she noted how his handsome face darkened with anger, a white line of fury forming about the lips she'd once loved to kiss. But she was so very angry with him, and determined to call his bluff. 'You think you can bully or blackmail me into obeying you? Damn it, you can't. I'll never belong to you, Billy Quinn. I didn't entirely believe Jinnie when she told me what you'd done to her while she was still so young. Now I do believe

281

her, every word. I would *never* go out with you again, not if you paid me.'

'Oh, and isn't that the shame of it because I'd be happy to pay, if'n it would help. I know yer finding money tight just now. Wouldn't a new career be a good idea, in the circumstances? You've talent enough in that direction, I should think.'

Bella struck out. Driven to the ends of her patience, rather as Jinnie had been before her, she flung back her hand and made to strike him right across his arrogant face. Sadly, she did not possess Jinnie's speed, or her skill at fighting. Quinn easily blocked the blow long before it reached him and Bella recognised at once her own mistake. With casual ease he thrust her back into the stinking clarts of filth and rubbish, holding her down with one hand while he slid the belt from his waist with the other. She gagged for air as desperately she tried to fight him off.

'You're a stuck-up little bitch, and isn't that the truth! Yer no more'n a tart, like all women when ye want attention from some man, and then when ye've had yer bit of fun, ye bleedin' well turn yer dainty nose up.' In that instant Bella knew, not only from the tone of his voice and the hard light in his brilliant blue eyes but by the very fact that he swore at her, she was in desperate trouble.

She made not a sound when the first stripe of his belt came, full across her back. She'd curled herself into a tight ball, tense and fearful but burying her face in the reeking filth, protecting herself as best she could with hands and arms, resolving to survive whatever punishment he meted upon her. But she could do nothing to protect her back. Even as she thanked her good fortune at choosing to wear her thickest coat on this cold morning, the second stripe came, this time to the backs of her legs. She screamed as the pain struck home through the thin stockings she wore. With one fluid movement, he ripped off her boots and beat her feet and legs with the buckle end of his belt till her screams and

cries were silenced only when Bella finally slid into uncon-
sciousness.

It must have been the cries of a hungry and frightened baby
which woke her but Bella opened her eyes upon darkness; cold,
icy rain beating down upon them both. It was her concern for
the child which gave her the strength to move but when she
put her feet to the ground, she screamed as a searing hot pain
shot through her. Leaning heavily on the bassinet, she fought to
gather her strength for a moment before slowly starting to push
Holly, the child now screaming in open-mouthed desperation,
step by agonising step out of the entry and along the street,
gritting her teeth against the pain. How she managed to stagger
even the few hundred yards to her own front door, she would
never afterwards be able to explain. Somehow Bella reached it
and crumpled to the ground once more in a dead faint. Had it
not been for the goodness of her neighbour, who immediately
dragged her inside and sent her youngest boy running with a
message to fetch Violet, she might well have remained there
until she perished of cold.

By the time Violet arrived, puffing and blowing with
exertion, her plump cheeks wobbling with concern, Holly had
been fed and changed by the friendly neighbour and Bella was
sitting with her feet in a tub of warm salt water, crying softly into
her hands. Never, in all her life, had she known such anguish.

'Jumping Jehosephat, what the hecky thump's happened
here?' Even Violet ran out of suitable epithets and exclamations
as she examined the raw crimson stripes on the soles of Bella's
feet; the bruises and open wounds on the backs of her legs; even
the tell-tale ribbons of stockings heaped beside her on the rag
rug. 'Christ almighty, who's done this to you?'

Bella told her everything, sparing herself not one ounce of
shame as she spoke of Quinn's attempts at blackmail, and the
reason he thought he could succeed with his threat. As she

listened, Violet sucked in her breath so hard that her mouth all but disappeared into the folds of flesh that comprised her round, usually jolly face. 'By heck, tha's in a proper pickle.'

'I think that's an understatement, Violet. I've been unbelievably stupid, and I really don't know how to deal with it.'

'Don't thee worry about that none, not just now. What thee has to do is rest up them feet o'yourn. I'll just pop back home for a bit of goose grease, that'll happen cure it.'

'Goose grease?'

'It's either that or iodine.'

Wincing at the prospect of either 'cure', Bella hastily suggested that Dr Syd might be called. Bella's colleague came right away. So shocked was she by what she saw that she insisted the police also be called.

'And what good will they do?' Violet scathingly commented, as she watched Dr Syd's ministrations with critical attention. 'They'll class it as a domestic. A chap can do pretty well owt he likes to a lass, wi'out complaint. Theer were a woman in our street got belted every day of her married life by her husband so she started seeing another chap and nobody would speak to her. They called her a loose woman. You can't win. Either t'coppers get yer, or t'gossips do.'

'I really don't want any fuss,' Bella insisted. 'Violet's right. What good would it do? They couldn't lock him up for ever, even if they were prepared to do anything at all. Once he was out, he'd take his revenge and I'd never be free of looking over my shoulder.'

Dr Syd continued to protest as she tended her patient but was firmly overruled on all counts. 'Least said, soonest mended,' was Bella's view.

Violet said, 'Our Dan'll sort out yon nasty piece of goods. Mark my words. He'll be far more effective than any bobby.'

The salt foot baths were repeated at regular intervals throughout each day, then layers of Dr Syd's salve were plastered over the wounds to protect against the possibility of infection and prevent the peeling of too much skin. After that, Bella's legs and feet were bound up in clean strips of cotton, making her feel rather like an Egyptian mummy. She might have laughed at the incongruity of it all, had it not been for the excruciating agony she suffered.

Even on that first day, Violet offered no opinion or judgement upon Bella's behaviour. She took Holly away with her, since Bella was no longer capable of properly caring for the child. Bella was anxious to speak to Dan, though, to explain that nothing untoward had taken place. Despite what his mother might say, she'd no wish for him to get involved with Billy Quinn. She was disappointed and somewhat puzzled when he did not call to see her that day, nor the one after that. By the time he did call, some three days after the event, Bella was so depressed, so filled with shame and remorse, that she could hardly bear to open her eyes and meet what she expected to be his condemnatory gaze.

'Bella, are you awake, luv?' he tentatively enquired as he tapped softly on her bedroom door and crept into the room. Bella kept her eyes shut fast, breathed softly and evenly. Thinking her asleep, he crept silently away. He did not come again.

It was two weeks later that Jinnie brought her the news. Dan had challenged Quinn to a bare-knuckle fight. Bella accepted this grim piece of information as if she had known it all along. Perhaps, in a way, she had. Apart from Dan's odd reluctance to visit, and her own to speak of the attack, she had observed the way even the frank and honest Violet had recently avoided direct eye contract with her. Deep inside, she had guessed that something was afoot.

'When?' Jinnie looked away, unwilling to answer. 'It's tonight, isn't it?'

'There's nothing you can do about it, luv. Leave them to it. Dan's a big chap. He can handle himself.'

'And Billy Quinn? Would he fight fair, do you reckon?'

The two girls looked at each other, a knowing anguish in both pairs of eyes. 'When has he ever?' Jinnie admitted, in a small, quiet voice. 'Perhaps that's why I thought you should know.'

Bella pushed herself up from her chair. It had taken the best part of a week for her to feel well enough to put on her shoes and stockings but she hadn't once ventured out of doors, still wouldn't if it weren't absolutely necessary.

Jinnie was appalled. 'You weren't thinking of going?'

'I just need a little practice, a walk in the sun. If I manage that without falling down, I'll be there tonight, come what may.'

Jinnie helped her to dress because she was perfectly certain that Bella meant every word and would do it anyway, with or without her help. Once outside, Bella breathed a huge sigh of relief. She walked out of the confines of the narrow court, leaning only slightly on Jinnie for support, and on to Liverpool Street, smiling and nodding with pleasure at familiar faces, responding to cheery greetings. It felt good to be able to move about freely and taste the soot-tainted air of dear old Salford. Bella pushed her fingers through her red-gold curls and shook them free, as if brushing the staleness of her confinement out of her head.

Somewhere in the distance she heard the sound of a ship's hooter which brought back her concern over Dan. Turning to walk back to her little house, she tightened her grasp upon Jinnie's arm. 'If anything were to happen to him, I don't know what I'd do.'

Not for one moment did Jinnie imagine she was speaking of Quinn.

The room where the fight was to take place was situated in the beer cellar of one of Quinn's favourite haunts. The vaulted ceiling was shrouded in gloom and the smoke from a hundred cigarettes. The place stank not only of beer and baccy, but of unclean drains and male sweat. Len Jackson stood at the door, charging threepence per person to everyone who entered. Trust Quinn to try to make money out of this. Bella could see that Len was also taking bets, continually licking the point of his pencil before scribbling numbers in his little pocket book.

And where was Quinn himself? Where was Dan? She scanned the crowd of shabbily dressed men who'd come along tonight to add a bit of excitement to their dull lives, not in the least interested in the reason behind the fight, only its outcome.

'There he is.'

Dan was standing on the edge of a group of men who all seemed to be fussing around him, offering advice, massaging his shoulders and arms, flexing his fingers. Bare to the waist, where his thick leather belt was strapped tightly around dark trousers, Dan's bulk seemed impressive, glistening with a pale but robust beauty in the light of the acetylene lamps. Bella couldn't tear her eyes away, she loved him so much. If anything were to happen to him this night, she would never forgive herself. It was all her fault that he was in this situation. She should have known better than to involve herself with the likes of Billy Quinn. As if knowing instinctively that she was there, he turned his gaze to hers, gave her a cheeky wink and the flicker of a smile, as if to reassure her all would be well, before turning away again to take careful note of his comrades' instructions.

Quinn was nowhere in sight.

'Perhaps he isn't going to show up,' Bella whispered to Jinnie, the two girls clinging to each other for moral support. Without her friend beside her, Bella thought she might well have been tempted to turn tail and run. Edward too was with them, not because he condoned the fight, or Bella's insistence on being present, but because he felt it his duty to be there to protect them. Bella appreciated his uncritical, solid presence.

Jinnie was saying, 'Not a chance. He'll turn up all right, like a bleedin' bad penny.'

'We could leave now,' Edward quietly informed them. 'We don't have to go through with this. It's primitive, evil, illegal.'

'If Dan is going through with it, I must be here for him.'

'Talk to him then. Make him change his mind. It's not too late.' But Bella shook her head, knowing that Dan would never back down, much as she might want him to. How could he without losing face? But before she had the chance to say any of this, a great roar went up from the watching crowd. Quinn had arrived. Space was made for him as he swaggered in, deliberately late in order to make the greatest impact. He looked what he was: a mean, lean rat of a man who would as easily strike a mate dead as shake his hand in friendship.

Bella looked at him and shuddered.

There were no ropes, no boundaries other than that provided by the eager spectators. Tom Linx, the cellar man, had evidently been selected to act as referee and he now brought the two men together and made them shake hands. Dan did so with reluctance, Quinn with a snarling grin of contempt. Another roar from the crowd, echoing upwards into the vaulted ceiling; last bets were furiously being placed, though no doubt Len would not close the book until the last blow had been struck. Quinn meant to win, as always, and make money in the process.

The referee held up his hands and a cathedral-like hush fell upon the crowd though in this place they were present not to worship life but to challenge death. Fear gripped Bella's stomach and she resisted an overwhelming urge to vomit.

The signal came and it was Dan who flung the first punch. Quinn ducked and it missed its target. Again Dan lunged, this time connecting smartly with Quinn's jaw, the crack of the blow snapping his head back. Dan gave the hand a little shake, as if he'd suffered as much from its impact as had the recipient. Then he flexed it, struck again and the hush of the crowd was broken by a roar of approval. There were plenty present eager to see Quinn brought down tonight. But where Dan had bulk, Billy Quinn had skill. He was spry, he moved well, he ducked and weaved and too often caught Dan off guard, not caring if a blow went below the belt, punching hard wherever he could and often holding on to his opponent with grim fury so that Dan couldn't break free or position himself properly to strike.

Blood was spilled, a tooth cracked, and the murmurs and jeers of the crowd grew in volume, their excitement palpable as many voices shouted out instructions.

'Punch him in the puddin's!'

'Watch him, Dan, he'd skin a flea for 'alfpenny.'

'Eeh, that were a belter!'

'Bluddy Nora, doan't stand theer like a stonejug. Put one on 'im, lad.'

There was worse language used but Bella fortunately either didn't hear or didn't understand more than half of it, so concerned was she with Dan remaining on his feet.

Suddenly he wasn't any more but sprawling backwards on to the sawdust-strewn floor. There were groans from the partisan crowd but the referee was holding Quinn back and counting. Dan staggered to his feet, swaying slightly, rocking on his heels, and Quinn knocked him down again. This time he moved in swiftly before the referee could stop him and began to kick Dan where he lay on the filthy floor, the toe of one steel-tipped clog hammering against his rib cage.

'Oh, dear God, he'll break his ribs. Dan will lose! Why won't Quinn allow time for him to get up?'

Edward said with bitter irony, 'It's a fight, Bella, not a picnic.'

But there were other cries of protest. 'Bloody cheat!' 'Stop him, ref.' 'He'll punce him to death ...' Before the referee had time to move in, Dan caught hold of Quinn's foot and yanked on it hard, toppling him to the ground. Then they were both sprawling on the floor, grappling and flinging punches as they rolled in the dirt and cigarette ends, just

missing being trampled on by the feet of the noisy spectators.

The referee finally managed to drag them apart, holding
up one hand to allow Dan to struggle back on his feet and
take a breather. His mates grabbed him, wiped the sweat from
his face and the blood from his chin as he spat out a tooth,
then began to whisper furiously in his ear, offering advice and
encouragement. Quinn stood watching, grinning from ear to ear
like the devil himself.

'Ye shouldn't come out to play with the big boys, Howarth.
Stay home with yer mammy in future and leave Bella Ashton to
a man who is a man, through and through. One who has tasted
her charms and means to do so again.'

Inflamed by the taunt, Dan let out a great roar and launched
himself forward to plant one huge, clenched fist in the middle
of Quinn's face. It caught him off balance, the force of the blow
taking him completely by surprise, and it was Quinn's turn now
to be sprawling flat on his back in the filthy straw. The referee
began to count. 'One – two –'

The crowd jeered and yelled, counting with him. 'Three –
four – five . . .'

Quinn was up, flailing his arms about helplessly like a
man drunk but still ready to fight. Dan walked up to him,
grabbed a fistful of his thick hair and almost spat in his
face. 'How about that for a taster then, just to let you see
what you're up against? I'm going to be kind and let you
live but you keep your filthy hands off my girl in future.
Right? Or you'll learn to your cost what I'm really like when
roused.' With a contemptuous flick of his wrist, he thrust
the other man away. Quinn's knees buckled and he seemed
about to fall but as Dan turned to go, lifting his arms in
readiness to meet the jubilation of his appreciative audience,
they shouted a warning. Dan swung round just in time to find
Quinn hurtling towards him like a steam train. He tensed and
with no time to plan, not a second to think, flung a random

punch, putting everything he had into it. His fist met Quinn head on.

The crack of knuckle on jawbone resounded throughout the cellar and there was a sharp, collective indrawing of breath as Quinn's feet lifted from the ground and he seemed to float backwards, almost in slow motion, falling in an unconscious heap on the floor. It didn't take the referee's meticulous counting to tell them that the fight was over and Dan had won. The roar that greeted this result could surely have been heard down at the Police Station, had they bothered to listen. Len Jackson found himself instantly under siege as eager men yelled for their winnings, or blamed him for losing their hard-earned cash.

Dan was clapped on the back, hugged, thumped, congratulated, and finally lifted shoulder-high to be heralded as a hero. At last, Quinn had been given a well-deserved walloping.

Bella pushed her way through the crowd till she reached Dan. The next moment she was in his arms, touching his face, the tender bruises on his skin, the cut on his mouth. She could feel the hard muscles of his young body, smell his sweat, was furious with him for taking such a stupid risk, and loving him for it all at the same time. 'Are you all right?'

He tried to grin at her, put a hand to his own face and winced. 'I think so. I love you, Bella.'

'And I you.'

'Keep the child if you must, but don't ever leave me.'

'Oh, never, my darling. Never, never, never.'

Chapter Twenty-four

It was late February, the melted slush of dirty snow on the ground, by the time Bella peered through the cracks in the workhouse's dirty wooden fence and watched the long weary line of men and women standing in line, each with enamel mug in hand, hoping for a sup of tea or hot soup to ease the ache of their hunger. The scrape of clog irons as they shuffled forward cut her to the heart; grubby, tattered clothes, grey faces and grim expressions; above all the atmosphere of silent oppression that hung over the scene, were terrible to behold. For all her current state of unexpected poverty, she did at least have a roof over her head, and Dan by her side. They were seriously walking out together now and she felt happy and excited about their planned future together, relieved that Quinn was no longer a part of her life. But there was still the unresolved problem of Tilly.

Bella could smell the appetising aroma of vegetable broth and felt her own stomach rumble, reminding her that she too had eaten nothing that day, for all there was food in the house. She had sausage, cheese and streaky bacon in the meat safe down the yard. One of Aunt Edie's fresh loaves stood untouched in the blue and white enamel bread bin but Bella knew that her purse held nothing more than a few coppers, so whatever she had in her cupboards must be made to last for as long as possible. It was a chastening thought and a chill crawled down her spine. How near was she to that line?

The money she earned from the clinic was barely enough to pay her rent and buy food for herself at the best of times, and she'd earned little above subsistence level over these last weeks while she was recovering from the attack. She still hadn't found Holly's mother and although it was a great relief that Dan had dropped his opposition to her keeping the child, temporarily at least, Bella did worry about how she would ever manage. What kind of future was she building for herself, let alone an abandoned baby?

Her one aim had been to help women lead a better life, safe from the yearly drag of child rearing. She had risked everything to bring this about. She'd suffered vilification in the press, been attacked at meetings, had bricks thrown through her window and been largely cast out by her own family. Bella knew what it was to feel alone, unappreciated and unwanted. Had it not been for Violet, where would she have gone that day her father had flung her out on the street? How would she have survived? How would she have got through these last weeks without her good friends, who'd repaid her a thousand fold with their good will and kindness, since only Jinnie and Edward had visited from Seedley Park Road.

Bella made her way into the workhouse yard, pushing the bassinet before her as she walked the length of the line. A few dull eyes glanced her way, though with no real interest. A woman with a child was not an unusual sight but as she neared the front of the queue, their attitude subtly changed.

''Ere, missus, th'end o'queue is back theer. We haven't stood 'ere all day for thee to shove in front of us.'

'Oh no, I'm not. Really, I was only ...'

'Hey, get back. 'Oo the bleedin' hell dusta think thee is?'

The crowd, once so passive, now appeared threatening. Several men broke away from the queue to move towards her, their faces hard and angry, and Bella backed away, suddenly afraid. 'I'm looking for someone, that's all.'

'Leave her be, it's Miss Isabella from the clinic,' a voice called out and some of the men backed off while others looked confused, still not too sure who she might be but noting the respect others held for her.

'Miss Isabella? Is it really you?'

Bella didn't at first recognise Tilly and then there she was, standing in line open-mouthed, a hunched and shivering figure patiently waiting to be fed. The little housemaid seemed like a scrawny child or, worse, a browbeaten animal, drawn, grey-faced and ill, so unlike her normal round-cheeked, cheerful self that Bella was appalled. One glance told all. Tilly was starving. Without pause for thought, uncaring now about the curious men who still hovered around, Bella elbowed her way through, calling the girl's name above the murmurs of protest.

'Tilly. Oh, *Tilly!*' Then Tilly was in her arms, sobbing and crying her thankfulness, and Bella's one desire was to get the poor girl safely home beside a warming fire and with a good meal inside her, all thoughts of economy forgotten.

When her visitor had eaten every scrap of the sausages and mash placed before her, as well as two slices of Aunt Edie's bread, all washed down by several cups of strong tea, Bella handed over Simeon's Christmas gift which she'd kept safe all these weeks. Tilly sat bemused before Bella's fire, face flushed with happiness for all huge fat tears slid silently down her grubby cheeks. At first Bella was horrified, thinking she truly was ill, but then the words of gratitude came spluttering out through the gush of tears and running nose.

'Eeh, I can't tell you how I app . . .' Words deserted her in a fresh paroxysm of gasping sobs. 'I thought I'd done summat wrong for him to dismiss me like that. It's not like Mr Ashton, I sez to mesel'. He were allus that good to me, your pa, once of a time, miss. I swear he changed when you left home. Never stopped sniping over summat from dawn to dusk, he didn't. Not himself at all. Then he up and chucks me out, just as he did you. I couldn't believe it, I really couldn't.'

Bella sat rocking Holly gently on her lap, half smiling as the child suckled hungrily from a curved feeding bottle, half listening to Tilly's tale and inwardly growing increasingly worried by her words. Could there be something seriously wrong with Pa? Surely not. What could possibly go awry with the safe and ordered life of Simeon Ashton? It was really long past time he got over these silly moods. Though, as Tilly said, it was unlike him. As this thought took root in her mind, Bella began to worry that perhaps there was something wrong after all. She still called regularly every other Sunday afternoon and had seen no indication of a problem, except for a certain tightening of the belt which was fair enough in these straitened times.

Suddenly Tilly got to her feet, rubbing one hand over her face to wipe away the tears. 'Nay, look at me. Crying when I should be smiling. You feeds me a good meal and all I do is grizzle and complain. I'm that grateful, really I am, but I'd best be off now.' So saying, she snatched up her coat and made for the door.

Bella sat up abruptly, making the baby jump as she called after Tilly, 'Where are you going? To your grandmother's?'

Tilly hesitated with her hand on the door knob and gave a little shake of the head. 'She couldn't manage to put me up, much as she'd like to. Gran hasn't two halfpennies to rub together, can barely manage to feed herself let alone ...' Her expression looked suddenly hunted. 'Not that I asked her to, you understand. 'Twouldn't have been right. No, I med out I'd just dropped by to see how she were like, it being Christmas. I give her some of me wages and ...'

'Some?'

'Well, most of 'em. But she's old, Miss Bella, and I'm young enough to work for me keep. I'll be right as ninepence now wi' what you've just given me.'

'But it won't last for ever. Where have you been sleeping?'

'Here and there. Don't worry, this'll tide me over nicely till I manage to find work, eh?'

'But what if you *don't* find any work?'

'Why shouldn't I?' Tilly seemed to have forgotten that she'd been looking for nearly three months, with no sign of a job. 'I've been given a good character, after all. Anyway, thanks again.' She pulled open the front door and a blast of ice cold air gushed into the tiny house, blowing the baby's nappies off the wooden clothes maiden that stood drying by the fire. Tilly bent to pick them up and smooth them back into place.

Bella said, 'How do you feel about being a nursemaid to a small baby, just until I find the mother? I've been a bit under the weather myself but now that I'm better, I'm itching to get back to work. I've calls to make, a clinic to run, yet I can't bring myself to just hand her over to the Board of Guardians. I keep hoping I'll find Holly's poor mother. I can't pay you, I'm afraid. Just your food, so long as we're not too greedy, and a bed of course. I'm offering you a home, Tilly, if you're prepared to work for your keep, at least until things improve. We could ride out this slump together, what do you say?'

The tears this time were pitiful little sobs and hiccups which became more and more effusive, threatening ultimately to turn into a flood of adoration which Bella would find hugely embarrassing. She forestalled such a scene by promptly putting the baby into Tilly's outstretched arms and, after planting a kiss on Holly's cheek, then one on Tilly's, said, 'Right, that's settled then. I'll get back to work.' And gathering her coat, she almost ran from the house.

Bella went thankfully back to her old routine, the sessions at the clinic and her regular home visits. One of her first calls was upon the new Mrs Clarke. Bella was appalled to discover that the girl was already far gone in her first pregnancy and didn't seem to be thriving on the condition. She was far too thin and looked thoroughly washed out, if her pasty face and hollow eyes were anything to go by.

'If only you'd agreed to come to the clinic for help,' Bella said, glancing despairingly around the stinking hovel Reg Clarke called home. There seemed barely a stick of furniture in the room beyond a kitchen table cluttered with unwashed pots despite the presence of a brown, slopstone sink. One wall was taken up with a filthy old range in which a pitiful fire burned and the other by a bed upon which several bare-bottomed children crawled, fought, screamed or sat eating large jam butties along with the snot from their runny noses.

The smell of stale urine emanating from the tumble of bed-clothes almost made her gag.

Restraining a shudder, Bella turned a deliberately bright smile upon the young girl whose name, she learned, was Alice. Bella explained how she'd chanced to be in the street anyway, so thought she'd call to see how the second Mrs Clarke was coping with the children. 'Sally was always telling me what a handful they were.' In fact, Bella had been hovering for an hour or more, hoping Reg would go off to work as, eventually, he had, thus giving her the opportunity to take advantage of his absence and pay a call upon his new wife.

The girl's expression was sulky and mutinous and Bella could tell that she was making little impression. 'We can manage. Reg'll help. He's already said so. Children are a blessing and a woman's labour is only a part of the cross we are all expected to bear,' she recited, as if she'd learned the words off by heart.

No offer of a cuppa had been made, though after an hour in a draughty street Bella was gasping for one. 'How about a brew?' She was glancing along the mantel-shelf in search of the tea caddy.

'Shurrup, you lot!' Alice screamed, struggling to separate a tangle of arms and legs and make the children sit still. Little more than a child herself, she seemed on the verge of tears. Bella helped her to restore order then swung the kettle over the fire.

'Have you not brought any with yer?' Alice wanted to know, watching her fill the pot with boiling water. 'Reg says that were th'only reason he ever let you in th' house. 'Cause yer'd happen brought summat.'

'Sorry but times are hard.' It was surely true that at one time she might have brought the girl a packet of tea or a loaf of bread to help eke out the family's pitiful resources but Bella was in almost as dire a state herself these days. No, not quite, she corrected herself, as another scream issued from the heap of filthy bedclothes.

'You'll have to wet the used tea leaves in the pot.'

Bella did so, recalling it wasn't the first time she'd enjoyed the dregs of a pot. Hot and wet at least, it was welcome on this chill day, though without even a drop of milk it would bring little sustenance to this poor girl.

They sat on the edge of the bed, which seemed the only place available in the overcrowded room, and sipped at the scalding weak brew. Bella looked at the children and saw hunger in their wizened faces, open sores on their stick-like limbs and an alarming pink rash all over their small bottoms. 'Does he help you now, with the four you've already got?'

The girls bleak expression became hunted. 'Like I say, Reg hasn't much time when he's on nights. Needs his sleep during the day and I has to keep the childer quiet.' Just where, exactly, Reg slept, Bella didn't care to consider.

'Well, five children will be enough for anyone to cope with, Alice. So you must come to see me after the birth.'

'Reg says I should've sat up straight after – after, you know – and coughed.'

'Coughed? What on earth for?'

'That would've saved me from getting caught. It's me own fault I'm up the spout 'cause I forgot to cough.'

Bella closed her eyes in momentary despair and disbelief. Education was indeed the answer, as Dr Syd said, but the most difficult part was always to get the women to venture up those stairs. 'You really must come to the clinic for help, or this child could be but the first of many.'

Alice bit her lip, looked as if she were about to say something of importance and then changed her mind. She set down her mug, scarcely touched. 'You'd best go. If anybody sees you here, they might tell him and then I'd be for it. Reg don't like no interference.'

'Unless it provides a free packet of tea. All right, I'll bring some next time. I'll go now, Alice, but remember what I said. See that you come to the clinic.' But as Bella left the house with a sigh of guilty relief, she held out little hope.

Despite every effort on Bella's part as well as those of her 'ladies', Holly's mother could not be found. Time went by and still Bella continued to put off the proposed visit to the Board of Guardians. Perhaps tomorrow, or the next day, or the one after that the woman would turn up or some other, better solution might present itself.

'What are you going to do with her?' Tilly would ask, cradling the child against her shoulder while she gently rubbed her back. She'd taken quite a shine to Holly, Bella could tell, and like herself was almost beginning to dread the prospect of having to give her up. 'She's a survivor, this one,' Tilly would laugh and so she was, a part of Bella's family now.

For Tilly, there was the added worry that she would then be out of a job and on the streets again.

Times were hard, as Bella knew only too well. Sometimes she could actually feel herself sinking lower and lower with less money in her purse and cupboards that were almost bare, a frightening sensation which often kept her awake at night. This had certainly not been what she'd intended when she'd first set out on her mission. She'd meant to make other women's lives better, not her own worse.

She spent a good deal of time scouring the local papers, half expecting to see her own scandalous behaviour emblazoned across the headlines for everyone to see. People tended to believe what they read in print, however inaccurate it might be, and if Quinn persuaded one of his cronies, or a female friend perhaps, to pass on this tale of their supposed intimacy to some tin-pot newspaper reporter, what hope would she have of refuting it? It would take only a scandal of that sort for someone, and not her father this time, to close the clinic down for good. Each day she sighed with relief when she found that Quinn had not carried out this particular threat.

Ever since his latest attack on her Bella had become increasingly jumpy and was glad of Tilly's company. Dan, of course, was also a regular visitor to her little house, though for a different reason. She took great care to give him lots of attention, even leaving Holly with Tilly at least one evening a week so they could go out together, alone. She loved him so much and didn't want him to feel hurt or neglected, his nose pushed out of joint by all the fuss the baby was receiving. They would walk through the park, or along the canal towpath, happily planning their future for all no date had yet been fixed for the wedding. Bella didn't mind. She was content to wait, knowing that Dan was a good man with a strong sense of pride, anxious to do things properly.

He often spoke of his family: of baby Joe having a special pair of clogs made to encourage him to walk, of the squabbling twins and young Pete's desperate desire to have a dog and Violet's equal determination that she'd enough on her plate. At other times Dan would speak of his mates at the docks and the difficulties of getting started in married life.

Though relations between them were warm and loving, and he'd accepted her decision not to do anything drastic with the child until she'd tried a little longer to find her mother, Bella could tell, by the way his mouth tightened and his jaw jutted with characteristic stubbornness, that there was much more he would like to have said upon the subject. 'It'll be different for us. We'll do things proper,' he'd say and Bella would happily agree since this was only evidence of his natural caution. They would wait till things picked up, he'd say. 'Once this slump is over, we'll marry in double quick time, make no mistake about that.'

Bella hoped that Holly herself would win him over completely in the end, as she certainly seemed to be doing. He would sit happily dangling her on his knee whenever he came round, which he did quite frequently these days. From time to time, though, he too asked the same question as Tilly, and Bella gave him the same answer.

'Whoever the mother is, she must have been desperate to abandon such a lovely child. But then it's a harsh world out there at the moment, for some women in particular. I shall keep her safe for as long as I can, since her mother trusted me to do so. Besides, I enjoy having her.'

'The longer you keep her, the harder it will be for you to part with her. It'll only hurt all the more when you have to let her go.' A fact that, sadly, Bella could not deny. She loved the child already, absolutely adored her, and deep in her heart dreaded taking her to the Guardians.

'She's not a pet dog,' Dan said, to which Bella responded with outrage.

'For goodness' sake, what do you take me for? Do you imagine that I'm going to grow bored with her after a month or two and suddenly abandon her like an unwanted pup? If I don't find the mother, then of course I'll take her to the Board of Guardians. I promise.'

What she did not say was how she loved to wake up and find the baby lying peacefully in the crib beside her, her gaze bright with interest, taking everything in. How she adored to watch her tiny pursed mouth hungrily grasp the teat of the feeding bottle, her trusting hands as fragile as pale rose petals but with a grip of steel. Bella could not, and would not, simply hand the baby over to an orphanage. The very idea seemed heartless in the extreme when she could offer both love and a good home.

It was one morning a few weeks later that Bella found

another parcel on her doorstep. This one contained baby clothes and a scribbled, ill-spelled note. The writer stated that word had got about that Bella Ashton took in babies now and had taken on a nursemaid to care for them. It told her that if she searched around she might find something of interest and finished with a stark warning: 'Dun't leave it too long.'

Bella searched frantically everywhere she could think of and finally ran to the ash pit at the bottom of the shared back yard, pushed open the small wooden door and searched in the filthy, murky gloom within. Only when she heard a thin, mewing cry were her worst fears confirmed. Pinned to the baby's grubby shawl was a second note. 'Doan't try to find me 'cos I doan't want her back. I've more'n enough already.'

Bella did not dare to tell Dan. He was only just getting used to the idea of keeping one baby. Two he would never accept. It was too much to ask of any man. She went instead to her sister-in-law.

Jinnie said she would love to take the new baby, a fine healthy boy, but Edward would never agree. 'He's quite certain that we'll have our own one day, despite everything that happened – you know – with me. I can't get him to see ... I daresn't push him too hard.' Jinnie blinked back tears as she held this tiny scrap of humanity in her arms, touching its frail cheeks, its tiny mouth hopefully sucking her finger. 'I would take him, you know I would, only it'd be like forcing Edward to admit there was no hope for us to have our own.'

'Would you like me to ask him?'

Jinnie gazed up at her out of eyes grown dark with sadness. 'He's your brother. You decide.'

Bella did speak to Edward and in the most tactful, gentle way suggested that it might be a good idea for them to take this child, just in case Jinnie couldn't have any of her own. The idea was greeted with complete and stark refusal. Jinnie would be fine, he told her, she was young yet. There was plenty of time and if Bella had got herself into a mess by having a stream of babies left on her doorstep, the fault was entirely her own. She should have taken the first baby to the orphanage as Dan had suggested, and have done with the matter.

'Two babies is hardly a stream.'

'I don't wish to sound harsh, Bella, but someone in this family has to be practical. Your head is constantly in some dreamy, socially do-gooding world. No wonder you and Dan are so often at odds. It drives him to distraction, as it would me in similar circumstances. It really is time you came down to earth and saw things as they are.'

'I dare say you're right,' Bella dolefully agreed, and took the baby back home since it was time for its feed.

When the third child was left in a shopping basket beside her wash tub, Bella realised that perhaps everyone was right after all, and she was indeed being foolish. If she wasn't careful she would soon have an orphanage of her own.

Chapter Twenty-five

It always surprised Bella how quickly word got about. In no time at all, it seemed, Dan was knocking at her door asking if it was true that she'd found another baby.

Sighing with resignation, she agreed that it was and let him into the house to see for himself.

He stood fidgeting at the door, cap in hand, and nodded at Tilly, happily feeding one baby, while behind her in the crib he could see a hump of bedclothes, indicating a second. He didn't approach to examine it. Didn't need to. He'd seen all he wanted to see. Deep in his belly, Dan felt a nub of fear. Matters were escalating out of control and there didn't seem to be any way to stop them. He had to get through to Bella what she'd got landed with; the years of toil and scrimping ahead, the effect these childer had on their own plans. 'Yer weren't thinking of keeping this one an' all, were you?'

'No decisions of any sort have been made yet.'

'I thought I said that I didn't want any childer for a year or two, let alone take on anyone else's. That happen I'd think about keeping little Holly but two is stretching it a bit, don't you reckon?'

'Three actually.'

Dan's eyes grew wide with shock. 'Three? Nay, lass. I'm stumped for words. Bloody hell. Who do you reckon I am? Rockefeller?' It seemed to be the final straw.

Bella glanced at Tilly's anxious face and suggested that perhaps they should take a walk. At least they could then exchange their views in private. They walked through the court and out on to Liverpool Street, both aware of the curious gaze of neighbours, rumour being rife in these quarters.

'Don't worry, I've put Mrs Blundell on the job. She's like a bloodhound and will soon sniff out these two mothers, make no mistake.'

Dan very reasonably pointed out that she'd had little success in finding Holly's mother.

'Perhaps, but this time I mean to try harder. I won't name these children, or allow myself to grow fond of them, I promise. Once their mothers are found, assuming they are fit and proper persons to have care of a child which will all have to be gone into, of course, the babies will at once be returned.'

'And what if they aren't fit and proper persons?'

Bella frowned. 'That *is* a problem, yes, I do agree. Or what if they are sick, or dying, or simply won't have the babies back? Or if I never find the mothers at all? What then?'

'Tek them to the orphanage now, love. What else can you do? It's not your job to find mothers or check them out. Don't listen to me mam. There's nowt wrong with Ignatius House, even if one or two of the nuns are a bit sour-faced. They look after childer well enough. Some of them even get sent to live in the country. You'd like that for them. Best you hand 'em over now rather than risk getting too attached.'

As so many times before when someone told Bella what she must do, she perversely wished to do the very opposite.

'Once we get the Board of Guardians involved, they might take Holly as well though, mightn't they?'

'Why shouldn't they take her? It'd happen be for the best.'

A long silence, with only the click of Dan's toe caps on the setts, tapping out her thoughts. To lose Holly now seemed unthinkable. Bella loved her as though she were her own child; after nearly three months caring for her, it felt as if she were. 'I haven't made any decisions about Holly yet. She's a living, breathing person with a right to a good life and I shall do my utmost to see that she gets one. I can't bear to think of her in an institution with no one of her own to love. She's so bright and full of fun. She's already sitting up and taking notice. She'll be walking in no time, I can tell.'

Recognising the maternal pride in her voice, Dan's heart sank still further. 'You have to face facts, Bella. You can't afford to keep her. And aren't your hands full enough, with your work at the clinic?'

She desperately sought another solution. 'Well, surely there must be any number of women who would be glad to have such a lovely child for their own.'

They both knew the answer to this one. If it might have been true once, it certainly wasn't an option now, with the slump biting hard.

Dan pulled her into his arms, eyes bright with desire, hands smoothing her back and shoulders as if he cherished every part of her. 'You know how I feel about thee, Bella. I love thee. I'd do owt for thee, tha knows I would – except tek on this child. I've had me fill o' minding childer over the years. When you and me wed, as I hope and pray that we will one day soon as I've saved up enough brass, then I want us to start off proper. I've a good job, a regular wage coming in. Let's hope I can keep it. When times get better, I want to find us a decent house to live in, give us a few years on our own afore we start a family and not have 'em raining down on us year after year as they did with me mam and dad. I've seen the toll childer take, how tired and weary me mam gets, despite her cheeriness. Underneath all that banter, she's exhausted, near wore out with worry and hard work. I'll not risk putting that on you. So, if tekking on another woman's child means we'd have one more mouth to feed, or would have to have one less of us own one day, then I'd say no, we're not having it. I want to marry you, Bella, because I do love you, with all my heart. But not that child.'

She was staring at him in a state of disbelief. 'Are you saying that you've changed your mind, that you won't take Holly, even if I found homes for the other two?'

'I said I'd think about it. Now I've decided. I couldn't agree to taking on another mouth to feed, not permanent like.'

A small stunned silence. 'I see. And if I refuse to give her up?'

'I'd hope that it wouldn't come to that.'

'But if it did?'

He took a step back from her, his eyes as full of hurt as a wounded animal's. 'I can't see me changing my mind.'

A breathless, agonising pause. 'Well – at least I know where I stand.'

'Aye. Happen we both do.'

That night, as she and Tilly were both fully employed feeding, changing and bathing babies, Bella explained that first thing the next morning she intended to take all three to the Guardians. Tilly went quite pale and her usually capable hands grew clumsy so that she accidentally pricked the baby she was tending with a nappy pin, making him cry out. 'Oh, I'm sorry, luv. There, there, don't cry.' She picked up the baby and began to nurse it, the gaze she fixed upon Bella filled with desperate appeal. 'You can't mean it. What, not our Holly an' all?'

'Yes. Even Holly. If I don't, I could be inundated with abandoned babies and . . . and there could be other – repercussions.' She'd thought hard about what Dan had said and saw now that he was right. It would put too much of a strain on them. The Board of Guardians would never allow her, a single woman, to take on a child and she couldn't force Dan to agree. It was asking too much of any man, and she really couldn't bear to lose him. 'It simply won't do, Tilly. How would I ever manage to feed and keep them all? That's why their mothers abandoned them in the first place, because they've proved to be one child too many to keep. The clinic was supposed to stop all of that but now things seem to be getting worse, not better.'

'It's the slump. That's what it is. Happen the baby's ma's will turn up one day, when it's all over and everyone's got jobs again.'

'And if that doesn't happen?'

'I don't know, do I? But you can't send these lovely children to be fetched up by them hard-hearted nuns.'

'They aren't all hard-hearted. Some are terribly kind and sweet. Violet is wrong about that. She feels that way because she's such a strict Methodist.'

'Aye, but she's right in one respect. What sort of a life is it for a child? To grow up in an orphanage, an institution, with no mam or dad. I've heard about them places. Thin porridge every morning for yer breakfast, nobody to kiss you good night or give you a bit of a cuddle. Bad as the workhouse. Would you like it?'

Bella could bear to hear no more. However calm and sensible she might appear on the outside, inside she was crying with the pain of it all. The decision was made and there was an end to it. 'If I don't take action now then I could lose everything that matters to me, including Dan, and I can't risk that, Tilly. It's time to accept the inevitable and face reality.' She got briskly to her feet and went to lay Holly in her crib, tenderly tucking in the blankets and kissing her sweet-smelling cheek. First thing in the morning, the babies would all be taken to the Board of Guardians, come what may.

The woman at the Board of Guardians' office appeared devastated by the depositing of three babies on her desk, as well she might. It seemed that they had been inundated in recent weeks, either by children they'd had to remove from family care because of near starvation, or their not being able to cope, or else a parent starting to take out their frustration on their nearest and dearest. Sometimes they'd simply been abandoned, as these had. Whatever the cause of the slump, whatever misery and hardships it created, the children were the real victims, the ones who were suffering most.

'These babies appear to be reasonably well fed and contented,' she said, gazing upon them as if they were specimens in a laboratory. Holly chose that moment to kick aside her shawl and beam delightedly at the nice lady.

Bella's heart contracted. 'We've done our best but we obviously can't go on indefinitely. I have a job to do, a clinic to run, and I'm not married.'

The woman considered her not unsympathetically. 'A pity. Looks like you were doing a good job. But you have a clinic, you say. Ah, yes, I remember, a Mothers' Clinic. Splendid job you're doing there, Miss Ashton. Much needed.' The woman was already turning her attention back to her overloaded in-tray, filing papers, signing letters even as she talked. 'Couldn't you house these three at your clinic for a little while? We could overlook the fact you weren't married if you could get one of your nurses to mind them. Temporarily at least. Otherwise, well, we'll see what we can do but I don't hold out much hope. Ignatius House is certainly full. I'd have to search further afield for suitable accommodation. Orphanages don't provide many facilities for very young babies, they prefer them to be adopted, and with the country in the state it's in at present, the number of prospective parents has seriously reduced in number. And of course they have to be housed and fed in the meantime while we check out suitable adopters, have they not?'

It was all sounding far more complicated than even Bella had anticipated but one fact stood out amongst this morass of detail. 'Further afield? How much further?' She'd nursed a secret hope of being at least able to visit Holly once or twice a week, perhaps have her to stay occasionally.

The woman shrugged, said she really couldn't say. Manchester, Preston, Blackburn Orphanage, who knew where they might end up? All good places, she assured Bella, but because of the slump, Salford, for the moment at least, was full.

As if on cue, one of the babies gave a whimper of distress and the other two tuned up in sympathy. Bella gathered them up, placed them back in the bassinet and took them home again. She'd keep them for a short while longer, she promised. Just until suitable accommodation could be found.

The clinic over the cook shop was not at all a suitable place to accommodate small babies and Bella had no intention of keeping them there. They would continue to be cared for at her own house by Tilly, until alternative accommodation had been found. 'What else could I do?' she asked of her stalwart group of 'ladies'.

'Nay, nowt.'

'Not wi' your soft heart, luv.'

If they had any other opinion on the matter, for once they had the good sense to keep it to themselves. Only Violet sucked in her breath long and hard and warned Bella she was dicing with fate. 'Tha con do owt but wheel theesel' in a barrow.'

Translated this meant that Violet was of the opinion Bella had taken too much on and there was a limit to even her capabilities. Bella hugged her friend and agreed that she probably had but that it was only temporary. 'The Board of Guardians are involved now and will find all the babies new parents.'

'Including your Holly?'

Bella swallowed. 'Yes, even Holly.'

Violet gave this due consideration. 'Our Dan'll be glad to hear it. He's been a bit low since he heard. It's summat of a facer, though, to be saddled wi' three childer even afore thee's wed. It's like gettin' drunk without the pleasure of suppin' the beer, eh?' She cackled with laughter and Bella was relieved to see that she hadn't lost her sense of humour. 'Aye, weel, in the meantime tha'll just have to hope thee hasn't started a flood.'

Mrs Blundell, however, had come up trumps. She had indeed located the mother of the second child. He belonged to Alice Clarke. Unfortunately, she'd given birth without assistance, had told her husband that the child had died and been taken away. She was now more than ready to accept help from Bella's clinic as she simply couldn't cope with the prospect of another. 'She'll not have the child back, though, not at any price. Sez she has her hands full with his little buggers. It'd only starve to death if she kept it.'

'He must go for adoption then, with the rest.'

'Aye. That's the ticket.'

'And the third baby?'

'No luck there, not yet, but I'm still asking around. Someone must know of a pregnancy that hasn't borne fruit.'

Within days the size of the task she'd taken on became all too clear to Bella. The babies ate, as Tilly remarked, like young gannets. From dawn to dusk and all through the night, the two girls seemed to be fully employed washing, changing, feeding and nursing babies. Yet because Bella was determined that her work at the clinic didn't suffer, she insisted on taking on most of the night shift, so that Tilly could at least get some sleep as she carried the brunt of the work during the day.

'You can't burn the candle at both ends, Miss Isabella.'

'I can cope for a little while.'

But it was a gargantuan task and, feeding the babies took money. The woman at the Board of Guardians' office agreed to make a small contribution to their welfare but it never seemed to be enough. Bella didn't need to examine her empty savings account to know she was in dire difficulties there too.

She felt so desperate that she wrote a letter to her father, reminding him how pleased she was that they'd got on so much better over Christmas. It wasn't strictly true since the good will had come entirely from her side but Bella felt it was worth a try. She explained that she was acting as temporary guardian for three children until adoptive parents could be found and begged Simeon for help, perhaps to make a small contribution or even to restore her allowance so that she could better cope with the situation. She was disappointed but not entirely surprised when he did not respond.

Unwilling to accept defeat or to believe that he could so easily ignore her, she called at the house in Seedley Park Road. It looked cold and unfriendly, the parlour blind half down, as usual, and the brass knocker daring anyone to tarnish its polished brightness. The door was opened by Mrs Dyson, since they had not taken on another maid to replace Tilly. But rather than exhibiting her usual degree of pleasure, the old housekeeper seemed unexpectedly troubled, even embarrassed, to find Bella standing before her. She half glanced back over her shoulder, drawing the door to as she hovered on the step and explained in a low whisper that she couldn't let Bella in.

'I'm sorry to have to be the one to tell you this but the mistress has left strict instructions that should you ever appear on her doorstep, you are to be turned away and not permitted inside the house. Not at any price.'

'Good heavens.' Bella half laughed, for all this information came as a shock. Despite all their differences, she had never actually been refused admittance before, not to what was still, in effect, her own home. 'What on earth have I done now? I thought we were on the way towards a reconciliation.'

'Summat to do with your being — you know — *shamed!*'

Bella frowned, not understanding. 'Shamed? What do you mean by that? In what way have I been shamed? Stop talking in riddles, Mrs D, and tell me straight.'

Mrs Dyson heaved a deep sigh, folded her hands in her pinny as if to stop them pulling Bella into her arms and, in a hoarse whisper, gently explained that she couldn't let her in because Madam had received a letter. It told how her daughter had been the mistress of the notorious Billy Quinn and was even now carrying his child. As a result, Emily had issued instructions that she no longer recognised Isabella as her own daughter. 'Certainly not one who's turned herself into a fallen woman. Those were her words exactly, miss. I'm that sorry.'

Bella was reeling in shock, struggling to come to terms with this news. A voice in the back of her head told her that the letter could only have come from Quinn himself, that instead of writing to the papers he'd decided on making mischief within her own family. He'd carried out his vicious threat to ruin her reputation, despite having been beaten in a fair fight. But then, as Jinnie had said, when did Billy Quinn ever fight fair? Before she had time to offer any sort of defence, let alone an apology for her parents having been dragged into this mire, the housekeeper murmured an apology and closed the door in her face. Bella hammered on it for some minutes before finally admitting defeat and accepting that Mrs Dyson would not open it again.

She turned away, stunned and more upset by this rejection than she could express. Bella walked home in a more sober frame of mind than ever before, all her usual optimism and cheerful determination to make the best of things quite deserting her.

Once back home she got out her writing paper and wrote yet another note to her father, explaining that any letter they had received making such an accusation had been sent with mischief in mind.

Dear Pa,
You know how I love you and would never for a moment intentionally bring shame upon you. If you would but grant me the opportunity, I could explain who wrote the letter and why. I can assure you that it was done by someone seeking to harm me. It is nothing but poison and completely untrue. I ask only for your love and forgiveness as I offer my humble apologies that this should cause you any distress.

It was a cry from the heart but it brought forth not a word in response. Bella received no reply to this letter either.

By telling these nasty, anonymous lies to her parents, Quinn had robbed her of the last chance to breach the gulf between them. Bella was less surprised by her mother's stiff-necked attitude but she wept for the loss of her beloved father.

Throughout their estrangement, Bella had always hoped Simeon would come round in the end, just as soon as he understood the good she was doing at the clinic. She could see no way now to heal the wound.

And then, quite out of the blue, it occurred to her that if Quinn had written such a poisonous letter to her mother, what in heaven's name had he said to Dan? Would she lose him too?

1931

Chapter Twenty-six

Dan had heard the rumours and made no secret of his disappointment in her. Even had he not expressed what he felt in those terms, Bella could sense it in him. His eyes held such sadness, such loss of hope, that her heart gave a tiny flip of despair.

'But you must believe me when I tell you that it isn't true. Of course I'm not pregnant! The very idea is ridiculous.'

The pair sat on a bench in the park, several freezing inches of cold ironwork between them, and talked as they never had before, Dan finally opening up the floodgates of suspicion that cluttered up his head.

At first he'd refused to believe it, he told her, but his mates said there was no smoke without fire, and now he was beginning to think they might be right. Perhaps it had been a mistake to champion Bella by fighting for her cause. What had it proved? 'Nowt. For all I know, you could've been Quinn's mistress all along, still might be, encouraging him and laughing up yer sleeve at me being such a daft 'aporth. After all,' he concluded, 'it's evident to everyone that you and him were close, often seen in each other's company.' It pained him so much to have to say these things, yet the words poured out of him, born of hurt and jealousy.

Bella was devastated. She had never felt more alone. She begged him to believe in her, to understand how stupidly she'd behaved and how sorry she was. 'But he tried to *rape* me! I don't love Quinn. I never did. I was obsessed, intrigued, excited ... oh, I don't know why I went out with him. It was all a terrible mistake.'

Dan stared out across the park, the smell of new spring grass in the air, feeling the pit of misery deepen in his belly. He'd believed her innocent when he fought Quinn, now he found himself quite unable to do so. Even so, he longed to reach out and pull her into his arms, to kiss some warmth into her cold, pinched face. Yet he couldn't. He felt frozen himself, chilled to the bone, all faith in her gone. No smoke without fire. He'd been made a fool of. A cuckold, wasn't that the word? For all they weren't wed yet, they were promised to each other, so it was just as bad. All his mates said so.

Even his own mother had refused to give him the assurance he sought that Bella had never actually let Quinn touch her. That it'd all been purely platonic. Violet had told him not to ask too many questions but to get on with life. Yet how could he? Bella expected him to believe in her innocence, had no objection to his fighting to defend it, and yet she'd offered no proof of her innocence. He felt riddled with suspicion, embittered by it.

Bella was saying, 'You'd take Quinn's word against mine?'

'I'm not saying that, only why would he want to go on hurting you in this way unless he felt he had the right? It doesn't mek sense. What would he get out of telling a lie?'

'You only think this way because you never would tell a lie, you would always play fair. Quinn never does. He enjoys inflicting hurt, doing as much damage as he can.' For a second, Bella thought that she'd won through as Dan seemed seriously to consider this point, his eyes desperate with appeal, quietly begging her to convince him.

'So you never ...?'

'No, we never did anything like that.'

'But he kissed you.'

'Y-yes, he kissed me.'

Dan's mouth tightened ominously. 'And what else?'

'For God's sake . . .' Bella got up off the bench, strode away from him, walked back, sat down, clasped her hands in her lap, attempting to be calm. 'Look, where is the point in going over what I did or didn't do? It's over. Finished. It meant nothing.'

'How can you say so? Women aren't like that. Not decent ones anyroad. Happen no man means owt to you, except as a bit of fun. Do you really love *me*, that's the question? Do you care a jot what I think or feel?'

Bella stared at him askance. 'Of course I do. I love you.'

'Happen you do, and happen you care only for yourself. Mebbe I was right all along. There's too much of a difference between us and happen you only bothered with me in the first place, and with Quinn, because you like to tease a chap, to enjoy a bit of rough. Mebbe you just like having a bit of fun. Life isn't serious to you, is it? You need a challenge, a campaign to fight for and win, to prove you can do it. That you're as good as any man.'

'Oh, Dan. That's a cruel thing to say and absolutely untrue.'

They'd talked for half the day in a desperate need to reach an agreement. Now they sat in pained silence for long moments watching the sun slide swiftly down the sky, hoping and praying for something, anything, to bring them together again yet failing to find it. They seemed further apart than ever.

Bella spent a long and lonely night weeping for what-might-have-been. She couldn't believe that Dan would choose to believe the rumours rather than her. But then she realised it was more than that. He was jealous, had all along resented the idea of her seeing Billy Quinn. Hadn't he trailed and tracked her constantly after that first meeting, as if appointing himself her guardian angel? In the end, of course, she'd come to love knowing that he was never far away. Come to love him deeply. Now he was out of her life completely, and inside she felt raw and cold with fear.

By the first light of dawn she'd given up all hope of sleeping and sat wrapped in her shawl by the bedroom window, looking out over the broken stone walls and back yard gates, thinking their lovely times together — the kites on Dawney's Hill, the fishing trips, the kisses.

They'd had their difficulties, it was true, their backgrounds being so different. Yet they'd been in the process of overcoming all of that. Their love had been far more important than any social differences between them. She couldn't imagine life without him. How would she manage? Even the day ahead seemed grey and colourless without the prospect of seeing him this evening.

At breakfast, Tilly remarked on her pale, drawn face, asking if she was sickening for something but Bella said she'd simply slept badly. In the cold light of a new day she'd convinced herself that Dan would have suffered a change of heart. He surely needed her as much as she needed him. She'd call and see him later and perhaps the quarrel would have been forgotten.

Cheered by the thought, Bella helped feed all the lovely babies, laughing at their antics, kissing and cuddling them far too long so that she had to run to get to the clinic on time.

As if to add insult to injury, Dr Lisle was standing in Mrs Heap's cook shop when she arrived, quite out of breath and rather flustered. He refused to wait any longer and followed her upstairs, hovering about as she unlocked doors and cupboards. He cleared his throat, insisting she sit down and listen to what he had to say. Bella was in the process of explaining how very busy she was when they were interrupted by Dr Syd who whirled in, took in the little scene at a glance and made herself scarce behind a screen.

In suitably hushed tones, since Bella refused point blank to find a more private place, Dr Lisle very seriously and courteously informed her that he could no longer consider her as a possible wife. Utterly flabbergasted, Bella simply gaped at him. It took several seconds but eventually she managed to find her voice.

'I wasn't under the impression that I still was — being

considered, I mean. Following that disastrous episode in the Picture House.'

'I am aware that I have neglected you somewhat recently,' he admitted, clearly choosing not to comment on that unfortunate matter. 'But my offer has never been withdrawn, you understand. I was simply waiting for the right moment to pursue it. However, in the light of new information which has now come to my attention I fear that you and I, Miss Isabella, would not suit. Would not suit at all.'

'I'm most rel ... er, sorry to hear you say so. But I can understand your reservations.' She picked up a stack of papers, hoping he would take the hint and depart. He stepped closer and the powerful aroma of fish almost overwhelmed her.

'Indeed, I have most severe reservations, my dear. I was prepared to overlook the little difficulty of the clinic as a passing fancy but I fear your morals are somewhat lower than even I had bargained for.'

For once Bella made no attempt to defend herself. She simply smiled sadly and shook her head in despair at her own scandalous behaviour.

'Of course, if you were to repent and seek forgiveness then, in time, I might reconsider. There could still be hope for us.'

'No, no, I fear I am quite beyond redemption. I do believe you were correct, Dr Lisle. We are not at all suited.' And she hastily showed the little man to the door. 'It's an ill wind,' she said to Dr Syd, who was doubled up with suppressed laughter behind the curtained screen.

'Thank your lucky stars you're off his list.' But then the laughter faded and her brow puckered into a frown. 'You don't think he'll take the matter any further, do you? I mean, use this as a means to make difficulties for the clinic?'

'Why should he? If he's no longer interested in me, he can no longer have any concerns over the clinic, can he? He only wanted to close it to force my hand, or rather my finger into a wedding ring. Ugh, I shudder at the thought!'

Both women accepted this theory as sound. Within days, however, they discovered otherwise. Bella was woken by a frantic knocking at her front door early one morning which startled the babies and set them all off yelling. The caller was Dr Syd who rushed in on a blast of cold air, scattering briefcase, scarf and hat, and flopping into the chair in an unusually distressed state.

'He's done it. He's succeeded.'

'Who has? Succeeded in what?'

'In getting his revenge.'

Bella stared at Dr Syd's booted feet depositing mud on the rag rug and her thoughts flew at once to Quinn. She knew he'd been too quiet lately, that he wouldn't be satisfied with simply ruining her last vestige of hope for a reconciliation with her father, as well as the destruction of her relationship with Dan. Blast him. He had to find some other way to hurt her. Dr Syd began to talk and it took some moments before Bella could follow what she was saying.

'She couldn't admit to being married, you see, or she would have lost her job. Thrown out of the profession. An absolutely archaic rule but there we are. So many nurses have to keep their marriages secret. It's not uncommon.'

'What on earth are you talking about? Start again. Who's married?'

'Oh, do pay attention, Bella dear. I'm talking about Mary. Nurse Shaw. That brother of hers that you met . . . well, he isn't her brother at all, of course, he's her husband and the supposed nieces are in fact her own daughters. It's an unbreakable rule that if a nurse marries she must leave the profession. Makes my blood boil. Some day we'll succeed in getting it changed, though God knows how. It's taken long enough to win the bloody vote. Women worked all through the war in all sorts of jobs, and yet they still think that once a woman marries she should give it all up. They call us pin-money wives. It's ludicrous.'

Dr Syd ranted on for some time while Bella brewed tea and listened with increasing sympathy, though all she could truly think of was that it meant the clinic was now without a nurse. 'It never rains but it pours. But what has all of this got to do with Billy Quinn?'

'Billy Quinn?' Dr Syd choked on her tea and looked up in amazement. 'I know it's early in the morning but do try to concentrate, girl. I'm talking about Dr Lisle. God knows how he found out but he's spilled the beans to the local press. Here it is in black and white. I picked a paper up on my way to the surgery as usual. We're ruined.' She drew the newspaper from her briefcase and flung it on to the table. Bella saw at once that it wasn't a rain shower they'd been hit by, or even a storm, this was a tornado.

Bella hardly needed to read every word to know what it would say, yet she did so, unable to tear her riveted gaze from the page as it informed its concerned readers about the *Scandal at Mothers' Clinic.*

The clinic is being run by Jezebels. By a nurse who has committed the cardinal sin of breaking one of this noble profession's most important rules; and by a scarlet woman who not only has been mistress to a notorious bookmaker well known in the area but has also given birth to his child, passing it off as a waif and stray abandoned on her doorstep. It has even been rumoured that she is expecting another.

'What utter tosh! These stupid rumours grow worse by the day. They'll be saying all three of these babies are mine before we're done.'

Now having been joined by Tilly, looking somewhat bemused and befuddled, jiggling a baby on each hip, all three women looked at each other appalled, for of course that was exactly what they would say.

Bella felt sick. It was as if the whole world had turned against her. With this kind of press, what hope did she have of winning even Dan's support? Why on earth should be choose to believe her above the facts he read in the paper?

Because, if he truly loved her, he should surely take her word above all others.

Dan knew perfectly well that Holly wasn't hers. How could she possibly be? Though Bella knew that for all he understood the fallacy of this particular part of the tale and might long to believe in her, his mates were constantly dripping doubt like poison in his ear. She still hoped she might win him round, though it would take time. But as well as the upset these lies had caused in her relationship with Dan, there was their effect upon the clinic.

'Read the rest,' Dr Syd said, her voice bleak.

Two other babies have been found abandoned, one of whom appears to be the child of a clinic patient. So much for the beneficial effect upon families of our Mothers' Clinic.

'Where in heaven's name did they get that story from? Has Mrs Blundell been gossiping? It's not true anyway. The new Mrs Clarke wasn't a patient at the clinic. Everyone knows how desperately hard I tried to persuade her to come, yet failed.'

'No one is going to believe that because she's certainly a patient now. Anyway, mud sticks. They, he – we can only guess the source of these tales for we've no proof – have thrown enough at us this time to make sure of that. How our various benefactors will view this sort of scandal, I dread to think. They are hardly going to be pleased and may withdraw their support altogether.'

Bella wrote again to her father, risked further rejection by calling at Seedley Park Road time after time to beg for the support of her family, using every pretext she could think of. She pleaded with Mrs Dyson, with Emily, even with Sam when once he came to the door, for a brief moment of her father's time so that she could explain the facts to him. Bella felt certain that if she could only win him over then she could convince anyone. Besides, Simeon Ashton still had influence. If people saw him standing by her they would think twice, but he remained obdurate. There was no response. This man, her adored pa who had once believed that the sun shone out of his daughter's lovely hazel eyes, refused even to speak with her.

Within days Bella received a rather stiff and formal letter from Mrs Lawton, the magistrate's wife who had been on the committee with them from the beginning, coldly informing them that she was withdrawing her financial support, as were her many friends. In frighteningly quick time all their other benefactors melted away; a weeping Nurse Shaw departed not only from the clinic but from her hospital post to be a full-time mother and Dr Syd was informed by the Medical Council that if she did not resign her position at the clinic forthwith, her days as a GP would be numbered.

Bowing to pressure, Bella closed the clinic. Her 'ladies' were horrified. 'Nay, tha can't close us down,' Violet said, appalled.

Poor Mrs Stobbs began to quake with fear at the thought of having nowhere left to come for help. 'Hecky thump, ah'd be off again in no time without you to keep me on the straight and narrow.' Even Mrs Solomon, the perennial optimist, began to wail and complain that if the clinic closed, the blessed Eli would be sure to ask her to try for another boy and she was exhausted and simply couldn't face it. Not again.

Mrs Blundell was full of contrition that she might have inadvertently caused this furore, while denying she'd gossiped to anyone but her own churns. 'Nay, thee only has to break wind and someone in t'next street'll hear about it,' she added, in her robust way. Heartened by her friends' response, she reopened it within days.

Reg Clarke came personally to see Bella, and she suffered a difficult hour while he preached and bemoaned his lot in life; how he needed his comforts but his wives had let him down, either by inconveniently dying or by lying to him. Alice, apparently, had disgraced herself to such an extent that he no longer felt he could care for her and she'd been returned to her mother, like an unsatisfactory gift. Bella had heard that in fact Alice had packed her frugal belongings and fled, thankful to be free of the responsibility of all those children. She'd vowed never to have another, poor girl.

Despite his vaunted Christian charity, Reg refused to take back his son and somehow managed to put the blame for being left with four motherless babies at Bella's door. She promised to find him a good woman to help him look after them but he must not on any account, she warned, mistake a child-minder for a wife again. The woman would be available only to help him care for the children. He must look elsewhere for his other 'comforts', and this time use proper precautions. He went away somewhat chastened.

The following week the two unnamed babies were found new homes. One was also offered to Holly and at first Bella refused it. The child was all she had left now. She represented someone to love and build a new future for. But the woman at the Board of Guardians tactfully reminded Bella of her single status, which was highly irregular, and of the fact that guardianship had only been granted on a temporary basis. With the Mothers' Clinic now closed she could not even claim to have a nurse for the child. Tilly, apparently, did not count.

On the day she had to hand her over, Bella felt as if her heart must surely break so tight was the band of pain across her breast. She lifted little Holly from her crib to say goodbye, cuddling her close to savour the sweet scent of her for the last time. Even the warm weight of the baby in her lap brought a gush of tears to her eyes. How could she bear to give her up? It was like having a part of herself torn away. She took the child to the Guardians' office and walked away like a woman sleepwalking, returning home to an oddly silent house.

Tilly, sobbing into her handkerchief, asked if Bella wanted her to leave now that there was no reason for her to stay.

'Oh, Tilly, I do hope you won't. I could do with a friend right now. We'll sort all this out, I promise. Somehow we'll start again. I'm not giving up. I shall rise again out of the ashes, just like the phoenix, see if I don't.' Tilly, who knew nothing at all about mythology, blew her nose and trusted in friendship.

Billy Quinn stood at the corner of Liverpool Street and watched Bella striding along. She was a fine figure of a woman, her lovely red-gold hair flying free in the breeze. Pity really that she was so damned stubborn.

He knew where she was going. For all she'd supposedly closed that dratted clinic, she was heading in that direction. He'd used everything he could find against her and what he couldn't find, he'd made up. He'd fired anonymous letters here, there and everywhere, the most productive being to that little weed Dr Lisle, and still she defeated him. She'd no intention of giving up. You had to admire the girl, obstinate as she was. He wouldn't put it past her to reopen that clinic, and to keep it open if it killed her.

And mebbe it would in the end. Mebbe she had it coming to her.

He took some satisfaction from the havoc he had created. She'd lost the children she doted on. He'd scuppered any chance of her being welcomed back into the bosom of her family. Even Dan Howarth had soon lost interest, once he heard the embroidered version of the story which had been fed to him through Len and other useful contacts. All in all, things were going well.

And didn't Bella owe him this revenge? It was surely a fair price for her to pay, for hadn't she stolen Quinn's best girl from him? Hadn't she refused even to consider the very reasonable offer he'd made for her to share his new home and help him go up in the world and climb the ladder of success? Oh, no, Isabella Ashton thought herself too fancy for him. Too hoity-toity by half. She'd toyed with him like a cat plays with a mouse and then dropped him. Well, who was the cat and who the mouse now?

For the moment Quinn was prepared to bide his time, to see how things panned out. Trade was slack what with the slump, jobs being hard to find and money being tight. He was having to squeeze people hard to get even a threepenny bet out of the punters, money he badly needed to pay the mortgage on his new house in Weaste, but he fully expected his affairs to improve. He'd keep an eye on Bella, continue to make his presence felt every now and then, just to let her know that he hadn't forgotten about her. It was a ploy he'd used many times before. Wear a person down over a number of weeks or months and they rolled over sweet as pie, exactly when he wanted them to.

Isabella Ashton would either come to him willingly in the end, or have no life left worth clinging on to. He'd have his revenge in full, so he would.

Arriving at the clinic just moments after Quinn had watched her walk the length of Liverpool Street, Bella finally allowed herself to glance back the way she had come. Was that him, lurking in the shadows? Heart beating fast and hard against her ribs, she sent up a silent prayer that it was no more than her imagination. Would she never fully recover her nerve? It was truly dreadful the effect that man had on her. But she'd no intention of allowing him to ruin her life. She'd beat him yet.

So deciding, Bella gave a deliberately cheery wave to Aunt Edie, gratefully accepting a slab of parkin and heading up the stairs where she knew Dr Syd would be waiting for her. They'd agreed on a counsel of war, determined somehow to find a solution to their problems. Not for one moment could she allow her 'ladies' to be so easily abandoned. Bella felt that if she was to be denied love in her life, from Dan and even from Holly, then she could at least hang on to her precious clinic, no matter what the cost. She would give her life to that, and to the mothers who so desperately needed her help.

Chapter Twenty-seven

Bella began by sitting down with Dr Syd to study the clinic's accounts. Together they examined what it cost for rent, cleaning, gas, nursing staff, stationery, postage and other sundry expenses. After that they considered their projected income. Now that their usual sponsors had withdrawn support, the result was not encouraging. It cost more than £600 a year to run the clinic, not counting their own expenses which, until Bella's recent troubles, had been borne by themselves. If they could not call upon the usual subscriptions and donations, then there seemed little hope the clinic could continue.

Bella was distraught. 'It's so unfair. We're a professional organisation affiliated to the National Society for the Provision of Birth Control Clinics, we can't just give up.'

'Nor can we survive without proper funding,' Dr Syd sadly pointed out, 'and all our sponsors have been scared off by the scandalous reports in the newspapers.'

'Then we must fight back. If people complain because I'm not qualified, we should remind them that Marie Stopes herself has suffered similar criticism just because her doctorate isn't a medical one. As for this nonsense of my carrying Quinn's child, well, it's all lies which deserve to be treated with contempt.' The more she argued her case, the more heated Bella became till she was pacing about the floor in an agitated state, thumping one fist into the other. 'Our achievements here are too important to lose, certainly not as a result of nasty gossip. Where once we used to be the ones asking for help, now other, newer clinics come to us for advice. The women of Salford depend upon us. We must *not* allow this vindictive campaign of gossip and innuendo against *me* to destroy the Mothers' Clinic.'

'Fervent sentiments with which I heartily agree but what can we do?' Dr Syd asked, holding out her elegant hands in despair.

Bella chewed on her lip, paced the floor some more, wrung her hands and finally said, 'We need to prove the cynics wrong. We must convince everyone that the clinic is worth keeping open; that it's not only needed by our patients but means we can put our valuable experience at the disposal of other establishments.'

'But how do we convince them of that?'

'We must get the people who really matter on our side.'

'And they are . . .'

' . . . *Salford City Council!*' The two friends spoke the words together and then grinned at each other in delight.

The very next day Bella called at the Municipal Offices and asked for the clinic to be inspected. They came in droves: doctors, nurses, medical students, social workers, Members of Parliament, and numerous other interested parties. Bella and Dr Syd spent an anxious few weeks while these various observers sat and watched them at work, talked to the women, examined every record card and patient file, studied their statistics of success and failure.

They'd been compelled to find a replacement nurse for Mary Shaw, but she proved her worth a dozen times over in those weeks. Completely unflustered by events, uninterested in scandal, Nurse Hughes simply pressed on, concerned only for her precious patients.

Even the likes of Violet and her merry band of helpers were thoroughly investigated. Not an easy task, as Violet herself admitted, though for once she managed to curb her wicked sense of humour and answer the inspector's questions in a proper fashion.

'And how long have you been working here, Mrs Howarth?'

Too long, Violet thought. Time I retired and put me feet up. 'Since it started,' she answered with a polite smile.

'And it is your task to encourage the patients to express their needs? To talk about their problems?'

You try and stop 'em. 'That's right, sir.'

'And do you ever offer advice?'

Nay, I tells 'em straight what they should do. 'No, sir. I h-advises them to speak to the doctor.'

'Good, good.'

Throughout the period of the inspection, nasty little pieces of gossip continued to appear from time to time in the local press, which often left Bella feeling sick to the pit of her stomach. She could only hope that when this mythical pregnancy of hers did not materialise into a living, breathing child, the gossipmongers would grow bored. In the meantime, people would turn their curious gaze upon her as she passed by and whisper behind their hands. But Bella held her head high and walked tall, determined not to be cast down by anyone.

'I've done nothing to be ashamed of,' she repeated, over and over. 'Let people think what they like.' There were still days when she jumped at the sound of clog irons scraping on the setts behind her, when she would glance sharply down a back entry and imagine she saw movement in the shadows, though fewer and fewer these days. Bella told herself she was far too busy to worry over such as Billy Quinn; that she must put the past firmly behind her.

When all the visits, questions and reports were made and written, they suffered another long wait while their case was considered.

The verdict came at last. Bella took the envelope, handed to her by Mrs Heap, and was forced to sit down in order to gather

her strength. The future of the Mothers' Clinic hung now on the decision of Salford City Council.

'Well, at least their decision will be fair, unlike that of Billy Quinn or the vindictive Dr Lisle.'

Bella unfolded the single sheet of paper which held their fate with some trepidation, feeling everyone's eyes upon her. Quickly, she scanned the contents, her jaw falling slack with shock. Then she began to read out loud.

The Salford City Council, following public opinion as referred to in the attitude of the press and the action of other towns, hes decided that birth-control advice can now be given for 'medical reasons' at the municipal welfare centres. Private clinics are, however, still necessary for cases not covered by the narrow interpretation liable to be placed on the phrase 'medical reasons'. For instance, for economic reasons where the wage earner is unemployed. Such clinics can act as a centre for the instruction of doctors and nurses, where they have not had such teaching in medical school. And thirdly, they may be involved in research.

Below this statement was added a single sentence: '*The Liverpool Street Mothers' Clinic has been passed as a fit and proper place for this purpose.*'

Can you believe it? 'We've won!' Bella cried and, squealing with delight, hugged Dr Syd, Tilly, Violet and all of her 'ladies', even Mrs Blundell.

Following this excellent news, matters quickly escalated. Just as the protesters had once helped them to launch the clinic in the first place, now it seemed almost as if the scandal had lifted it on to a higher plane. Quite the opposite of what had been intended. They'd been checked, inspected and fully approved. Bella had no doubt that the controversy over the rights and wrongs of their work would continue for some years but the future of the Mothers' Clinic was assured. It could continue, in spite of petty sniping. They were now free to concentrate on what they did best: provide good health care for the women of Salford.

Inspired by this approval, Bella sought and found new sponsors. She opened a second clinic in new and better premises, this time fully equipped with surgical couches, screens and everything needed for the staff to do their job. There was even a suggestion that the City Council may well consider offering a grant in a year or two, should everything proceed smoothly. Which meant that, in time, the clinic would be able to pay proper salaries to its medical staff.

Bella's name, and her achievements, became much more widely known as a result of this success and she was often called upon to give talks and lectures, to describe and explain the work they did at the clinic. She put all her heart and soul into this cause, for here was something she could do without qualifications. She seemed to know instinctively how to communicate, how to educate. This was her métier and her strength, and she embraced the task with enthusiasm and renewed energy. She still suffered opposition at public meetings but by now Bella was a seasoned campaigner, willing to take on anyone in this great debate. Her eyes would glow with passion and intensity, her tawny hair crackle with new life as she spoke of her deeply held belief that all women should, by right, have full access to birth control and to ante-natal care. This last was, of course, set to be her next campaign.

The winter of 1932 was bitter and if it was thought that times were hard before, the people of Salford soon discovered that they could get harder yet. Unemployment allowance had been cut and a means test brought in, which was disastrous for those living hand to mouth in and around Liverpool Street. Britain had narrowly avoided bankruptcy by coming off the Gold Standard but the last dregs of optimism and hope finally melted, bringing with it news of several suicides in the homes of the upper classes and yet more thousands of unemployed to add to the two and half million already drawing the dole.

Bella was even invited to speak on the wireless, which she did so well that she was asked to come back. Soon she became a regular, doing a weekly 'Chat to Mothers' in which she was supposed to confine herself to topics of interest to women though she would often stray into discussing politics, gambling, or the iniquities of the means test, which were previously considered not to be women's business at all.

She was fearless, unafraid of overstepping the mark and speaking her mind; talked tough but with a real sense of compassion. Only Bella could get away with such effrontery. The more controversial her comments, the more her listeners loved her. She developed a reputation for courage, intelligence, and for being an ardent feminist, someone prepared to fight for the ordinary woman in the street.

As a result, the people of Salford came to hold a special place for her in their hearts, all thoughts of past scandal long forgotten.

Manchester and Salford, two proud cities where once much of the country's wealth had been created, now faced their most testing time. By early-May of that year, so did Simeon when Josiah Collins shut his mill gates for the last time and the operatives spilled out on to a street where there was nothing waiting for them but a bleak and hungry future.

Even Emily took the news in complete silence.

'You realise what this means, my dear,' Simeon gently explained. 'We shall have to sell the house and, since we must earn a living somehow, I thought we could buy a business.'

She stared at him from wide, frightened eyes. 'Business? What kind of business?'

'A shop. Now I want you to stay quite calm, my dear, because the matter is not only decided, the deal is done. I have found a buyer for the house and purchased an excellent little business on the corner of Liverpool Street.'

The silence which followed this terrible announcement was so awesome those present could almost sense the aspidistra start to tremble. '*A corner shop?*' You would have thought, Edward later told Bella, that he'd informed Mother he'd bought a brothel at the very least.

'You needn't give up your friends, my dear. It's only just down the road.'

'My friends will give *me* up!' Her scream of outrage and anguish was such that it must have been heard at the other end of Seedley Park Road.

'Shall you go into the business with him?' Jinnie asked her husband as they stood in the kitchen helping Mrs Dyson to wrap pots and pans and pack them in boxes, preparatory to moving. Not that the housekeeper was getting much packing done as she spent a good deal of time lamenting the loss of her beloved kitchen and comfortable way of life, every jelly mould bringing forth a fresh outpouring of memories and further tears.

Edward smiled softly at his adored wife, then shook his head. 'No, I feel it's time for us to branch out on our own. I've found us a house to rent not too far away from the Quays. We'll manage.'

'And I still have my job,' she added, smiling confidently back. It sounded little enough on which to embark upon this new phase of married life but at least it gave them the chance to be independent at last, free from Emily's influence. She was not with them this morning, nor helping in any way with the move in fact. On hearing that she was to lose the last of her servants, she had taken to her bed.

Sam had been given his notice and left some weeks ago, now it was the turn of Mrs Dyson. Having nowhere else to go, the housekeeper was to retire to Scarborough and help her sister run a small boarding house. This wasn't what she'd planned for her retirement but she found she had no choice in the matter. Apart from what little she'd managed to save throughout a long lifetime in service, Mrs Dyson had no home of her own to go to, couldn't even remember the last time Mr Ashton had paid her any wages beyond her excellent keep and the comforts of her beloved kitchen, of course. It would all be different in Scarborough with sister Olive in charge.

Emily showed not a shred of sympathy for her faithful servant's plight. She considered their own downward progress into Liverpool Street to be far worse; even Tilly's fate, ending up begging for soup at the workhouse, paled into insignificance beside this ignominy. It was a disaster of calamitous proportions. This was the end. She could see no hint of salvation for them in the future. Any friends who had clung on through the shame of Bella's shockingly immoral behaviour and Edward's scandalous marriage would now desert them entirely. They would become outcasts in their own city.

While his wife lay weeping in bed and his servant and family packed up his home around him, Simeon sat in his study and wrote to inform Bella that, as the only unmarried daughter, she would be expected to move back in with them and look after her mother. She could always help in the shop as well, now that she was unemployed, and stop wasting her time on lost causes.

Bella read the letter in a state of shock. 'He only ever contacts me when *he* wants something,' she raged. 'Never when *I* ask for *his* support. Maybe that's how it's always been, all I ever was to him: a by-product of his life to show what a fine man he is; to parade before his guests and business acquaintances as his ladylike daughter to be admired and petted, or else to perform some menial task and be made use of in a practical way.' She was incensed by the suggestion. 'How dare he order my return to do his bidding? Why can't he admit for once that I'm right, that I'm a success? I'm my own person with a life of my own to lead. So have Edward and Jinnie. Thank goodness they're leaving at last. It's time they too got on with their own lives.'

After which display of temper, she burst into tears.

✳   ✳   ✳

Edward and Jinnie settled quite comfortably in their modest two up and two down on Cross Lane. The house was clean and sound, comfortably furnished with items from Seedley Park Road and, best of all, completely private. If they wanted to make love on the rug before the fire, they could. They could eat whenever they felt like it, without having to sit in formal splendour at Emily's mahogany table being careful not to spill wine on her pristine white damask tablecloth. On Sundays they could get up when they pleased instead of having to be down to eat breakfast *en famille*, though they did miss Mrs Dyson's crisp bacon and devilled kidneys. Or they could stay in bed all morning, if they preferred.

Not that there was much time to linger there the rest of the week. They both of them worked hard to keep their jobs, ill paid though they might be.

'Things can only improve. We can climb the ladder again, all the way to the top,' Edward would constantly remark and Jinnie would adoringly agree. If in his terms they were now poor, in Jinnie's they were rich. In that respect they would always see the world through different eyes.

From Cross Lane it was but a short walk to the Quays each morning where he would stand in line with Dan and the rest of the men, hoping to be taken on for a day's labour on the docks. Dan was always more fortunate in this respect than himself but he was gaining a name for reliability. Edward didn't intend to spend the rest of his life as a dock labourer. Once this slump was over, he had plans. He was saving every penny and one day meant to have a business of his own. Then Jinnie could give up her job as a cleaner and help him to run it. But he certainly had no intention of getting involved with his father's plans.

The important thing was that he and his wife were happy, deliciously content together. Not for a moment had he ever regretted marrying her, for all he realised now that there would be no children. What did that matter when he had Jinnie, his lovely sweet wife? Each evening as they sat cosily together before the shining black kitchen range where a bright fire burned, she would happily plan the painting and refurbishment of their front parlour, reminding him that it was the first time in her entire life that she'd ever possessed such a room.

'And I've no intention of putting up a green paper blind to block out the sunshine. I shall buy some pretty cotton off the market and make curtains. Do you think we should paint the walls cream, Edward, or can we afford to paper them?'

'Whatever you wish, my love.'

Simeon and Emily, on the other hand, were finding life in Liverpool Street very different from Seedley Park Road. They were not managing quite so well. For one thing, Emily had to rise early each morning and sweep the shop and pavement outside before opening sharp at eight. This had come as a great shock since she had expected Simeon to do all of these menial tasks. But it was a part of his job to visit the markets and buy in fresh fruit and vegetables for them to sell, and since Bella remained stubborn, who else could open the shop except Emily?

'It's teamwork,' Simeon would say, bringing her a cup of tea each morning before he left at six, to encourage her out of bed. 'I depend upon you utterly, my dear, as you depend upon me. Fear not, we shall prevail.'

So Emily would stand behind the counter in her twin-set and pearls and sniff disapprovingly at anybody who dared to touch her apples with no intention of buying. 'They aren't put there to be pawed about,' she'd crisply remark and too often the poor miscreant would hastily depart without buying anything.

Simeon painstakingly explained to her on numerous occasions how the customer was always right but Emily couldn't quite seem to grasp this maxim. Customers, in her opinion, were but an evil to be endured.

Edward and Jinnie were expected for tea every alternate Sunday. Never to lunch. Emily did not cook lunch. It was, she explained, quite beyond her. 'Some things,' Simeon would regretfully explain to Edward, 'never change.' During the week, he would get by on pies or black puddings while Emily picked at the odd piece of haddock which he kindly poached for her. Sometimes Jinnie would call in with a dish of hotpot or liver and onions for them. These were treats that they both looked forward to and enjoyed. On Sundays they always took lunch at the Midland Hotel. They certainly couldn't afford to but Simeon felt it was the least he could do for his long-suffering wife.

At tea time, the four of them would sit around the table eating tinned salmon and bread and butter with whatever fresh salad was left over from the week's trading, followed by tinned peaches and cake. Jinnie would always bring a cake she had baked 'specially, knowing that Emily didn't bake either. There was never a great deal to eat, not that this mattered as the atmosphere was so oppressive, Jinnie's appetite on these occasions was always small. Her mother-in-law, surprisingly enough, was not ungrateful for her efforts.

'What a blessing she is,' Emily would murmur as Jinnie sliced the cake and handed her a sizeable piece. Emily was exceedingly fond of cake. She seemed long since to have forgotten her initial objections to this girl, a one-time street urchin. But then not only had Jinnie made her beloved son happy, she'd also proved to be an excellent daughter-in-law.

Isabella, once their only daughter and Simeon's favourite child, was never mentioned.

Chapter Twenty-eight

Dan judged the moment to make his approach with care. He'd spent a miserable winter deeply regretting the critical attitude he'd so foolishly adopted yet unable to abandon his pride sufficiently to heal the breach between them. With the coming of spring and the prospect of this bleak life without Bella continuing throughout summer and beyond, he made up his mind that the time had come.

He chose one evening in late-June and waited, as he often used to do, in the cook shop for Bella to emerge from the rooms above. For all she now had a much larger, grander clinic, he knew she still spent a great deal of time up there working with Dr Syd, presumably seeing some of her local ladies or making plans for further fund raising. He lingered for an hour or more chatting to Mrs Heap and the women who came and went buying pies, a currant tea cake or half a loaf, eyeing him up and down with critical amusement.

'Tha favvors tha's been dug up,' Mrs Blundell said, commenting that he looked pale as death. Supporting her bosom on her folded arms from which a large basket dangled, she winked at Mrs Heap and concluded, 'It's surprising what tha sees when t'weather turns nasty.'

Mrs Heap rolled her eyes ceilingwards and drily remarked, 'He's after a bite of th'apple,' which brought a crimson rush of colour to his cheeks, much to the ladies' delight.

Bella emerged down the stairs at a run, as always, dashing

out into the street and striding away before Dan had realised she'd even appeared.

'Na then, lad, shape thissen, tha'll niver get thee feet under table if thee stands theer like a wooden clothes horse.'

Dan was off like a shot, racing out of the door and at once skidding to a halt to check in which direction Bella had gone. He caught a fleeting glimpse of the hem of her coat as she turned a corner and vanished from view. Off at the gallop again, he finally caught up with her, out of breath and startling her by his abrupt and sudden appearance at her elbow.

'Bella, I thought it was you. What a bit of luck.' He was glad now that she hadn't spotted him hanging around in the shop. Much better that their meeting appeared accidental.

She was staring up at him, eyebrows raised as if asking a question, yet she said nothing. Not even hello.

Dan filled the silence by clearing his throat. 'Sorry to make you jump but I'm glad I ran into you.'

'You're not still following me, are you?' She half glanced back over her shoulder, seeming suddenly nervous. 'I thought somebody was but ... Never mind. What did you want?'

'I was hoping for a word.'

'Oh?'

So she wasn't going to be very helpful then. She was carrying a large carpet bag that seemed stuffed with papers and books but when he offered to carry it for her, she shook her head. He gathered his courage and ploughed on. 'Could I happen buy you a drink? In the Ship. We used to enjoy going in there.'

'We used to enjoy a good many things.' She turned from him and began to walk away. Startled, he remained where he was for a full half second before rushing to catch up with her, measuring his pace to hers.

All those months of agonising over whether he should take up with her again, endlessly asking his mother for advice and being irritated when she refused to give it. He'd watched events at Seedley Park Road, seen her family fall on hard times and face life in 'ordinary street'. He'd noted how Bella had struggled to piece her life back together, even read the further nasty pieces which had appeared from time to time in the local paper until it finally became clear that Bella Ashton was not pregnant with Quinn's or anyone else's child. After a while, the paper had grown bored with its campaign and someone else was put in the firing line to be gossiped over. He'd felt some shame then over his jealousy, though Dan told himself that he'd believed less than half of it, and never once stopped loving her.

And you had to hand it to her, not for a minute had she given up.

Then, seemingly overnight, she'd turned a corner and changed herself into an icon, a popular public figure who couldn't put a foot wrong. It no longer seemed to matter that some might try to bring her down. The Liverpool Street Mothers' Clinic had been given the stamp of approval and folk of consequence were falling over themselves to donate to it. He'd felt pleased for her, proud he'd once been able to call himself a friend. Wished he still was.

Now he felt nervous about making this first approach. Dan worried that he'd maybe left it too late. 'Happen we could again. Enjoy many things. I mean ...' He stopped, kicking himself for sounding so gormless but all common sense, along with the carefully rehearsed phrases, had deserted him now that he was actually with her.

'I know what you mean. At least, I think I do, and the answer's no.'

'I beg your pardon?'

'You think because the babies are all gone to new homes and I am, once again, unfettered by the responsibilities of children, we can pick up where we left off. Well, it's not quite so simple, Dan.'

'I didn't expect it to be simple.' He could feel his confidence seeping away.

'Good.'

She hitched the bag higher up her arm but not for a second did she slow her pace. He'd forgotten how quickly she walked, bobbed hair flying wildly in the cool breeze, crocheted hat screwed up tight in one fist. Perhaps an indication of her feelings? Glancing sideways he studied the smooth line of her cheek, flushed with exertion or emotion, he wasn't sure which; the tilt of her firm chin, as forceful as ever but adding to rather than detracting from her beauty. How he loved her! Dear God, why had he ever listened to those so-called mates of his? Why hadn't he taken her word rather than theirs? Why hadn't he believed in her, stood by her, been the friend she needed? No wonder she'd have nowt to do with him now. He'd let her down good and proper.

'I was hoping time would have healed matters between us, that we might at least behave like friends. Mebbe more than friends. One day. When you'd forgiven me like.'

She stopped then to consider him, the expression on her lovely face giving him no clue to the feelings within, but hope was strong in him, refusing to burn out completely. 'And what about Quinn?'

'What about him?'

'You're not still jealous of him then?'

'You said it was all over.'

'And you believe me now, do you? Don't you still want to know what we got up to when we were together? What I let him do? Or do you imagine that I might give you a taste of it too, now that I'm a woman with a reputation? Is that the way of it?'

'The only reputation you have is for doing good. You're a woman of influence now, Bella. One who can make things happen; make people sit up and tek notice. Nay, luv, you know that I'd never think bad of you. Never.'

'Do I? I'm not sure that I know you at all, Dan Howarth, or even want to.' So saying she strode away, leaving him standing alone in the middle of the road, and this time he knew better than to hurry after her.

✻   ✻   ✻

Violet strove to keep her opinions on the differences between her son and her young friend to herself, for all it went against the grain to do so. She appreciated that, if anything, the gulf between them had widened in recent months but it broke her heart to see Dan sitting around the house night after night, mooching about the place, looking as miserable as a wet washing day. When he wasn't doing that, he was fretting and sulking, or sitting with his head in his hands as if he carried the weight of the whole world on his great shoulders.

'I seen it comin', this. Warrer you gonna do about it?'

'Leave it be, Mother. I don't know, do I?'

'Eeh, tha's as daft as a tackler. Anyone would think tha's had thi brains tekken out. Thee has to do summat. It won't fettle itself.'

'How can I fettle it? How can I ever make it right again? She won't have anything to do with me. I've blown me chances and that's that.'

Cyril said, 'Leave well alone, Mother. Nowt to do wi' us.'

Violet buttoned her lip and said no more. Men! Where was the point in argufying with the daft hap'orth? She'd sat back all through a long cold winter and into spring, waiting to see how events shaped up, yet still there was no sign of improvement on either side. Violet came at last to the conclusion that her intervention was called for. If the pair couldn't see what was plain as a pikestaff to everyone else, that they were meant for each other, then they'd have to be told straight. And who better than the lad's own mother for the job? She wrapped her shawl about her head and went to call on Bella, to tell her, in the kind of blunt language for which Violet was famous, that if she didn't think on, she'd lose all chance of snapping up Dan.

'And he's a gradely lad, no doubt about it. Thee has to tek a leap in t'dark one day, lass. Give lad a chance, at least. He's chucked his cap in, what more con he do?'

Bella had the grace to smile, albeit sheepishly. 'I don't know,

Violet. I really would like us to be friends again but I'm not sure. He let me down, do you see? He believed all those nasty stories about me. Wouldn't even consider keeping little Holly so I lost her too. I'm not sure it would be wise for us to – to try to get back to the way we were.'

Violet shook her head in doleful despair, her chubby jowls vibrating in sympathy. 'Nay, that sounds bad, I will admit.' And then, brightening, added, 'But he's been up to his oxters in childer all his life. Thee can't blame t'lad fer wanting a rest, now can ya?'

'No, I do see that. I do really but ...'

'And your behaviour weren't exactly the soul of discretion, were it? Bothering wi' that piece of muck. Tha needs thee head lookin' at.'

Bella sighed. 'We both made mistakes, I do agree, but ...'

'Don't you miss Dan? Thee was allus laughin' over summat, pair on you. Happy as sandboys, you were. Not that it's any of my business,' she added, as if she hadn't made it such.

'Yes, of course I miss him. How could I not? He's in my mind day and night. It's as if I've lost a part of myself. Oh, I'll think about it, I will really, but I'm not making any promises so don't grin at me like that. Violet, don't you dare give him any hope. I need time to think.'

'Me lips is sealed.' Her bright little eyes, however, sunk within their layers of flesh, were shining with new hope.

Dan stood on the canal towpath facing his enemy. Recalling all too clearly Bella's startled reaction to his approach, the way she'd constantly glanced back over her shoulder throughout their brief conversation, he felt he could at least make sure she was safe. Even if she no longer loved him, never wanted to speak to him again, he could at least do this much for her.

He told Quinn, in no uncertain terms, to stay out of Bella's life. 'Don't you see what you've done? You've damaged her. She used to be full of confidence and happiness, a lovely, laughing girl with a free spirit. Now, despite her having come up in the world, which is more'n you'll ever do, Quinn, she's still nervous, allus looking over her shoulder as if expecting to find your ugly face not far behind. I thought I'd made it clear, when I beat you fair and square in that fight, that you were to leave her well alone. Were you wanting another pasting, happen?'

Quinn gave a wolfish grin. 'It might prove interesting.'

'Don't push yer luck, Quinn. I'll have your head on a platter if you so much as touch her.' Reaching forward with both hands, Dan grasped him by the collar and almost lifted him off his feet. 'Yer frightening her – lay off. Or I'll teach you the real meaning of fear. And just in case that message still hasn't got through, let's wash yer ears out.' After dangling him for a few precarious seconds by his lapels, Dan casually dropped him into the canal. Quinn sank in the filthy brown water, came spluttering back to the surface to find a sea of faces on the canal bank all laughing down at him, their mouths agape with the pleasure of witnessing the Irishman get a taste of his own medicine.

By the time he'd climbed out to stand dripping on the path, Dan had gone.

'Len! Where the bloody 'ell are you when yer needed?' Len came hurrying over, looking anxious. 'Look at me. Why didn't you stop him, ye great eejit? Don't stand there gawping – get me some bleedin' clothes. You and me has to talk.'

Dusk was falling as Bella walked home later that same afternoon. Still too early for the lamplighter, the streets were surprisingly quiet as people gathered indoors eating their supper or preparing for the night shift. She hurried on her way, as always these days, her gaze darting to right and left, constantly checking that she wasn't being followed. The moment she heard the scrape of clog irons on the setts behind her, she half swung about to see who it was. Perhaps Dan, coming to make yet another apology.

She never got the chance to see before everything went black. Someone had thrown a sack over her head. Arms were holding her tight, lifting her off her feet, and the next instant she was being slung over someone's shoulder. Then she was being carried away, her abductor running at a fair lick over the cobbles. Though she kicked, screamed and shouted as hard as she could, she held out little hope that anyone would hear her.

Emily gazed at Violet as if she'd dropped in from another planet. 'Abducted? What on earth are you talking about? Have you women nothing better to do than to spread tittle-tattle about my daughter? Who is it she's supposedly run off with this time?'

Violet stood stolidly in the centre of the small shop which was as yet only dimly lit as dawn peeped in through the shutters. She folded her arms and planted her legs firmly. Only a tank could have shifted her and stopped her from speaking her mind. 'Tha were ready enough to believe the gossip last time, when it weren't true, so why not now when it is? Bella's gone. Vanished. Disappeared off the face of the earth. She didn't land home last night. Tilly's been going frantic. Then this morning she should've met Dr Syd at the new clinic and hasn't turned up for that neither. We've looked everywhere and don't know where to look next. I'd call in the police, 'ceptin' they'd be no use. She's a grown woman and con do owt she likes in their opinion, include vanish for no reason.'

'Perhaps she's with this – this man she took up with.' Emily spoke as if there were a nasty smell under her nose.

'No, we've been to Quinn's house on Bromley Street. He in't there. Hasn't been seen for months, or so his neighbours say. Though theer's talk he's happen tekken another house, some place else. We're trying to find out if anyone knows where that might be. I wondered if you'd heard owt?'

'Why should I know anything? I'm only her mother.'

Violet ignored the caustic remark and, looking about the dark little shop, asked if Mr Ashton was at home. On being told he was at the market going about his business, she gave up and left. It seemed nobody cared one way or the other what had happened to Bella, except her friends. And Dan. He was out of his mind with worry.

Bella's 'ladies' all gathered together in the rooms over Aunt Edie's shop to chew the matter over. They all knew, in their hearts, that Bella wouldn't simply disappear. Not for a moment would she consider running off or going anywhere without telling one of them where. Wilful and headstrong she may be but never reckless, never stupid. They also knew that ever since the attack by Quinn, she'd lost some of her usual confidence and took even greater care. It was obvious to all who was the most likely culprit, particularly once Dan had confessed to his latest encounter with him. The question was how best to deal with the matter.

Dan said, 'I've checked out all Quinn's usual haunts. He's not at any of them. He must be somewhere we haven't thought of.'

'He'll be keeping his head down, lying low for a bit,' Violet agreed.

'But *why* would he take her? What has she ever done to him? I thought he was keen on her, even fond of her in his way.'

'Obsessed more like. 'Oo knows how that rat's mind works, but she did throw him over. Happen he objects to that, or to you giving him a ducking.'

'He deserved it. I was telling him to lay off.'

'Aye, well, you didn't succeed. Tha's only made matters worse.' His mother wagged one finger in his face.

Mrs Solomon politely intervened in the family row. 'It's

pointless to speculate. What matters is how we deal with it. We have to find the poor lass before it's too late.'

'Too late?' Dan's face went chalk white.

'Aye. Too late,' Mrs Stobbs solemnly repeated. 'Remember what happened to Sadie, and there's some as say he were behind Harold's disappearance.'

'I'd like to see his bits and pieces fried on toast.' This from Mrs Blundell, who else?

'Mrs Solomon is right. Stop argufying and put yer brains to steep.' Violet propped her rolls of fat against the edge of the table, making it creak in agony while she chewed on her lip, deep in her thoughts. Almost at once she began to speak them out loud. 'He must have her hidden somewhere, mebbe in some secret place he doesn't use very often, or a place he used to call his own. A cellar or pub perhaps, or else a room somewhere. The question is where, and who would know?'

Dan said, 'Jinnie! Of course. Why the hell didn't I think of her before!' He was off like a shot, flying out of the door and halfway down the stairs before his mother's shouted words gave him pause.

'When you finds her, lad, come back here and tell us what she has to say. Any plans have to be made careful like, or the bugger'll win.'

Chapter Twenty-nine

The cellar was cold and damp. It smelled of dogs and fear. That fear, Bella realised, was her own. She couldn't see anything because of the blindfold but she could hear the animals whimpering outside the cupboard into which she'd been locked and felt a kinship with them. They were being kept in this hell hole to do their master's bidding, as was she. No, she wasn't quite like them. She had a will of her own and would make certain that she exercised it. What Quinn's plans were for her she daren't even think, but she'd make damn' sure that he never carried them out.

First he'd locked her in a room overnight which hadn't been too bad for all there'd been little air and the stink of drains, the windows being boarded up. It was no wonder that she'd barely slept a wink. Len had even brought her breakfast though of course she'd declined to eat it. All Bella could feel was a strong sense of outrage. She had asked Len why she'd been taken, what Quinn was intending to do with her.

'He's tried blackmail and ruining my reputation. If he hopes to get money from my family for my release, he'll be disappointed. Even if my father had any left, which he hasn't, he wouldn't pay a penny to get me back. Quinn has seen to that too. So what does he hope to achieve?'

'Nay, lass. It's safer not to ask. Eat up. It might be your last chance today.'

But she'd stubbornly ignored the plate of bacon sandwiches, despite their tantalising smell. Len hadn't returned until late afternoon and then only to put the sack back over her head and bring her here. All he'd said when she'd asked him where he was taking her was that there'd been a change of plan. Now she felt so sick and weak, with fear as much as hunger, that Bella wondered if she'd been wise to refuse the food. She would need all her strength to survive this ordeal.

She had been aware at one point that Quinn was present; had smelled that unmistakable combination of Player's Weights and Irish whiskey, though he hadn't touched her. Not yet. Perhaps she could persuade him, even now, to let her go.

Bella concentrated on breathing slowly and calmly, which wasn't easy through the filthy gag bound tightly between her teeth. Only a deep resolve to survive made her steel herself against whatever she might have to face. She could hear her heart pounding in her ears, sounding as if it came from somewhere other than her own body. But then everything felt unreal, as if this were happening to someone else and not to her at all.

She could hear a sound growing louder. The clatter of clogs and rumble of deep voices. Men, coming into the cellar, laughing and talking. Dear Lord, Quinn was holding a dog fight now, this evening, while she was hidden away in this damned cupboard. She could hear Len calling the odds, encouraging them to lay their bets. How long did Quinn mean to keep her here? Would she be able to alert anyone? Bella began to kick against the door. The noise beyond rumbled on, louder than ever. She kicked harder, praying someone would hear. Though how could they possibly through the din they were making? They were cheering now as the dogs fought. She could hear the barking, snapping and snarling, the terrible screaming yelps of one hapless victim. Her stomach lurched and it took every ounce of will-power not to vomit. As the noise dropped between fights, Bella kicked the door with her heel again, using all her strength.

Suddenly the door opened and a hand grasped her neck, making her squeal in surprise. 'Shut it, if'n ye know what's good for ye. Jest ye stay there nice and quiet, m'lovely, till I'm ready to deal with ye.'

Darkness closed in again and despair settled upon her heart. How long did he intend to keep her prisoner? How would he deal with her? She didn't care to consider.

Jinnie told them about the room off Liverpool Street, the one where Sadie had done her worst, but by the time Dan got there, it was empty and clearly had been for some time with the windows all boarded up. He tried Bromley Street again and even, once more as a result of Jinnie's enquiries among the women who used to work in the mill, discovered Quinn's new house in Weaste. So far as he could tell from a swift recce, that too appeared empty.

Nor were Bella's 'ladies' idle. Violet scoured the canal bank. Mrs Stobbs toured the public houses, chivvying her husband to act as escort and offer a bit of support along the way by asking questions here and there. Mrs Heap, for the first time ever, closed her little cook shop and she and Mrs Solomon visited everyone they could think of who'd had some contact with Quinn in the past. Mrs Blundell, being the only one amongst them who had the courage, tackled the street gangs and bands of youths who prowled the neighbourhood.

They all drew a blank.

Back at the rooms over the cook shop Dan said, 'The problem is there are so many possibilities. We need to persuade Quinn to come to us, instead of us looking for Quinn.'

Violet snorted. 'How? He in't stupid. He'll guess what we're up to.'

'He'd come fast enough if there were money to be made,' Jinnie said, and they all looked at her in surprise.

'Of course, that's it. That's the answer. He needs to get wind that there's a game on, at which he can make a bob or two. Jinnie's right, he'd come fast enough then.'

Mrs Blundell volunteered her husband to act as decoy. It was far easier to swindle a bookie if he trusted you and Quinn would have no reason to be suspicious of Fred Blundell, who was known for his partiality to a hand of poker and a jar or two. Word was sent through a network of contacts which finally reached Len, and a time was fixed for later that day.

The game was to be held, like many previous, in the back entry near Collins Mill, a favourite haunt of card schools. Their hope was that, unable to resist the lure of a profit, Quinn would come along.

'Though I'm still not sure how luring him to a card game will help us find our Bella,' Violet protested as the final details were put into place.

Dan said, 'Let's get our hands on the bastard first. We'll drag, squeeze or beat the information out of him if necessary.' And since no one had any better ideas, this was agreed upon.

Simeon, stubborn as ever, absolutely refused Edward's request that he join the valiant group of friends gathering together to find his elder child. He calmly faced his outraged son and told him that he had no daughter, or none that he recognised.

'Sometimes, Father, you're a damned fool. What is it that Bella has done which is so terrible? Opened a clinic to help women less fortunate than herself, that's all. She's battled against bigoted husbands, the tittle-tattle of the press, the Church, the medical profession, worked every hour God sends, and yet you've done nothing to help. Now her work has finally been recognised as a success by all except you, her own father. All right, so she made one mistake. She got herself involved with a ne'er-do-well like Billy Quinn. You should ask yourself if that isn't your fault too. Yours and Mother's.'

Emily, keeping well behind the counter as if for protection against this uncharacteristic display of anger from her normally gentle boy, gave a little gasp of outrage. 'We did everything we could for that child. Gave her every advantage.'

Edward rounded on her. 'No, you didn't. You gave her what *you* wanted. Bella wanted an education, which you denied her. She wanted to be a nurse. You objected to that too. Unlike Father, you viewed the clinic as a temporary rebellion, a phase you assumed would quickly pass, then she'd come scurrying home and continue to wait upon you, hand, foot and finger, as you have Jinnie doing now.'

Emily let out a terrible wail and, clutching her handkerchief to her wide-open mouth, fled to the sanctuary of her sitting room.

'Nay, lad, that were a bit close to the knuckle.'

'I'm sorry, Father, but you've driven me to it. If Bella had been blessed with a loving home, parents who cared about her and listened to her troubles, maybe she wouldn't have gone seeking love and attention in the wrong places.'

'That's a damned insult and you know it!'

'Did you leave the door open, or offer any opportunity for her to come home?' Recognising the shame in his father's face Edward nodded. 'I thought not. Did you offer your forgiveness or loving support? No, you damned well didn't. You sat back and left her to stew in her own juice. Well, Bella's a modern woman with her own way of going about things. At least she has the guts to do what she wants with her life while I've always gone along with whatever you've arranged for me, for all I've often hated it.'

'I never made you do anything that wasn't for your own good,' Simeon protested, but Edward had his dander up now. It was long past time he stood up to his father and he did so, at long last.

'You sent me to an awful school where I spent many miserable, unhappy years. You didn't care that I wanted to work with my hands, to be a carpenter, so to please you I tried to learn Greek and Latin and Mathematics, loathing every minute of it. I wanted to *be* somebody you might be proud of. *You* decided that I should work in the mill office, not me. You might give the outward impression that you're soft and accommodating, gently nurturing your womenfolk, but that only applies when everyone is playing by your rules. Otherwise you ignore and reject them, as you rejected me. As you have now rejected Bella, when all she ever wanted was to live a useful and productive life. One you were hell-bent on denying her.'

Simeon's face was near purple with rage as he listened to these uncomfortable home truths. 'I only wanted to protect her from the worst of life. A woman shouldn't have to toil and labour every God-given day. She should have a good husband to mind her.'

Edward half turned away in disgust. 'Oh, for pity's sake, Father, listen to yourself. You might call your behaviour protective – I call it sanctimonious, self-opinionated and old-fashioned. That what your problem is, Father. Along with your damned pig-headedness.' Whereupon Edward stormed out, slamming the door behind him so hard that he heard the shop window rattle. For a terrible moment he thought it might break.

The session began with a harmless game of pitch and toss, the stakes fairly low. After that they moved on to Black Jack and finally to poker. They sat in a close huddle, half a dozen men in shabby jackets and patched trousers, the only sounds that of their heavy breathing, the snap of the cards on stone and the wind howling through the broken walls around them. Tension held them silent.

They weren't the only ones with nerves stretched to breaking point. From where Dan and his stalwarts watched through the cracks in a back yard gate, the group might have been entirely invisible in the shadows save for the glowing tip of a cigarette and the stink of beer growing stronger by the minute as jug after jug was refilled at the nearby tap room and duly consumed.

You had to hand it to him, Dan thought, Quinn was slick. If he was manipulating the cards in any way, there was no sign of it. And in contrast to the rest of the men who comprised the card school, he seemed completely relaxed, without any fear of discovery since he had his usual runners stationed about, keeping a weather eye open for the rozzers.

In no time at all Fred Blundell had grown loud and boisterous in his drink. No one was surprised. He was, after all, well known for it. His wife, for one, could give testament to that, He'd lost, as usual, though not heavily. Without any sign of rancour he leaned heavily against Quinn and began to sing, 'When Irish Eyes are Smiling'.

Quinn shrugged him off and told him to place his stakes and hold his noise.

Whispering under his breath to Edward crouched beside him, Dan said, 'Can you see her? Did he bring Bella with him?'

'No chance.'

'Fred looks like he's getting restless. I hope his nerve holds. We mustn't make a move until Jinnie gives us the signal.'

Edward was fidgeting from one foot to another. 'Let's go *now*, Dan. I've had enough of this. He could just up and leave at any minute. Every second that ticks by, Bella is in more danger.'

'Do you think I don't know that?' Dan's frustration was making him irritable. The whole sorry plan now seemed useless, pointless in the extreme. Of course Quinn wouldn't have brought Bella with him. They were still no nearer to knowing where she was being kept. He thought he might very well explode if he wasn't able to take action soon.

Bella's 'ladies' were already taking theirs. Moving softly on clogs wrapped in flannel to deaden the sound, the shawl-shrouded figures crept through the darkness like ghosts. It would be their task to deal with Quinn's boys and give them the fright of their miserable lives. When each of them had a runner in their sights, a soft cough echoed down the back street and finally Dan saw it, the flicker of light at a bedroom window which was Jinnie's signal.

'They're in place. Let's go.'

Their timing was superb. As Dan and Edward burst open the back yard gate, Fred Blundell wrapped his octopus arms about Quinn's shoulders and gave him a hefty drunken smacker on the cheek. Quinn's roar of protest was cut off in mid-voice as Dan added his weight to Fred's and Edward flattened Len. Both men were pinned to the ground, their faces in the dirt. Seconds later, Quinn was back on his feet and utter mayhem broke out with fists and clogs flying everywhere while the rest of the punters at the card school took the opportunity to scarper. Dan felt the rough cloth of a familiar collar and held on to it like grim death.

At the very same moment, unfortunate runners secreted in shadowed corners of the back entry were to discover that whatever they might fear from the police was as nothing in comparison with the treatment they might expect at the hands of their womenfolk. Rolling pins and rolled up stockings were wielded with reckless abandon and, in no time at all, the cobbles were ringing with the sound of running feet.

'That's got rid of them buggers, for now at least,' Violet said with some satisfaction. 'Now let's see what that nasty piece of goods has to say for hissen.'

Quinn had very little to say. Nothing at all in fact, because when order was finally restored Dan discovered that it was Len he was holding on to and not Quinn at all. Billy Quinn had given them the slip, as always.

'Slippy as a bloody eel,' was the general consensus. Always was, always will be. 'No one should expect to catch the bookmaker,' Len drily remarked, though he was soon persuaded to change his tune. In fact, after Dan and Edward had enjoyed a little 'chat' with him, he proved almost eager to talk.

✻   ✻   ✻

The sound came first. The familiar scrape of metal toe caps on the stone floor of the cellar, the familiar tread of booted feet. Heart in mouth, Bella listened. She heard the turn of a key in the lock, then she was being dragged out and flung on to the wet floor.

The sack was pulled from her head, the gag and blindfold removed. How many hours she had lain in that cupboard Bella couldn't tell but the dogs had gone from the cellar, along with the noisy spectators. She and Quinn were quite alone.

Bella got unsteadily to her feet and stood before him, legs shaking with the unaccustomed effort but her chin held high. She meant to let him see that she would not be cowed by him. 'You can't keep me a prisoner for ever. You'll have to let me go some time.'

'When I'm good and ready. When I say you can go and not before.' His voice was little more than a snarl. He sounded like a mad dog himself, one who'd been cornered and was indeed fighting for his life. Had he come to take his fill of her as he'd threatened? To enjoy his rights, as he termed them? Or would he relent, now that he'd scared the living daylights out of her, and release her?

'You're going to come with me and do exactly as I tell ye. Didn't I explain to ye long since how I'm in need of someone to help me improve me life? You and me, Bella, is meant for each other. Sure, and won't ye be thankful for this day in a year or two's time when yer living in the finest house on the Polygon and with the wealthiest bookmaker in the business?'

'Over my dead body.'

'Tch! There you are, saying those dratted words again. All right, if that's the way ye want it, that's the way ye can have it.'

It happened before she had time to draw breath. One minute he was smiling down into her eyes, the next he had smacked her across the head, sending her sprawling on her stomach across the floor. Blood spurted from her nose and Bella was sure it must be broken. Her head spun but her brain was working fast, faster than ever before. From the corner of her eye she spotted a thick spar of wood. She snatched it up, and as he lunged for her a second time Bella turned on to her back and struck out. It caught him full in the face, bringing with it a look of complete surprise as he dropped to his knees and then fell flat on the ground.

The next instant the cellar door burst open and a whole crowd of shouting people flowed in, a sea of faces that washed towards her like a great tide, but Bella saw only one face, only one pair of outstretched arms. 'Pa,' she cried and half fell as he gathered her close.

'I'm glad that Simeon thought better of his decision not to help, and that you are reconciled. But what about us?'

Bella looked into Dan's face and thought how very much she loved him. She regretted the differences that had torn them apart and welcomed, with all her heart, the fact that he was again a part of her life. But was she yet ready to contemplate a future for them both?

It was the following morning and they were sitting on their favourite park bench, close together this time. Somewhere she could even hear a lark singing.

'I'm glad about Pa too. Sometimes he's far too stubborn for his own good. You're very much the same, Dan Haworth, in that respect.' She smiled teasingly at him to soften her words, laughing still more when she saw his blush. 'We had a long talk last night when he took me back home to his new business premises. Mother made me a sandwich, would you believe, and a cup of tea. Unprecedented.' Bella chuckled at the memory of her mother struggling with the bread knife and her own silent plea to her father to leave her to it. Given time, who knows, Emily might even take up housewifery. 'Pa was full of apologies for his behaviour towards me this last year or so, which of course I generously accepted.'

'You haven't offered to give everything up and go and help in his shop, have you?'

'As if I would!' Bella pulled off her crocheted hat to run her fingers through her hair as she laughed out loud. 'Not unless I had a death wish, for there would certainly be blue murder done if Mother and I were ever to share a house again. Actually, I was hugely impressed that Pa didn't even ask me to. Very noble of him. He swears he is more than ready to accept that I'm now a grown woman with a mind and a life of my own. He's making progress, eh?'

Bella wondered if the same could be said of Dan. As if reading her mind he said, 'I've learned a few lessons too. I understand now that material differences aren't important, it's how two people are inside that counts. And I do realise that I should've trusted you and not listened to the gossipmongers. As for them childer, well, I'm sorry about that but perhaps I just felt it was all happening a bit too fast.'

'As if you were being landed with somebody else's cast-offs? They were babies, Dan, in need of love and care.'

'I know. I needed a bit of time to adjust, that's all.' He gazed at her, his expression soulful though the soft grey-blue eyes held just a glimmer of hope. 'I do love you, Bella. Can we start again? It's not too late for us, is it?'

For a long moment, endlessly long in Dan's mind, she sat in silent contemplation. He could hear the wind sighing through the branches above their heads, a hauntingly lonely sound. Then, clasping her hands in her lap, she began to talk. 'You are aware of what I've been doing all these months, all through this long, hard winter?'

'I am, lass. How could I help it? And I want you to know that I'm proud of you. Real proud.'

'What I've achieved so far is only the beginning. I want to work in ante-natal care as well as with birth-control. If we give women the care and education that they deserve to look after themselves properly, to enable them to have just the right number of children, then that's the best way to ensure a safe future for all tomorrow's generation. That's what I want to do. What I mean to do.'

'I understand that ...'

'No, don't interrupt. Hear me out. Many more women are volunteering for this sort of work, all wanting to do their bit. In order to justify their faith in me, and to achieve my aims, I need to improve my own credentials. I can't lecture to others unless I have studied too. I need to talk to doctors and university students, nurses and others who work with the poor. The message has to reach those who count, who actually treat women on a regular basis. Dr Syd has been coaching me, whenever she can spare a moment from the clinic and her family. I mean to take a degree at the University. Perhaps in Social Economics.'

Dan took a slow breath. 'I see. And what about us?' It was a repetition of the same question. This time, casting him a shy, sideways glance, Bella answered it.

'I was hoping, though I know it's a lot to ask, that you might wait for me. There's nothing in the university rule book to say I can't have a boy friend. At least, I don't think so. Anyway, if there is, rules can be changed. It could be part of my next campaign.' Her voice sounded almost flirtatious, filled with optimism, and something else. 'So, it's up to you. Will you wait for me, Dan? Is our love strong enough, do you think?'

'Oh, aye, my love, it's strong enough all right. I'll be glad to wait, just as long as it takes.'

Bella was laughing with soft affection now as Dan reached out for her and she moved gladly into his arms, eager for his kiss. 'So long as it doesn't take too long, eh?'

'Aye, that's the ticket.'